OLD TOWN
Symphony

I0582761

MILLA HOLT

Published by Reinbok Limited, 111 Wolsey Drive, Kingston Upon Thames, Greater London, KT2 5DR

Publisher's Note: This is a work of fiction. Names, characters, places, and incidents are a product of the author's imagination. Locales and public names are sometimes used for atmospheric purposes. Any resemblance to actual people, living or dead, or to businesses, companies, events, institutions, or locales is completely coincidental.

Cover by Willette Cruz

Editing by Sara Turnquist

Small Town Harmony / Milla Holt. -- 1st ed.

ISBN 978-1-913416-33-1 Print ISBN 978-1-913416-34-8

Old Town Symphony

A WHOLESOME CHRISTIAN ROMANCE
RHAPSODY OF GRACE BOOK 3

Milla Holt

REINBOK LIMITED
United Kingdom

Welcome to
the Mosaic Collection

W E ARE SISTERS, A beautiful mosaic united by the love of God through the blood of Christ.

Each month The Mosaic Collection releases one or more faith-based novels or anthologies exploring our theme, Family by His Design, and sharing stories that feature diverse, God-designed families. Stories range from mystery and women's fiction to comedic and literary fiction. We hope you'll join our Mosaic family as we explore together what truly defines a family.

If you're like us, loneliness and suffering have touched your life in ways you never imagined; but Dear One, while you may feel alone in your suffering—whatever it is—you are never alone!

Learn more about The Mosaic Collection at

www.mosaiccollectionbooks.com

Join our Reader Community, too!

www.facebook.com/groups/TheMosaicCollection

Mosaic Collection Books

ELEANOR BERTIN

Unbound (The Ties that Bind #1)
Tethered (The Ties that Bind #2)
Lifelines (The Ties that Bind #3)
Flame of Mercy (Burning Bright #1)
Flicker of Trust (Burning Bright #2)

SARA DAVISON

Lost Down Deep (The Rose Tattoo Trilogy #1)
Written in Ink (The Rose Tattoo Trilogy #2)
Every Star in the Sky (two sparrows for a penny #1)
Every Flower of the Field (two sparrows for a penny #2)
The Color of Sky and Stone (In the Shadows #1)
This Little Nowhere, Nothing Town (The Rose Tattoo Trilogy short story collection)

JANICE L. DICK

The Road to Happenstance (Happenstance Chronicles #1)
Crazy About Maisie (Happenstance Chronicles #2)
Calm Before the Storm (The Storm Series #1)
Eye of the Storm (The Storm Series #2)
Out of the Storm (The Storm Series #3)

DEB ELKINK

The Red Journal
The Third Grace
Vagabond Come Home

CHAUTONA HAVIG
Spines & Leaves (Bookstrings introduction)
Hart of Noel (Bookstrings "Noella")
Twice Sold Tales (Bookstrings #1)
Clock Tower Bound (Bookstrings #2)

MILLA HOLT
Into the Flood (Seasons of Faith # 1)
Through the Blaze (Seasons of Faith # 2)
Within the Storm (Seasons of Faith # 3)
Amid the Ashes (Seasons of Faith # 4)
After the Frost (Seasons of Faith # 5)
Home Town Melody (Rhapsody of Grace #1)
Small Town Harmony (Rhapsody of Grace #2)
Old Town Symphony (Rhapsody of Grace #3)

ANGELA D. MEYER
This Side of Yesterday
Where Hope Starts (Applewood Hill #1)
Where Healing Starts (Applewood Hill #2)
Where Joy Starts (Applewood Hill #3)

STACY MONSON
When Mountains Sing (My Father's House #1)
Open Circle
Shattered Image

LORNA SEILSTAD
More Than Enough
Watercolors

CANDACE WEST

To my husband, who is my biggest cheerleader. Special thanks to my beta readers: Brenda, Rebekah, Kathy, Carmen, Rose, and the HG Three, I owe you so much. This story wouldn't be what it is without your tough love. Thank you also to Susan, my eagle-eyed friend.

Chapter 1

*K*EZIA BLAIR CLOSED HER eyes and let the music swallow her whole. The cool leather of the studio headphones pressed gently against her ears, sealing out the world until only the song remained. Layered instrumentation wrapped around her, but she was listening for something deeper: pockets of space where her voice could slip in, weaving light through shadow.

"Higher Ground" would be pop star Verity James's next single. But for now, the only vocals on the track were Kezia's—a clean, steady guideline bathed in the textured harmonies she'd already recorded.

When Verity finally bothered to show up to the studio and do her part, her voice would replace Kezia's lead. But the backing vocals would stay. Kezia's voice—every rise, every blend—would still be there, propping up the final product.

She didn't mind. This was the kind of work she loved. Art and arithmetic fused into one—calculating intervals, sculpting tone, shaping emotion without stealing focus. She could do this all day—build exquisite cathedrals out of sound, then hand someone else the spotlight.

Head tilted, she swayed slightly, fingers tapping in time. There—in the pre-chorus—a tiny pocket of air. If she added a high descant right there, it would catch the melody's light and throw it back like stained glass.

She signaled to producer Sam Crawford that she was ready, her reflection ghosting in the control room glass. Inhaling on cue, she added the new harmony with practiced precision.

A glance at the booth clock confirmed it was nearly two. Verity was almost two hours late, even by London standards. Sam was too professional to grumble out loud, but Kezia knew every minute of studio time cost him money. He was paying for Verity to keep them all waiting, and the label expected the completed track tonight.

"One more for insurance? If your voice is feeling good?" Sam asked. "That last run was gorgeous, but it's always nice to have options."

She nodded. Her throat still felt strong. Three hours in, and her special throat coat tea was holding up its end of the bargain. The warm licorice and slippery elm had kept her voice supple.

"From the bridge?" she asked, already knowing the answer.

"You read my mind. Rolling in three, two..."

Kezia let the main vocal track wash over her, waiting for her entrance. Her fingertips tapped lightly against her thigh, keeping time with the click track in her left ear. On cue, she opened her mouth and let the new harmony slip into the mix—clean, precise, threading beneath the melody like silk.

The red light blinked off. Sam's voice returned. "Perfect. Want to try that alternate bridge harmony? The one where the third drops out on the second repeat? No pressure. We've got everything we need from you, but since we've got the time…"

"Copy that," Kezia said. "Just the fifth and octave, light on the vibrato."

She was halfway through the variation when the studio door burst open.

A petite woman stumbled in, sunglasses still on despite the dim lighting, clutching an oversized coffee like a life preserver.

"Why isn't my booth ready?" Her voice sliced through Kezia's harmony line. "We're already behind schedule."

Kezia had only seen her on magazine covers and in music videos. So this was Verity James in the flesh, somehow both smaller and louder than expected.

Sam's diplomatic tone crackled through the headphones. "Good to see you, Verity. We're just wrapping up with Kezia. She's been laying down some beautiful—"

"Whatever." Verity waved a manicured hand and marched into the booth, invading Kezia's space in a cloud of designer perfume. Jasmine, patchouli...and vodka?

Verity's complexion had a sickly gray undertone beneath the makeup, and sweat dotted her hairline despite the air conditioning. She shoved her sunglasses onto her forehead and winced at the lights with bloodshot eyes.

She didn't bother with introductions. Just scanned Kezia from head to toe like she was part of the furniture.

Then she pushed in front of Kezia, reaching for the mic stand. "Can someone fix this? It's set up for a giraffe."

Kezia tucked her session notes into a folder, packing up slowly. Looked like her work was done. She'd built Verity's backing vocals for weeks, but this was the first time they'd shared a room. Funny how you could know someone's voice so intimately—its breaks and its sweet spots—without knowing the person at all.

She reached for her thermos and her package of premium throat coat tea—just as Verity's hand shot out toward the box.

"Oh good," Verity said, "I need this."

Kezia got there first, pulling the box of tea toward her. "I'm sorry, this is my personal supply."

"Are you serious?" Verity's voice rose. "I need that for my session. My throat is killing me." She turned toward the glass. "Sam!"

Sam winced behind the console. "Kezia, would you mind leaving a few teabags? We'll make sure you're compensated."

Kezia frowned. The specialty tea from Harrod's wasn't cheap, and she had just enough to last the week. But Sam's eyes held a silent plea—the look of a man trying to keep the peace.

She sighed and pulled three bags from the box, setting them on a napkin.

As she stepped out of the booth, Sam leaned toward her. "I hate to ask, but would you mind making the tea for her? You know how long to steep it and..." He nodded toward the glass, where Verity was complaining again about the mic stand, which had been adjusted for Kezia's 5'10" frame. "We really need as little friction as possible."

Irritation flared. Apparently, tea service was now part of her job. But Sam had given her steady work for three years. He never lowballed her rates or haggled over hours. In a career stitched together from zero-hours contracts and last-minute gigs across London's studios, his loyalty mattered. Especially with her housing situation hanging by a thread.

She'd do it for him. Not for Verity.

"Of course," she said. "I'll bring it right in."

"Thanks. And—would you mind sticking around a while longer? I have a feeling we might need you."

The sound engineer entered the booth with Verity and cranked the mic stand down several notches. "Would you like to warm up before we check levels?"

Verity scowled. "Warm up? I've been ready for hours. Not my fault everyone else is behind. Where are my lyrics, Sam?"

He slid the lyric sheet through the window. "We've highlighted the changes from the demo."

Verity frowned. "You changed the second verse? I thought the original was better."

"The label wanted the new lyrics. They tested better in focus groups," Sam said, calm as ever. "And remember, there's a quick turnaround in the pre-chorus. We struggled with that timing in rehearsals."

"Whatever," Verity muttered, scanning the lyrics.

Sam pressed the talkback button. "Let's do a quick level check, and then we'll get started."

"I need that tea first."

"On it," Kezia said, moving toward the door.

But before she could exit, a studio assistant stepped in. "Sam, Zach Falconer is here for your two o'clock."

Sam cursed softly. "Already? Please tell him I apologize for the delay. Ask him to give us a few minutes."

Wow. Working with Verity James was already a feather in Sam's cap. But he had enough pull to keep an industry powerhouse like Zach Falconer waiting?

Kezia slipped out and headed for the break room. After all her training at the Guildhall School of Music and Drama, here she was...fetching tea for a singer who couldn't be bothered to show up on time to record a track due tonight.

All that education. All that talent. And she was still invisible—the ghost in the machine, making stars like Verity sound better than they were.

She'd better get that tea before the star imploded.

Chapter 2

ZACH FALCONER PACED THE waiting area of Cadence Studios while his PA, Simon Vale, juggled calls and emails on his tablet. Sleek navy-blue leather couches surrounded a minimalist glass coffee table strewn with industry magazines and music catalogs. Lo-Fi instrumental music drifted from unseen speakers—meant to soothe, no doubt.

It didn't work on Zach.

Sam Crawford's assistant had just delivered an apologetic message in person. The recording session was running long. Sam was still tied up.

Zach didn't have time for this. But what choice did he have?

With just over a month until filming began, there was a massive producer-shaped hole in the staffing roster of his reality music show, *Starbound*. He was desperate for Sam to take over from the man who'd pulled out due to a health crisis.

The role needed someone of Sam's caliber. And at this late stage, Zach wasn't here to pitch. He was here to beg, fully prepared to trade on their long friendship.

There wasn't time to vet unknowns. He needed someone he trusted implicitly, someone whose talent and work ethic he'd seen firsthand. Sam had already turned him down months ago, but maybe things had shifted since then. The freelance world always did.

Still, Zach couldn't afford to waste the day. Not with half a dozen fires already burning.

As if on cue, his phone rang. Zach suppressed a sigh. Here was one of the arsonists responsible for those fires. Ryan Sterling, one of the mentors on the show...and the most high maintenance of the lot. Likely calling to follow up on the laundry list of demands he'd already emailed.

Zach answered. "Hi, Ryan. I was just about to email you, but you beat me to it."

"Were you? Glad to hear it. Some of the issues I raised are deal breakers. I need answers before I can confirm my participation in *Starbound*."

Good thing Ryan couldn't see his scowl. If Zach had his way, Ryan wouldn't be anywhere near the show. But Albion Broadcasting Network had insisted on Ryan's inclusion. They wanted the industry heavyweight for gravitas.

And, boy, was the man throwing that weight around—like a wrecking ball aimed at Zach's sanity. Some of his demands beggared belief. Still, maybe if Zach gave way on the smaller stuff, Ryan would back off on his more outrageous asks.

"I'll just pull your email up while we talk," Zach said, signaling to his assistant Simon to pass his tablet over.

He skimmed the list. "All right, let's see what we can do. Your accommodation requests are fine. I'll let the interior designer know about your specifications for the cottage: linens, furniture, everything. But I'll have to say no to the personal chef. We've hired an excellent culinary team for production. They'll accommodate any dietary requirements."

He scrolled down. "An assistant is reasonable. We've lined up someone with five years' industry experience and all the resume specs you requested. But you'll need to share them with another mentor."

Ryan sighed. "I suppose that's acceptable."

"I'm glad you think so." Zach kept his voice even as he scanned further. "We can't cover weekly first-class flights from Los Angeles to London for your stylist. But we've sourced a highly respected local stylist. Your LA guy can come in once for the finals, but we'll fly him business class. And he'll need to stay at the *Starbound* campus, not the Hilton."

Ryan sniffed. "Well, I suppose if you don't have the budget. I'm doing you a favor even taking part in this pet project of yours, and I've been talking it up to some of my contacts. I just had lunch with Renee Johnson. She says they're watching the show's development with interest, looking at Canadian licensing rights. So I think my requests are far from unreasonable. I'm going over and above my contracted duties."

"Thanks, Ryan. I appreciate that." Zach forced civility into his voice. The truth? He needed Ryan...and Ryan knew it. That was a big part of the problem.

"Well, what about the other things I requested?"

"Let's see..." Zach glanced back at the email. "I have no issues with your name appearing first in the show's listings."

Although Zach was the creator and executive producer, the name order was cosmetic. If it got Ryan to play nice, fine.

"And the co-creator credit?" Ryan asked.

"No."

"Fair enough."

The speed with which Ryan had let that go told Zach that even the man's massive ego knew he was pushing it with that particular request.

He scrolled to the end of Ryan's email. "Glad we're on the same page. I think that's everything?"

"For now," Ryan said smoothly. "Here's to a successful and prosperous partnership, Zach."

Partnership? Not a chance. Ryan was a contracted employee—one who'd happily take over the whole show if Zach gave him the chance.

Zach ended the call. That went better than he'd expected.

Across the room, Simon ended his own call. His brow was furrowed. "That was the location manager. He says Lady Harrington's threatening to file a formal complaint with the council. Too much congestion from production vehicles on the village lanes. She's also worried the camera lighting will affect local bat populations. And she doesn't like that we might film in the direction of her property."

Zach groaned. "Threatening? Has she submitted the paperwork yet?"

"Not yet. But she says she will unless we address her concerns before the end of the day."

Of course she would.

Zach checked his watch. "It's already after two? I'll go down there myself. If she escalates this, there's no telling how long the council will take to resolve it. We can't afford more delays."

Charm the neighbor. Appease the bats. Preserve the peace before a council complaint brought his show to a screeching halt.

He glanced at Simon. "Would you mind checking with Sam to see how much longer he's going to be? If it's more than ten minutes, we'll need to reschedule."

Simon nodded. "I'll go over there and get a time estimate."

"Thanks."

As his assistant left, Zach let out a slow breath and sent a silent prayer heavenward.

He was so close to getting this thing off the ground. But even with so many pieces miraculously falling into place, a dozen more could still derail it.

Starbound was supposed to be something different—a reality singing show with integrity. Not just another over-produced ratings-chasing spectacle. But to get there, he had to survive egos, lighting permits, and an unexpected bat crisis.

And he still had to convince Sam to say yes.

Chapter 3

KEZIA WINCED AS VERITY belted the chorus of her song into the mic.

"There's a fire... burning...deep in my heart."

Sam and his assistant Jeff exchanged glances.

Were they just going to let her go on with this? Verity was so far off key, Kezia doubted whether even production magic could fix it.

"Reaching a fever pitch and it just can't be healed!" The star's voice cracked on the high note, and she slammed down the lyric sheet. "Ugh! Sam, this isn't the key we worked on before. It's way too high."

Sam pushed the talkback button, his voice still calm despite the countless useless takes and the looming deadline. "Same key we've always used. Just relax and focus on the notes, please. From the top."

"Make me feel like it's the end of the wo—" Verity made another attempt, barely reaching the chorus before stopping. "What is with this track? It's totally throwing me off. Sam, how am I supposed to do my job when you guys don't do yours? I'm telling you, this is the wrong key. And the levels are all off. You should really prep better if you want me to perform at my best."

Sam's eyelid twitched. He took a slow, deep breath. "Verity, I know you're having a rough day. But we're running out of time here. Can you just give me one clean take? We'll deal with it from there."

"Seriously?" she shot back. "You know how hard it is to get in the zone when you're all stressing me out with this impatience? The song's in the wrong key. And I can't deal with this pressure right now."

She pulled off her headphones and crossed her arms, glaring.

Sam pinched the bridge of his nose.

Kezia held her breath. Was this the moment Sam would finally lose it?

No. Apparently, he had a bottomless well of patience. "Okay, Verity. If we lower the key, could you come back and try again in a couple of hours?"

Verity shrugged. "Fine. Just don't waste my time like this again, okay?"

She flounced out of the booth, shoving her shades back on. "Call me when you've got your stuff in order."

When she was gone, Sam turned to Jeff. "We'll have to lower the key digitally. Take it down a full tone. Thank God we used all digital instruments for this one."

Jeff nodded. "Will it hold up if we do it that way? I mean...what about the feel?"

"It'll hold," Sam said. "Digital instruments can handle the shift without losing quality. If we move fast, we can still get this to the label tonight."

He turned to Kezia. "We'll need a new guide vocal and backing vocals in the new key. Can you do it?"

"Ready when you are," she said.

Sam clapped her shoulder. "You're a star. Seriously. I don't know what we'd do without you today. Give us a few minutes to get the track adjusted."

Kezia stretched and did a few vocal warm-ups while Sam pulled up the digital audio workstation on the main screen. He and Jeff quickly got to work, fingers flying over the controls to transpose the key.

As they adjusted the settings, Kezia settled back into the booth, raised the mic to her height, and scanned the lyrics again, mentally preparing. Through her headphones, she could hear the faint beeps and clicks of the track being modified.

"We're just about there," Jeff said, glancing at Sam. "Patching in the new key now."

"Do it," Sam replied, eyes still on the screen.

Kezia sighed. So many people breaking their backs over Verity's song. And the woman whose name would be on it might earn hundreds of thousands for less than half an hour's work.

But nobody said showbiz was fair. Kezia had known that going in. She saw it every day.

Those were the breaks.

"We're good to go," Jeff said. "Key's lower. Sounds solid."

"Perfect." Sam looked through the glass at Kezia. "We're set."

She took a deep breath. "I'm ready."

"Okay." Sam nodded and clicked a button, letting the intro roll through the talkback. "Follow the flow of the new key and give it your all."

As the music began, Kezia immersed herself in the rhythm, her voice flowing out with confidence and clarity. "There's a fire burning deep in my heart."

With each phrase, she felt herself connecting more deeply with the song.

The take was going well, so she was surprised when Sam stopped her after the first chorus. "Hey, would you mind taking it from the top? Try to match Verity's style— breathier, no runs. Let your voice hitch a little on the big notes. Think you can do it?"

Kezia nodded. "I'll try."

She launched in again, adapting her voice to sound more like Verity's.

When she finished the second verse, Sam came into the booth with a sheet of paper. "Do you mind signing this?"

Kezia glanced at it. A release form. She'd signed a few before. But this one told her something more. If Verity failed to deliver a usable take today—and the odds weren't looking great—this contract would give the label permission to use Kezia's voice in the final mix. It was Sam's insurance policy. He wanted the option to use Kezia's vocals to heavily supplement or possibly replace Verity's. Kezia would get no credit and no royalties. Just a flat fee and a vanishing act.

Sam ran a hand through his hair, meeting her eyes. "I know this isn't what we originally discussed, but we're in a bind. It has to go to the label tonight, and you've seen what we're up against. How about I pay you for two full sessions instead of one?"

Kezia crossed her arms. "Make it three. And don't forget the throat coat tea comes on top of that."

"Deal. But officially, this never happened."

Kezia smiled. "What never happened? I don't know what you're talking about."

Sam chuckled. "I owe you big time."

"Yeah, you do."

She signed the form. Thank God—this little financial windfall would come in handy.

As Sam collected the release, a slight man with a crew cut and designer glasses stepped into the control room.

Sam gestured for Kezia to wait, then stepped out of the booth to greet the visitor, closing the door behind him.

Through the glass, Kezia could see their conversation—serious expressions, animated gestures—but couldn't hear a word.

She adjusted her headphones and turned back to the lyrics, prepping for the next take.

A moment later, Sam returned to the console and pressed the talkback. "Kezia, I need to step out to meet with Zach Falconer. Jeff will take over."

"Got it." Zach Falconer was still here? Must be important.

The visitor remained in the control room as Sam left.

"Okay, let's keep the momentum going," Jeff said, sliding into Sam's chair. "Whenever you're ready."

Kezia inhaled deeply, centering herself as the music faded in.

Sing it like Verity, she told herself. Breathy, no runs, a hitch on the big notes.

"There's a fire burning deep in my heart..."

Jeff held two thumbs up as the song ended. "That was fantastic! Perfect take!"

To her surprise, the stranger was still in the room, watching.

"Okay," Jeff said. "I'm happy with that. Let's lay down the backups next."

"Okay," Kezia replied. "But can I take five?" She could use a comfort break before the next stretch.

"Of course," Jeff said. "Take your time. I'll cue the next take when you're back."

As she stepped out of the booth, the stranger approached with a smile. "That was really impressive," he said, extending a hand. "I'm Simon Vale. I work with Zach Falconer. From the Falconers Christian music band."

Kezia shook his hand. "Thank you. I've heard of him. I'm Kezia."

"I know," he said with a grin. "I had to stay and listen. Your vocals are something else."

Her face warmed. "Thank you. I just wanted to make sure it worked for the project."

He pulled a business card from his wallet and handed it to her. "Zach's working on a new singing competition. It's serious stuff. Not one of those shows where people go to make fools of themselves."

Kezia turned over the card, studying the silver and blue logo. "*Starbound*?"

Simon nodded. "They're hand-picking vocalists to audition. If you're interested, call me in the next couple of days. The shortlist's already finalized, but I'll make sure you get a shot at an audition if you want it."

A reality show? Really? That was how Verity got her record deal. Did Kezia want to follow that path?

Then again, despite all her Guildhall training, she was still the one singing backing vocals.

She smiled. "Thanks for the opportunity. I'll think about it."

"Don't think too long." Simon gave a quick wave and stepped out the door.

Chapter 4

*K*EZIA TOOK A MOMENT to catch her breath outside the front door of her family home. She'd come straight from Cadence Studios after her marathon recording session and still carried the stale tang of studio air and recycled tea. No time to shower or change—she was late enough already.

She raised her hand to the doorbell. Although she still had the same spare key she'd carried since she was fifteen, it felt wrong to just let herself in.

She glanced around. The Byaruhanga family home nestled among a row of substantial houses on Westcott's Parsonage Lane, their Georgian façades lined up like well-pressed matrons—upright, composed, and quietly judging.

Her parents had recently added a tasteful stone pathway leading through the front garden, flanked by carefully pruned hydrangeas basking in the summer evening light. Nothing too showy, of course. In Westcott, understated affluence was the watchword. Ostentatious displays were considered vulgar among the surgeons, barristers, and corporate executives who called this corner of Surrey home.

The door swung open to reveal her mother, elegant in a powder-pink twinset and gray slacks, her pearls glowing in the light. Freshly permed hair framed her face in sleek waves.

Kezia resisted the urge to touch her own Afro. Mum had long since given up pestering Kezia to "do something" with her hair. "Something" meaning chemical straightening, wearing a wig, or weaving in extensions.

Mum came from a generation in which "professional" hair for a Black woman in corporate Britain meant doing everything possible to obliterate or hide the natural tight and coarse curls of her African heritage.

But Kezia's hair, like her career path, didn't fit her mother's tidy definition of well-ordered propriety.

"Sorry I'm late," Kezia said, giving Mum a quick hug. "The recording session went a lot longer than I expected. I had to stay and do some extra work."

"Mm, okay. Come in." She stepped aside for Kezia to pass. "Actually, it worked out just fine. Dorcas dropped in unexpectedly, so we ate with her. But I kept you a plate."

"Dorcas is here?" Kezia rarely saw her youngest sister these days. A neurosurgical resident at King's College Hospital, Dorcas was usually buried in trauma shifts or complex spinal procedures.

She'd followed their father into neurosurgery with the same single-minded dedication that had taken him from first-generation Ugandan immigrant to one of the Royal Surrey County Hospital's top cranial specialists.

Meanwhile, their middle sister Salome had taken up their mother's legal legacy—though she'd traded corporate law for human rights work with the United Nations Human Rights Council in Geneva.

Kezia followed Mum into the open-plan living area, where Dorcas and Dad sat at the dining table with dessert plates in front of them, each bearing a generous helping of treacle tart and custard.

"Sit and I'll get your plate," Mum said.

Dad nodded. "Hello, Kezia. Sorry we couldn't wait. Dorcas has to leave soon."

"That's all right. Work took longer than I expected. Hi, Dorcas."

"Hi! I love those trousers—so comfy-looking."

Kezia glanced down at her outfit, uneasy that Dorcas was drawing attention to her clothes. She'd dressed for a long day in the studio, not a family dinner. Mum thought sweatpants were low-class—marginally acceptable at a high-end gym or on the rugby pitch. Certainly not at her dinner table.

Dorcas, by contrast, wore hospital scrubs—technically casual, but clearly the uniform of an approved Byaruhanga profession.

"Thanks." Kezia settled at the table, hiding her pants under a linen napkin. "What's up with you?"

"Had a rare free afternoon and thought I'd swing by. How's work? Done anything interesting lately?"

She'd love to brag—just a little—about how she'd just been recording backing vocals for Verity James. But the NDA prohibited her from so much as whispering the star's name. So, she just shrugged. "Yes. Plenty to keep me busy."

"And Claire? How's she doing?"

"Swamped with wedding planning." Kezia's best friend Claire was getting married in a week, which meant Kezia would lose both her housemate and the flat they'd shared for five years.

Without Claire's half of the rent—and with a looming twenty percent increase from their landlord—there was no way Kezia could afford to stay in the flat. She didn't blame the landlord. The rate hadn't changed in years. But the timing couldn't be worse.

She was working as hard as she could, booking as many jobs as she could handle while still being careful not to overstrain her voice. But it wasn't enough. Her options were stark—find a new flatmate or move out next month.

She'd hoped to quietly ask if she could move back home for a month or two, just until she found another suitable place to live. Preferably in London. Rent prices were punishing, and she still had student loans.

Her voice was not just her instrument but her livelihood, which meant the place where she lived needed specific conditions to protect and maintain it. It might take a while until she could find another home that ticked every non-negotiable on her list.

The flat she'd shared with Claire was perfect—sound-proofed with space for her vocal warm-ups and remote recording work, well-ventilated, and in a quiet street close to transport links.

And, above all, she'd had a nonsmoking housemate who understood her need for vocal rest periods and quiet times before important sessions.

But how to bring it up to her parents? They probably wouldn't say no to her living at home for a short while, but it was so hard to work up the boldness to ask. It would mean admitting that her financial situation was precarious. That music wasn't quite paying the bills.

She shifted uneasily in her chair as Dorcas turned back to their father, her voice animated as she continued whatever they'd been talking about before Kezia showed up.

"I wanted to tell you about this incredible case we had yesterday. Fifty-eight-year-old male with a glioblastoma extending into the motor strip. Mr. Hayworth let me assist with the resection—we used that new 5-ALA fluorescence-guided technique you mentioned at Christmas."

Dad's eyes lit up. "And how was the tumor-brain interface visualization?"

"Remarkable clarity. We achieved near-gross total re-section while preserving all function in the eloquent cortex."

"That's the sweet spot." Dad broke into a smile. "There's a reason why Hayworth's one of the best. You're fortunate to be learning under him."

Mum returned from the kitchen with an Instagram-worthy plate of roast chicken, potatoes, and vegetables. She set it down in front of Kezia. "Here you are, darling. I've warmed it through properly."

"Thanks, Mum," Kezia said, suddenly aware of how hungry she was after the marathon recording session.

As she took her first bite, Mum settled back into her chair, her face brightening. "Oh! Now that you're here, Kezia, I can tell everyone about Salome's news. She called this afternoon to say she and Edward have finally decided on their wedding venue—Lake Como! Can you imagine? It's going to be absolutely stunning."

Dad smiled over his coffee. "A fitting location. Edward's family has that villa near Bellagio, I believe."

"Yes, and they've offered to host the rehearsal dinner," Mum said. "We'll need to book flights and accommodation soon. The wedding's in June, but everything books up fast around the lake."

Kezia's fork paused halfway to her mouth. Lake Como? She'd seen the photos Salome had shared in the family

WhatsApp group from her last vacation—the crystal blue lake, historic villas, and eye-watering price tags. Even with a year to save, the flights, hotel, appropriate attire, and gift would easily cost over a thousand pounds. Money Kezia didn't have.

Dad turned to Dorcas. "Your mother and I will cover your travel. I know your stipend barely covers London rent, let alone international travel."

"Thanks, Dad. That's really generous," Dorcas said.

He patted her hand. "That's what parents are for. You might need help now, but you'll be standing on your own two feet soon enough. That's how we've raised our daughters—to be independent."

Kezia took a sip of water, trying not to wince. Independent...and here she was, about to ask to move back home.

Mum turned to her. "Salome said you've agreed to sing at the ceremony."

"Yes." She had—before the location was announced. Now, attending meant turning down work and scraping together funds out of nowhere. She wanted to sing for her sister—but she didn't see how she could afford it without asking for help. And she couldn't bring herself to do that.

As the conversation carried on, her carefully rehearsed pitch—just a temporary stay until she found somewhere else—dissolved in her throat.

Her father's words rang in her head. Independence. How could she admit that at twenty-nine, she couldn't make rent? That her music career wasn't covering the basics? That they'd been right all along about how precarious it would be?

As she picked at her chicken, her diamond tennis bracelet glinted on her wrist. The gift her parents gave her for her outstanding A-Level exam results. Just before she'd turned down law programs at King's College London and UCL and chosen Guildhall School of Music and Drama instead, causing a rift in her relationship with them that had never quite healed.

She made her decision. She would not be asking to move back home. She would sell her diamond bracelet and the earrings that came with it. That should cover the shortfall and pay for one month's rent in her current home. Buy her enough time to find other options.

She could pick up more session work, or maybe even look for a retail job. Anything would be better than confirming what her family already believed—that her choice to pursue music had been a mistake.

And—wait—there was that other opportunity Simon mentioned today at the studio, after he'd praised her vocals on the Verity James track.

A reality TV singing competition seemed desperate and commercial—everything she'd tried to avoid in her pursuit of authentic musicianship. But what kind of "authentic musicianship" was she really doing now? Backing vocals for a lazy and entitled pop princess? Ad jingles? That nine-month stint at Butlins?

And "desperate" pretty much described her financial situation right now.

What had he told her again? *If you're interested, call me within the next couple of days.*

As soon as she left here tonight, she would make that call.

Chapter 5

*M*IDMORNING SUN ILLUMINATED THE warm oak-paneled walls of what had once been the drawing room of Glenmere Hall, now repurposed as the main conference room for the *Starbound* production team.

Zach, as executive producer and show creator, sat at the head of the polished meeting table, where coffee cups and laptops mingled with thick production binders—organized chaos that mirrored the scale of what they were about to launch.

Filming would begin in just a few days with a hand-selected group of singers auditioning for a spot in the competition. Unlike other talent shows that threw contestants into the spotlight unprepared, *Starbound's* twelve-week format would focus on real artist development: songwriting workshops, producer collaborations, and performance coaching from industry veterans. The contestants would leave with more than exposure. They'd have tangible skills and a portfolio of original music—whether they won or not.

Zach's brother, Ezra, and sister-in-law, Martha, sat together near the door—a quiet reminder of the family support that had made this dream possible.

Victoria Harlow from the Albion Broadcasting Network sat opposite him, her tablet propped between her water bottle and phone. The rest of the production team filled the remaining seats—Hugo Murray as showrunner, Daniel from legal, Jennifer Randall managing the budget, and a half dozen other specialists whose combined expertise would shape the next three months of their lives.

And the success or failure of Zach's biggest business gamble to date. It wasn't just his life savings on the line—his entire family had invested in *Starbound*. Their confidence in him meant failure wasn't an option. Not while he had breath in his body to make this work.

His vision for a music show that developed artists instead of exploiting them was finally coming to life.

If they could just get through this final meeting without surprises.

So far, everything was falling into place. Maybe too smoothly. And experience had taught Zach that's usually when things went sideways.

Hugo wrapped up his staffing update. "Sam Crawford is confirmed as Team Zach's music producer. Three of the mentor contracts are finalized, including Ryan's amended terms." He glanced at Jennifer. "Which the budget accommodated nicely."

Jennifer nodded. "We managed Ryan's new terms by reallocating from the guest mentor fund. And thanks to

Martha and Ezra waiving their coaching fees, we're still tracking on target."

Zach nodded. "Thanks, both of you. While we're on staffing—Victoria, any word on whom Albion has chosen as the fourth mentor?"

Along with a couple of competition elements they insisted on keeping top secret—even from Zach—Albion Broadcasting reserved the right to appoint the show's four mentors. Each contestant would be assigned to a mentor: an industry professional who would guide song choices, artistic development, and potentially make or break a contestant's journey.

As the show's creator, Zach was automatically one of the mentors. But in order to prevent his team of contestants from having any unfair advantage, Albion would keep him in the dark about some "surprise twists."

It rankled that he didn't have complete creative control over his own show, but he understood why it had to be this way.

And surely, whoever they chose couldn't be worse than Ryan.

Victoria tapped her tablet with a manicured nail. "We've been in negotiations with two candidates. Our first choice has been hesitant to commit, but she's promised to give us a final answer today."

"Are we allowed to know who the first choice is?" Zach asked.

Victoria smiled. "Yes, of course. I'm sure you're familiar with her. Verity James."

Zach's hands clenched under the table, though his voice stayed even. "Yes. I know her."

He could feel Ezra's eyes on him. Could almost hear the sympathy radiating from Martha. But he kept his focus on Victoria. Just hearing Verity's name shouldn't matter. He was over it. Over *her*.

Victoria's phone buzzed. "Speak of the devil. It's Verity. Excuse me." She stepped out to take the call.

Zach stared at the closed door. Verity. On his show.

Martha cleared her throat, a gentle cue to remind him the meeting hadn't ended.

Right. He was chairing it.

He turned to the casting director. "Maya, how are we doing on contestant profiles? The network needs those press packets ready as soon as we make our selections."

"Almost complete." Maya tucked a lock of hair behind her ear. "We just need one more. Simon added someone to the audition list."

Zach frowned. "We finalized that list last week. Why are we making exceptions now?"

Maya shifted in her chair. "Simon said you wouldn't mind. He was very insistent. Said she's exceptionally talented."

"Name?"

"Karen...no, Kenzie...something unusual with a K." She rustled her notes. "I have it here somewhere..."

Hugo cut in smoothly. "We're only adding her to the audition pool, Zach. Not guaranteeing her a spot. Listening to one more person audition this weekend won't kill us."

Zach pinched the bridge of his nose. A silly, meaningless change like this shouldn't bother him. But the thought of Verity being part of *Starbound* had him on edge. "Fine. She can audition. Let's move on. Daniel, legal protocols?"

Daniel launched into a summary of the key policies, particularly the no-fraternization clause.

"I'm sure I don't need to remind anyone about the mess on *Chart Topper* and *Pop Royalty* when judges got too cozy with contestants," he concluded.

Martha caught Zach's eye. "You'd better pay attention to those rules. You've always been the biggest heartthrob of the Falconer Brothers, and now you're the only eligible one."

"I'm here to make music, not scandalous headlines," Zach said drily. "Save the romance for the tabloids."

Victoria returned, phone still in hand. "Apologies. Verity's declined the offer. Said the development-focused format was, in her words, 'tediously boring compared to what audiences want.'"

Zach blew out a slow breath, the tension seeping out of his body. Thank God. Let Verity insult his concept as much as she liked. She wasn't part of it. That was all that mattered.

"Tyler Reed has accepted the role," Victoria added. "Contract's *en route*. She'll need a couple of trips home to Canada during filming, but she can work around our schedule."

"She's a much better fit anyway," Martha said. "A producer and songwriter. She'll bring real substance."

Martha and Ezra were the only ones in the room who understood just how much it meant to Zach that Verity wouldn't be involved.

The meeting wrapped soon after Victoria outlined the promotional rollout and international licensing discussions.

As the others filed out, Ezra and Martha lingered behind.

Ezra leaned against the table. "That 'boring' comment? Bit rich coming from Verity. Back when you were dating, she'd turn up at the opening of an envelope."

Zach tried to smile. It came out stiff. "She's moved up in the world, apparently. And her opinion stopped mattering a long time ago." He stacked his papers—too hard—sending them sliding across the table again.

As he gathered them, he noticed his hands were shaking. For crying out loud. Six years. And Verity could still rattle him.

Not because he still cared. He didn't. But because of what she represented—the version of himself he wanted to forget. The fool who mistook charm for character. Who followed his feelings straight off a cliff.

What unnerved him wasn't Verity. It was the memory of how easily and completely she'd duped him. He hadn't seen her clearly until it was too late.

And he couldn't afford a mistake like that again.

That was the past. *Starbound* was the future, and he had work to do. Beginning with auditions this weekend.

Chapter 6

*K*EZIA SAT PERFECTLY STILL while a makeup artist dabbed powder across her forehead to fight the shine from the studio lights. After four years of session work—not to mention stints at Disneyland Paris, Butlins, and touring as a backup vocalist—she knew the drill. Stay calm, stay focused, deliver.

But this wasn't just another backing gig. This was *Starbound*—her chance to be seen by a national TV audience, and maybe add rocket fuel to her career.

The holding room buzzed with nervous energy as production assistants herded contestants through.

On the mounted TV monitor, Kezia watched the current singer finish her number. The girl couldn't have been more than nineteen, all fresh-faced enthusiasm as she belted out a Taylor Swift song to the panel of judges. Muffled applause filtered through the walls—soft, but encouraging.

A dark-haired woman whose name Kezia couldn't remember called out, "Two minutes." She approached with a tablet. "Kezia Blair? You're our final audition of the day."

Kezia nodded, careful not to disturb the makeup artist's work. Her heart thundered against her ribs, but her hands were steady. She'd prepared. She'd chosen a song well within her range—one she could nail even with adrenaline in her system.

The teenager burst back into the holding room, immediately engulfed by family members. Their excited whispers carried across the space. "They loved you!" and "Did you see Ryan's face?"

A camera crew filmed their reunion while a producer moved in for an interview.

The woman with the tablet gestured. "Places, please." She led Kezia to the stage door.

Kezia rose, smoothing her jewel-toned wrap dress—chosen for how it complemented her dark skin and flattered her tall, curvy frame. She caught her reflection in a makeup mirror. Her short natural hair was impeccably styled, the curls defined and gleaming under the lights. Professional. Polished. Perfect.

Everything she'd trained to be. Would it be enough?

The stage door opened onto darkness. Guided by blue floor lights, Kezia stepped out and followed the marked path to her spot. The spotlight hit, momentarily dazzling after the shadows of the wings. Polite applause rippled through the studio audience.

As her eyes adjusted, the judging panel came into focus. And there he was—Zach Falconer.

Her breath quickened.

Anyone familiar with Christian music knew the Falconer family name. Their worship songs were staples in churches across the UK. The light caught the angles of his face and gleamed off his black hair. He'd always been the most photogenic of the brothers, but in person, he was something else entirely. So gorgeous it was almost unreal. But there was something else too, an intensity in his expression as he studied her, that made her skin prickle.

Focus, she told herself. She'd performed for plenty of attractive men before. This was about her voice, her talent, her future. The only thing that mattered was what his ears thought of her voice.

Rather nice ears, actually.

"Welcome to *Starbound*," Zach said, his warm baritone resonating through the studio. "Could you introduce yourself—your name, age, and what you do?"

"I'm Kezia Blair." Her voice was clear and steady—just as she'd practiced. She'd been using her middle name as a stage name since her earliest auditions, because English tongues always stumbled over *Byaruhanga*. "I'm twenty-nine and work as a session vocalist in London."

Something flickered across Zach's face. "Ah," he said, making a note on the paper in front of him. "So you're our special last-minute discovery."

"And what will you be singing today?" a voice as smooth as velvet asked.

Kezia turned to Diana Morris. The industry veteran leaned forward with interest. Even after thirty years, the multi-Grammy winner was radiant under studio lighting, her dark skin glowing.

"'And I'm Telling You' from *Dreamgirls*," Kezia said.

A murmur rippled through the audience. She knew it was a bold choice. The kind of number that either made or broke auditions.

She'd already touched base with the band during her brief sound check. The key was confirmed, the intro rehearsed.

As the famous opening bars filled the studio, Kezia took a steadying breath, and her training kicked in. Back straight. Shoulders relaxed. Breath from the diaphragm.

The first phrase came out pure and controlled. No nerves, no strain—just clean technique and perfect pitch. As she built through the verses, muscle memory took over. Every crescendo, every run, every dynamic landed exactly as rehearsed.

By the time she reached the bridge, the audience was with her, their energy feeding hers. When she hit the final notes, they were on their feet before the song ended.

Kezia couldn't stop her grin. She'd nailed it.

The Canadian judge—Tyler something?—spoke first, her voice cutting through the cheers. "That was masterful.

Your control is extraordinary, even in the upper register. We all know how extremely hard that is."

"Absolutely phenomenal." Diana pressed a hand to her chest. "You have such command of your instrument. I'd love to know where you trained."

Kezia felt like she was floating six feet above the stage. "Guildhall. Both undergrad and master's."

Ryan Sterling's dazzling smile lit up his face. She recognized him from countless album credits and industry profiles. "Well, that explains the polish. But what I loved, Kezia, is how you made such a well-known song your own. When I heard your song choice, I thought, 'Here we go again.' But wow—your arrangement was inspired. You blew me away."

Kezia beamed. "Thank you. That means the world."

Three positive responses. Only Zach remained.

She looked at him.

He was studying his notes, his expression unreadable.

After a long pause, he looked up. "There's no question about your vocal ability. I can hear that Guildhall training. But here's the thing—*Starbound* isn't looking for a dime-a-dozen session singer."

His words hit like a gut punch. It took every ounce of willpower to keep her expression neutral.

Gasps rippled through the audience even as her grip tightened around the microphone.

But Zach Falconer wasn't finished.

The owner, creator, and lead mentor of *Starbound* waved a dismissive hand. "We're looking for the full package, not just someone who tries to blow up the speakers with power and vocal acrobatics. I'm not entirely convinced you belong here, Miss Blair."

Chapter 7

Z ACH CAUGHT THE TIGHTENING of the session singer's well-formed lips, and the way her brown eyes widened. The flash of emotion lasted only a heartbeat, before a neutral mask lay over her features, hiding whatever she really felt. For just a second, something raw had surfaced. Something unscripted.

The audience's boos grew louder. So, they didn't like his critique, either. He hadn't meant to go in so hard. Not really. But that emotion was the first hint of genuineness he'd seen in her, despite the song she'd chosen.

He stood by his words. She was too perfect, too polished. He'd seen technical brilliance before. It never got under his skin like this, and he couldn't quite explain why. She was Session Singer Barbie, immaculately presented with her edgy curly Afro and a blue dress draping her statuesque hourglass figure. He noticed that, didn't he? More than he should have.

He shook it off. Everything about her screamed "hired talent" rather than "artist."

Ryan was the first of the other mentors to find his voice. "Are you sure you don't need a hearing aid, Zach?"

The audience cheered loudly before Ryan continued. "That was a flawless performance. She definitely belongs in this competition. It's a firm yes from me. What do you have against perfect technique, Zach?"

Zach waited for the audience to quiet down, then faced Kezia. "It appears that I need to explain, so I will. Here's the thing: you hit every note, you nailed all those runs, but I felt...nothing. You kept your eyes closed through most of the performance. It's technically impressive, but where's the connection? The audience needs to feel something beyond vocal acrobatics."

As the audience got noisy again, Ryan jumped in again. "That's what development is for. Her voice is exceptional. One of the strongest we've heard."

"I'm with Ryan," Diana said. "Technical foundation like hers is rare. The performance aspects can be taught."

Tyler chimed in. "Not saying there isn't room to grow, but I'd rather start with extraordinary talent we can shape than the other way around."

As the audience clapped and whistled, Zach watched the session singer, looking for any cracks in her professional demeanor. But she maintained an unflappable poise as she listened to the other judges speak, mouthing her thanks with a soft smile.

Olivia Chang, the hostess, said, "Well, Zach? What do you say?"

Zach shrugged. "Fine. She's got a spot. But..." He met her gaze squarely. "You need to prove you've got what it takes to be more than just another good voice. *Starbound* isn't looking for performers who hide behind technical perfection."

The audience cheered raucously and the session singer's smile widened.

Olivia turned to her. "Kezia, you've just received some strong feedback from our judges. Ryan, Diana, and Tyler see exceptional talent, while Zach has his reservations. What's going through your mind right now?"

Zach crossed his arms as he studied her. If she were following the reality show playbook, this is where she would turn on the waterworks and play up to the camera.

She drew a deep breath. "I appreciate the opportunity and all the judges' feedback." She shot a fleeting glance at Zach, then turned back to Olivia. "I've spent years perfecting my technique because that's what's expected in my professional world—to be reliable, consistent, technically flawless."

Turning again, she met Zach's gaze. "But I understand what Mr. Falconer is saying. Technical skill isn't enough by itself. I'm here because I want more than being background support for someone else's vision. I want to learn how to bring my own voice forward. And I'm willing to do whatever it takes to prove I belong here."

Whatever it takes. Zach's jaw clenched. How many times had he heard that exact phrase? From Verity, from countless hopeful with ambition that outweighed their integrity. People willing to compromise anything—including themselves—for success.

Kezia Blair was cranked out of the same mold as all the others—hungry for fame and success. Right up Ryan's alley, judging by the way the man was practically salivating.

The audience, too, was eating it up.

Fine. Let him have her. Zach was looking for something more.

He leaned toward his mic. "Thank you for your time, Miss Blair. The *Starbound* team will let you know about the next steps."

Chapter 8

"HANK YOU FOR YOUR time, Miss Blair. The *Starbound* team will let you know about the next steps."

As Zach Falconer dismissed her with a flick of his wrist, Kezia nodded graciously, the way she'd been trained.

Always thank the client, even when they've been difficult. "Thank you for the opportunity."

She walked off stage with measured steps, the thunderous applause washing over her as she followed the lighted path back the way she'd come.

The stage door clicked shut behind her. Only then did she let her shoulders drop, resting her forehead against the wall as Zach's words echoed in her mind. *Dime-a-dozen session singer.* Years of training...dismissed with a flick of his wrist.

He and Dad would get along great. They had the same opinion of what her career amounted to. But Ryan, Tyler, and Diana—all influential players in the industry—had given her enthusiastic praise. Were they just being kind? Playing their roles for the cameras?

"Kezia!" A pretty, dark-haired woman hurried toward her with a thick folder. "I'm Maya Patel, casting director for

Starbound. Congratulations! You're one of only four who've received an on-the-spot offer to join the show today."

"Really?" Kezia straightened. "Even after what Mr. Falconer said?"

"Zach? He's demanding with everyone, but..." Maya hesitated, adjusting her grip on the folder. "He usually doesn't come out quite that strongly right away. He's passionate about developing genuine artists, not just good singers. Trust me, if he didn't see potential in you, you wouldn't be here at all."

Maya pulled out a stack of documents. "Before we get into any details, I need you to sign this NDA. It's non-negotiable, and I can't share anything else about the show until you do."

She slid across a document and a pen. Kezia scanned the first page, familiar enough with entertainment industry contracts to know what to expect. Her signature was steady. If she was going to leap, she might as well do it with both feet.

"Perfect." Maya's smile widened. "Now I can tell you about where you'll be staying. The show is filmed at the Starbound Campus, formerly known as Glenmere Hall in Surrey. It's this gorgeous historic estate with extensive grounds. Absolutely beautiful location. You'll be staying in dormitory-style accommodation in what used to be the carriage house, all newly renovated with wonderful facilities. Zach's spared no expense. All meals are provided."

Kezia knew where Glenmere Hall was. It was about forty minutes from her parents' place in Westcott. "Will we be able to leave the grounds?"

"No, it's a closed set. Complete seclusion for the duration of your time on the show. It helps create the right atmosphere, builds those connections between contestants." Maya paused. "The financial side is quite attractive. Base stipend starts at £800 weekly for the first round, increasing to £1,000 for rounds two and three, and £1,500 for the semifinals. Finalists receive £2,000 per week. Plus performance bonuses once the challenges begin."

Kezia did some quick mental calculations. The initial stipend was less than she'd make from a busy week of session work, but with accommodation and meals covered, it would balance out, and she could still cover her student loans and storage fees. And if she made it past the first few rounds...

"There's more paperwork we'll need to sort out over the next few days." Maya shuffled through her folder. "Medical waivers, publicity releases, social media policies. But today I need three things: the NDA you've just signed, this participant agreement that confirms you're joining the show, and this contract of engagement that covers your employment terms, including the stipend structure we just discussed."

She laid out the documents. "Take your time to read through these. They're legally binding, so make sure you're comfortable with everything. The rest can wait until you arrive at the Starbound Campus at Glenmere, but these are essential today."

Kezia nodded, pulling the contracts closer. The participant agreement was fairly standard reality show fare. She'd seen similar documents before. Contestants had to agree to being filmed 24/7, follow production schedules, comply with house rules. There was a clause about potential elimination at any stage, and another about following the mentors' creative direction.

The engagement contract was more complex. Beyond the payment terms, it outlined rehearsal requirements and restrictions during the show's run. Contestants couldn't accept other performance work, give interviews, or post on social media without production approval. Any original songs created during the show would be subject to a royalty-sharing agreement between the artist and *Starbound*.

"Filming starts exactly one month from today," Maya said. "That's August 14th, the day you arrive on the Starbound Campus."

Kezia glanced up from the document. "I have some commitments booked before then." Including performing at Claire's wedding. "And some ongoing contracts. Would that be an issue if I sign this?"

"You'll need to take a leave of absence for however long you're on the show," Maya said. "The competition runs for twelve weeks, though of course, how long you'll be here depends on how far you advance. But contestants need to be fully committed while they're on the show. No outside work allowed."

An open-ended absence, potentially twelve weeks long? Kezia's mind raced through the practicalities. She'd have to contact all her regular clients, explain the situation, recommend replacements. Some might understand, but others would not be as forgiving.

The trickiest situation was the four-track EP she'd signed to record with Archer Productions. She was contracted to provide backing vocals for an indie artist's debut, scheduled for mid-September studio time. Maybe she could convince the producer to move the session up before *Starbound* began? She'd have to be careful not to strain her voice right before the competition, though.

Then there was the theme song for that new children's television show she'd been recording from her home studio. The production company needed the final harmonies by next week, which was manageable. But they'd already booked her for the "learning moment" songs that appeared in each episode, expecting her to record six of them by early September. The advance had paid for her new microphone.

And the regular commercial work through Soundwave Productions would certainly disappear. She'd been their go-to vocalist for nearly two years, recording jingles and voice-overs for everything from shopping centers to insurance companies. That steady income would be gone, and they'd certainly find someone else during her absence.

"Is there any flexibility at all for existing contracts?" Kezia asked. "I've committed to an EP that's due to record in September, and I have theme songs already paid for."

Maya's expression was sympathetic but firm. "I'm sorry, but the contract is clear. No outside professional commitments during filming. The rehearsal and performance schedules are intense, and we need contestants fully focused."

Kezia nodded. She'd asked God to open the door if this was His will. And it was open—though squeezing through might take some wriggling.

She'd have to work double-time over the next few weeks. Call Malcolm at Archer tomorrow about rescheduling the EP. Finish the *Poppy's Purple Playhouse* theme song harmonies and "learning moment" songs before August 14th, even if it meant late nights. All while arranging to move out of the flat she could no longer afford to keep.

At least she could sing at Claire's wedding next weekend. The initial stipend would just cover her student loan payments and storage for her furniture.

She glanced at the elimination clause again. If she crashed out in the first round, she'd be back to square one, scrambling for session work. But if she made it through even half the show, the exposure alone would be worth more than a year of session work. And the later rounds' stipends and performance bonuses could give her a financial cushion even if she went back to her regular gigs.

She couldn't see a real, permanent downside. And after Zach's dismissive critique, something in her was burning to show him she could be more than a backup vocalist.

"Outstanding audition, Kezia."

She looked up to see James Robson, the musical director, pause as he walked past. He was in charge of the live band who'd backed her audition today.

He gave her a thumbs-up. "Your breath control on those sustained notes was impeccable. Best I've heard all day."

That simple compliment from someone who understood the technicalities of her craft hit her harder than all the mentors' feedback combined. He'd been sitting there with the band, had witnessed everything Zach had said to her.

Her eyes stung. She swallowed hard before managing a quiet, "Thank you."

As James continued down the corridor, Kezia stared at the contract in her hands. This was the opportunity she'd been looking for—a chance to break out of the session singer cycle. Could she prove Zach and her dad wrong?

Even if she crashed out early, it would still be valuable experience for her resume. She signed her name on the two additional documents needed today.

"Excellent!" Maya pulled some vouchers from her folder. "And these are dinner vouchers for you and your family at Bramble & Rose. Zach likes us to treat our new contestants to a celebration meal. Take enough for you and whoever came with you to the audition today. The restaurant is just down the street."

Kezia hesitated before taking one voucher. "It's just me today."

Maya's smile faltered slightly as she glanced around the now-quiet corridor. Only crew members remained, breaking down equipment and carrying clipboards, paying them no attention. Her cheeks colored.

"Well," she said brightly, tucking the remaining vouchers away, "you should still celebrate. This is a big moment."

Kezia nodded, slipping the single voucher into her bag alongside her newly signed contracts. A big moment, yes. But like most of the milestone moments in her music career, she'd mark it alone. It was okay—she was used to it. Someday, her talent would demand celebration—and not in solitude. Maybe *Starbound* was the first step toward that day.

Chapter 9

*K*EZIA'S HEART THUDDED LIKE a kettle drum as the black SUV crunched up the gravel drive and Glenmere Hall came into view. Late summer sunshine gilded the honey-colored stone, making the Georgian mansion glow against the backdrop of ancient oaks. Ivy climbed between the tall windows, softening the building's grandeur into something almost fairytale-like.

This would be home for...however long she lasted in the competition.

The driver pulled up at the sweeping entrance, where broad limestone steps led up to imposing double doors. Twin stone urns overflowed with deep purple heliotrope and ruby-red dahlias, their rich colors punctuated by cascading sprays of white jasmine. The freshly pressure-washed façade spoke of the careful restoration that had transformed this historic estate into the Starbound Campus. Through the windows, Kezia caught glimpses of what looked like original paintings and elegant furniture. Clearly no expense had been spared in maintaining Glenmere's heritage.

"Here we are. Best of luck, Miss," the driver said.

She flashed him a smile. "Thanks."

She stepped out of the car, smoothing down her navy wrap dress. The production team's note recommended that she wear something comfortable but camera-ready for Arrival Day. Her dress was professional without being fussy, and her leather ballet-style pumps would see her through whatever the day might bring.

She'd splurged a full day's pay getting her Afro trimmed and styled at a specialist London salon, one she normally couldn't afford. To be honest, she still couldn't. But she needed the confidence boost of knowing she looked her best.

Before she could reach for her luggage, a young woman with a pixie cut the color of cotton candy bounded down the limestone steps to meet her.

Clipboard in hand, headset around her neck, and wearing an impossibly bright smile, the woman's energy fizzed around her like champagne bubbles. "Hi, Kezia! I'm Sophie, your Contestant Coordinator. We are so excited to have you here!"

"Lovely to meet you, Sophie."

"Don't worry about your bags!" Sophie waved to someone behind Kezia. "Our crew will take them to your room in the residence block. We'll get you settled in there later, but first we need to handle some paperwork and get you properly oriented. Follow me!" She gestured toward the impressive double doors.

Sophie led Kezia into what must have been the original library, now transformed into a bright welcome area. Ornate bookshelves still lined the walls, but modern tables had been set up to create workstations.

"Grab a seat, please, and let's do this! Okay, so first things first." Sophie pulled out a chair at one of the tables, her enthusiasm never wavering. "You'll need to hand over your phone. You got the email about our no-electronics policy, right? Since you're all being sequestered for the duration?"

Kezia nodded, pulling out her phone. "Do you need me to—?"

"Yes, please power it down completely." Sophie held out a labeled envelope. "And you didn't bring any other devices? Laptop, tablet?"

"No, I left those at home as requested." Well, in storage, anyway. Along with the rest of her belongings.

"Perfect! Don't worry, you'll still be able to contact your family and loved ones. We have designated phone times twice a week in the communication room. Twenty minutes per call, all supervised of course. We need to keep internet and social media access strictly controlled during filming." Sophie sealed the phone envelope. "Zach was super specific about this. He wants everyone to focus on their artistic development without outside distractions. He's thought of everything, you know?"

Kezia managed not to roll her eyes. Zach was certainly hands-on. But Sophie's fangirling made it clear she'd never been on the receiving end of one of his razor-edged remarks.

After Kezia handed over her powered-down phone, Sophie spread out several documents. "Just a few forms to sign. Zach reviewed all these procedures personally. He's been so hands-on with every detail. Did you know he even selected the grand piano in the main performance space himself? Flew to Vienna just to test it out!"

Was everyone here this starry-eyed about Zach? The man she'd met had been precise to the point of clinical, not this paragon of artistic vision Sophie was describing.

While Kezia worked through the paperwork, Sophie pulled out a thick welcome packet from a black leather portfolio. The embossed *Starbound* logo caught the library's natural light. A stylized star ascending in deep blue and silver.

"This has everything you need to know for your time here. Let me walk you through it." Sophie flipped open the portfolio. "First, there's your daily schedule template. Breakfast is served from six to eight every morning in the communal dining room. Then you've got your practice room assignments. Zach made sure everyone gets equal studio time."

She pointed to a detailed map. "This shows all the areas you'll need to know. The residence block is here, practice rooms here, and the main assembly space is in what used to be the ballroom. Red zones are production areas and strictly off-limits to contestants. Don't worry if it all seems like a lot to take in. You'll have a full orientation later today when all the other contestants are here. Oh, and here's the contact sheet for all the key staff. I'm your main point of contact, available 24/7, but you've also got numbers for medical, technical support, and your assigned vocal coach."

Kezia nodded along, trying to focus on the map Sophie was pointing to, but the information was coming at her like a blast from a fire hose. Practice rooms, red zones, vocal coaches... She'd have to review all this later when her head stopped spinning.

Sophie tapped another section. "These are the filming guidelines. Really important. Like, super important. Green lights mean cameras are rolling, red means we're between takes. Zach wants everyone to feel completely natural on camera, but it helps to know when you're actually being filmed. And these tabs mark the house rules, performance protocols, and elimination procedures. But, like I said, don't worry about taking it all in yet. You'll have plenty of time to absorb all that, and you're getting a full orientation later. Now, if you're done signing all those documents, I'll grab them off you. Ready to see your room?"

Good, her room. Some space of her own. Between the endless stream of information and Sophie's apparent conviction that Zach Falconer walked on water, Kezia was more than ready for a moment of quiet to process it all.

Sophie gathered up the signed forms. "Right! Let's get you settled in. The contestants are staying in the converted carriage house. It's four to a room, dormitory style, but don't worry, we've made sure everyone has their own space. You'll get a proper tour of the grounds during orientation later, but first things first."

They stepped out into the late morning sunshine. A gravel path curved across manicured lawns toward an impressive stone building where the original carriage house and stable block had been connected by a modern glass atrium. Ivy softened sections of the honey-colored walls, and what had once been stable doorways now housed elegant arched windows. The *Starbound* logo gleamed above the entrance, and through the glass atrium, Kezia glimpsed a courtyard with outdoor seating arranged around a fire pit.

"The building's been completely renovated inside," Sophie explained as they approached the entrance. "But they've kept all the character features. Wait until you see the main living area. It's stunning."

She wasn't exaggerating. As they passed through the atrium, the former carriage bay took Kezia's breath away. A double-height ceiling with exposed wooden beams soared overhead, and floor-to-ceiling windows flooded the space with natural light. Enormous slate blue sectional sofas formed conversation areas beneath a spectacular modern fireplace feature wall. A massive television screen mounted nearby suggested this was where they'd gather for group activities.

Sophie led her past a state-of-the-art kitchen with a dining area that could have come straight from a luxury magazine, all anchored by a stunning chandelier above a table that could easily seat twenty. "The bedrooms are upstairs," she said. "I'll show you to yours."

At the top of the stairs, Sophie led Kezia to a bedroom at the far end of the floor. The door opened to reveal a bright, airy room with large windows overlooking the gardens. Four single beds with crisp white linens and navy accent pillows were spaced comfortably along the walls, each with its own desk, reading lamp, and privacy curtain. Storage trunks in dark wood sat at the foot of each bed. Kezia's suitcase waited beside one of them.

"This looks really nice," Kezia said, appreciating the thoughtful layout and neutral decor. Then she noticed the small camera crew already set up inside—a camera operator, sound technician, and a young female producer with a clipboard.

"Hi, guys. This is Kezia." Sophie turned toward her. "The crew will be filming first impressions. Laura here will guide you through it. I need to head back down because we've got another arrival due any minute."

With a bright smile and wave, Sophie disappeared like a pink-haired whirlwind, leaving Kezia with the production team.

"So," Laura said, approaching with an encouraging smile, "if you could just take your suitcase back outside, we'll capture your genuine reaction to seeing your room for the first time."

Kezia blinked. "I'm sorry?"

"Just step outside with your suitcase, then come back in and react naturally. Maybe a little gasp of excitement when you see the space?"

The reality hit like a splash of cold water. This wasn't just about singing anymore. Every moment, even something as simple as entering a bedroom, was going to be choreographed and filmed. The cameras wouldn't just be there for performances or group activities; they would be capturing everything, manufacturing "authentic" moments out of thin air.

"You want me to...pretend I'm seeing the room for the first time?"

"Just give us an authentic first-time reaction," Laura said, as if this request wasn't fundamentally contradictory. "It helps viewers connect with your journey."

Feeling ridiculous, Kezia wheeled her suitcase back into the hall. At Laura's signal, she re-entered, attempting an enthusiastic "Wow!" that sounded stiff even to her own ears.

"Great effort," Laura said, "but could we try once more with a bit more excitement? Remember, this gorgeous space you've just laid your eyes on is your home for the next several weeks."

By the third take, Kezia's "spontaneous" reaction had become increasingly awkward. She was a professional vocalist, not an actress, and the fakeness of the situation was throwing her off balance.

Laura said, "Okay, we need to keep things moving. Why don't you unpack your suitcase while just chatting naturally about what you're doing?"

"You mean show my stuff on camera?"

"Nothing too personal—just something with emotional significance. A photo of a loved one, maybe a childhood keepsake, something like that?"

Kezia looked down at her suitcase. "I brought my humidifier."

Laura blinked. "Not what I was expecting... but sure. Let's go with that. Why do you travel with a humidifier?"

Kezia pulled out the appliance, carefully unwrapping it from the protective towel she'd packed around it. "Because

I make a living with my voice. I need to do everything I can to protect my instrument. Maintaining optimal humidity is crucial for vocal cord health."

Laura nodded encouragingly and Kezia continued talking. Finally, she could discuss something she actually knew about. "In older buildings like this, the air can get quite dry. And with the amount of singing we'll be doing..." She retrieved her hygrometer next, placing it precisely on the corner of her desk. She leaned forward to read the digital display. "See? Only thirty-two percent humidity right now. I always keep track of the room's humidity levels. Anything below forty percent can cause strain on the vocal folds."

"Could you explain a bit more about that?" Laura prompted from behind the camera.

"Well, when people talk about hydration, they normally just think about drinking water. But proper hydration is about so much more." Kezia set up the humidifier with practiced efficiency, measuring the exact distance from her bed with her hand spans. "The vocal cords need surface hydration too. Think of them like violin strings. They need to be at the right tension to produce clear sound. Too dry, and they become stiff and prone to damage. That's why I also brought my steam inhaler. Once I get the humidifier running, we should see these numbers improve within the hour."

Were Laura's eyes glazing over? Maybe that's because Kezia wasn't explaining this in enough detail. She raised a finger. "It's also really important to monitor the mucus membrane's hydration levels." She began arranging her collection of saline sprays in a neat row on her desk, ordering them by frequency of use. "I have this whole routine with my saline sprays and—"

The door swung open.

"Oh my goodness, this place is incredible!"

The gasp of delight sounded so natural that Kezia almost forgot there were cameras rolling. A young woman with expertly styled honey-blond waves swept into the room with the kind of effortless grace Kezia associated with Instagram influencers. Her designer athleisure wear looked both comfortable and expensive, and her "natural" makeup was flawless.

"Hi! You must be one of my roommates. I'm Brianna!" She approached Kezia with a warm smile, somehow making what should have been an awkward on-camera introduction feel completely spontaneous.

Laura brightened at Brianna's arrival, and the cameras started to track the young woman.

Without missing a beat, Brianna floated around the room, exclaiming over the garden view and asking Kezia questions.

The camera crew followed her around, letting her talk without interruption. Clearly, they liked what she was doing. They never had to scold her once for looking at the camera.

When her gaze landed on Kezia's desk, Brianna's head tilted with curiosity. "Oh, look at all these gadgets. Is this a humidifier? You must be one of those singers who's really into the science of it all."

Kezia nodded. "Yes, I take a scientific approach to my vocal health."

"Mm. I prefer to let my muse lead," Brianna said with a giggle. "So exciting to be here, though, isn't it? I was on pins for days after my audition waiting for the callback. When did you find out you'd made it?"

"Oh, um, they actually offered me a place right after I finished my audition."

Something flickered behind Brianna's bright smile. "Wow, that's amazing! You must have really impressed them. I guess that makes you a real front-runner here."

When the crew finally packed up their equipment and left, the room felt suddenly larger. Kezia exhaled slowly, only now realizing how tense she'd been.

Brianna's demeanor shifted, too. She was still friendly, but somehow less...sparkly.

"First time with reality TV cameras?" Brianna asked, arranging her makeup collection on her desk with an efficiency that suggested long practice.

"Is it that obvious?" Kezia said. "You weren't even here when they made me re-enter the room three times because I was failing to get my spontaneous excitement right."

"You'll get used to it," Brianna said with a shrug. "By week two, you'll barely notice them. And don't worry about that whole re-entry thing. When I was on *Breakout*, they made me do five takes of meeting my roommate because I didn't look 'surprised enough.'"

She paused, then let out a pitch-perfect gasp of feigned surprise.

Kezia laughed.

Brianna patted her arm. "I'm an old hand at this. Stick with me, and I'll show you the ropes. Guess we'd better finish unpacking."

As Kezia turned back to her suitcase, a thought struck her. Which version of Brianna was the performance? The one for the cameras, or this one?

Chapter 10

As Kezia put the last of her blouses away in her assigned drawer, she listened to Brianna telling war stories to their two other roommates.

"So there I was, center stage at the O2," Brianna said, perched elegantly on her bed. "Waiting for my backing track to begin. But seconds before my cue, complete technical failure."

Lily Wang, cross-legged on her own bed with the perfect posture that screamed "classical musician," covered her mouth with her hand. "No way! So, what did you do?"

"Performed it *a cappella*, of course." Brianna shrugged as if improvising with no backing instruments in front of thousands was nothing special. "That's the thing about live TV. You have to be ready for anything."

At just twenty-three, Brianna already had more reality TV experience than the rest of them combined.

Jasmine Lopez sat on the floor between the beds, drinking in every word. "I can't believe you've done this before. I mean, I've been in every production our community theater has put on since I was fourteen, so I'm used to performing live, but television is so different."

"Oh, it's a whole other world," Brianna said. "But not to worry. I can show you all the little insider hacks."

A chime sounded through the intercom system, followed by Sophie's bright voice: "All contestants, please gather on the front lawn for your official welcome and compound tour!"

Brianna was on her feet instantly. "This is it, ladies. First impression time. Just need to touch up my lip gloss."

While Jasmine and Lily fussed with their appearances, Kezia checked the room's humidity levels. They were finally where she wanted them.

"Come on, Kezia," Brianna called from the doorway. "We want to time our entrance perfectly. They'll want reaction shots of everyone arriving, so let's not be first or last. We're after somewhere in the sweet spot where they can get good coverage."

They waited another minute before heading downstairs and out onto the front yard. Brianna was right—camera operators were positioned to catch contestants' entrances from multiple angles.

The early afternoon sun warmed the limestone steps where Maya, the elegant woman Kezia met at the audition, stood to address them. Behind her, Glenmere Hall's imposing façade provided a perfect backdrop for the cameras.

"Welcome to *Starbound*," Maya said, her voice carrying naturally across the lawn. "Some of you already met me as the casting director at your auditions, but I'm acting as your talent producer now. This isn't just another singing competition. What you're about to experience is the most comprehensive artist development program ever captured on television."

"Cut!" A spiky-haired man with horn-rimmed glasses stepped forward. "Sorry, everyone, but we need more energy from you all. Remember, this is exciting! You've made it onto *Starbound*! Big smiles. React to what Maya's saying."

Brianna nudged Kezia. "They'll cut between our reactions for the final edit," she whispered around a wide grin. "Try to look impressed, but not desperate."

Maya resumed her welcome with the same polished delivery. "Over the next twelve weeks, you'll face challenges designed to transform you into launch-ready artists. Vocal performance, image development, songwriting—every aspect of your craft will be tested and refined."

"The prize package reflects our commitment to real artist development," she continued. "The winner receives not just a record deal, but a complete launch package: professionally produced music, music video, and a tour-ready performance set."

Kezia's throat tightened. That kind of launch package could change everything for her.

The other contestants nodded enthusiastically, exchanging excited glances.

Kezia caught Brianna's sparkling gaze and grinned back. How many takes would they need to get their "natural" reactions right?

Just two turned out to be enough. After that, Maya led them across the manicured lawns toward a complex of buildings that wrapped around a courtyard. "The main house is reserved for production offices and you won't spend much, if any, time there," she explained, "but this is where the real work happens. We've converted the original service buildings and added purpose-built facilities to create a state-of-the-art rehearsal complex."

The first building, a converted stable block, housed a row of individual practice rooms. "These are your personal rehearsal spaces," Maya said. "You'll have designated time slots, and yes..." She smiled as several hands went up. "They're all soundproofed."

Kezia peered through an open door at a room equipped with recording equipment and acoustic panels. This was more professional than some of the studios she'd recorded in.

"See that guy standing to Maya's left?" Brianna whispered. "Jamie Collins."

Kezia glanced at the lanky young man with tousled dirty blond hair as Brianna continued talking. "He had a couple of hit albums when he was a kid. He launched his third one when he was fourteen, but it tanked. Big time.

He's been in the wilderness ever since, and this is definitely his last shot."

Kezia sneaked another look at the man—more a boy, really—taking in his fitted shirt, designer jeans, and peach fuzz facial hair. He couldn't be more than twenty-one, and Brianna was already writing him off as a has-been? What did that make Kezia at twenty-nine? A never-was?

They crossed the courtyard to a modern glass and steel structure that connected to the old coach house. Inside was a full performance space complete with stage lighting and a professional sound system.

"Your mentors will work with you here for your onstage presence and performance skills," Maya said. "We've replicated exactly what you'll encounter during the live shows."

Brianna seemed more interested in dishing out information about their fellow contestants than in hearing about the facilities. "The girl with the red hair?" she murmured to Kezia. "Sandra Cassidy. Two million followers on TikTok. Her covers are everywhere, and she's actually pretty good. She's got the online audience but needs industry legitimacy. I've heard she was also given an on-the-spot offer at the auditions."

How on earth had Brianna got the inside scoop on people this fast?

"Watch how they're filming us walking through the courtyard," Brianna said. "They'll speed this up with music underneath. Classic reality TV transition shot. Keep your steps smooth and elegant so you don't end up looking like a Smurf."

Next, they came to the newly constructed recording studio wing. Through the glass, Kezia could see multiple isolation booths and a control room filled with top-of-the-line equipment.

"This is where you'll record your performances for on-line streaming," Maya said. "Our technical team will be available around the clock to support your development."

Brianna inclined her head toward a tall, striking man at the mixing board—biracial, maybe, judging from his tawny complexion and silky brown curls. "That's Neil Phillips. Been gigging since he was fifteen, along with some model-ing work. Management's already sniffing around, but I don't think he's signed with anyone before. Good voice—but his ego barely fits in the room."

Kezia was only half-listening to Brianna now, mentally cataloging the facilities. The humidity controls in the prac-tice rooms, the acoustic treatment, the monitoring system-s...everything a serious vocalist could want. *Starbound* had really gone all out.

"Remember," Maya concluded, "you'll have more re-sources here than anywhere else in the industry. Use them."

As the tour wound down, the contestants naturally drifted into small groups in the courtyard. Camera operators circulated among them, and the spiky-haired producer called out, "Just chat naturally about your first impressions of the facilities and the mentors. You'll be getting your mentor assignments tomorrow. Who are you hoping to work with? Keep the energy up."

Kezia found herself with her roommates near a stone bench.

Lily's eyes were bright with enthusiasm. "Diana Morris would be amazing to work with. She's an absolute legend. You don't have a decades-long career like hers for nothing. Did you see her Wembley show last year?"

Jasmine nodded. "Diana's great, but I'm hoping to get Tyler Reed. Imagine getting a song crafted by her." She grinned. "But I wouldn't say no to Zach Falconer. Have you seen his arms? He's so hot." She giggled, and Brianna and Lily joined in.

Kezia crossed her arms. She used to think Zach Falconer was hot, too. Right up until she'd met him.

"What about you, Kezia?" Brianna turned to her. "Who do you want as your mentor?"

Kezia answered without thinking. "I'll gladly work with anyone but Zach Falconer. Did you hear what he said to me at auditions?"

The moment the words left her mouth, Kezia froze, her gaze darting to the nearby camera operator she'd momentarily forgotten. Oh, no.

Brianna's eyes brightened. "No, I didn't hear. What did he say?"

Before Kezia could think of a suitable way to extract her foot from her mouth, Maya spoke up. "That's it for our tour, everyone. The only other scheduled activity for today is dinner at six o'clock. Make sure you all get some rest, because tomorrow will be intense. The mentors will select their teams, and your *Starbound* journey truly begins."

The group began to disperse and Laura approached Kezia.

"Kezia? We'd like to get you in the confession room now for a quick interview."

Brianna grabbed Kezia's arm. "Confession room already? Oh honey, it must have been that juicy comment you made about Zach." She lowered her voice. "Get ready, babe. They're going to milk this for all it's worth."

Chapter 11

*T*HE SOUND-PROOFED CONFESSION room, located in a corner of the contestants' house, was barely larger than a walk-in closet, but it had been transformed into a professional interview space.

A single leather chair sat positioned against a dark backdrop emblazoned with the metallic *Starbound* logo. Three cameras were arranged to catch every angle. One straight on, two for profile shots. The lighting setup was intense, making the small space uncomfortably warm.

Kezia perched on the edge of the chair, hyper-aware of her posture. Why did this feel like an interrogation room?

Mark, the spiky-haired producer with horn-rimmed glasses, sat just off-camera with a clipboard.

Now that he wasn't barking orders, his calm presence suggested years of coaxing nervous contestants to open up. While the camera operator made final adjustments to the lighting, Mark chatted casually about the weather and asked if she was comfortable.

"I'm okay," she said. It couldn't be farther from the truth.

"Try to relax. Let's start with a few questions about your first impressions." Mark's tone was warm and conversational. "So, Kezia, what do you think of the Starbound Campus?"

The easy question helped her relax slightly. "I was really impressed by—"

"Sorry," Mark interrupted gently. "When I ask a question, it won't show up in the show. So, could you try and repeat the question in your answer? And keep the answers in the present tense? So, say, 'I think the Starbound Campus is' and so on. Do you want to try again?"

"Right, of course." Kezia took a breath. "I'm really impressed by the facilities on the Starbound Campus. They've got everything we need to develop as artists."

"And the other contestants? Tell us your thoughts about the ones you've met."

"The other contestants were all so welcoming—"

"Present tense," Mark reminded her with a smile.

"Sorry. The other contestants are all so welcoming," she said, navigating carefully. "And everyone's so talented. They all bring something unique to the competition. The level of talent is incredible." She was starting to feel more confident. This wasn't so different from a regular interview, after all.

Mark shifted his tone slightly, leaning toward her with increased interest. "We noticed your comment about Zach Falconer earlier. Can you elaborate on that?"

The change in energy was subtle but unmistakable. Kezia straightened in her chair, professional instincts kicking in. The warm-up was over. This was what they'd really brought her in for.

She swallowed. "I probably shouldn't have said that about Zach. It wasn't professional. It's just that..." She paused, choosing her words carefully, conscious of the camera catching her every expression. "I think I'd work better with a mentor who immediately sees my potential rather than just my technical background."

"So you don't want to work with Zach?" Mark pushed, exactly as she'd suspected he would. His casual demeanor had shifted to something more focused, like a detective who'd caught a witness in a revealing statement.

"All the mentors have incredible expertise to offer, and I'd be fortunate to work with any of them." She fought to keep her expression neutral, but even as the words left her mouth, she knew no one would buy it.

"Zach had some strong opinions at your audition. Why do you think he's wrong about you?" Mark's tone was gentle again. "How are you going to show him that you do belong here?"

The questions caught her off guard. She'd been prepared to be defensive, but this...this touched something deeper. "I've spent years... I spend every day working to be the best vocalist I can be. My technical background isn't a limitation. It's the foundation everything else stands on."

Her throat tightened, and she blinked away the sudden rush of moisture in her eyes. "But Mr. Falconer doesn't see that. He just sees another session singer who should stay in her lane."

The moment the words left her mouth, she knew she'd given them exactly what they wanted.

"This really means a lot to you, doesn't it?" Mark asked softly.

Kezia tried to backtrack. "What I mean is—"

"No, that was perfect," Mark cut in smoothly. "Just one more question. What if Zach chooses you to be on his team tomorrow?"

A small, incredulous laugh escaped her before she could stop it. "I don't think that'll happen."

"Why not?"

"There are fifteen other very talented singers here. I imagine he'll choose contestants whose styles align more with his vision." Even as she tried to sound professional, she could hear the hint of bitterness creeping into her words.

"Thanks a lot, Kezia," Mark said. "That'll be all for today. Great job."

As Kezia left the confession room, the cooler air of the hallway was a relief. But she couldn't shake the feeling that she'd just provided exactly the kind of content the producers wanted. She'd tried to be careful. But her heart had spoken louder than her caution—and the cameras had caught every word. Brianna was right. They were going to milk this for all it was worth.

Chapter 12

*E*ARLY THE NEXT MORNING, Kezia and the other fifteen *Starbound* contestants stood on a raised platform behind a heavy velvet curtain in what had once been Glenmere Hall's grand ballroom.

The nervous energy was palpable, contestants shifting from foot to foot or smoothing invisible wrinkles from their carefully chosen outfits. Today was the day they'd find out who would be mentoring them.

Production assistants had arranged them in even rows, fussing over their spacing like florists arranging a display.

"Two minutes, everyone," a floor manager called out. "Remember—big smiles when the curtain opens!"

Kezia stood in the back row, just behind Brianna. Her hands were cold, though the studio lights blazed hot on the other side of the curtain. After that confession room interview, she wasn't sure whether to hope Zach picked her or pray he didn't.

"This is the fun part," Brianna whispered, somehow managing to look perfectly relaxed. "They love these big reveal moments. Pure drama." She lowered her voice further. "And after what you said about Zach? The cameras are going to be all over your reactions, babe. Keep that in mind."

Kezia's stomach dropped. She hadn't thought about that.

The curtain slowly parted. Blinding lights momentarily dazzled her before the ballroom came into view. The mentors sat facing the contestants, seated on four throne-like chairs, illuminated by dramatic spotlights that cast their silhouettes across the polished floor.

Diana Morris exuded regal elegance in a stunning crimson pantsuit, her silver jewelry casting sparkles of light with every slight movement. Ryan Sterling slouched with practiced casualness in his chair, designer sneakers paired incongruously with a tailored suit. Tyler Reed sat forward, her cropped hair styled beautifully, studying the contestants with a slight smile. And at the end, Zach Falconer, expressionless, arms crossed, his gaze scanning as if systematically assessing each potential team member.

His eyes slid past Kezia as if she didn't exist. Not even a flicker of recognition. And somehow, that stung more than it should have. Had he already dismissed her?

The show's host Olivia Chang strode onto the platform, carrying herself with an easy confidence that made Kezia stand straighter just watching her. She wore her sharp tailored suit with the perfectly styled elegance of a clothes mannequin.

"Welcome to the *Starbound* Mentor Selection!" Olivia's voice filled the space. "Today, our mentors will each select four contestants to guide through this competition."

She turned to the contestants. "The mentors have been reviewing your auditions, gauging and assessing whom they want on their team. Your mentor will serve as your artistic guide, helping you develop and grow as you progress through the competition. Each comes with solid industry expertise and a strong philosophy of music."

What was Zach's philosophy of music? Did she fit?

Olivia said, "The selection works like this: mentors choose one artist at a time. To ensure complete fairness, we've randomized the selection order. And our random draw has determined that the selection order will begin with Zach, followed by Ryan, Diana, and Tyler."

A ripple of excitement went through the contestants. Kezia's fingernails dug into her palms. Zach got first pick. Of course he did.

"To level the playing field," Olivia continued, "when a mentor chooses a singer, any other mentor can speak up if they want the same contestant. If multiple mentors want the same contestant, the contestant will choose between them. This is your journey, after all." She smiled warmly at the group. "Each mentor must select four contestants by the end of the process. Are you ready?"

Ready? Kezia had never felt less ready in her life. But the cameras were rolling, and this was happening whether she was ready or not.

"Zach, you get to choose first," Olivia said. "Who will it be?"

The cameras swept across their faces, and Kezia forced herself to breathe normally. Brianna's warning echoed in her mind. They'd be watching for her reaction no matter what happened.

Zach took his time responding, a finger resting on his chin as he surveyed the group. His gaze skimmed past her again, and she hated the way her pulse skipped. Why did she care what he thought?

"I'm looking for someone with untapped potential," he said finally. "Someone ready to transform their approach to artistry." He paused, and Kezia's heart hammered against her ribs. "For my first pick, I choose Jamie Collins."

"Interesting choice," Brianna murmured. "The ex-child star. Didn't see that coming."

As Jamie made his way down to the platform, Kezia released a breath.

"Ryan..." Olivia turned to the next mentor. "It's your turn."

Ryan smiled, relaxed and confident. "I'm impressed by technical excellence and professional-level skill. This artist has both in abundance. For my first pick, I choose Kezia Blair."

Relief washed over Kezia. Ryan was a solid presence in the music industry. And she was his first pick!

As she stepped forward, her legs steadier than she'd expected, Olivia's voice cut through the moment. "Hold on, Kezia. Don't move just yet. We have another mentor interested!"

Diana's hand was raised, her elegant posture commanding attention even from her seated position. A collective gasp went up from the other contestants, followed by excited whispers.

"Diana is also interested in working with Kezia," Olivia said. "This means, Kezia, you have a choice to make."

Two of them wanted her? That was beyond anything she'd dared to hope for. And Ryan and Diana were the most influential and established of the four. After spending the whole morning dreading being picked last, being the contestant no one wanted, Kezia found herself with an actual choice to make.

Ryan held up his hand. "Before you choose, Kezia, let me say this. You've got the technical chops of Whitney, Mariah, Christina. I can put you on exactly the same path they took. With your training and my connections, we could create the next great vocal diva. I hope you'll choose me."

"Excuse me." Diana placed her hands on her hips. "If Ryan gets to pitch, then I want to pitch, too."

The contestants chuckled as Diana continued speaking. "Kezia, your voice is extraordinary. I can hear your training and your technical mastery. As a fellow vocalist, I thoroughly understand what you can do, as well as your potential. Because amazing as you are, I know we haven't yet seen your full capabilities. I'd love to work with you on bringing more of your heart into those impressive runs, and help you connect with the audience on a deeper level."

Kezia bit her lip. They weren't making this easy. Ryan's industry connections versus Diana's experience in the trenches.

"Kezia," Olivia said, "it's up to you. Would you prefer to work with Ryan or Diana?"

Her pulse thundered in her ears as she looked between them.

Ryan sat forward in his chair, one eyebrow raised expectantly.

Diana's smile was warm, genuine.

Both were incredible in their own right. Both could teach her so much.

"They're both incredible mentors," Kezia said, proud her voice came out clear and steady. "But I think I need someone who has a clear vision of where I want to be." She held Ryan's gaze. "I choose Ryan."

Ryan gave a satisfied nod while Diana's smile turned gracious.

"A loss for me," Diana said, "but a good match for you both."

Kezia's cheeks warmed at the praise as she made her way to stand behind Ryan's chair. Despite her best intentions, her gaze drifted to Zach. His expression didn't change. No sign that her choice—or her presence—meant anything to him at all. She lifted her chin slightly. Fine. She'd show him exactly what he'd overlooked.

"Diana," Olivia said, "you have the next pick. Who would you like on your team?"

"For my first pick," Diana said, "I choose Sandra Cassidy."

As Sandra's shoulders relaxed, a movement caught everyone's attention. Zach had raised his hand.

"We have another challenge!" Olivia said. "Zach is also interested in working with Sandra." She paused as Tyler's hand shot up as well. "And Tyler too! Three mentors vying for one contestant."

A buzz of excitement rippled through the remaining contestants.

Sandra's face flushed pink beneath her freckles, making her look even younger than sixteen. With copper-red hair falling in waves around her heart-shaped face and those huge green eyes, Sandra was exactly what casting directors dreamed of—the perfect mix of innocence and raw talent. The girl just needed the right mentor to help her handle the pressure that came with that kind of attention.

And Kezia had heard Sandra practicing in the one of the rehearsal rooms yesterday. Her voice had the kind of natural soul that couldn't be manufactured, wrapped in vocal cords that could handle Adele's most challenging runs.

"Sandra," Olivia said, "you have quite a choice ahead of you. Would you prefer to work with Diana, Tyler, or Zach?"

Sandra's small hands twisted together as she looked between the three mentors. "This is such an honor," she said, her voice trembling slightly. "All of you are incredible artists, but..." She took a deep breath, and Kezia found herself holding hers in sympathy. "I grew up listening to Diana, and I've been a fan for years. My mum says I sang 'This is Us' before I could talk. I choose Diana."

Diana's face lit up while Zach inclined his head.

"Tyler..." Olivia turned to the final mentor. "It's your turn to choose."

The rest of the draft unfolded like a carefully choreographed dance. Tyler chose Michael Grant, a jazz pianist whose arrangements had caught everyone's attention during auditions.

Kezia glanced at Brianna, suddenly aware she'd been so caught up in her own drama that she hadn't considered how her roommate must be feeling, still waiting to be chosen.

But Brianna maintained her camera-ready smile, perfectly poised despite the pressure.

"For my second pick," Zach said, "I choose Lily Wang."

Kezia's other roommate. Lily flushed and smiled as she made her way to Zach. Interesting pick. Though classically trained on violin, Lily had taught herself to sing, developing a crystalline soprano that could shatter glass.

As the selections continued, Kezia felt Ryan shift in his chair. "Brianna Taylor," he announced for his second pick, and Kezia's heart lifted. She'd grown closer to Brianna than anyone else here, and now they'd be on the same team.

Brianna's confident stride to join them matched her broad smile. "Told you the cameras would be watching," she whispered as she took her place beside Kezia. "But you handled it like a pro." She glanced over at Sandra standing behind Diana's chair. "Though not quite as much drama as Little Miss Three Mentors over there. Must be nice to have millions of followers before you even start."

When Zach chose Neil Phillips for his third pick—a soulful guitarist with a voice like warm honey, Kezia noticed a pattern emerging. Every one of Zach's choices was a musician who'd found their own way to their voices, whether through self-teaching or unconventional paths. There wasn't a traditionally trained vocalist among them.

Ryan completed his team with Dominic Carter and Jordan Hayes, both strong vocalists with professional experience. Diana and Tyler filled out their teams with their final selections, and suddenly it was done.

"These are your *Starbound* teams," Olivia announced. "Tomorrow, you'll begin working with your mentors. For now, take some time to get to know your teammates."

Brianna threw an arm around Kezia's shoulders. "Team Ryan all the way."

The nearest cameraman swung to capture the celebratory moment. Of course, the show would want footage of teammates bonding.

Brianna leaned closer, still grinning. "Between your technique and my stage presence, we're going to be unstoppable."

Chapter 13

*L*ATER THAT EVENING, KEZIA sat in a private dining room with Ryan and her new teammates.

Dinner with Team Ryan had been pleasant enough, if a bit stilted at first. They'd started the process of getting to know each other over expertly prepared food that Kezia had barely tasted, too aware of the cameras capturing every bite, every laugh, every "natural" moment of team bonding. Ryan and Brianna carried most of the conversation, telling entertaining stories that eventually had everyone chuckling. They had all had started to relax by dessert, including Jordan, who'd been quiet since the team selection.

Perhaps it was because Jordan was among the last contestants to be chosen. That had to be weighing on the young woman's mind.

As waiters cleared the dishes, Ryan announced he wanted individual time with each team member to discuss their development strategies.

"Let's make use of these beautiful grounds," he said. "I find walking conversations more productive than sitting in stuffy rooms, especially after such a wonderful meal. I'll start with you, Brianna."

Kezia watched as each of her teammates took their turns. Brianna returned from her walk looking triumphant, and Dominic seemed quietly pleased after his one-on-one with their mentor. Neither of them volunteered to share what they'd discussed with Ryan, instead making small talk about everything else. Jordan was the third to go. When she returned, her expression was tight, though she, too, gave nothing away when Kezia caught her gaze.

"Kezia," Ryan called from the terrace doors. "Ready for our strategy session?"

Kezia's pulse quickened as she stepped toward Ryan and the ever-present camera crew.

He flashed her a warm smile.

The evening air carried the sweet scent of late-blooming jasmine as they stepped onto one of the gravel paths winding through the estate gardens. Their footsteps crunched in sync while behind them, the camera operator navigated carefully around pruned shrubs and ornamental borders.

"I've saved the best for last," Ryan said as they walked, angling himself slightly toward the camera. She was the same height as he, although she was wearing flats. But he had a solid physique that gave the impression of confidence and strength. "There's a reason I picked you first, Kezia. You've got the potential to win this entire competition."

His words soothed all the places bruised since Zach Falconer had put her down. Ryan Sterling, the man who'd launched multiple chart-topping careers, saw her potential.

Pride flowered in her chest like a rare tropical bloom, unfamiliar after years of being in the background. "Wow. Thank you."

"I don't say that lightly," he said. "Your technical foundation is phenomenal." He gestured expressively as they strolled past a row of carefully pruned hedges.

The setting sun stretched their shadows along the path. Somewhere, a blackbird sang.

"I've worked with Grammy winners who don't have your control and range. You're already at a professional level most contestants will never reach."

Did he really mean that? "Thank you. That means a lot coming from you."

Ryan stopped beside a stone bench and turned to face her.

The camera operator circled to catch both their profiles.

"And let's be honest. You have so much more going for you. The complete package." He gestured appreciatively. "You're stunning. You've got the kind of bone structure that lets you pull off that short-haired Afro look, which tells me the stylists will be able to do anything with you.

And you photograph extremely well. We're talking about serious marketability here."

Kezia didn't know what to say to that. Agree with him? That would be too conceited. Deny her awareness of her looks? False humility would be even worse. And yet accepting his compliment felt equally weird as he assessed her features like items on a checklist. She masked her discomfort with a nod, unsure how to receive a compliment that felt more like an appraisal.

Thankfully, Ryan didn't seem to expect an answer. "All of that means you've got a huge head start compared to the rest of the pack."

Ryan started walking again, and she fell into step beside him. "Here's what I'm thinking for your journey on *Starbound*. While others will work on basics, we can focus immediately on your market positioning. You're versatile enough to excel in multiple genres—adult contemporary, R&B, pop, soul, and a laundry list of others that'll come to me if I think about it a bit more."

They came up to a small fountain, its gentle splashing providing perfect background ambiance for filming.

Ryan paused again. "I'm sure you've heard of some of my greatest success stories—Xander Robinson, Gray Cartwright, Billy Rodriguez. We identified the right lane, created the right image, and boom, chart success followed. I plan to do the same for you."

Kezia nodded, absorbing his strategy. It made logical sense. Her versatility as a session singer meant she could adapt to whatever would be most commercially viable. It was what she'd done for years—shaping herself to fit other people's visions. Taking direction.

"The question is which market will give you the quickest path to success," Ryan continued. "I'm thinking adult contemporary with R&B influences. Sophisticated enough to showcase your technical skills but accessible enough for broad appeal."

As they rounded a corner in the path, movement caught her eye. Zach was coming toward them. His shirtsleeves were rolled up, and he carried a leather-bound notebook. He slowed as he approached, nodding a professional greeting.

Ryan, mid-flow in a description of marketing demographics, barely acknowledged his presence.

Zach stepped around them and continued on his way, the sound of his footsteps fading into the evening quiet.

Kezia said, "I'd also like to also work on finding my unique voice as an artist beyond the technique. I'm hoping that being here will give me a chance to do that."

Ryan's enthusiasm dimmed slightly, though his camera-ready smile remained. "Of course, but the artistry will evolve once you've achieved a certain level of success. You have to earn the right to do that. First, we build your career, then you can explore those nuances."

They stopped by a stone balustrade overlooking the rear gardens of the estate. Moths fluttered around the garden lights that were just beginning to illuminate the deepening dusk.

"So you're more focused on building my market profile than helping me discover my artistic voice?" Kezia asked, trying to frame it as curiosity rather than criticism.

Ryan's smile widened. "That's what sets me apart. I don't just develop voices. I develop careers. I pick winners." He paused, as though choosing his next words carefully, and Kezia noticed his eyes flick briefly toward the camera. "And considering how brutal this industry is, we need to move efficiently. You have extraordinary talent, Kezia, but at twenty-nine, you don't have the luxury of the extended development time that someone like Sandra or even Brianna might have."

His words hit like a bucket of ice water. Twenty-nine. Not exactly ancient, but in pop music terms, she was practically geriatric.

Ryan sighed. "I just finished a similar conversation with Jordan. She's very...committed to her specific artistic vision. While I respect that, it limits what I can do to help her succeed in this industry. I find I work best with artists who understand the value of being open to guidance."

His implication was clear—as a mentor, he meant to call the shots. But wasn't that what she was here for? To get the sort of guidance he was offering?

Kezia maintained her professional smile as they began walking back toward the main building in the deepening twilight. "I understand. The industry expertise you bring is exactly why I want to work with you."

"Excellent," Ryan said, his enthusiasm returning. "Tomorrow we start the real work. You have incredible commercial potential, and I'm going to push you to become the best you can be."

The producer called out, "Can you just stand there for a few more seconds, framed against the terrace doors?"

Kezia stood still, meeting Ryan's warm smile.

She should be thrilled. Ryan, famous for his sixth sense about what would make an artist sell, thought she could be a star. And that's what she wanted after years of paying her dues as a session singer and backing vocalist.

He knew what the market was, and his point about her age was valid. She didn't have much time left, or many chances. She needed to make the most of this opportunity. She just prayed she'd made the right choice.

Zach had stayed later than intended in the common room, mulling over what he'd learned about his team during their dinner. Each presented unique challenges and opportunities.

Lily, a savant with the violin, now finding her range with a voice whose ethereal beauty intrigued him. Her quiet intensity masked a deep musicality that few would recognize at first glance.

Neil might be a problem. His confidence, bordering on arrogant self-assurance, almost overshadowed his talent. Would he be willing to learn what Zach could teach him?

And Jamie. The vulnerability in the young man's eyes as he'd shared about the lost years after his time as a child star—there was something there waiting to be nurtured, once Jamie learned to trust himself again.

Lost in thought, Zach almost didn't notice the pair walking along the garden path until he was nearly upon them. Ryan Sterling with his first pick—the tall, note-perfect session singer.

Zach slowed his pace, professional courtesy requiring at least a nod of acknowledgment.

Ryan was in full pitch mode, gesturing with the confident flair that had made him famous in the industry.

The woman beside him was listening with rapt attention, her striking features composed in an expression of earnest engagement.

"...marketing analytics show this approach has a sixty-three percent higher success rate..." Ryan said.

Exactly what he'd expected. Ryan's approach was always the same—identify marketable talent, package it for optimal commercial appeal, and push it relentlessly. No conversations about personal journeys or emotional foundations, just straight to market positioning.

And the session singer was clearly buying into it, hanging on his every word. Another technically gifted performer looking for the fastest route to commercial success rather than artistic development.

As he passed them, something made Zach look directly at her. For just a moment, he caught something unexpected in her gaze. Not the blind ambition he'd anticipated, but a flicker of something more thoughtful, more questioning.

He nodded briefly and continued walking, dismissing the impression. He'd seen countless technically proficient performers come and go in this industry. People who could hit every note perfectly but never make an audience feel anything real. He'd been right to choose Jamie instead, despite the challenges ahead.

Still, as he made his way back to the main building, Zach found himself replaying her audition in his mind. Flawless—too flawless. All technical precision, but no emotional spark. All technical proficiency with nothing genuine behind it. Yet for a split second, he'd seen something different in her eyes just now.

Probably just a trick of the evening light.

Ryan would mold her into exactly the kind of commercially viable, emotionally vacant performer that the charts were already full of. That perfect technique would never be matched with authentic feeling.

So why did that brief glance bother him?

What would he do with a contestant of that caliber? How would he train her, develop her artistry? Elevate that technical skill into something that resonated on a bone deep level. Peel off the layers of perfection and—

Zach caught himself and shook his head. What was he doing? She wasn't his mentee. She'd chosen Ryan, and Ryan had chosen her. They were perfectly matched, both prioritizing commercial success over artistic authenticity.

She was exactly where she belonged. And he had four contestants who actually wanted the kind of development he offered. That's where his focus needed to be.

With a final glance back at the pair still deep in conversation, Zach quickened his pace toward the main building, determined to put the session singer out of his mind.

Chapter 14

HE MORNING AFTER THE mentor draft, Kezia sat in *Starbound's* medical examination room. A vocal health assessment usually cost her hundreds of pounds, but the show was providing one to every contestant.

She'd expected a cursory checkup, not a full ENT exam. The converted bedroom still held echoes of Glenmere Hall's grandeur—ornate crown molding, a crystal chandelier—but the sleek medical equipment and high-end laryngoscopy station signaled just how seriously *Starbound* took vocal care.

Brianna, who'd been on two other singing competitions, had been amazed when she heard about it. "Usually they just make you sign a form saying you're healthy enough to perform," she'd told Kezia that morning. "I've never heard of a show bringing in specialists."

Now, seated across from Dr. Elaine Park—a petite woman with calm, efficient movements—Kezia understood Brianna's shock. This kind of thorough screening wasn't standard on any show she knew.

"Isn't this unusually comprehensive for a TV production?" Kezia said. "Most of my friends haven't had anything close to this."

Dr. Park glanced up from her laptop, smiling slightly. "This isn't most shows. Mr. Falconer was quite insistent about having proper medical oversight for all contestants. And you've given me some very thorough documentation here. I see you've listed your maintenance routines in detail. Tell me more about your approach to vocal care."

"I keep a strict regimen," Kezia said. "Humidifier in my bedroom, proper hydration schedule, regular vocal rest periods. Session work taught me early on that consistency is crucial. I also do saline sprays. Three times a day, precisely six hours apart."

Dr. Park's eyebrows lifted. "That's...impressively regimented."

"I know it probably seems excessive. But I've found it helps maintain consistent vocal quality, especially during long recording sessions."

Dr. Park nodded approvingly while her assistant made notes. "And how long have you been doing professional vocal work?"

"I've been doing session work for the past four years," Kezia said. "Plus other bookings when I can get them. Before that, I sang backup for Lara Jackson for six months on the Europe and Asia legs of her 'Shimmer' tour. I did some theme park work—Disneyland Paris and Butlins. A stint on a cruise ship. Plus five years of training at Guildhall for undergraduate and master's degrees."

"So, would you say you work full time as a vocalist?"

"Yes, thankfully. Between the regular studio clients and picking up other gigs, I've got all the work I can handle." Kezia was grateful for that, even if it meant juggling multiple clients and learning her limits for the sake of her vocal health. A tricky balance when bills had to be paid.

"Let's take a look at those vocal folds, shall we?" Dr. Park positioned the equipment. "I'll need you to stick your tongue out and say '*eee*'—"

"—and hold that position while breathing normally through my nose," Kezia finished, already moving into position.

"I get the feeling you've done this before," Dr. Park said, a smile in her voice. "Perfect. Now just try to relax. I know it's not exactly pleasant."

Kezia made herself relax as the scope entered her nasal passage. Not painful, but definitely uncomfortable. She focused on keeping her breathing steady through her nose while maintaining the "*eee*" position with her tongue. The slight pressure and strange tickling sensation as the scope moved down to view her larynx was always the worst part, but she'd learned long ago how to stay still and calm through the procedure.

The examination proceeded in focused silence. Dr. Park worked efficiently, making small adjustments to get different views while her assistant recorded observations.

A camera operator stood unobtrusively in the corner, recording everything for the show's medical documentation.

Finally, Dr. Park withdrew the scope—triggering the telltale urge to sneeze Kezia had learned to suppress.

"Remarkable," the doctor said, turning to make notes in her file. "Your vocal folds are in exceptional condition. You clearly take your instrument seriously."

"It's what puts food on the table," Kezia said, accepting the water the assistant offered and taking a sip to ease the residual tickle in her throat. "I can't afford not to take care of my voice."

The doctor sat back. "Most performers I see only come in once they're already having problems. You're clearly doing the work to protect your voice before things go wrong." Steepling her fingers, she regarded Kezia thoughtfully. "With vocal care this meticulous and your steady work history, I'm surprised you're not already headlining."

The doctor's words touched a nerve Kezia usually kept buried. It was the same old frustration. She'd done everything right—trained properly, maintained her instrument, built a solid reputation in the industry. Her entire life revolved around working and keeping her voice healthy. Yet here she was, still trying to break through.

"I'm grateful that session work is steady," she said. "There's always demand for reliable vocals."

"Indeed." Dr. Park made a final note in her file. "Well, you're in excellent vocal health. Whatever happens in the competition, keep doing what you're doing. It's clearly working."

Kezia smiled and thanked her, but as she left the converted bedroom, Dr. Park's words echoed in her mind. *I'm surprised you're not already headlining.*

Maybe that was about to change.

Zach settled into the chair across from Dr. Park's desk, notebook at the ready. Late afternoon sun slanted through the tall windows, casting long shadows across the spread of medical files. Dr. Park's reports on his team's vocal health were in those manila folders.

"Three of your team members show potential issues we'll need to manage closely," Dr. Park said, flipping to the top folder. "The fourth looks fine—routine care should be enough."

Zach nodded. "Okay."

"Let's start with Jamie," Dr. Park said, adjusting her reading glasses. "His vocal folds appear healthy, though I observed some laryngeal tension during the examination. Our voice specialist will want to address that."

Zach made careful notes. Jamie's raw talent had caught his attention during auditions, but untrained voices often came with hidden problems.

"Now," Dr. Park's tone grew more serious as she opened another file. "I have concerns about Neil. There's visible muscle tension dysphonia—excessive tension in the laryngeal muscles. Sarah Matthews, our speech pathologist, will need to work with him on this before it causes lasting damage."

"How serious is it?"

"Left unchecked, it could develop into chronic issues. I'll have Sarah design a treatment plan. She's excellent with this type of problem."

Zach nodded, adding more notes. Neil's powerful voice was one of his greatest assets, but it was clear no one had taught him how to use it without grinding it down. They'd have to intervene before it cost him.

Dr. Park paused before opening the next file. "About Lily." She looked up at Zach over her glasses. "I'm seeing early signs of vocal nodules."

Zach's pen stilled. "How early?"

"Early enough to prevent serious damage, if we act now. Her classical violin training seems to be working against her here. She's approaching singing with the same intensity and push-through-pain mentality that served her well as a violinist, but without the technical foundation to support it. I'm referring her to Sarah for immediate voice therapy, and Teresa Winters will need to modify her training schedule significantly. No belting, limited practice time, and absolutely no pushing through fatigue."

A knot tightened in Zach's stomach. He'd seen promising careers derailed by nodules. "What are our options?"

"From a medical standpoint, she needs immediate voice therapy and modified vocal load. I'll work with Sarah and Teresa to create specific guidelines." Dr. Park handed him a preliminary report. "The question is, can she remain competitive under these restrictions?"

Zach studied the report. Maybe a stripped-down acoustic arrangement? Or a duet to lighten Lily's load? His mind was already working through alternatives. "We'll adapt her arrangements, focus on her musicianship rather than power. But I won't risk her long-term vocal health for a competition."

"That's why we do these assessments," Dr. Park said. "I'll have detailed recommendations from our voice team by tomorrow morning. It's refreshing to see this level of medical oversight in a competition setting."

"Their development as artists matters more than any single performance. These assessments..." He gestured at the files. "They're exactly why we insisted on proper medical support."

Zach pulled out his phone and checked the production schedule. The first challenge started in less than a week. "I'll need to coordinate with Hugo about scheduling the therapy sessions around rehearsals and filming," he said. "And brief Teresa on the modifications for each of them before training begins."

"The sooner the better," Dr. Park said. "Particularly for Lily."

"I'll speak to Hugo tonight. We built in flexibility for medical support. Now we'll make sure we use it."

Zach made a final note. He'd have to be strategic about song selection for the first challenge too, choosing pieces that would work within his team's current limitations while still showcasing their talents.

As he left the office, Zach reviewed his notes. Three talented artists, three different challenges. Now came the real work: helping each of them grow while protecting their instruments. It wouldn't be easy, but then, nothing worthwhile ever was.

Zach strode down the hallway from Dr. Park's office, medical reports and his notebook tucked under his arm. Priority number one was going to be supporting Lily, given that news about her vocal nodules. As soon as he spoke with Sarah, they would—wait. What was that?

A remarkable vocal run stopped him in his tracks. The precision was extraordinary, with each note perfectly placed, the transitions liquid smooth. The sound came from the main rehearsal space. His feet were moving toward the sound before he even registered the decision. Who was singing?

He told himself it was just professional curiosity. That run had been...something else. Anyone would want to know who it came from. But his pulse was already ticking up.

He reached the doorway...and saw her.

Ryan's session singer, center stage, surrounded by the specialized equipment they'd brought in for the performance section of the contestant vocal assessments. Teresa Winters, the *Starbound* vocal coach, circled the taller woman with focused attention while a sound engineer monitored acoustic readings.

Ryan lounged against the piano, arms crossed, a satisfied smile on his face.

Zach couldn't blame him for looking so smug. The sound coming out of that woman...

Several other contestants, including Brianna, watched from the sides of the room while cameras captured everything.

"Excellent Kezia," Teresa said, making a note on her tablet. "Outstanding. Your breath support is remarkably consistent across your range. Let's take it up a third. Same pattern, but add the mixed voice transition on the descent."

Kezia nodded and executed the passage flawlessly. Grasping what Teresa wanted instantly, singing it back with no effort or strain.

The sound engineer's eyebrows lifted as he checked his readings. "Clean signal all the way through the upper belt. Zero clipping, zero pitch drift. That's pro-level control. Cleanest upper register I've seen without it being auto tuned to death."

Zach took a few steps forward.

"Yes, that's remarkable control," Teresa murmured, making notes. "Now let's test your style versatility. Give me the first verse of 'Someone Like You.' Raw emotion, like Adele."

Kezia's posture shifted subtly as she began to sing. Her execution was, again, technically perfect, every note pure, every phrase beautifully shaped. But...

Teresa held up her hand. "Beautiful execution. But could you try it again? Show me more vulnerability this time."

There it was again—that flicker. Not fear. Not defiance. Something more elusive. Something aching. It vanished as quickly as it came, but it pulled at Zach, a thread left dangling in an otherwise seamless performance.

Kezia started again, and while the technical precision remained impeccable, the emotional distance was, if anything, more pronounced.

"That's enough," Ryan interrupted, pushing away from the piano. "The technical foundation is exceptional. We can work on performance aspects later."

But Zach had seen something in that moment of hesitation. Not just technical excellence, but a carefully constructed barrier. He'd missed it during her audition, too focused on what he perceived as her playing it safe. Now he found himself automatically analyzing approaches that might help her break through that wall. Song choices to crack the veneer. Exercises to coax the ache beneath the armor...

He caught himself. She wasn't his contestant to mentor. And, given how their last interaction had gone, she probably wouldn't welcome his input, anyway.

As he turned to leave, he heard Ryan talking to his singer. "Ignore that critique, Kezia. Technical excellence is what separates professionals from amateurs. Everything else is just window dressing."

Zach shook his head as he walked away. Ryan was wrong about that, but that wasn't Zach's problem. He had his own team to worry about. Three of his four artists had pressing vocal health issues, and all of them needed his full attention.

Still, as he headed toward his office, he couldn't quite shake the echo of that perfectly executed run. What, exactly, was buried beneath that gleaming wall of control? It shouldn't have mattered. But it did. And that, more than her technique or her poise, was what unsettled him most.

Chapter 15

*O*N SUNDAY MORNING, KEZIA stood with her roommate Lily and the rest of the small group of *Starbound* contestants who were attending church.

Sophie, the pink-haired contestant coordinator, consulted her tablet in the circular drive of the Starbound Campus. "Those going to Mass, you'll ride with José in the blue van. Elena, Patrick, Nicole, he's waiting for you by the gate." She looked up at Kezia and Lily. "Grace Community Church transport will be here for you in five minutes."

Most of the other contestants were taking advantage of the quiet morning to have a lie in. Given that tonight was the watch party for the first episode of the show, Kezia suspected they were conserving their energy. Her voice felt refreshed after Saturday's vocal rest—a welcome recovery from Friday's intensive assessments.

Lily smoothed her skirt. "I can't believe we're going to see ourselves on TV tonight. Are you nervous?"

"A bit," Kezia said. "No idea how I'll come across on TV. You?"

"Terrified. Zach says the first episode will probably focus on auditions."

"Mm hm," Kezia said. Since joining his team, Lily was now a fully paid-up member of the Zach Falconer fan club. It was Zach this, Zach that, all day long.

Lily yawned. "Speaking of Zach, we spent ages yesterday going over my vocal care plan point by point. And it's got so many notes on it. He made sure Dr. Park included specific warm-up modifications and everything and didn't end the session until I showed him I understood every single point. Did Ryan do the same thing with you guys?"

Kezia shook her head. Ryan hadn't even mentioned her vocal care plan. But maybe that was because it was just a standard one. No modifications needed, just the usual guidance about hydration and rest periods. Things she was already doing.

Lily said, "The no-belting rule is going to be challenging, but Zach promised to help arrange songs to work around it."

"Nice that he's giving you that kind of support," Kezia said. Either he genuinely cared about his team, or he just liked to micromanage. She leaned toward the latter. Ryan seemed to be a big picture guy, one who expected his team members to be mature enough to handle their own vocal health, just like she'd been doing for the last decade.

Lily peeked into her bag. "Oh, good, I didn't forget my Bible. I'm really looking forward to church."

"Grace Community's not far from where I grew up, actually," Kezia said. "About twenty minutes away."

"Oh? Did you ever go there?"

"No. We attended St. James in Westcott while I was growing up." The genteel mid-sized church was favored by the well-heeled professionals of the village, and generally devoid of anyone aged between sixteen and forty. "I've heard of Grace Community, though. They have a strong music program."

"I just hope it's not one of those massive productions," Lily said. "You know, fog machines and light shows."

Kezia chuckled. "Says the girl who's competing on a reality TV music show."

"That's different," Lily protested, but she was grinning too. "I like church to be a bit, you know, reverent. Not feel like a nightclub or a concert."

Their driver arrived on schedule. Judging by the first appearances, Lily would get her wish. The church, although modern and well-maintained, wasn't as large as Kezia had imagined.

The interior welcomed them with warm oak paneling and cream walls, natural light streaming through tall windows. No dramatic lighting rigs in sight, just tasteful pendant lamps hanging from exposed beams. A grand piano and acoustic guitar stood ready on the simple platform, alongside a modest drum kit partially enclosed in clear panels.

As they found seats in the middle section, Lily's hand suddenly clamped onto Kezia's arm. "Please pinch me. Is that Morgan?"

Kezia followed Lily's gaze. Even from a distance, Morgan, the chart-topping pop artist, was unmistakable. Wearing a blazer over a silk blouse and A-line skirt, her elegant presence drew attention without seeming to try.

Lily whispered, "Her real name is Martha, and she's married to Zach's brother, Ezra. Do you think—"

Kezia's stomach flipflopped as she spotted Zach a few feet away from Morgan, speaking to someone she recognized from press photos and album covers as his youngest brother Levi.

"Of all the churches in the area," she murmured, sinking into her seat as much as a 5'10" person could. Though really, she should have joined the dots. The Falconers were based in this part of Surrey and were known for their involvement in their local church. It was part of their public image. She just hadn't realized *this* was their local church.

"Do you think Zach will notice us?" Lily's excitement was palpable.

Kezia hoped not. What if he imagined they'd come here specifically to see him or rubberneck at his famous family? "Let's just focus on why we're here."

But focusing proved challenging as the service got underway. Zach seemed different here—more relaxed, less the stern mentor she knew from *Starbound*.

When the first song began, she caught herself watching him sing, noting how freely he expressed himself in worship compared to his usual controlled demeanor. But as the familiar words of "How Great Thou Art" filled the sanctuary, Kezia found herself drawn into worship. Here, she could just be another voice lifted in praise, her focus fully on God. No critiques. No cameras. No pressure to perform.

The pastor, an open-faced man not much older than she was, based his sermon on Psalm 13. Going through it verse by verse, he talked about how David wasn't afraid to pour out his open, unvarnished feelings to God in that deeply emotional and honest prayer.

"This brief psalm is a beautiful example of honest, vulnerable prayer and song, capturing both despair and hope, anguish and faith—the unfiltered heart of a believer pouring himself out to God," the pastor said. "David expresses intense distress, confusion, and frustration to God, openly questioning why God seems distant and silent."

Kezia's pen moved across her notebook, the earlier awkwardness forgotten as she focused on the message.

"How many of us have felt that same impatience?" the pastor continued. "I know I have. When injustice seems to flourish unchecked, when our personal struggles drag on and on, when God's silence feels deafening. Like David, we wonder 'How long, O Lord?' Yet by the end of this short psalm, through the very act of crying out to God, David finds his way to trust and joy."

Kezia knew that impatience well. The frustration of waiting, of working hard and seeing no results, of wondering if God had forgotten her entirely. Yet David's path from despair to trust felt like a map she could follow.

The whole message was a lifeline, reminding her that even in all the uncertainty—her dwindling savings, the competition, her future—she wasn't alone. God was with her. Like David, she would remember God's goodness and His unfailing love...and put her trust in Him.

As they sang the final hymn, her gaze snagged on Zach again, and the quiet peace she'd found slipped away.

Gathering her things, she said to Lily, "We should head out."

But her roommate looked reluctant. "Right now? I was hoping to say hello to Zach. Maybe thank him again for being so careful with my vocal care plan."

Kezia shook her head. "You saw him yesterday evening, and I'm sure you'll see him tomorrow at rehearsal. Let's go."

They made their way toward the exit, but the foyer was crowded. Through the sea of people, Kezia saw the Falconers surrounded by a happy knot of friends. Martha laughed at something someone said while Zach listened with an easy smile she'd never seen at *Starbound*. Relaxed, confident, and too annoyingly handsome to pretend she didn't notice.

Then, before she could look away, his gaze met hers across the space. For a single heartbeat, time stilled—just the two of them across the crowded room.

His eyes widened, the smile vanishing in a blink. He gave her the tiniest possible nod before he turned back to his conversation.

Face burning, Kezia hustled Lily toward the doors. Did he think she was stalking him? Was he annoyed? Surprised? Ugh, the cringe was unbearable.

Their driver was already waiting outside, and Kezia had never been more grateful for *Starbound*'s precise scheduling.

As they pulled away from the church, Lily sighed. "I still think we should have said hello."

"Sometimes hello just makes things more complicated." Kezia watched the building recede through the rear window.

She really liked Grace Community Church. She really liked Grace Community Church. The music, the message—it had been almost perfect. Pity Zach Falconer had been there.

Martha elbowed Zach in the side. "So, who was that pretty girl you were looking at?"

He turned to find her watching him with those eyes that always saw too much. He kept his tone neutral. "Just one of the *Starbound* contestants. Lily Wang. She's on my team."

"You know perfectly well I wasn't talking about the cute one with the long hair." Martha's eyes sparkled with mischief. "I meant the tall one with the amazing bone structure and the Afro. The one you were staring at."

"Oh." He didn't bother to deny Martha's allegations about staring. "That's Kezia Blair. She's also a contestant on *Starbound*."

"Really?" Martha's interest sharpened. "Is she good?"

"She's technically skilled. Ryan picked her for his team." He was doing very well with his casual tone.

Since spotting her during the second hymn, he'd had ample time to compose both face and voice. The session singer he'd seen today was different from the woman who'd auditioned.

In worship, when she thought no one was watching, evaluating, or judging her, her natural musicality flowed effortlessly. The genuine emotion in her expression spoke of something deeper than mere performance.

It unsettled him. He'd filed her away as another technically proficient performer playing the industry game. Yet here she was, in church on a competition Sunday when she could have been resting, singing with an authenticity he hadn't believed she possessed.

Martha said, "Well, if she's as talented as she is striking, Ryan found himself a winner. You need to up your game."

"Technical skill isn't everything. And sure, looks help, but they're not enough," Zach said.

Martha arched an eyebrow. "Uh-huh. Spoken like a man who definitely hasn't noticed how gorgeous she is."

"Of course I noticed. I've got eyes in my head. But being flawless—technically or visually—doesn't guarantee staying power." He sounded confident, but the words rang hollow.

He couldn't shake the image of Kezia lost in worship, her face transformed by genuine connection to something that moved her.

Not performance. Not ambition. Just...reverence.

It was the most compelling thing he'd seen all week— and it hadn't been on stage. How did she really sing when nobody was looking? And why did she hide that authenticity behind technical precision?

Chapter 16

THE PHONE ROOM AT the Starbound Campus reminded Kezia of a miniature call center, with its row of private booths along the walls. Each cubicle contained just enough space for a chair and a phone.

Through the glass panel of the nearest booth, she watched Jamie finishing his call. His animated gestures suggested he was talking to family. She checked her watch. Five minutes until her scheduled slot.

Sophie approached her, tablet in hand. "Hey, Kezia. Ready to call your loved ones? Remember the rules: twenty minutes maximum, approved contacts only from your pre-submitted list. No discussion of competition details, other contestants, or anything covered by your NDA." Only Sophie, with her bubbly voice, could make a list of regulations sound like steps in a thrilling adventure.

Kezia nodded. Her approved contact list in her hand was short—just Claire and her parents. She'd call Claire first. At least that ought to be a relaxing conversation.

The moment Jamie emerged, she slipped into the booth, still warm from his presence, and dialed Claire's number.

"Hi, Claire, it's me. How's married life?"

"Kezia! It's so good to hear from you. How are you?"

"I'm okay. But tell me about your honeymoon first," Kezia said.

For a few precious minutes, she let herself be swept up in Claire's stories about the white beaches and crystal-clear waters of the Maldives. It felt almost normal, like their regular Sunday catchups.

Homesickness tugged at her with a dull ache. But the home she missed didn't exist anymore. Claire had moved out of the flat they'd shared on Bermondsey Street and was settling into her new home with Tom. And Kezia's belongings sat in a storage unit in Croydon.

She didn't like the word "homeless," but the fact was, she didn't have a home right now. Something she'd need to deal with as soon as her run on *Starbound* ended. However soon that happened.

"And then Tom tried snorkeling for the first time and completely panicked—" Claire broke off. "But enough about me. You have to tell me about *Starbound*. And Zach Falconer. Have you met him yet? He is absolutely gorgeous in person, isn't he?"

"I can't really talk about the mentors or what's happening here." Kezia glanced nervously at Sophie, who was pretending to study her tablet while obviously monitoring the calls.

"Come on, just tell me if he's as gorgeous in real life. And he'd be perfect for you."

"What?" Kezia nearly dropped the phone. "We can't—"

"Not only because he's a Christian, but he actually understands music, not just the commercial stuff. As a mentor, he'd get what you're trying to do."

"As a mentor?" Heat crept up Kezia's neck. "Oh, right. Um, well, I'm not really allowed to talk about that. NDA and all."

Claire's laugh rang through the line. "Of course, I was talking about him as a mentor. Why? What did you think I meant? Though now that you mention it..."

"I mentioned nothing! Claire, I literally can't talk about any of this. NDA, remember?" Kezia pressed her free hand against her burning cheek.

"Fine, fine. I can't wait for tonight's episode though. I've invited everyone from the wedding party."

"I don't know how much of me you'll see," Kezia warned. "There are sixteen of us."

"Stop being so modest. The house feels weirdly quiet without your endless scales and arpeggios. I keep expecting to hear you practicing when I wake up. Never thought I'd miss that."

"I miss you too." Kezia's throat tightened. "Even the K-Pop you blast in the kitchen when you're cooking."

Claire laughed. "Tom just sings along with it. He's definitely a keeper. So what's it like there?"

Kezia shifted the phone to her other ear. "Strange. Sometimes I forget about the cameras, and then suddenly I'll remember and get all self-conscious again. But some of the people are really nice."

They chatted for a couple more minutes, then Kezia glanced at her watch. She'd used up two-thirds of her phone time. "Sorry, but I have to go. They limit our phone access and I still need to talk to Mum."

"Of course! Give my love to her. And Kezia? You're going to be amazing tonight. We'll all be watching and cheering you on."

"Thanks, Claire. Really."

Hanging up the phone, Kezia sat for a moment, soaking in Claire's warmth and enthusiasm. Then she straightened her shoulders and picked up the receiver again. Time to call her parents.

Her finger hovered over each digit of her parents' landline, as if delaying the inevitable.

"Hello, Kezia." Her mother's crisp tone came through. "We were beginning to wonder if we would hear from you."

"Sorry, Mum. They only let us make calls at specific times. We're not allowed our phones during filming."

"Well, I hope this television program isn't taking up too much of your time. Have you spoken to Salome about her engagement party?"

Kezia's stomach clenched. There it was—the conversation she'd been dreading since her sister had settled the date, announcing it just days before Kezia left for the Starbound Campus. "That's actually why I'm calling. If I'm still on the show, I won't be able to come."

"I see." Mum's tone was chilly. "So your sister's engagement isn't important enough."

"It's not that." Kezia pressed her fingertips against her temple. "I can't come. Not if I'm still in the competition. We're not allowed to leave during filming, apart from going to church. This is my career, Mum."

"A singing competition is hardly a career, Kezia." Her mother's voice grew distant, as if she'd moved the phone away from her mouth. "Yes, Richard, it's Kezia. She's calling from that TV show. Saying she won't be attending Salome's engagement party."

Kezia heard her father's muffled voice in the background, followed by her mother's clipped explanation.

"Salome will be disappointed." Her mother's voice returned at full volume. "But I guess you've shown your priorities."

"Mum, please."

"I should go. Your sister's calling on the other line."

The call ended and Kezia stared at the phone, throat aching, eyes burning. She'd planned to tell them about the first episode of *Starbound* airing tonight, but what was the point? They'd just see it as another of Kezia's pointless endeavors that would ultimately lead nowhere.

Through the glass panel, she could see Sophie gesturing that her time was up.

Kezia nodded, not trusting herself to speak. She replaced the receiver, gathered her composure, and stepped out of the booth.

At least she wouldn't have to make any more calls until next Sunday.

"Tough call?" Brianna was waiting for her turn to phone home, leaning against the wall with her arms crossed.

"Mm." Kezia managed what she hoped was a neutral smile.

"Family stuff? Or boyfriend drama?"

"Just family." Kezia shifted her weight, ready to escape. "No boyfriend to worry about."

"Really?" Brianna's perfectly shaped eyebrows rose. "Hard to believe someone like you isn't taken. Especially at your age."

Kezia shrugged. No, even at her age, she didn't have anyone. No boyfriend, no flat, no certainty about her future...no distractions. The one thing she did have was this opportunity. And she was going to give it everything she had.

Chapter 17

*T*HE MAIN COMMON ROOM of the contestants' house had been transformed for the evening. Comfortable seating clustered around a large screen, and tables laden with snacks and soft drinks lined the walls. The familiar space felt different, more like a private cinema than their usual hangout spot.

Kezia helped herself to some popcorn as she walked past one of the snack tables. The nervous energy in the room was palpable. A group of the boys lounged across the furniture with studied casualness. Sandra couldn't seem to stay still, pacing between the snack tables.

"Over here!" Lily waved from a loveseat, and Kezia gratefully claimed the space beside her.

"Ready for your television debut?" Lily asked, tucking her feet underneath herself.

"Not really." Kezia watched the production team positioning cameras around the room to capture their reactions. "I keep thinking about all the things I said in my interview that could be edited strangely."

"At least we know how it ends. Because we're all still here." Lily grinned. "Well, for now anyway."

A producer called for quiet as the screen flickered to life. A dramatic orchestral theme filled the room, the first time any of the contestants had heard it, as the *Starbound* logo appeared.

Olivia Chang faced the camera, stunning in a midnight blue cocktail dress. "Welcome to *Starbound*, where we're about to discover Britain's next great artist. Yes, I know what you're thinking. But this isn't just another singing competition."

The screen cut to Zach Falconer, perched on a tall stool with a guitar on his knee. He wore a dress shirt with a loosened tie, his sleeves rolled up to reveal his muscled arms. "We're not here to create disposable pop stars. We're looking for artists who can sustain real careers in this industry."

"They've made it look amazing," Lily whispered. "My family is going to freak out when they see this."

Kezia nodded, trying not to think about whether her own family would be watching.

"We've hand-picked singers from all across Britain," Zach continued in voiceover, as the screen showed glimpses of contestants in waiting areas, some pacing nervously, others warming up their voices. "Each one brings something unique—raw talent that just needs the right guidance to develop."

Kezia caught a fleeting glimpse of herself, head bent over sheet music. She hadn't even noticed that being filmed. Nobody else would even guess it was her.

Ryan Sterling appeared on the screen, lounging against a piano in his signature leather jacket. "It's not about finding someone who's already perfect. We already know these guys can sing well. It's about spotting that spark of star quality." His grin flashed. "And I've never been wrong about that."

Kezia's heart rate quickened. Everyone knew Ryan's track record, how he'd discovered Jade Rooney at an open mic night, how he'd spotted Dylan Ross when he was still playing pub gigs. Both were selling out arenas now. And she'd been his first pick for his team.

The show cut to Brianna's pre-audition package, with shots of her striding confidently through London streets. "I've been working toward this my whole life," her voice declared over the footage. "Music isn't just what I do. It's who I am."

In the common room, Brianna preened, a satisfied smile playing across her face as the editors cut together her best moments. Her audition song, a stylish, contemporary take on "Royals," had been perfectly edited to highlight her strengths.

Brianna had mastered a few clever tricks: careful breath control that made her light, breathy tone seem effortless, and the way she used speak-singing to mask the breaks in her passaggio. She had an instinctive ability to stay just within her comfortable range. What Brianna lacked in vocal power, she made up for in artistic choices that made each phrase sound intimate and intentional. She was definitely making the most of what she had.

"That's what I call star quality," Ryan said on screen, leading the judges' enthusiasm as Brianna finished her song. "She knows exactly who she is as an artist."

The mood shifted as gentle piano music introduced Jamie's segment. Home video footage showed a young boy performing on children's television, followed by newspaper headlines about "Britain's Youngest Chart Success."

"I thought they'd focus more on the singing," Jamie muttered, shrinking into his seat as the show delved into his subsequent struggles with anxiety and his retreat from public performance.

His audition performance of "Ordinary People" had been trimmed to just the emotional crescendo, but the cameras lingered on Tyler wiping away tears and Zach's intense expression.

Jamie's experience showed in his clear tone and command of vocal dynamics, even if nerves had made his vibrato a bit unsteady at points, and he had some pitch issues at the start. But it was now clear to Kezia why the young man was Zach's first pick.

Sandra's segment opened with a montage of her viral singing videos, the follower count ticking up into the millions.

Her performance of "The Prayer" showcased a voice that made Kezia sit up straighter in her seat. For someone just sixteen years old and entirely self-taught, Sandra's natural instincts were remarkable. Her pitch was near perfect, and she had an innate sense of how to support those high notes.

A few small technical adjustments could make Sandra's performance even better—a slight modification to her breathing pattern here, a more efficient placement there. But the raw talent was undeniable. It was incredible that the girl had developed this level of control purely through intuition and practice.

That three-way mentor bidding war made complete sense now. Sandra was exceptional. And Zach had clearly seen something in her that Kezia lacked.

"With that range and that following," Olivia's voiceover explained, "Sandra was already marked as one to watch."

Sandra ducked her head, but Kezia could see she was pleased with how they'd portrayed her. And why wouldn't she be? That setup was perfectly pitched.

Olivia's polished smile filled the screen. "Join us next week as we continue our journey through the *Starbound* auditions, on this quest to discover Britain's next great artist."

The screen went dark as the production team shut off the TV. Conversations erupted around the room, most centered on the production choices—who'd been featured, how they'd been portrayed, which moments had been highlighted or cut.

Kezia felt a strange twist in her stomach.

That was it.

Her own audition hadn't made the cut. No interview segment. No reaction shot. Nothing.

She'd known it was possible—only a few of them would be featured in the first episode—but still, the absence stung. She forced herself to sit straighter. This wasn't about screen time. It was about the long game. She was still here. That was what mattered.

Lily bounced in her seat. "My family's going to go mental when they see this. Mum's probably already calling everyone she knows as we speak."

On the other side of the room, Brianna held court, perched on the arm of a sofa. "They can only show a handful of auditions in the first episode. It's all about creating narratives the audience can follow. Trust me, I've done this before." She launched into a detailed analysis of reality TV editing techniques.

Kezia tuned her out, heading over to Sandra, who was helping herself to more popcorn by the snack table. "Your control is incredible," she said. "I can't believe you've had so little formal training."

Sandra's face lit up. "Thanks! Coming from you, that means a lot. Your performance assessment the other day was based. The way you handled those exercises Teresa gave us? I don't think anyone else was able to nail them."

Sophie appeared in the doorway, clipboard in hand. "All right, everyone, big day tomorrow. We start preparation for the first challenge at nine sharp. You're all big boys and girls, so I'm not telling you it's lights out, but you should all get some rest."

As others began dispersing to their rooms, Kezia reached for the small bag she'd placed beside her chair.

"You're not going to sleep yet?" Lily asked.

"I always do my evening vocal exercises," Kezia replied. "Need to keep my voice ready for tomorrow." It wasn't something she thought about. Like brushing her teeth or warming up before a session, it was just part of life—second nature by now.

"Kezia?"

She turned around to see Sandra watching her.

The young girl twisted her fingers together. "Um, are you heading to one of the practice rooms?"

Kezia nodded.

Sandra stepped closer. "Teresa mentioned something about diaphragmatic breathing during my assessment. She said my breath support needs work, but I'm not sure I understand what she meant. I know you're really familiar with all this stuff. Could you...I mean, if you don't mind, could you explain it to me?"

Kezia felt a spark of surprise. This talented young singer who had over two million social media followers, and whom every mentor wanted, was coming to her for advice. It felt...good. Everyone else around here zoned out the moment she started talking about the technical and physiological dimensions of singing. And Sandra was actually interested?

Kezia smiled. "Of course. I'm just doing maintenance work, but you're welcome to join. I can explain it to you while I show you how."

"You two have fun with your...breathing," Lily said with a theatrical yawn. "Some of us need our beauty sleep."

As Lily headed upstairs, Kezia led Sandra toward the practice rooms, already mentally organizing how best to explain proper breathing technique to the young girl. For once, her extensive technical knowledge wouldn't be met with glazed eyes or polite nods. Sandra genuinely wanted to learn. And Kezia found herself looking forward to sharing what she knew.

Chapter 18

"HOLD THOSE POSITIONS, EVERYONE," the *Starbound* senior producer, Steve Wilson, called out.

The contestants stood in two camera-friendly rows on the lawn in front of Glenmere Hall, Kezia in the back line between Jamie and Dominic. As usual, her height made her an obvious choice for the rear placement.

The production crew had already spent twenty minutes filming the sixteen contestants as they repeatedly walked onto the lawn and arranged themselves into lines. First, their walk was too haphazard. Then, they were marching in lockstep and looked unnatural. Then Lily had a sneezing fit, and they had to redo the take. But it seemed Steve was finally happy with the result.

Was everything going to take this long? Crew members bustled around them, making tiny camera adjustments while tension crackled in the air.

Kezia blew out a slow breath. This was where the actual competition began. She'd been up since six, going through her usual morning vocal exercises and warm-ups, then enduring an hour in hair and makeup.

Olivia Chang stood in front of the contestants, effortlessly polished in a coral dress as she reviewed notes with a producer.

"And...action," Steve barked.

Olivia's smile flashed as she spoke to the contestants. "Welcome to your first *Starbound* challenge! The theme of this challenge is 'Finding Your Voice.' You will be tested on your vocal foundation as well as your ability to collaborate musically with others. Each of you will showcase both a duet with one of your peers and a solo performance. Your mentors will take a comprehensive evaluation of your baseline abilities. And the stakes are high." She paused for dramatic effect. "Because one contestant from each team will be eliminated."

A cold weight settled low in Kezia's belly. She'd known eliminations would start soon, but hearing it made official sent a chill through her.

"Cut." Steve Wilson strode forward. "People, this is monumental news. Four of you are going home!" He jabbed his finger at them. "It could be any of you. I need to see genuine concern when Olivia mentions elimination. Let's try again."

"This is silly," Jamie muttered.

Kezia understood the feeling. Manufacturing reactions felt dishonest somehow, even if the concern was real enough.

In the front row, Brianna was already road-testing her shocked expression.

Kezia bit her lip to stifle a giggle.

"From the top," Steve barked. "And... action."

"Welcome to your first *Starbound* challenge!" Olivia's voice carried even more dramatic weight this time. "This week will test your vocal performance through both duets and solos. And the stakes are high. Because one contestant from each team will be eliminated."

Brianna's gasp was perfectly timed and exactly the right volume to be picked up by the microphones. The other contestants managed varying degrees of concern and surprise.

Kezia did her best, hoping she didn't look like she'd wandered on from a Telenovela set.

"Perfect," Steve called. "Bring in the mentors."

Olivia waited as the production assistants made final adjustments to the equipment.

"And...action."

"And now," Olivia's voice rang out, "please welcome your *Starbound* mentors."

The double doors of Glenmere Hall swung open. Ryan Sterling strode through first, confident and casual in his signature leather jacket, until his foot caught on a stray cable. He stumbled, catching himself before he face-planted.

"Cut!" Steve glared around him. "Who left that cable there?"

Kezia pressed her lips together, trying not to laugh. Beside her, Jamie wasn't quite as successful at hiding his amusement.

A production assistant rushed to secure the offending cable while Ryan, scowling, retreated to his starting position.

"From the top," Steve called. "And...action!"

"And now, please welcome your *Starbound* mentors."

The doors swung open again. This time, nobody tripped. Zach and Diana were perfectly synchronized, but Tyler lagged a half-step behind.

"Cut." Steve sighed. "Tyler, you need to be in time with the others. One more time, and I'll count you in."

Kezia watched as the mentors reset their positions. For someone who seemed to despise technical perfection, Zach sure seemed okay with doing endless takes of a walk through a pair of doors.

"And...three, two, one...action."

"And now, please welcome your *Starbound* mentors."

This time, all four mentors emerged in perfect sync, joining Olivia and the contestants to form the three points of a triangle.

After what felt like hours of filming entrances, introductions, and reactions, they finally split into their teams.

Ryan led his four contestants—Kezia, Brianna, Dominic, and Jordan—to a bright rehearsal room. A grand piano dominated one corner, while chairs had been arranged in a semicircle facing a small performance area.

A team of production assistants were already there, with the camera and lighting in place.

Ryan paced the floor with restless energy while they settled into their seats.

"This is where we make our mark," he announced. "Vocal Performance week isn't just about showing you can sing. It's about proving you're a complete artist."

He outlined the two-part challenge, each word carrying more weight than the last. "Your duet will demonstrate your ability to perform with another artist, a skill that's essential in this industry. Your solo is your first real showcase with full production behind you."

His expression grew serious.

"Your journey to success starts right here. Make no mistake—one of you is going home after this challenge. That's the reality of this business." He didn't soften the blow with platitudes or apologies. "I don't back losers. I create winners. Show me you have what it takes to go all the way."

Ryan's directness was both refreshing and terrifying.

A prickle of unease crawled up Kezia's spine.

"Right." Ryan pointed at Kezia and Brianna. "You two are doing 'No More Tears (Enough is Enough)'. Your contrasting styles will make for a dynamic performance."

Brianna's face lit up. She turned to Kezia with an eager smile.

Kezia's mind raced through the technical challenges of the Barbra Streisand/Donna Summer duet. The song would require both precision and drama. She thought she'd be up to it. But did Brianna have the range needed to tackle this song?

"Dominic, Jordan," Ryan continued, "you'll do 'Rewrite the Stars' from *The Greatest Showman*. It's current, romantic, and showcases range."

"The real work starts now," Ryan continued. "You'll have today and tomorrow to familiarize yourselves with your assigned songs individually. Your tablets have practice tracks with your individual parts isolated. Learn them thoroughly. You'll work with our vocal coach separately before coming together for your first joint rehearsal on the 22nd. By then, I expect both parts to be performance ready. That's when we'll start refining the arrangement."

Ryan's gaze swept across the group.

"And remember—this isn't just about the performance on elimination day. You'll be recording studio versions that will be released on streaming platforms. These tracks represent your first commercial releases under the *Starbound* brand. They need to be flawless. And I will pay very close attention to how your singles perform. It'll form part of the basis by which I consider who stays and who goes back home."

He looked at each of his teammates in turn.

Kezia held his gaze despite the rioting churn in her gut. Hopefully, her studio experience would stand her in good stead with this aspect of the competition.

"The recording sessions are scheduled for the 27th and 28th, after we've locked in the arrangements," Ryan said. "This isn't just a singing competition. It's artist development at warp speed. I expect you to use every resource *Starbound* provides." His urgency hadn't diminished. "Work on your voice. Work on your performance. Work on your recording technique. Every aspect matters."

Kezia's mind was already breaking down the schedule. Nine days to master both the duet and her solo, develop the arrangements, nail the performances, and create flawless recordings. She'd handled complex projects before in her session work, but this was different. This time, her name wouldn't be buried in the liner notes. It would be front and center, with her future in the competition riding on every note.

She was ready.

Chapter 19

FTER TWO DAYS DRILLING her part of the "No More Tears" duet, Kezia could sing it in her sleep. The practice tracks Ryan had provided helped her lock down the precise timing of each phrase, though she'd already known most of Barbra's parts from previous session work. Now, standing in the rehearsal room, she did her final warm-up exercises, waiting for Brianna to arrive so they could run through the song together for the first time.

Ryan and the choreographer Dani stood near the sound equipment, deep in conversation while gesturing toward the performance area. Mike, the vocal coach, sat at a small table in the corner, reviewing notes. The production crew had already set up three camera positions, with a boom mic operator standing ready.

Everything was in place for their nine o'clock start. Everything except Brianna.

Kezia glanced at the wall clock: 8:57.

Ryan's watch-check and slight frown didn't escape her.

At precisely nine o'clock, the door swung open and Brianna entered with a bright smile that lit up the room. "Good morning, everyone," she called cheerfully, her voice filled with enthusiasm. Her vibrant tank top and leggings were the very picture of camera readiness.

"Perfect timing," Ryan said, moving to the center of the room. "Let's get started. I want to hear where we are with the duet. Mike, can you give us the backing track?"

He gestured for Kezia and Brianna to take their positions in front of the main camera.

Kezia moved into place, taking a deep breath as she centered herself. Beside her, Brianna bounced lightly on her toes, shaking out her hands.

The gentle piano intro began, and Kezia sang the opening lines, matching Barbra Streisand's languid, intimate delivery, her voice clear, controlled, smooth as velvet.

Brianna joined in, going for an airy, breathy tone, but she made some strange phrasing choices, her pitch wavering slightly on the transitions between notes.

When they hit the climactic transition point between the smooth opening and the break into the disco beats, Kezia sustained the single, powerful, high note with her part, starting at close to a whisper and building it to a perfect crescendo.

Brianna was supposed to be doing something similar to Donna Summer's vocal flourishes underneath, but her runs were uneven, some notes blurring together while others stood out too sharply against Kezia's sustained tone.

When they reached the anthemic chorus, Kezia let her voice soar into the higher part of the duet, each note landing exactly where it needed to be.

Brianna sang the lower harmony, but she wasn't projecting her voice enough to balance the duet. Each time Kezia opened up to hit the powerful notes, her voice filled the room—too much, too easily—dwarfing Brianna's contribution.

Ryan exchanged a glance with Mike, who was writing furiously on his notepad.

Ryan raised his hand as they got to the second chorus. "Cut the track, please. Ladies, give us a moment."

He and Mike huddled in the corner, speaking in low tones.

Brianna turned to Kezia with a sheepish giggle. "Now I know what runners feel like when they get lapped on the track. I feel like I'm trying to run a marathon next to an Olympic sprinter. Try and leave some song for me, okay?" She laughed again.

Kezia wasn't sure how to respond. "This is just the first run through, and we're here to work on it and get it right. You've got the performance energy down perfectly."

Mike gestured emphatically at his notes while Ryan nodded, occasionally glancing their way. After a minute of consultation, they approached.

"Ladies, there's good material to work with here," Ryan said. "I'm convinced we've picked the perfect song for both of you. But we need to make some adjustments to create a more cohesive duet."

Mike stepped forward, notebook in hand. "We're going to swap your parts. Brianna, you'll take Barbra's higher melodic line. Kezia, you'll handle Donna's part, but—" he glanced at Ryan, who nodded in confirmation, "—no runs. Just straight notes on the chorus. Keep it clean and straightforward."

Kezia blinked, processing what this meant. They were giving Brianna the more prominent part with the sustained notes that showcased vocal control, while relegating Kezia to a stripped-down version of the more technically challenging part. The very flourishes that showcased her skill were now off-limits.

She was being relegated to Brianna's backing vocalist.

"This will create a more balanced performance," Mike said. "Sometimes the arrangement needs adjusting to suit the performers."

Ryan watched Kezia's reaction carefully. "Remember, this is the duet portion of the challenge. We want both of you to shine."

Brianna nodded enthusiastically. "Let's do it."

"Try it again with these adjustments," Ryan said, already moving back toward the sound equipment. "From the top."

The piano intro began again, and this time Brianna took the lead with Barbra's opening lines. Her voice was pleasant enough, but she lacked the technical control to deliver the languid phrasing properly. Instead of the restrained power the opening needed, Brianna's interpretation was breathy and rushed. But Ryan was digging it, based on the way he nodded along.

When Kezia joined in with Donna's simplified part, she had to hold herself back from the runs that would have elevated the performance. Instead, she delivered clean, straight notes as instructed. It felt like asking a concert pianist to plink out "Chopsticks" and pretend it was art.

As they approached the bridge section where Kezia had a few solo lines, she threw in some gentle inflections to build the emotional tension of the song.

"Cut!" Ryan held up his hand. "Kezia, we need you to stick strictly to the melody."

"But don't we need some variation to build the emotional arc?" Kezia turned her appeal to Mike. Surely, as the vocal coach, he'd back her up. "It's what makes the song work. That contrast between the straightforward verses and the more complex bridge."

Mike shook his head. "We're looking for consistency across the performance."

"A duet is all about balance, Kezia." Ryan's tone was firm. "You two need to sound like you're singing the same song, not like you're from different musical worlds. Brianna is giving us a straightforward, emotional performance. Your embellishments, while impressive, are creating a disconnect."

"But I think—"

He cut her off with a wave of his hand, holding her gaze. "The melody. Nothing more."

Kezia nodded, pressing her lips together to keep from arguing further. She was a professional. She could follow direction, even when every musical instinct screamed that it was the wrong choice.

They started again from the bridge. This time, Kezia delivered her solo lines with plain precision that reflected none of the seething irritation within her. She knew how to be the perfect session musician, doing exactly what was asked, nothing more and nothing less.

As the final notes faded, Ryan broke into applause.

"That's exactly what we're looking for. Great chemistry, ladies. Brianna, I loved that emotional turn during the transition. Very dramatic. Kezia, much better."

Brianna bounced on her toes, grinning widely. "That felt amazing. I really connected with the song this time. It's so much easier when we're in the same musical space." She turned to Kezia. "Don't you think?"

Kezia managed a smile. "It certainly had a different feel."

Ryan checked his watch. "Now that you sound like a real duet, let's talk about your movement. This isn't a dance number, but we need you both to have presence on stage. Dani, come help us, please."

A petite woman with a sleek chestnut brown bob stepped forward. "With a duet, it's all about how you share the stage. When Brianna has her solo lines, Kezia, you'll need to pull back physically. Step slightly upstage but remain engaged. Then you'll switch positions when your moment comes."

Dani walked them through the basic positioning, showing how they should create visual interest by occupying different parts of the performance space. "It's a conversation between two divas. Each commanding attention in turn, then coming together for the powerful moments."

They ran through the number again, following Dani's directions for how to move around the stage.

Dani held up her hand, stopping the music. "Brianna, you're doing great. But, Kezia, when Brianna is singing, you're standing there like you're waiting for a bus. You need to stay in the performance, react to what she's giving you."

Kezia gritted her teeth. This was so much harder than singing in a booth where you didn't have to look interesting and perform even while silent.

Ryan nodded. "A duet is about connection. Even when you're not singing, you're still performing."

After a couple more run-throughs, Ryan was finally satisfied. "That's a wrap for now."

He turned to Kezia. "I need you to work on loosening up, but otherwise, I'm pleased. Brianna, perfect energy. Keep that up. We'll refine this over the next few days, but the framework is solid."

Kezia gritted her teeth as she gathered her things. This was what Ryan called a solid framework? The vocal arrangement had been adjusted to hide Brianna's limitations while diminishing Kezia's strengths. And in a performance where the visuals mattered, she was failing to match Brianna's movement and stage presence.

She'd thought being on *Starbound* would finally put her in the spotlight, but they were already dimming it before she'd even had a chance to shine.

Chapter 20

ZACH ARRANGED THE LAST of the snack bowls on his coffee table. Cashew nuts for Levi, his sister-in-law Adria's favorite popcorn, and crudités and dip for the health-conscious Ezra and Martha. It was Sunday evening, and they were all going to watch the second episode of *Starbound* together. They were at his own home, rather than his mentor's cottage on the Starbound Campus.

Martha and Ezra were already settled on the sectional sofa, Martha typing rapidly on her phone.

She glanced up at Zach. "Episode two, baby! Are you ready? Social media response to the premiere is still trending upward."

"I'm more than ready." Albion Broadcasting Network was cautiously pleased with the numbers for episode one. Zach prayed there wouldn't be a steep drop-off tonight.

The doorbell rang just as he was adjusting the television settings. "That'll be Levi and Adria," he said, already moving to the door.

His youngest brother stood on the doorstep with his wife beside him. Levi held up a Tupperware box. "We brought cookies."

Zach placed his hands on his hips. "Not that I don't want to see you, but where's Owen?"

"Last minute change of plan," Adria said. "He's spending the evening at Noah and Eden's."

Zach shook his head. "That cuts me to the quick. He'd rather go there than visit his Uncle Zach?" Four-year-old Owen was best friends with their pastor's little daughter.

"Sorry, bro." Levi walked past him into the house. "Between you and a play date with Linda Chaplin, there's no contest."

He and Adria exchanged greetings with Martha and Ezra.

"Mum got away okay?" Ezra asked. Their mother lived in the guest lodge on the family estate, while Levi and his family occupied the main house.

Levi nodded, his usual cheerful expression sobering. "We saw her off around three. She was planning to drive straight to Harrowgate."

"Any update on Greg's condition?" Ezra asked.

Adria shook her head. "The prison hospital isn't exactly forthcoming with information. Beth said she'd call once she knew more."

"They're saying it's serious this time?" Martha asked quietly.

"Apparently." Zach kept his tone measured. "But with Greg, you never know if it's real or just another act."

No one responded to that. Their stepfather's history of deception hung in the air between them, alongside the complicated truth that, despite all he'd done, their mother still loved him.

"It's starting," Ezra announced as the *Starbound* theme music filled the room.

Zach leaned back, pushing thoughts of his stepfather aside. Time to watch what the public would be seeing of his vision for *Starbound*.

The episode opened with a montage of hopeful contestants arriving at the audition venue, interspersed with dramatic close-ups of the mentors.

"Your hair looks good there," Adria commented as the camera lingered on Zach's profile.

"Stylist did something different that day," Zach replied, watching himself critically. He always noticed the tiny flaws no one else would see—a gesture that seemed forced, a comment that could have been worded better.

The first few auditions passed with casual commentary from the family.

"He's pitchy, but I love that gravely tone," Levi said as a nervous young man sang "Use Somebody."

Ezra nodded. "I have to say the standard is pretty high, though."

"No major train wrecks," Adria said. "The drama's coming from their personal stories."

After a commercial break, Martha sat up straighter. "Hey, that's the girl who came to church again today."

On screen, the session singer stood center stage as she introduced herself to the panel. The camera loved her, capturing the warmth in her skin, the striking set of her eyes, the gentle curve of her mouth. But it couldn't replicate the quiet presence she carried in person.

"And what will you be singing for us today?" TV Zach asked.

"'And I'm Telling You' from *Dreamgirls*," Kezia replied.

Leaning forward, Martha shook her head. "Ooh, bold choice."

As the first note came out of Kezia's mouth, the atmosphere shifted in Zach's living room.

The editors had chosen to play her performance in full. It was obvious why. It was just as outstanding as Zach remembered. The camera occasionally cut to the mentors' reactions—Ryan's raised eyebrows, Tyler's grin, Diana's shining eyes, and Zach's own intense concentration.

As the TV audience applauded, Martha was the first to speak. "She's extraordinary. That control is phenomenal."

Levi nodded. "Solid technique. That doesn't happen by accident."

On screen, the mentors began their feedback, one by one giving their effusive praise.

The camera cut to Zach. "There's no question about your vocal ability. I can hear that Guildhall training. But here's the thing. *Starbound* isn't looking for a dime-a-dozen session singer."

In the living room, Ezra turned to give Zach a disbelieving look.

Zach stared back at him. "What?"

"Seriously? Dime-a-dozen?" Martha said. "She was the best technical vocalist of the day. Scratch that—in every audition I've seen so far. I'm not even sure I could have pulled that song off so flawlessly under that kind of pressure."

Zach crossed his arms. "I didn't say she's not good. But technical excellence isn't enough. This isn't a competition for who can hit the most perfect notes."

"I'm not musical like you guys," Adria said, "but I loved listening to her. I'd buy her record in a heartbeat."

"She's hiding behind perfection." Why did he always have to justify his opinion about Kezia to everyone? He was getting sick of this. "Every note is calculated. I need to know there's something real beneath all that polish."

Ezra stroked his chin. "There's something there beyond technique, though."

Of course there was something there. Zach had glimpsed it as she'd sung, unguarded, during the church service. "The question is whether she can access that consistently. Or if she retreats to technical perfection when she's uncomfortable."

On screen, Kezia received unanimous approval to continue in the competition, despite Zach's reservations.

The auditions were being shown out of order, and the show moved on to the next contestant.

Zach's phone vibrated in his pocket. One glance at the screen made his chest tighten. "It's Mum."

Martha muted the television, and the room fell silent as he read the message.

"What does she say?" she asked.

Zach looked up. "Greg's stable for now. But the doctors are concerned about his liver function, so she's staying at Harrowgate for a few days. Sounds like he really is poorly this time. She wants to speak to the specialist."

Ezra sighed. "I still don't understand why she goes every time he claims he's dying. After all his lies..."

"Because she loves him," Levi said softly. "Despite everything."

Zach stared at his phone. "It's their twentieth anniversary in October."

Had Greg always been a selfish conman? Or did he become one only after he'd earned their trust?

As the eldest of the brothers, Zach had the clearest memory of when Greg had first come into their lives. Their mother, widowed young with three boys to raise, had been swept off her feet by his charm and confidence. They'd all been taken in by it.

Zach hadn't seen past Greg's surface charm. Or Verity's. But the signs had been there. He just didn't want to see Verity's single-minded ambition beneath her declarations of love. How she was using him and his family name to advance her career.

An uncomfortable silence lay over the room. Then Ezra asked whether anyone wanted coffee while, at the same time, Martha suggested they carry on watching the show.

"Yes, to both," Zach said. "I'll get the coffee."

As the show resumed and he filled the coffeemaker, Zach thought about Verity and Greg. He'd been burned too many times by people whose perfect façades were the ideal cover for their hidden agendas. Never again. He'd rather have something imperfect but real. Then at least he knew where he stood. That went for relationships and for the vocalists he mentored.

Chapter 21

ON THE FIRST PERFORMANCE day of *Starbound's* Round One challenge, Zach shifted in his mentor's chair, taking in the full spectacle of what he'd created. Applause swelled around him as two of Tyler's mentees left the stage. Their rendition of "Up Where We Belong" had been competent if not spectacular, and the studio audience was generous with their appreciation.

The stage gleamed under the powerful lighting. Tiered seating surrounded three sides of the stage, filled with an enthusiastic audience, while cameras captured every angle for the episode that would air in a couple of weeks.

With the first elimination challenge well underway, things were getting real, and the atmosphere crackled with nervous energy. Contestants from Team Ryan and Team Tyler were performing today, with Zach and Diana's teams scheduled for tomorrow. When all the contestants had done their solo performances and duets, each mentor would have the difficult task of eliminating one contestant from their team.

Zach frowned. He wasn't looking forward to that. Based on what he'd seen in rehearsals and mentoring sessions, he already knew who he would drop from his team, unless an extraordinary performance tomorrow changed his mind.

Olivia glided onto the stage in a shimmering blue gown. Her poise and warmth had made her the perfect host.

"Wasn't that lovely?" she said into her microphone. "That was the last of Team Tyler's performances tonight. Now we move on to Team Ryan for our next duet. Ryan, you've mentioned you've been working intensively with these two contestants."

Ryan flashed a smile. "I have, indeed. And, boy, has it paid off. You're all in for a treat today."

Olivia turned back to the audience. "Next up, performing Barbra Streisand and Donna Summer's 'No More Tears,' please welcome Brianna Taylor and Kezia Blair!"

Zach sat up straighter. The session singer was up. His family thought he'd given her an unfair critique on her audition. He'd pay close attention today—and see if he'd misjudged her.

The lights dimmed, then rose on Brianna and Kezia, posed at opposite ends of the stage.

Brianna shimmered in a gold sequined mini dress that caught and reflected every beam of light.

Kezia appeared subdued, in contrast, wearing a high-necked black jumpsuit. Understated. Elegant, but restrained. Like she was determined not to be noticed.

Brianna was dressed like a star, Kezia as a background vocalist.

Ryan had made a smart song choice, though. The diva anthem should be the perfect showcase for Kezia's powerful voice.

The opening notes filled the arena, and Zach settled in to watch.

Brianna immediately commanded attention, her movements dynamic and theatrical as she launched into the opening lines. She wasn't the strongest vocalist, but what she lacked in power and range she made up for in performance energy. The effect was surprisingly entertaining.

Then Kezia entered with Donna Summer's part—flawless, every note perfectly placed, her control impeccable. But Zach had expected her to make more of those iconic lines than the simple, almost Spartan delivery she gave.

As the chorus approached and the women sang together, it became even more clear that Kezia was holding back. Despite Brianna's weaker voice, the petite blonde was the dominant one, commanding attention, owning the stage with her fluid movements.

The audience responded enthusiastically to Brianna's energy, cheering when she hit a particularly dramatic pose. Zach glanced at Ryan, who was watching with obvious satisfaction, head nodding in time to the music.

What was going on here? Something didn't add up. Kezia could easily sing the stuffing out of this song. But instead, Brianna was killing it with showmanship while Kezia faded into the background.

As they approached the climax of the song, Brianna suddenly spun away from her marked position, extending her arm in a dramatic sweep. Eyes widening, Kezia stepped back. The gold sequins on Brianna's dress caught the spotlight as she dropped into an unexpected dip, then rose with a hair flip that sent her honey blond waves cascading around her shoulders.

The song ended with Brianna center stage in a dramatic pose, Kezia positioned behind her. The audience erupted in applause, Brianna soaking it in with a beaming grin.

Kezia's smile was tight-lipped.

Zach studied her carefully. The technical perfection was there, but she'd subdued her abilities. Why?

"Ladies, that was fantastic!" Olivia exclaimed as the applause died down. "Let's hear what our mentors thought. Diana?"

"What a dynamic performance," Diana said. "I think all of us were expecting Kezia to knock this out of the park, but, Brianna, what a revelation. You two really complemented each other's strengths."

Tyler nodded in agreement. "Well done holding your own out there, Brianna. You absolutely slayed."

Ryan grinned. "This is exactly what we worked on in rehearsals. Finding that balance as performers, understanding when to step forward and when to support. I'm incredibly proud of both of you."

Olivia turned toward Zach. "Zach?"

He tapped his chin. "Brianna, you commanded that stage. Your energy was excellent."

Brianna beamed her thanks.

Zach faced the session singer. "Kezia, you were underwhelming. You disappeared up there. Brianna completely outshone you."

Her lips tightened as her chin raised up.

The studio audience reacted with shocked "*oohs*" and scattered booing.

Olivia shifted uncomfortably, but Zach continued despite the reaction. "At your level, I expect you to do more than just phone it in. Brianna left everything on that stage, but you gave almost nothing. I thought you were here to prove you're more than a backup singer."

Something flashed in Kezia's eyes, but her professional mask remained firmly in place as she nodded politely.

Ryan jumped in. "Zach, I have to disagree. What you're seeing are two artists who've worked to blend perfectly. Kezia showed tremendous professionalism in creating a balanced performance."

"Balance doesn't mean one performer becomes invisible," Zach said.

Olivia spoke up. "Well, we certainly have some differing opinions tonight. Let's thank Brianna and Kezia for that performance."

The audience cheered the two women.

As they left the stage, Zach sat back. Why would a vocalist of Kezia's caliber deliberately diminish her performance? And why did Ryan seem so pleased about it?

He was disappointed in what he'd seen, but even more disturbed by what he hadn't. She was holding something back. Not just vocally, but emotionally. And part of him hated that he cared.

Because if she were just another contestant, she wouldn't still be in his head.

Chapter 22

*K*EZIA PACED THE NARROW corridor back-stage, her chest tight. Ryan, with his dumb "coaching," set her up as Brianna's backup singer. And as if that didn't make Kezia look pathetic enough, Brianna decided to bust out those flashy dance steps out of nowhere and practically shove her off the stage. And to top it all off, those cutting, humiliating words from Zach, calling her out in front of everyone.

Kezia, you were underwhelming. You disappeared up there. Brianna completely outshone you.

Her hands tightened into fists. The worst thing was, he was right.

And why had she been a total pushover and gone along with all of it? This was *her* opportunity, her career. Why did she give her power away?

"Five minutes, Kezia," a production assistant called, clipboard in hand.

She nodded, smoothing down the simple black dress she'd changed into for her solo performance. She would be performing "Vision of Love." Unlike the duet, Ryan had given her almost no direction for this performance beyond choosing the song and expressing confidence in her ability to handle it.

"Mariah's in your wheelhouse," he'd said. "Just do your thing."

Well, she would. She was done with diminishing herself to make someone else look better. Zach Falconer had accused her of "phoning in" her last performance. Well, she hoped he had his ears wide open, because she was going to give him something worth listening to.

"Kezia, you're up," the stage manager said, gesturing her toward the wings.

She squared her shoulders. Zach Falconer wanted a show? She'd give him one, with or without his approval. And if he didn't like it? Good. Let him choke on the perfection he claimed to despise.

Olivia's voice rang out across the stage. "Next up, performing Mariah Carey's 'Vision of Love,' please welcome back Kezia Blair."

The audience applauded politely as Kezia walked to center stage.

Ryan grinned at her, giving a thumbs-up.

She scanned the mentors' panel, her gaze lingering briefly on Zach. His expression was neutral, expectant. She'd show him "backup singer."

The intro of "Vision of Love" started, and Kezia closed her eyes for a second, letting everything else fall away.

From the first note, she let her voice flow freely, the opening vocalization with its intricate runs gliding smooth as silk.

As she progressed into the first verse, she deliberately unleashed her full technical arsenal, each phrase more intricate than the last. Every run and vocal flourish executed with the precision of a virtuoso.

She felt it shift—the audience, the energy, the atmosphere. Polite attention turned to awe.

For the first time in this competition, she wasn't wondering how she came across. She *knew*. This was what she was born to do. Not fading into the background, not supporting someone else's moment, but standing in her own light and showing what she was capable of.

As she moved into the second verse, certainty grew within her. She was fully in the zone, aware that she was delivering something exceptional. The vocal runs became more complex, yet she executed them with perfect control. The music was her plaything, her servant. She was in total command.

She didn't look at Zach, but she felt his focus like heat on the side of her face.

When the moment came for the whistle register notes—the stratospheric high notes that were Mariah Carey's signature—Kezia hit them perfectly, soaring above everything else, clear, pure, and trilling.

The audience reaction was electric. They leaped to their feet as they applauded, their energy flowing toward her, lifting her even higher.

Ryan nodded with satisfaction, as if he'd expected nothing less. Diana pointed a hand high in the air, eyes closed as she vibed with the music, while Tyler grinned. Zach's expression remained enigmatic, but his focus on her was absolute. Unblinking. Unyielding.

It was time for the final vocal run, a moment where the music cut out and it was only her voice. Kezia delivered it flawlessly, each note distinct and deliberate. She held the last note with perfect control and tone as the instruments burst back in.

As she finished, the crowd's standing ovation washed over her. After years of background work, the warmth of their validation was like a physical force that left her body trembling.

Diana and Ryan were on their feet immediately, Tyler joining them with a head-shaking grin, mouthing the word, "What?"

Zach remained seated, but his intense gaze never left her face.

Kezia inclined her head, exhilarated, as she accepted the applause. Nobody could say she'd phoned that in. She'd just delivered a masterclass.

As the applause finally subsided, Olivia came to stand next to Kezia. "Wow. Let's hear what our mentors thought of that incredible performance. Diana?"

Diana's eyes were still wide. "Are you sure you're human, Kezia?"

Kezia chuckled along with the audience. What a compliment, coming from an artist of Diana's pedigree.

"That's a serious question," Diana said. "Your vocal control is out of this world. You have fully mastered your instrument. That was technically flawless."

Tyler nodded. "That was truly special. Few singers would dare attempt that song, and even fewer could execute it. Those whistle notes? Perfection."

Ryan's chest was puffed out like a proud father. "Thank you, Kezia. You're showing everyone yet again why you were my first pick. Completely breathtaking."

Kezia absorbed their praise but found herself waiting for one more opinion. The one that, for some reason, mattered most.

Draping an arm around Kezia's shoulders, Olivia turned to the final mentor. "Well, Zach? Has Kezia finally made a believer of you?"

The room quieted as Zach held Kezia's gaze. "You're all over the map today."

Her throat tightened, and murmurs rippled through the audience.

"Am I a believer?" he said. "The truth is, I don't know what to make of you. You took a complete back seat in the duet. Now, you're out-Mariah-ing Mariah. In this performance, you were so busy showing off every technical trick in your arsenal that there was no room left for anything authentic. First you hide behind Brianna, now you're hiding behind vocal gymnastics. All technique, zero connection."

Boos echoed across the studio, and Olivia squeezed Kezia's shoulder.

Heat rushed to Kezia's face. She felt like she'd been slapped. The critique was about her performance, but it felt like it was about her. How dare he! She'd just delivered a performance that most vocalists couldn't even attempt.

"I know this isn't a popular opinion," Zach said over the audience murmurs, "but I didn't come here to see how many runs you can fit into a three-minute song. I came to discover artists who have something to say. So far, all I'm hearing from you is 'look what I can do.'"

Tears stung Kezia's eyes, but she fought to keep her expression neutral. He would not make her cry.

Ryan jumped in. "That's completely unfair. What Kezia just did was extraordinary."

"Extraordinary technique," Zach interrupted. "I don't disagree with that."

Diana said, "We just witnessed a remarkable display of vocal prowess, and that deserves recognition."

Tyler nodded. "I know you're all about artistry, Zach, but technique at that level is artistry in itself."

But Kezia barely heard their defenses. She maintained her composed smile—or at least she kept her teeth out—and thanked them for their feedback, but inside she was reeling.

She walked offstage with measured steps. Not because she felt strong, but because she refused to fall apart in front of *him*. Please, let there not be an on-the-fly interview now. She couldn't handle a camera in her face.

Brianna appeared at her side, her eyebrows drawn together. "You poor thing. I don't know who put Zach's boxers in a twist. Don't listen to him. That was incredible." But her words rang hollow.

Kezia managed a tight response. "It's fine. He's entitled to his opinion."

"His loss," Brianna said with a shrug, drifting away to chat with other contestants.

Finding a quiet corner away from cameras and fellow contestants, Kezia huddled on a stool, facing the wall. She prayed nobody would interrupt her until she'd had a moment to compose herself.

It was crystal clear to her now. Zach Falconer, creator of *Starbound* and industry powerhouse, hated her as a performer. She'd delivered a perfect rendition of one of the most technically challenging songs in any singer's repertoire, and he'd still picked it apart and dismissed her.

Nothing she could do would ever be good enough for him. It shouldn't matter—she was on Team Ryan, after all. So why did Zach's opinion cut so deep?

Chapter 23

ZACH SAT ON ONE of the plush couches in the judges' green room, tablet in hand. It was quiet now that the day's performances had ended. The contestants were on their way back to the Starbound Campus, the audience had filed out of the studio, and most of the production crew were busy breaking down equipment and resetting for tomorrow's performances.

He should be gone, too, but he was waiting for Hugo, the showrunner, to arrive for their scheduled debrief. While he waited, he went over his critique notes for his team. They would perform in tomorrow's elimination challenge, and he needed to be prepared. Their final rehearsals showed promise, but there were still adjustments to make, points to emphasize before they took the stage.

The door swung open but instead of Hugo, Ryan strolled in, looking way too pleased with himself.

"Hi, Zach. That was quite the feedback you gave Kezia. Planning how to be equally encouraging to your contestants tomorrow?"

Zach set down his tablet. "Just preparing. Hugo's running late."

Ryan helped himself to a bottle of water from the mini-fridge and settled into an armchair opposite Zach. "'Out-Mariah-ing Mariah.' Creative."

"Just being honest," Zach said, keeping his voice measured. "Technical skill isn't the same as artistry."

Ryan laughed. "You can't recognize what's right in front of you, can you? Talent like hers doesn't happen every day, Zach. Even you should be able to see that."

"I never questioned her talent."

"No, you just passed on her in the draft." Ryan twisted the cap off his water bottle. "And now you can't admit she's exceptional. Is it pride? Or just that Christian music sensibility that can't recognize commercial potential?"

Zach bristled at the dig at his background. "I recognize her technical gifts better than you do. What I don't see is the artist behind the technique. She's all skill, no soul. Impressive tricks aren't enough for me."

"This industry runs on impressive tricks, Zach. Always has." Ryan's smile was sharp. "But you go ahead and search for 'authentic souls.' While you're doing that, I'll be developing marketable performers. I found exactly what the industry wants. Her name is Kezia Blair. You found what... Jamie Collins? A has-been former child star?"

Zach set down his tablet. It was too late in the evening, and he was too tired to be dealing with this guy. "That's the difference between us. You want products. I want artists."

Ryan rolled his eyes as he got to his feet. "Save the artistic integrity speech for your motley crew of contestants tomorrow. Meanwhile, I'll be deciding which three of my exceptionally talented team members to keep. Including the vocalist you claim has 'no soul' but everyone else recognized as the standout of the day."

He turned to go, then paused with his hand on the door. "You know what your problem is, Zach? You think there's only one right way to be an artist—your way. But the charts and the bank accounts tell a different story."

He walked out, clearly believing he'd delivered a mic drop.

Zach returned to his notes, but the bullet points blurred. Instead, a different image surfaced, uninvited and inconvenient—Kezia in church that first Sunday, eyes closed, face unguarded as she sang along with the worship music.

No flourishes, no posing. Just quiet surrender. It had caught him off guard then. It still did.

Was he being too harsh? Too uncompromising? Or was it just easier to critique her than to admit she affected him? That her voice—no, her presence—kept echoing, long after the music ended.

He shook his head, dismissing the thought. His standards were the bedrock of his career, what had allowed him to maintain artistic integrity in an industry that constantly pushed for compromise. If Kezia Blair had something real to offer beyond technical perfection, she hadn't shown it yet.

Tomorrow was about his team. They deserved his full attention. Not Ryan's star mentee.

Kezia had already taken up too much of his headspace. And the worst part? He hadn't even figured out why.

Chapter 24

THE STUDIO LIGHTS FELT hotter than usual as Kezia stood with Ryan's team on the *Starbound* stage. It was the second day of the Round One challenge, and everyone had done their duet and solo performances. Now, all sixteen contestants were lined up in four groups.

Four of them would be eliminated today, one from each team.

The studio audience sat in hushed anticipation.

Kezia maintained her professional mask, the one she'd perfected over years of session work. Smile: pleasant but not overeager. Posture: straight but not rigid.

A day had passed since Zach's critique, but his words still stung like a fresh wound. *All technique, zero connection. I came to discover artists who have something to say. So far, all I'm hearing is 'look what I can do.'*

She'd watched the day's earlier performances by Team Zach and Team Diana with a critical eye. Zach hadn't been nearly as harsh with anyone else, not even contestants with obvious technical flaws. His feedback to his own team members had been constructive and encouraging, nothing like the dismissive assessment he'd given her.

Olivia Chang walked to center stage in a sleek emerald dress, her tablet in hand.

The studio lights dimmed, spotlights focusing on her and the contestants.

"Good evening, everyone," she said, her voice carrying across the hushed studio. "Over the past two days, we've witnessed incredible performances from all sixteen of our talented contestants. But as you know, *Starbound* is not just about showcasing talent. It's about finding artists who can grow and evolve throughout this competition. And there will be only one winner."

She paused, letting the tension build.

"Tonight, we begin our first elimination. Each mentor will let one member of their team go."

Kezia clenched a fist. She hoped she'd done enough to be one of the three Ryan kept on his team. She didn't dare think which of her teammates he would cut.

Olivia continued, "However, there's a twist that none of you—including our mentors—are aware of."

Kezia glanced at the mentors. All of them stared at Olivia. Diana and Tyler looked surprised, but Zach and Ryan's expressions remained impassive.

Olivia said, "When a mentor eliminates a contestant, another mentor can choose to save that singer and add them to their team. Each mentor has one save they can use throughout the competition."

The contestants exchanged glances. Kezia felt a flicker of relief. It was a safety net, at least in theory.

"But..." Olivia held up a finger. "There's a cost. Mentors, if you save someone from another team, you must then eliminate an additional contestant from your own team in order to keep the balance. Choose wisely. Because once your save is used, it's gone."

Kezia felt the contestants around her shift nervously. Like her, they were probably weighing what this rule meant.

She took a deep breath, steadying herself. Despite Zach's criticism, she felt confident about her safety. Her solo performance had been technically flawless, and the audience response had been overwhelming. Ryan was effusive in his praise both on and off camera. And tonight, his opinion was the only one that mattered.

Olivia said, "Each mentor will declare two contestants from their team who are safe. The remaining two will be at risk, with one eliminated from the competition. Diana, you're up first. Which two of your contestants are safe from elimination tonight?"

Diana leaned forward in her chair, fingers interlaced. "This is never easy," she began, her voice gentle but firm as she addressed her team. "Each of you brought something special to the stage these past two days. And I want you to know that just because I'm eliminating one of you, it doesn't mean that person is flawed or deficient. It just means I can only take three of you forward."

She paused, scanning the four nervous faces before her. "Based on their solo and duet performances, I'm declaring Sandra Cassidy and Carter Shaw safe."

The two contestants broke into relieved smiles. No surprise there. Sandra's soulful rendition of "At Last" had brought the audience to their feet, while Carter had the butter-smooth sound of a young Luther Vandross.

"Jade, Nikki, please step forward," Diana continued.

The two young women moved to the front of the stage, their hands linked.

Kezia felt for them.

Jade Monroe had a trendy pop star vibe, and Kezia found her performances fun to watch. Between them, Nikki Vargas had a stronger voice. But although Nikki was a powerhouse vocalist with an impressive range, she had struggled with pitch issues and messy runs in her solo performance. If Diana was going by performances, Nikki was probably in trouble.

"This was a difficult decision," Diana said. "Jade, your commercial appeal is undeniable. Nikki, your talent is extraordinary, and you have moments of pure brilliance. But consistency is essential in this industry."

She took a deep breath. "I've decided to keep Jade. Nikki, I'm sorry, but I'm letting you go."

Nikki nodded, fighting back tears.

"Does any mentor wish to use their save for Nikki Vargas?" Olivia asked, scanning the panel.

The mentors remained still. Zach glanced briefly at Nikki but made no move.

After a moment of tense silence, Olivia nodded. "Nikki, we wish you the best in your future endeavors."

Nikki gave a final wave to the audience before exiting the stage.

It was Tyler's turn next, and she approached her decision with characteristic directness.

"I'm keeping Tessa and Devin," she announced without preamble.

After a brief deliberation focusing on vocal technique and performance quality, Tyler eliminated Leo Winters, a folk-rock artist with a distinctive raspy voice.

That surprised Kezia. She loved Leo's tone, so unique among all sixteen contestants.

Olivia asked if any mentor wished to use their save. Again, no one stepped forward.

Leo departed with a thumbs-up to the audience and his former teammates.

But there was no time to worry about other teams. Now it was Ryan's turn to cut one of his team members.

His expression somber, Ryan looked at Kezia, Brianna, Dominic, and Jordan in turn.

"After careful consideration of both duet and solo performances," he began, "I'm declaring Brianna and Kezia safe."

Although she expected this, a wave of relief washed over Kezia. She exchanged a quick smile with Brianna before they both stepped back, leaving Dominic and Jordan center stage.

Both were powerful performers, and she had no idea what Ryan would base his choice on. But if it were up to her, she'd keep Jordan, whose jazz sensibilities showed more musical complexity and technical skill. She held her breath in sympathy for her teammates whose fate still hung in the balance.

Ryan turned to face the two remaining singers. "Dominic, Jordan, you both brought unique qualities to this competition. Jordan, your talent is undeniable, but I question whether this is the right platform for your artistic direction. Your jazz influences are impressive, but they may be too niche for what we're looking for in a *Starbound* winner."

Jordan nodded, her expression resigned.

"Dominic," Ryan continued, "you've shown tremendous growth potential and audience appeal. Your performance yesterday connected with viewers in a way that suggests you could have a significant commercial impact."

Oh, no. Kezia knew how much this chance meant for Jordan, a single mum who'd hoped this would be a gateway to a better life. And, musically, she was stronger than Dominic.

Ryan paused, but Kezia knew what he would say before he spoke. "Niche" versus "significant commercial impact"? The writing was on the wall.

"I've decided to keep Dominic," Ryan said. "Jordan, I'm afraid your *Starbound* journey ends here."

Jordan stepped forward with a gracious smile. "Thank you for the opportunity, Ryan. I've learned so much already."

"Does any mentor wish to use their save for Jordan Hayes?" Olivia asked.

Tyler shifted in her seat. For a moment, it seemed she might speak up, but after glancing at her remaining team members, she stayed silent.

Poor Jordan. Her quiet professionalism and genuine love of music had been refreshing amid the bigger personalities on their team. Seeing someone with that kind of talent leave on the first round was unsettling. But Kezia couldn't deny the relief that it wasn't her walking off that stage.

Now it was Zach's turn.

Kezia watched as he addressed his team.

"Jamie and Neil, you're both safe based on your performances," he said.

No! That meant Lily was up for elimination. Kezia felt a rush of anxiety for her friend, who now stood alongside Liam, a self-taught guitarist with a raw, gravelly voice who'd spent years playing in pubs across northern England.

Lily's voice wasn't particularly powerful, but her tone had a haunting quality to it.

Zach's expression softened as he turned to the final two. "Both of you are outstanding singers in different ways. Lily, your vocal tone is unique. There's no one out there who sounds quite like you. Although your range is limited, I believe there's significant room for growth in developing your artistry within those boundaries."

He shifted his attention. "Liam, you've shown remarkable skill and professionalism in every challenge. Your authenticity and musicianship are undeniable."

He pressed his lips together, holding each of their gazes in turn. "Both of you are excellent vocalists and wonderful to work with. This decision comes down to artistic potential. I've decided to continue working with Lily. Liam, I have to let you go."

Liam nodded graciously despite the sheen evident in his eyes.

"Does any mentor wish to use their save for Liam Porter?" Olivia asked.

The panel remained silent.

As Liam began to exit, Zach leaned forward in his chair. "Liam, before you go—your musicianship is exceptional. See me after we wrap. I'd like to connect you with some colleagues who could use your skills."

That was unexpected. Zach Falconer actually being nice? The other mentors had offered kind words to their eliminated contestants—but none had extended a concrete opportunity.

Olivia stepped back to center stage. "Four talented contestants leave us tonight, but we have twelve remaining to continue their *Starbound* journey. Let's give them all a round of applause."

The audience responded enthusiastically as the remaining contestants regrouped with their mentors. Ryan gathered his team, already strategizing for the next challenge, his voice animated as he outlined what they needed to work on.

But Kezia's gaze drifted to Zach and his team.

He stood with his hand on Lily's shoulder, speaking quietly to her. Lily's eyes glistened with tears despite having just been declared safe. Jamie and Neil stood nearby, the three of them forming a tight circle around their mentor.

Why was she even noticing this? She quickly refocused on Ryan's instructions, setting her resolve to excel in the next challenge. He was her mentor. One who believed in her abilities and had just kept her in the competition.

What mattered now was continuing to prove Ryan right in making her his first pick.

Chapter 25

THE MORNING AFTER ELIMINATION night, Kezia joined the rest of Team Ryan in the rehearsal lounge. The room was bathed in September sunshine as Ryan stood next to the large wall-mounted screen, remote in hand.

Brianna sat beside Kezia, while Dominic took the armchair to their right. A carafe of coffee and a plate of untouched pastries sat on a table between them.

Ryan cued up the footage. "Let's watch last night's Episode 3 broadcast and talk strategy from there."

The episode began, showing the contestants' arrival at the Starbound Campus. Kezia watched as the cameras lingered on an effervescent Brianna stepping out of the SUV. There were quick cuts of various contestants exploring the facilities, with Brianna featured prominently in several segments, gushing over the resources and how no expenses had been spared in creating the perfect artist development environment.

In voiceover, Olivia Chang spoke about how mentors would soon choose which contestants would join their teams, based on what the mentors were looking for in an artist.

The footage cut to Lily. "Diana Morris would be amazing to work with. She's an absolute legend. You don't have a decades-long career like hers for nothing. Did you see her Wembley show last year?"

On screen, Brianna said, "What about you, Kezia?" Brianna turned to her. "Who do you want as your mentor?"

Oh no. They were showing this? Kezia's heart lurched as she heard herself say, "I'll gladly work with anyone but Zach Falconer. Did you hear what he said to me at auditions?"

Archive footage of her audition came on, showing Zach giving the lines that were branded onto Kezia's soul. "*Starbound* isn't looking for a dime-a-dozen session singer. I'm not entirely convinced you belong here, Miss Blair."

It took everything Kezia had not to bury her burning face in her hands as her confessional interview came on next. "I think I'd work better with a mentor who immediately sees my potential rather than just my technical background."

The footage flashed back to Zach at her audition. "You hit every note, you nailed all those runs, but I felt...nothing. You kept your eyes closed through most of the performance. It's technically impressive, but where's the connection? The audience needs to feel something beyond vocal acrobatics."

Back in the confessional booth, Mark's gentle voice probed off-camera. "So you don't want to work with Zach?"

Kezia's face filled the screen as she answered, blinking away tears, her voice trembling. "I've spent years...I spend every day working to be the best vocalist I can be. My technical background isn't a limitation, it's a foundation. But Mr. Falconer doesn't see that. He just sees another session singer who should stay in her lane."

It looked even worse than she'd thought. Now she really prayed her parents weren't watching.

Ryan paused the playback, fixing his gaze on Kezia. "The producers are clearly establishing a narrative between you and Zach. And after his comments during elimination night, they're definitely going to continue with it."

Brilliant. That's exactly what she didn't want to happen.

He hit "play" again as the episode continued with footage of the mentor draft. The production team had clearly focused on building stories around certain contestants. The bidding war over Sandra played out against the backdrop of her huge social media following. Jamie's emotional reaction to being Zach's first pick was the climax of a long buildup featuring his childhood career and years in the wilderness.

Brianna, too, got more screen time with her enthusiastic response over Ryan's selection.

Ryan clicked the screen off as the episode ended with a teaser for next week's performances and elimination. "First, congratulations again on making it through last night's elimination. All three of you delivered strong performances, and we'll get to that."

Turning to Brianna, he said, "You're a natural on camera. The way you interact with the other contestants, your enthusiasm during the tour. It's clear that you understand how to create moments the audience remembers." He glanced at Dominic. "You and Kezia could stand to learn from Brianna how to emote for the camera. When something happens, don't just process it internally. Let it show on your face. React visibly."

Brianna beamed at the praise, tucking a strand of blond hair behind her ear.

He turned to Kezia. "What's interesting is how quickly the producers have latched onto this tension between you and Zach. Did you notice how much screen time they gave to your 'Anyone but Zach Falconer' comment? That's gold for them. The audience loves a conflict, especially with someone they're positioning as the tough, uncompromising judge."

Kezia shifted uncomfortably. "A conflict? I didn't mean it to come across that way."

"Don't apologize," Ryan said with a wave of his hand. "This is exactly the kind of story that keeps viewers engaged. Viewers need someone to root for, and right now, they're setting you up as the technically brilliant vocalist who's being unfairly criticized by Zach, the show's creator and lead mentor. It's a powerful narrative, the underdog fighting against the establishment. We need to think about how to capitalize on that."

"I don't know," Kezia said, her discomfort growing.

"I want you to understand that this is as much about storytelling as it is about singing," Ryan replied. "Having Zach as your...enemy, for lack of a better word, gives you an identity in the competition. It's something viewers can latch onto beyond your vocal ability, which, let's be honest, is extraordinary but not always enough to create an emotional connection with the audience."

His words stung. So, he also thought her voice wasn't enough? That she needed this kind of manufactured drama to win fans?

Dominic nodded. "It's like in pro wrestling. The heroes and villains aren't real, but the audience eats it up."

"I'm not asking you to be inauthentic," Ryan said. "Just don't shy away from the narrative they're creating. When Zach criticizes you, defend yourself. Stand your ground. The audience will love it."

"Dominic," Ryan continued, "that friendship storyline with Tessa on Tyler's team is excellent television. The audience loves those personal connections. Make sure to keep developing those relationships. They're as important as your performances."

Dominic grinned. "We were just hanging out in the kitchen late one night. I didn't realize they were filming."

"They're always filming," Ryan replied with a knowing smile. "And that's something all of you need to remember. You may wonder why I'm going on and on about this. Here's why—this competition has a significant voting component once we reach the later stages. The public vote will ultimately decide who wins this show. And you need to do everything you can to win the audience over. Technical skill gets you in the door, but connection keeps you in the room. And these stories are building connection."

Brianna nodded vigorously, scribbling notes in a small notebook.

Kezia chewed her lip. This was a different world from the session work she knew, where the goal was an artist's skill, not the surrounding drama.

"I'll have one-on-one meetings with each of you over the next few days and we'll go into greater depth," Ryan continued. "In the meantime, Brianna, I want you working on extending your range. Dominic, focus on your breath control during movement. Kezia, vocally you're on point, but think about how you can own this narrative they're building about you and Zach. Are we clear?"

Kezia nodded along with the others, though she felt increasingly uneasy. The idea of leaning into a manufactured drama with Zach felt wrong, especially after seeing him at church, after glimpsing a different side of him than what was portrayed on camera.

The man didn't like her as an artist, and that stung. He was very vocal about how terrible he thought she was. But he was entitled to an opinion, just like anyone else. Did there have to be more to it than that?

But what if Ryan was right? He was the one who understood marketing and what audiences responded to. Was she shooting herself in the foot by not playing along?

Apparently, that was the nature of the game. *Starbound* wasn't just a singing competition...it was entertainment. And if she wanted to succeed here, to have the platform this show could provide for her career, she needed to adapt. And yet adapting felt...icky. Inauthentic. As though she was lying.

She headed toward the door. She needed time to think—and pray—through this.

Chapter 26

ZACH SETTLED ONTO A wooden bench beneath one of the sprawling oak trees that dotted the Starbound Campus. Now that they were into September, he wasn't sure how many warm mornings like this were left before fall set in, so he'd suggested they meet outside rather than in a rehearsal room.

His remaining team members arranged themselves around him. Jamie lay sprawled on the grass, his lanky frame stretched out in the dappled sunlight; Neil leaned against the tree trunk, and Lily perched on the edge of the bench beside Zach, her dark hair lifting slightly in the gentle breeze.

The setting was informal and private—away from the ever-present cameras inside the main buildings. Here, they could speak freely without performing for an audience.

"First, congratulations on making it through the elimination," Zach began, opening the folder of notes he'd compiled from their coaching sessions. "I know it wasn't easy saying goodbye to Liam."

Jamie nodded. "He was really talented."

"He *is* talented," Zach said. "And I meant what I said about connecting him with some colleagues. His musicianship is exceptional, and this isn't the end for him." He paused. "I also want to mention that Episode 3 aired last night. Did any of you watch it?"

They all nodded, Neil adding an eye roll.

Zach said, "Then you'll have seen how they've created their narratives. But don't get too caught up in how they edit things. Our focus is on your development, not television drama."

That went for him, too, especially when the producers were making a huge story out of his comments to Kezia. His conscience pinged him as he remembered how she'd spoken to the camera in her confessional interview, on the verge of tears, about his words to her. Perhaps he had spoken too harshly. He regretted that. But she needed to develop a thicker skin if she planned to stay in this industry.

And he didn't have time to worry about someone else's mentee when his own contestants needed his help.

He made eye contact with each team member. "Let's talk about where each of you stands and where we're going from here."

Zach turned to his folder, with its detailed assessments from Teresa and the other vocal coaches, along with his own observations from their rehearsals. "Although there will be only one overall winner of *Starbound*, that's not what this is really about for me. I'd love it if one of you won. But my intention is for each of you to learn something transformational while you're here and to leave with tools for continued growth."

Neil shifted against the tree, frowning.

"These resources—the vocal coaches, the production team, the recording facilities—they're not available to most developing artists," Zach said. "Use them while you can. The competition is the vehicle, but your development as artists is the destination."

He opened the folder and turned to the first page of notes. "Jamie, let's start with you. Teresa says that your technical foundation needs strengthening. The shortcuts you learned as a child performer won't serve you here. You've developed some habits that are putting strain on your vocal cords."

Jamie twisted his face. "I've noticed that. The exercises she's given me are helping, but they feel weird after doing things my way for so long."

"That's normal," Zach said. "It takes time to rewire those neural pathways. Keep at it. Your natural talent is exceptional, but good technique will ensure you can have a long, healthy career."

He turned to the next page. "Neil, the vocal coaches report you've missed two sessions. Is there something we need to address?"

Neil crossed his arms. "Those exercises are basic. I've been doing this stuff for years. I don't need to waste time on scales when I should be working on performance. I thought that's what a vocal coach does."

Zach maintained his cool. He was prepared for this response. Neil was a twenty-three-year-old with the attitude of a stroppy teen. He'd shown resistance to guidance from the beginning, confident in his self-taught methods that had served him well busking and singing at weddings. But they wouldn't hold up under professional scrutiny.

"There's a difference between knowing something and mastering it," Zach said. "Every professional I know still does their fundamentals. Every day. Including me."

Neil's expression turned mulish. "I know what works for my voice."

"I understand that perspective," Zach said, keeping his tone measured. "But this isn't optional. The coaching sessions are part of your development plan. If you have specific concerns about the exercises, we can address those with Teresa, but skipping sessions isn't the solution."

Neil held his gaze for a moment before looking away with a shrug.

Zach chose not to push further in the group setting. They would revisit this during their one-on-one. But Neil was on very thin ice.

Zach turned to Lily. "The feedback on your performances shows some areas we need to work on. Let's talk in more detail during our one-on-one later today." Her problems were more confidential, and he didn't want to bring them up in front of everyone else.

Lily nodded, her eyes reflecting that she already understood there were issues to discuss.

Zach closed the folder and placed it beside him on the bench. "I've outlined personalized development plans for each of you. Jamie, we're focusing on rebuilding your technical foundation while maintaining your natural expressiveness. Neil, we're working on expanding your range and developing sustainable techniques for the more demanding aspects of your style. Lily, we'll be addressing your vocal technique and finding ways to maximize your unique tonal qualities."

He glanced at each of them in turn. "We'll work individually on connecting your technique to your artistic expression. That's where the magic happens, when solid technique becomes invisible and all the audience experiences is the emotion and meaning of your performance. Any questions?"

Neil plucked at a blade of grass, but the other two shook their heads.

"In that case, we're done here," Zach said. "I want you to remember one thing, though. Whether or not you win, use every minute you have here to grow. That's the real prize. The winner gets a recording contract, but all of you can leave here as better artists than when you arrived, with the foundation and tools to build your careers."

He turned to face the young men. "Jamie, your session with Teresa is at eleven. Neil, you're scheduled for two this afternoon. I expect you to be there. And Lily, could you stay behind, please? I want to discuss your vocal plan."

As Jamie and Neil headed back toward the main building, Zach caught Neil's surly expression. He'd need to address the young man's attitude before it affected team dynamics, but that conversation could wait.

Right now, Lily's health was the priority, with the vocal nodules Dr. Park had identified. The last thing he wanted under his watch was for one of his artists to get an injury that could have been prevented.

As the others disappeared around the corner of the building, Zach turned to Lily. "How are you feeling after last night? *Really* feeling. Not just what you think I want to hear."

Lily tucked a strand of dark hair behind her ear, her gaze dropping to her lap. "My throat's a bit sore. But that's normal after performing, right?"

Zach frowned. No, that was not normal.

"How are you managing with the vocal care plan? I asked Dr. Park to attend yesterday's filming, and she was worried about your performance. She noticed some signs that you might be pushing beyond the safe limits we established."

"I followed everything in the plan," Lily said quickly, then hesitated. "Well, mostly. I did some extra rehearsals the night before. I was nervous about the elimination."

Zach sighed. "I know how tempting it is to push, especially under pressure. But those nodules we caught won't improve if you keep overworking your voice."

She bit her lip, still avoiding his gaze. "But everyone else gets to practice as much as they want. I feel like I'm falling behind, especially compared to singers like Kezia or Sandra who seem to have endless stamina."

"You don't need to compete on their terms," Zach said. "Sandra's a freak of nature and Kezia is a...she's a machine. Don't worry about them. We've been working with what makes your voice special without damaging it. Your tone is unique. It's haunting and evocative. Let's focus on that rather than pushing your range. That's what will set you apart, not how many hours you can push through practice."

He pulled out the modified practice schedule they'd developed with Teresa and Sarah, the voice therapist. "I think we need to revisit this. The competition is only going to get more intense, and we need to make sure we're protecting your voice while still giving you the preparation you need."

Lily looked at him. "Won't that put me at a disadvantage?"

"In some ways, perhaps." There was no getting around it. "But it will also force us to be more creative, to find what makes you distinctive. And, more importantly, it will protect your long-term career prospects."

He set the schedule aside, making sure he had her full attention. "How are the therapy sessions with Sarah going? Are you finding them helpful?"

"Yes," Lily said. "The exercises she's given me make my voice feel better. It's just..." She trailed off.

"Just what?" Zach prompted gently.

"It's hard to stick to the restrictions when everyone else is working so hard. I hear them practicing at all hours. Kezia's always in the rehearsal room working on her performance and whatever else she does. She's even got Sandra doing those drills with her."

Kezia was working with Sandra? Voluntarily helping her strongest competition? That didn't fit the narrative he'd constructed about her. A flicker of unease stirred in his chest. Either she was playing some deep strategic game...or he'd been wrong about her. Again. And he didn't like how much the second possibility unsettled him.

"I understand your frustration," he said. "But remember what we discussed when we first created your vocal care plan. This isn't just about *Starbound*. This is about setting you up for a sustainable career. What good is winning a competition if you damage your voice in the process?"

She nodded slowly. "You're right. I know you're right. It's just hard in the moment."

"That's why we're checking in regularly," Zach said. "I want you to promise me something. No more extra rehearsals without clearing them with Teresa or Sarah first. And if your voice feels strained, you stop immediately, no matter what's happening in the competition. Can you commit to that?"

Lily took a deep breath, the breeze lifting her hair in soft wisps. "Yes. I can do that."

"Good. Because your voice is extraordinary, Lily. Our job is to protect it while developing your artistry. That's what matters most. Not just for this competition, but for your future."

She nodded. "I appreciate that. More than I can say."

"Good." Zach stood to signal the end of their conversation. "For now, check in with Sarah this afternoon. I've asked her to reassess where you're at after yesterday's performance. And strictly no singing today. Use it as a rest day."

"I will. Thank you, Zach." Face flushed, Lily gathered her things and headed toward the main building.

As she left, Zach sat down again, not quite ready to give up this moment outside. He looked up, watching a pair of finches dart between the branches above him.

Each of his team members needed something different from him as a mentor. The challenge was providing that guidance while navigating the demands of the competition.

The show wanted drama and personalities. But he wanted artistic growth and development. Somehow, he needed to balance both without compromising his values or their potential.

At least with Lily, he was trying to make the right calls, even though the limits he was setting might affect her chances in the competition. Her health had to come first. Some things were more important than winning.

Chapter 27

*A*WEEK AFTER THE team feedback session with Ryan, Kezia stood in a semicircle with the eleven remaining contestants on the stage of *Starbound*'s main hall. Larger-than-life images of iconic artists dominated the backdrop—Madonna, David Bowie, Beyoncé.

Beside her, Brianna vibrated with barely contained excitement. "What do you think this next challenge is going to be?"

Before Kezia could respond, Steve, the senior producer, called out, "Quiet on set, please. Cameras rolling in five, four..." He continued the countdown silently with his fingers. "Action."

Olivia stepped forward, stunning in a shimmering blue pantsuit. "After a week of vocal rest and development workshops, I hope you're ready for your second *Starbound* challenge." Her smile was warm but held a hint of mischief that made Kezia's stomach tighten with anticipation.

"This week is all about taking your artistry to the next level." Olivia gestured to the images of iconic artists behind them. "These legendary performers aren't just great vocalists. They created complete artistic identities that defined their careers. Being a complete artist means knowing who you are and how to present yourself to the world."

A thrill of excitement made Kezia's skin tingle. This was exactly what she'd dreamed of when she decided to audition—the chance to step out of the background and define herself as an artist. After years of adapting her style to complement others, she could finally explore her own identity.

She remembered Ryan's advice about showing more personality on camera. *When something happens, don't just process it internally. Let it show on your face. React visibly.* How did one show enthusiasm? She sneaked a peek at Brianna, whose eyes were bright and shining, jaw almost down to her chest.

Kezia tried for a wide-eyed expression of wonder and hoped she didn't look like a buffoon.

"This week," Olivia said, "you'll develop and perform a song as the artist you want to be, not just the singer you are. We've brought in top industry image consultants to work with each team. They'll help you craft a cohesive look and develop your stage presence. But remember, authentic audience connection is key."

Authentic audience connection. Those words were the bane of Kezia's existence. But she oohed and aahed along with the other contestants.

Steve must be happy with the reactions he was getting, because he allowed the cameras to keep rolling.

The mentors were in on it, too, standing at the side of the stage. Ryan nodded with a grin, and even Zach cracked a smile.

"All right everyone," Olivia said, "please join your mentors for team briefings. They'll share the specific requirements for this week's challenge."

"And cut," Steve called. "Good reactions, everyone. Very natural."

Kezia suppressed a snort. Natural? If only he knew.

As she followed Ryan with Brianna and Dominic, she caught sight of Zach leading his team in the opposite direction.

Lily gave her a small wave and Kezia returned it with a smile.

Despite being on different teams, she and her roommate were growing closer—attending church together on Sundays and sharing a short prayer time each Wednesday evening, since they both missed their mid-week Bible studies. But although they hung out a lot, Lily wouldn't join Kezia and Sandra in their vocal drills, saying Zach had placed her on a restrictive vocal therapy plan.

What would Zach—Mr. Authenticity himself—make of this challenge? He would probably say—

"Come on, Kezia!" Brianna grabbed her arm. "I have so many ideas already. This is going to be amazing!"

Kezia quickened her pace to keep up as a camera tracked Brianna's exuberant stream of words. If this was what it took to get screen time, Kezia was doomed. There was no way she could look that manic.

Ryan ushered them into one of the smaller meeting rooms, tablet already in hand. "This challenge plays perfectly to our strengths," he said, standing where the cameras could capture both him and their reactions. "I chose each of you to be on my team because you have such powerful market potential, and image is all about that. Since day one, I've been developing positioning strategies for each of you."

Kezia didn't like the way Ryan was spinning this. The first time he'd talked about her marketability, it had sounded exciting. But after the duet fiasco with Brianna, she wasn't so sure his positioning of her would align with where she wanted to be.

"We're not playing around with guesswork," Ryan continued. "This is about identifying viable market niches and building your brand accordingly. I've done all the market research to help each of you define your authentic voice."

Wait. Was Ryan trying to be funny? Base their "authentic voices" on his market analysis? No, the man was dead serious.

He turned to Dominic. "You're our heartthrob with substance. Justin Timberlake meets John Legend. Accessible but with musical credibility."

Dominic's face lit up. "That's exactly the space I want to be in."

"Brianna." Ryan's grin widened. "You're our dynamic performer with mass appeal. The complete entertainment package. Bold, energetic, visually striking."

"Yes!" Brianna bounced on her toes. "That's totally me!"

"And Kezia." Ryan's gaze fixed on her. "You're our vocalist's vocalist with sultry sophistication. Refined, poised, with technical excellence that appeals to discerning listeners. I see you as the industry's secret weapon...elegant restraint, flawless technique, the kind of singer critics love."

She smiled because he expected it, but behind the show of enthusiasm, she weighed his words, tested them to see whether that was a mantle she wanted to wear. She wasn't going to do anything simply because Ryan said so. Look where that got her last time.

He was still talking. "Tomorrow you'll meet with our image consultants to develop your looks. I've already briefed them on these directions, so they'll have concepts prepared." He glanced at each of them in turn. "Remember, this is about creating a marketable artist identity. Trust the process. Trust *me*."

"I can't wait to see what they come up with!" Brianna clutched her hands together. "This is going to be incredible."

Ryan faced Kezia, waiting for her reaction.

Sorry, she couldn't be a zealot. But she'd try for engaged enthusiasm. "I'm really excited about this. It's exactly what I've been waiting for."

"Perfect." Ryan checked his tablet. "Start thinking about song selections that fit your prescribed identities. We'll review options tomorrow after your styling sessions."

As they filed out of the room, Brianna launched into a supercharged monologue about potential outfits and staging ideas. But Kezia barely heard her. Her mind was already racing. Not with how to fulfill Ryan's vision, but with how to figure out and present her own.

Refined. Elegant. Sophisticated. Not bad qualities—but not the whole story, either. There was fire in her soul, passion in her faith, steel in her spine. It was time to let that shine.

Chapter 28

EZIA STEPPED INTO *STARBOUND'S* styling suite, where ornate Victorian mirrors now shared space with professional lighting rigs and camera equipment. Mood boards covered every surface, and racks of clothing lined the walls. The air smelled of hair products and new fabric.

Alessandra Beale, the lead image consultant, swept forward to greet her. "You must be Kezia. Ryan's told us so much about your potential look." Her assistants bustled around, arranging materials, while the camera crew adjusted their positions.

Laura, one of the *Starbound* producers, stood in the background, watching with the camera crew.

"We've developed a sophisticated concept based on Ryan's direction." Alessandra guided her to an elaborate mood board. "You're 'the vocalist's vocalist with sultry sophistication'. Timeless elegance with a modern edge. I absolutely love it for you! Your height, your skin, your bone structure, your striking eyes—you're going to be incredible."

Kezia studied the images. Sade in a sleek gown. Alicia Keys from her straight-haired era. Whitney Houston and Toni Braxton in glamorous poses. The color palette was rich with deep burgundies, golds, and blacks. Fabric swatches of silk and velvet promised luxury and refinement.

"And now for the hair." Alessandra all but skipped to a separate board. "We're thinking long, sleek extensions. Very versatile and polished. My first thought was straight, but we could do soft silky waves." A styling assistant appeared with sample hairpieces in a range of colors. "These would give you gorgeous movement onstage."

Kezia's body tensed as Alessandra pulled up computer mockups showing her with long, straight hair. One of the camera operators subtly adjusted his position, angling for a better shot.

She shook her head. "I'm not changing my hair." Her voice was quiet but firm.

Alessandra blinked. "Oh, it's not permanent. Just extensions for the performance." She smiled reassuringly. "I think your natural hair is cool, but this is about creating a cohesive look. Hair is just another styling element, like clothing or makeup. It's a blank canvas we can transform."

"My hair isn't a blank canvas," Kezia said. "And this isn't a direction I'm willing to explore."

Laura stepped closer, clearly interested in the brewing conflict. She motioned one of the cameras to move in for a tighter shot.

Alessandra half-laughed, like she couldn't believe what she was hearing. "But it's standard practice in the industry."

"No."

Kezia kept her tone professional, but inside, a lifetime of memories fueled her resolve. This wasn't just about a hairstyle. This was about everything that had brought her to this moment, every hard lesson learned about staying true to herself.

Alessandra glanced down at her brief, then back at Kezia, her smile tight. "I understand this is important to you, but Ryan was very specific about the direction..." She looked to her assistants for support, but they suddenly seemed very interested in reorganizing fabric swatches.

The cameras edged closer, drinking in the tension.

Alessandra's smile wavered. She cleared her throat. "Let's take a step back from the hair question. What elements of this concept do work for you?"

Kezia moved to the mood board, pointing to the rich color palette and some of the clothing designs. "I'm open to creating a sophisticated look that works with my natural hair, not against it." She straightened her shoulders. "Since I'm planning to perform 'Golden' by Jill Scott, we could take inspiration from her natural hair styling."

Alessandra's eyes lit up. "That could work beautifully. Jill Scott embodies that neo-soul sophistication." She nodded to one of her assistants, who quickly pulled up reference images on a tablet. "We could incorporate gold accents to tie in with the song title and create a cohesive artistic statement."

She turned back to Kezia, her professional smile in place, although she still sounded uneasy. "Let me go back to the drawing board with your feedback. I'll need to discuss this with Ryan, of course, since it's a significant change from his direction."

"I understand." Kezia met her gaze steadily. "But my hair is non-negotiable." She was ready to die on this hill if she had to.

Laura gave her a thumbs up from behind the cameras.

Kezia resisted the urge to roll her eyes. Of course Laura loved this—it was exactly the kind of "moment" producers wanted the *Starbound* contestants to "create."

Alessandra consulted her tablet. "I can see you tomorrow at ten or two for the revised consultation."

"Ten works for me."

As Kezia left the styling suite, she could feel the cameras following her exit, probably already planning how they'd edit this scene. But that wasn't important. What mattered was that she'd stood her ground. Now she just had to prepare herself for Ryan's reaction.

"Kezia," Laura called out. "That was perfect. Can we get your thoughts on camera?"

She gestured to a small seating area they'd set up in an alcove.

Laura's eyes sparkled as she directed Kezia to a velvet armchair.

The second Kezia was seated, Laura said, "That was quite an exchange with Alessandra. Why are you so adamant about not changing your hair?"

Kezia took a deep breath. She hadn't planned to share this story, but maybe it was time. Authenticity, right?

She sat up straighter. "When I was eleven, I went to a boarding school where I was the only Black student."

St. Catherine's, Ashworth.

Her parents had been delighted when she got a place in that prestigious fee-paying school. The memories of those Gothic spires and immaculate playing fields still made her stomach clench.

"Everyone else had this soft, long, silky hair. I spent years chemically processing my hair to fit in. Then one day, just before the beginning of term, Mum couldn't get me an appointment at our regular salon. So we went somewhere else. They either had a bad batch of chemicals or the stylist didn't know what she was doing."

Kezia paused for a moment, the stench of lye and the agony of the chemical burns coming alive again in her mind.

"My scalp was badly burned, and I had to cut all my hair off. I was lucky it grew back."

She could still hear the whispers and giggles, see the finger-pointing, feel the toe-curling humiliation when she'd returned for the summer term in Year 10 with her close-cropped natural hair. How she'd held her chin high despite the murmuring, despite feeling like every eye was on her, a spotlight on her almost shaved head.

That was when she'd thrown herself into music, spending hours in the practice rooms where her voice, not her appearance, was what mattered.

Music had given her the confidence to stand proud, even when she thought her hair was ugly.

She touched her short, textured Afro, smiling despite a sudden rush of moisture to her eyes. "I finally learned to love my natural hair. This isn't just about aesthetics for me. It's about identity and self-acceptance." Her voice thickened. "I've come too far, worked too hard to accept myself. I won't go back to that."

Laura's eyes were shining. "I totally get that. But how do you think Ryan will react to this change in his vision for you?"

Kezia swallowed, working to get her emotions under control. "I respect Ryan as a mentor. I understand that he's a genius at marketing and image. But some things aren't up for negotiation. I can be sophisticated and polished without compromising who I am. And if I can't, then what am I doing here?"

Laura nodded, satisfied. "That's great, Kezia. Really great." She glanced at her notes. "One more thing. Tell me about your song choice."

"I'm planning to perform 'Golden' by Jill Scott." Kezia smiled. "It's about embracing who you are and taking ownership of your joy and your path. It felt...appropriate."

Ryan might have other ideas. But she was ready to fight for her own corner.

Chapter 29

*L*ATE AFTERNOON SUNLIGHT WARMED the polished wood of the upright piano in the rehearsal room. Kezia's fingers moved over the keys as she experimented with different voicings for the bridge of "Golden," her notebook propped open on the stand. The song's sheet music lay spread across the piano, covered in her neat annotations.

It was a good thing that music calmed her. Because she had a fight on her hands. Ryan would be showing up any moment to discuss song choice. She hadn't seen him since her meeting with the stylist.

When the door opened, she forced herself to finish the phrase before looking up.

Ryan strode in, tablet in one hand and a stack of sheet music in the other.

She studied his face. At least he didn't look mad.

"Sorry I'm a bit late. I've been finalizing your song selection for the image challenge." He spread several pieces of sheet music across the piano like a winning poker hand. "The audience hasn't forgotten 'Vision of Love,' and I want you to stamp your authority on that stage. We're going to lean into your abilities as a power vocalist—someone who delivers show-stopping performances."

Kezia glanced at the titles. Celine Dion's "The Power of Love." Whitney Houston's "I Have Nothing." Mariah Carey's "Without You."

"These songs showcase the vocalist's vocalist direction we discussed." Ryan tapped the title sheet of "The Power of Love." "This would be my top pick. We'll marry your technical excellence with a sophisticated, accessible image that's as broadly marketable as possible."

Kezia looked at his selections, then back at her own arrangement of "Golden." Zach's words echoed in her mind. *Hiding behind vocal gymnastics.*

"I've actually been working on 'Golden' by Jill Scott." She played a few bars of the introduction. "It aligns with a direction I'm exploring for myself."

Ryan's smile flickered. "That wasn't the direction we discussed yesterday." He set his tablet down. "The brief I gave Alessandra was for a commercially accessible vocal powerhouse."

"I want to show more than just technical ability," Kezia said. "I want to connect emotionally with the audience. This song means something to me. It has commercial appeal as well as artistic integrity. And it'll let me show control while allowing for emotional depth."

She met his gaze and spoke what she hoped was his language.

"It's marketable, too. Neo-soul has proven, consistent commercial viability."

Ryan's jaw tightened. "Kezia, Alessandra called me about your...concerns...regarding the styling direction." He leaned against the piano. "Part of being a successful artist is adaptability. Taking guidance from industry professionals who understand the market."

He crossed his arms. "First the hair, now the song. I'm seeing a pattern of resistance that concerns me." His voice lowered. "Look, we both know at twenty-nine, you can't count on another chance like this coming along. This is your opportunity to package yourself right and hit the market correctly. The window is closing."

His words stung, but Kezia kept her composure. "I'm not being resistant for the sake of it. I'm trying to develop an authentic artistic identity." She played the opening of "Golden" again, this time with more conviction. "Neo-soul artists like Jill Scott have successful careers spanning decades precisely because they don't chase fleeting trends. And you know I can sing. I can deliver a sophisticated, marketable performance."

Ryan studied her for a long moment. Finally, he said, "Fine. You can do 'Golden.' But it needs to be elevated— taken somewhere fresh, beyond the original."

"It will be."

He gathered his sheet music. "If you're going to deviate from my direction, the performance has to be flawless." Half under his breath, he added, "Between this and the styling issues, I'm already getting pushback. Don't need diversity and inclusion headaches on top of it."

Is that how he saw it? That she was playing the race card? Anger flared for a moment, but Kezia bit back a comment. If he thought her resistance was about identity politics, there was no point saying anything else. He could keep his lazy narrative. She knew the truth.

"You get your song choice and you keep your hair," he said louder, his tone clipped. "I'm giving you room to express your vision. Don't make me regret it." He paused at the door. "Make it work, Kezia. Prove me wrong."

After he left, Kezia sat in silence, her fingers trembling as they rested on the keys. She'd won this round, but at what cost? The expectations were even higher now. She had to prove that authenticity wasn't the enemy of success—that staying true to herself didn't mean she was hard to work with.

Hiding behind vocal gymnastics.

She straightened her spine and began to play "Golden" again, this time with renewed purpose. She wasn't hiding anymore. Not behind technique, not behind what other people wanted her to be. Make it work, Ryan had said. And she would.

Chapter 30

ZACH STUDIED THE LATEST viewing figures on his tablet. Four episodes in, and *Starbound* was holding strong, consistently capturing over twenty-five percent of the available audience. The elimination episodes were trending even higher.

But something in the most recent demographic data for last night's episode caught his eye. While they dominated the 18-34 age group, family viewing had dipped slightly. With their first live show just over a week away, they needed to keep that core audience engaged. He made a note to discuss tweaking the promotion strategy with Victoria from the network.

A knock at the door interrupted his analysis. Hugo, the showrunner, entered with the kind of expression Zach had learned meant trouble.

"We have a situation," Hugo said, closing the door behind him. "Ryan's requesting clothes for one of his mentees that go well beyond our approved styling parameters. Naomi says the outfits are completely inappropriate for our pre-watershed slot."

Zach's stomach tightened. Kezia? The thought surfaced before Hugo even finished speaking.

He knew her faith mattered to her. If Ryan was trying to push her into wearing something that crossed a line, especially under the guise of industry expectations, Zach would shut it down fast. As executive producer, it was absolutely his job to uphold the show's standards.

But this wasn't just about brand guidelines. The idea of her being cornered—coerced—made something twist in his gut.

"Which mentee?" His voice was sharp.

"Brianna."

Zach caught himself relaxing slightly. It wasn't Kezia, but this still wasn't good. "Define inappropriate." He was already dreading the answer.

"Too revealing, overtly sexualized." Hugo shifted uncomfortably. "Naomi says they wouldn't pass Albion's broadcast standards review. Naomi's team is caught in the middle, and Ryan's throwing his industry weight around. You're the only one he'll listen to."

Zach pinched the bridge of his nose. This was exactly what he'd been trying to avoid when he'd set up *Starbound's* guidelines. "She's right to escalate this. Where's Ryan now?"

"He left the styling department after making his demands. He's scheduled to work with his team in the Blues Studio this afternoon."

"I'll speak with him directly." Zach stood, already planning his approach. "This needs to be addressed before the styling team proceeds any further. Tell Naomi I've got her back, and to hold firm on the guidelines until she hears from me."

Hugo nodded gratefully. "She'll be relieved. Ryan can be...persistent when he wants something."

Persistent. Code for manipulating and pressuring junior staff, wearing them down until he got his way. Well, Zach was *not* junior staff.

He gathered his brand guidelines document from the desk. Time to remind everyone exactly what kind of show they'd signed up for.

An hour later, Zach positioned himself in the corridor between the cafeteria and the Blues Studio, doing his best to look casual—not like he was loitering with intent to intercept Ryan.

He'd spent the last hour reviewing the *Starbound* style guide and broadcast requirements. When it came to defending his show's standards, he intended to be on solid ground.

Ryan, like the creature of habit he was, approached right on schedule, tablet in hand, reviewing notes as he walked.

"Ryan, got a minute? Need to run something by you."

Surprise flickered across Ryan's face before settling into professional neutrality. "Sure, what's up?" His tone suggested he already knew.

"Let's use my office. It's about Brianna's styling concept."

Once the office door closed behind them, Ryan went immediately on the offensive. "The styling team shouldn't have gone over my head. I'm trying to give my contestant the best chance at making an impact."

"The guidelines were established with Albion before production began," Zach responded calmly. "Everyone, mentors included, signed off on them. They're non-negotiable for our pre-watershed slot."

Ryan crossed his arms. "Every other show pushes those boundaries. Standards have evolved."

"Not for this show." Zach's voice remained firm. "*Starbound* is positioning itself differently. That's part of what the network and our sponsors bought into. If you have concerns about the guidelines, you bring them to me directly. You don't put the styling team in an impossible position."

"Right, right...the Falconer family values." Ryan's tone became as sharp as a blade. "I should have remembered we're running the Osmonds 2.0 here."

Zach's jaw tightened. "This isn't about personal values, Ryan. It's about the show's positioning and our agreement with Albion."

"Come on," Ryan pressed, clearly sensing he'd found a pressure point. "We both know this is about more than broadcast regulations. Your family's fingerprints are all over this format. Wholesome entertainment for the whole family, right? Very on-brand for the Falconers."

"My family invested in this concept because it's commercially viable. Family-friendly content reaches a broader audience and attracts more diverse sponsorship. It's smart business, not just personal preference."

Ryan leaned back with a slight smile. "If you say so. But let's be honest—you're trying to break into mainstream entertainment while bringing your Sunday school sensibilities with you. That might have worked for your Christian music audience, but reality TV plays by different rules."

"I'm not *trying* to break into mainstream entertainment. I'm already in it." Zach tapped the report with the viewing figures. "You might want to check the latest ratings."

Ryan gathered his notes, his smile faltering.

As he reached the door, Zach added, "And, by the way, people love the Osmonds."

After Ryan left, Zach let the tension release from his shoulders. He made a quick call to Hugo. "It's handled. Tell Naomi and her team Ryan's back in line."

Brianna wouldn't be walking onstage in some racy out-fit designed to shock. Not on his watch. And if Ryan had similar plans for Kezia, he'd be ready for that, too.

Chapter 31

KEZIA STOOD IN THE wings of the *Starbound* stage, her heart beating steady and strong against her ribs. After two weeks of intensive prep, it was finally the first live show of the season. And she was opening it.

Alessandra and her team had outdone themselves. Her Afro was styled in well-defined tight coils and had never looked better.

The champagne-colored silk gown flowed to the floor, its clean lines complementing her curves. Delicate gold embroidery traced the sweetheart neckline and wrapped around her waist like evening sunlight on water. She'd gone with four-inch strappy gold heels, owning her height. Tonight was about authenticity, after all. And she was going to embrace everything that made her stand out.

Ryan's words echoed in her mind: *If you're going to deviate from my direction, the performance has to be flawless.*

It was almost time. She closed her eyes, centering herself. The band was in position. She'd worked with them all week to get the arrangement just right. Red lights blinked on cameras, reminding her again that for the first time, *Starbound* was broadcasting live. But she pushed that thought away. Focus on the audience here in the studio. Connect with them. That's what this song was about.

Her cue came from Olivia. "Performing 'Golden,' please welcome Kezia Blair."

Kezia stepped into the warm stage lights, the familiar weight of performance settling over her like a well-worn coat. The audience's welcome washed over her as she stepped into position center stage. The golden lighting design she'd fought for bathed the stage in warm amber tones—exactly as she'd envisioned.

The opening groove began, and Kezia felt the music in her bones. James, the music producer, had layered the arrangement beautifully, adding the vocal challenges she'd suggested without overwhelming the song's essence. At its heart, this was still "Golden." Still true.

She began the song with the opening vocalization, the notes perfectly placed, technically precise but carrying the warmth this song demanded. She moved with the rhythm, not choreographed steps, but letting the music guide her, her body an extension of her voice.

The verse built toward the chorus, and Kezia allowed herself to dig deeper as she sang about living life to the full, embracing freedom and joy. She wasn't singing a cover. This was her declaration.

The audience was with her, dancing, their energy lifting her up.

As the final chorus approached, Kezia reached for everything she had. Technical precision met emotional truth as her voice filled the studio.

Her last note hung in the air, perfectly controlled, perfectly felt. In the moment of silence before the audience's response, Kezia knew with absolute certainty—she'd done exactly what she set out to do.

The applause crashed over her like a wave and she laughed, riding it, still soaring high.

"Ladies and gentlemen, Kezia Blair!" Olivia's voice rang through the studio as she strode onto the stage in her signature six-inch heels. "What a way to open our first live show. Am I right?"

As the audience applauded again, Olivia turned to Kezia with a warm smile. "They seem to like it. How are you feeling?"

"Amazing." Her heart was still racing. "It felt right, you know? Like everything came together exactly as it should."

"Well, let's see what our mentors thought of that stunning performance. Diana, let's start with you."

"That was sophisticated, controlled, and yet I felt your soul in it," Diana said, beaming. "This is exactly the kind of artistry we're looking for."

Tyler nodded. "The neo-soul direction suits your voice perfectly. I mean, we all know you can sing bigger than that, but I enjoyed this. Smart artistic decision."

Kezia's heart was still racing. But when Ryan leaned forward, her pulse quickened for a different reason. His eyes were hard.

"It was well-executed," he said. "Very well-executed, just as we would expect from you. But I wonder if we missed an opportunity to showcase your full vocal range."

Cold fingers traced up Kezia's spine. He'd asked her to prove him wrong. It sounded like he still felt he was right.

He waved a hand toward her. "The styling looks good, though I still think we could have gone in a more broadly commercial direction. But good work on making this concept your own and trying something new."

Then it was Zach's turn. He sat back in his chair, gaze steady.

"Technically, this was your most polished performance yet. The neo-soul direction is interesting, and I liked the movement—it felt natural. You looked like you were enjoying yourself up there." He paused, his tone shifting. "But I still don't know who you are, Kezia."

The studio hushed.

"Every time I think I'm starting to see something real, something beyond the polish, it slips away. And I'm left wondering if there's a complete artist in there, or just a beautifully styled vessel with perfect technique and no center."

More murmurs. A few scattered boos.

"I know that's not what anyone wants to hear," he added, quieter now. "But I came here to find truth in the music. Not just skill. Truth."

She should be used to being his verbal punching bag by now. But this time, it felt like a TKO. What more did he want from her? After everything she'd put into this performance—choosing a song that meant something, fighting for her artistic vision—he still couldn't see past her technical ability. He still thought she was a human jukebox who could hit the notes, but had nothing to say.

She forced her face to remain neutral, aware of the cameras capturing every micro-expression. "Thank you for your feedback," she managed, speaking to all the mentors, her voice steady despite the tightness in her throat. Her gaze met Zach's for a moment, and she lifted her chin slightly. She wouldn't let him see how deeply his words had cut.

The walk offstage felt endless. As soon as she was out of sight of the cameras, she pressed a hand against the wall, trying to ground herself.

"That was so brave, Kezia," Brianna said, appearing beside her. "Going against Ryan's vision like that? I could never." Her voice dripped with sympathy that didn't quite ring true. "And Zach never has anything nice to say about you, anyway, so just ignore him."

Kezia straightened, pulling her professional mask back into place. "Thanks. I knew I was taking a risk." The words left a bitter, ashy taste in her mouth, like charcoal dust.

She watched the monitor as Olivia announced Brianna's name. The girl bounced onto the stage in the outfit Ryan had chosen for her, all sparkle and commercial appeal, ready to sing the Taylor Swift song he wanted.

Empty vessel.

Kezia pressed her hands together to stop them from shaking. She'd delivered exactly the performance she'd intended. She'd stood up for her artistic vision. She'd been true to herself.

So why did she feel like she'd failed?

Chapter 32

THE ROUND TWO PERFORMANCES were over. The lights bore down, hot and merciless, as Kezia stood with her teammates on the *Starbound* stage, her heart hammering against her ribs as they waited for the eliminations to begin. To her right, Brianna's nervous energy manifested in the constant click of her bracelet against her watch. To her left, Dominic's controlled breathing couldn't quite mask his anxiety.

Twelve contestants remained. After the mentors were done swinging their axes, there would be eight.

"As you know," Olivia's voice filled the studio, "four contestants have to leave us tonight." She paused, letting the weight of those words settle. "Tonight, each mentor must eliminate one contestant from their team. And it's only going to get tougher. Diana, please let us know which contestant you'll be letting go tonight."

Diana rose first, elegant in midnight blue. "This decision wasn't easy," she began, addressing her three contestants. She was letting Jade go. The girl's shoulders slumped before Diana even said her name, as if she already knew. Her elimination speech was gracious, if tearful.

Kezia's throat tightened as she watched her leave the stage. One down.

The studio felt smaller as Tyler stepped forward to face her team and send one home.

Two down. Kezia's turn next.

Her fingernails pressed half-moons into her palms as Ryan stood. His expression gave nothing away, but she knew. After tonight's performance, after every battle over artistic direction these past weeks, after his thinly veiled disappointment—she knew.

"This decision," Ryan said, his voice carrying to every corner of the silent studio, "comes down to potential and adaptability." He turned to address each of his team, and Kezia forced herself to breathe normally. To keep her face neutral. To stand tall.

"Brianna, I know you're here to win. You have consistently embraced direction and become better every week."

Brianna's breath caught audibly.

"Dominic, you've connected with the audience and showed versatility."

A muscle worked in Dominic's jaw.

Ryan's gaze settled on Kezia, and she squared her shoulders. She wouldn't look away. Wouldn't give him the satisfaction of seeing her fear.

"Kezia, you're technically flawless. But that can only take you so far. In fact, sometimes, being so talented sometimes leads to...resistance to guidance."

Resistance to guidance. A diplomatic way of saying she'd fought him on every attempt to reshape her into his vision of a commercial artist. The pause stretched out, though she already knew what was coming. Her prepared speech sat ready on her tongue. Thank you for the opportunity, I've learned so much...

"I've decided that Kezia's journey on *Starbound* ends tonight."

There it was.

Gasps rippled through the audience.

The words landed exactly as she'd expected, yet they still knocked the air from her lungs. She kept her spine straight, her expression composed, even as something crumbled inside her. She'd known the cost of standing her ground. Known it might come to this. So be it.

Pressing her lips together, she nodded.

"Kezia," Olivia said gently, "do you have any final words for your mentor?"

She drew breath to deliver her prepared speech. "Yes. I—"

"I'd like to use my save."

Zach's voice cut through the studio like a thunderclap.

A loud murmur bubbled up from the audience.

Kezia's gaze flew to his face.

He sat forward in his chair, expression unreadable. This had to be some kind of mistake. A joke. He was just mocking her now. Earlier this evening he'd called her an empty vessel, criticized her for hiding behind polish. Why would he...?

"To clarify," Olivia spoke over the audience, each word distinct and careful, "Zach, you're using your one save of the season on Kezia Blair?"

The entire studio went silent, holding its breath.

Kezia's pulse roared in her ears.

"Yes." No hesitation. No explanation. "She joins my team effective immediately."

The audience erupted in gasps and murmurs.

Kezia's legs went weak, and she locked her knees to stay upright. This couldn't be happening. Her harshest critic, the man who hated every single performance she'd delivered, had just saved her?

"Okay," Olivia said. "Kezia joins Team Zach. But, as you know, using a save requires an immediate double elimination from your existing team. Who will you let go?"

Double elimination. The words took a moment to penetrate the fog of shock in Kezia's mind. Then their meaning hit her with devastating clarity. Two people from Zach's team would go home because of her.

"I understand." Zach's voice remained steady. He faced his team. "Neil, Lily, you're truly exceptional artists, but we've gone as far as we can. It's been a privilege to work with you."

The shock rippled through the studio in waves. First came Neil's sharp intake of breath, then Lily's quiet "oh." Jamie, Zach's remaining contestant, put a hand over his mouth.

Kezia's chest constricted. Lily had become a friend during their weeks here. They'd shared late-night conversations about music and faith, encouraged each other through difficult rehearsals.

And Neil...his face was transforming into something hard and ugly, his glare burning into her with such ferocity she had to fight not to step back.

"Kezia," Olivia's voice drew her attention. "Please join your new team."

Her legs felt like lead as she began the long walk across the stage. The heat of the lights, the weight of hundreds of eyes watching, the sound of her heels against the floor...everything felt amplified, surreal.

Neil's shoulder slammed into hers as they passed. "Hope you're worth it," he muttered, voice thick with bitterness.

Before she could process that, Lily stepped forward and wrapped her in a hug, triggering a wave of loud applause from the audience.

Her unexpected kindness hit harder than Neil's bitterness. Kezia's carefully maintained composure cracked. Her throat closed up, and she had to swallow hard against the threat of tears.

"I'm so sorry," she whispered, her voice threatening to break. Sorry seemed inadequate for what had just happened, for being the cause of Lily's elimination.

But Lily pulled back, her smile tearful but genuine. "It's okay. It's not your fault." She squeezed Kezia's hands, her grip warm and steady. "You go win this thing."

Kezia forced herself to breathe slowly, deliberately, as she finally took her place beside Jamie. He looked as shell-shocked as she felt. Her hands trembled, and she clasped them tightly together, fighting to project the composure expected of a professional performer.

Her gaze darted toward Zach. He hadn't moved. He hadn't even looked at her.

His eyes were still on Lily and Neil as they walked off the stage. But the hand resting on the desk in front of him was clenched into a white-knuckled fist.

The weight of what had just happened settled over her like a heavy cloak. She blinked rapidly against the harsh stage lights, willing herself to hold it together for just a few minutes more.

What could Zach possibly see in her that was worth such sacrifice? The man who'd criticized her at every turn had just eliminated two of his own contestants to save her. And how could she possibly live up to Lily's faith in her?

The stage lights dimmed, but the questions blazed brighter than ever in her mind. She drew another careful breath, knowing her control was fragile as glass. Whatever came next, nothing would ever be the same.

Chapter 33

ACH STOOD AT HIS office window, staring at the darkness beyond the security lights. The events of the evening felt surreal, like watching someone else make that split-second decision to save Kezia. But the consequences of his actions were very real, and he needed to handle them properly. Professionally.

He turned at the soft knock on his door. "Come in, Lily."

She entered quietly, her eyes red-rimmed, but her face composed. Her small suitcase stood beside her, ready for her departure. He didn't blame her for crying. This was a sad day for him, too. He truly had wanted to help her develop her gift. But this was the only option, and he prayed he could help her see that.

"Please, sit." He gestured to one of the comfortable chairs grouped around the coffee table rather than the more formal ones in front of his desk. "I know you're hurt and confused about my decision," he began, choosing directness over platitudes. "And I owe you an explanation."

Lily held up her hand. "It's okay. I understand you saw something special in Kezia."

"This isn't about Kezia. This is about protecting your gift, Lily."

Her fingers went to her throat as he continued speaking.

"We've done our best to work within your limitations—keeping arrangements in a safer range, scheduling extra vocal therapy. But it doesn't seem to be helping. In fact, I'm worried that it's getting worse. After your performance tonight..." He met her gaze. "Another few weeks of competition intensity could cause permanent damage."

Tears filled her eyes, but she didn't argue with him. She couldn't deny the hoarseness in her voice tonight.

"You have something very special, Lily. A gift from God that deserves to be protected and nurtured." He crossed to his desk, collected a business card and a thick manila envelope, and handed them to her.

"This is Dr. Elena Reeves, one of the best vocal rehabilitation specialists in London. I've arranged for three sessions with her, fully covered. The envelope contains your full vocal assessment and medical files. Dr. Reeves will need to see these."

Lily stared at the card. "You're helping me even though you eliminated me?"

"I eliminated you from a competition, not from music. There's a difference." He sat in an armchair opposite her, making sure she was looking at him before he continued speaking. "And I eliminated you for your own good. Letting you continue would have been a mistake. I hope you'll come to see that in time."

"I'll...I'll try." A tear slipped down her cheek.

"Dr. Park thinks the nodules are at an early enough stage that you can recover. But your voice needs proper rehabilitation, not competition pressure. Elena will teach you how to sing without the damaging techniques you've developed. When you're ready—truly ready—I'd be happy to help you find professional opportunities. I'd even be open to you auditioning again for *Starbound* in two years, if the show is still airing, which I'm hopeful that it will be."

"I don't know what to say. Except..." She smiled tremulously. "If this had to happen, I'm happy you were able to save Kezia. She's really special."

Zach sat back, thrown by the shift in conversation. "I..." He still hadn't processed that part of his actions.

"I'll be praying for you both." Lily stood, gathering her composure. "And thank you. For caring enough to stop me before I did permanent damage."

"Your gift matters, Lily. Take time to heal, to grow stronger in your faith and your technique. The industry will still be here when you're ready."

She nodded. "Bye, Zach."

"Go get better. I expect to hear great things about you someday."

After she left, Zach remained seated, steeling his resolve. One difficult conversation down. But Neil would be a very different matter entirely.

Zach's office door burst open without a knock. Neil stalked in, tension radiating from every muscle. He remained standing, arms crossed, ignoring the chair Zach gestured to.

"Laura said you wanted to see me. I'm guessing this is where you justify keeping someone you barely know over someone who's been on your team from the start." Neil's voice vibrated with barely contained anger.

Zach kept his own posture relaxed, deliberately nonconfrontational. "I understand your frustration. But this isn't about Kezia."

"Right." Neil's laugh was harsh. "Nothing to do with the hot singer who—"

"This is about your vocal assessment and what you've done and not done about it." Zach's calm voice cut through Neil's building rant. He opened a folder on his desk. "This shouldn't come as a surprise to you. We've been over this already. You have significant technical issues that could be corrected with proper training."

Neil rolled his eyes. "Here we go again."

Zach spoke over his interruption. "But every time our coaches tried to address those issues, you pushed back. You insisted your way was better."

Neil's jaw tightened. "My style is what makes me unique. I wasn't going to let you water it down."

"There's a difference between artistic choice and technical error." Zach held Neil's gaze. "You weren't willing to recognize that difference. Your resistance wasn't about artistic integrity. It was about fear—fear that you might have to admit you don't know everything."

The words landed. Neil's crossed arms loosened slightly, a flicker of uncertainty crossing his face before he scowled again.

"Talent without teachability has a ceiling, Neil. You hit yours in this competition."

Silence stretched between them, their gazes locked in a contest of wills.

Zach reached for a business card. "This is Derek Wells. He runs a studio musician program that includes technical training." He placed the card on the edge of his desk. "He specializes in working with strong personalities. I think he might be a better fit than what we can offer here. This isn't me dismissing you. It's me recognizing you need a different approach than what *Starbound* provides."

Neil scoffed, snatching up the card, only to toss it back onto the desk. "Save the virtue signaling. This whole thing's been rigged from the start. You can't just eliminate someone to save somebody else's favorite."

Zach sighed. He'd hoped Neil would be wiser than this.

The younger man's voice rose. "My agent's going to have a field day with this. There are laws against arbitrary dismissal, you know." He stepped closer to Zach's desk, his tone threatening. "We'll see how your precious show holds up to legal scrutiny."

Zach didn't flinch. "You signed a comprehensive contract before joining *Starbound*. Section twelve, paragraph four specifically covers elimination procedures. Section seven includes non-disparagement and confidentiality clauses that you might want to review before making public statements."

He gestured to the contract copy on his desk.

"I'm under no obligation to offer you anything beyond what's in that document. I'm offering this opportunity with Derek because I believe in developing artists, even when they're difficult."

He slid the card back to the edge of the desk.

"Take it or leave it. That's your choice. I'll email you in two weeks after you've had time to cool down and process your options. That will be my last outreach."

Neil snatched the card, crumpling it in his fist. "Don't bother with the email. We're done here."

He stormed out, slamming the door hard enough to rattle the window blinds.

Zach released a long breath, the tension of maintaining his composure finally easing from his shoulders.

What a hotheaded fool. But he was young. Didn't they say the human brain wasn't fully developed until twenty-five? If that was true, Neil's brain still had three years' worth of maturing. He deserved another chance. If he was smart enough to take it.

Zach rubbed the back of his neck. Two very different conversations. Two very different futures ahead for those artists. He prayed he'd done right by both of them.

And somewhere in the compound, a third artist whose future he'd tied to his own on impulse.

And he still didn't understand why.

His phone screen lit up as he retrieved it from his desk drawer where it had sat silenced all evening. There was an avalanche of notifications. Missed calls and texts from the production team, network executives, and members of his family.

A text from Martha snagged his gaze.

Bold move. You okay? Call me.

Not tonight. He needed space to think, to process. Better to head home tonight than stay on campus. He powered his phone off.

The evening air had cooled as he walked across the compound, his footsteps echoing in the quiet. His mind churned with Lily's vocal issues, Neil's anger, and his impulsive save of Kezia. The network executives would be demanding explanations tomorrow. They were probably demanding explanations now, among the flood of messages doubtless queuing up on his powered-off phone. His life didn't need these complications.

A faint sound made him pause. Piano notes drifted from the rehearsal complex, so gentle he almost missed them. The melancholic opening phrases of Satie's Gymnopédie No. 1. Someone—clearly a well-trained someone—was playing with expression.

Despite his exhaustion, he followed the sound. The melody grew clearer as he approached, drawing him to one of the smaller practice rooms.

Kezia sat at the piano, playing with her eyes closed. Her shoulders moved with each phrase, lost in the gentle rise and fall of the music. She'd changed out of her glittering performance outfit and stripped off all her stage makeup. Instead, she wore...was that a Pokémon sweatshirt? No trace remained of her usual polished demeanor.

He couldn't tear his gaze away from her face, from the emotions that played across her features. The music flowed through her like breath, as natural as her worship had been that morning in church. That same intensity that had caught his attention then was here again—unguarded, pure, and honest.

Frustration prickled beneath his skin. Why couldn't she be like this on stage? Why was this side of her—the raw, aching, real side—covered up everywhere but in private? Why did she hide this soul-deep connection to her musicality behind technical perfection? He'd seen glimpses of it in church. But the moment she stepped onto that *Starbound* stage, everything genuine disappeared behind a polished facade.

What had possessed him to save her? To complicate his own life by adding her to his team when he already had his hands full? Lily had to go, but he could have kept Neil and wrestled with the boy's outsized ego.

He told himself it was Kezia's artistic potential. But maybe it was the way she made him feel when she let the mask fall. Like he was glimpsing something rare.

Kezia was talented, yes, but talent wasn't enough. Not when she seemed determined to bury her gift beneath layers of technical precision.

The music stopped abruptly and her eyes flew open. She'd sensed him in the doorway.

Their gazes clashed across the silent room.

Chapter 34

THE GYMNOPÉDIE FLOWED FROM Kezia's fingers, each gentle phrase a soothing balm. She'd retreated here, seeking solace in music, her happy place, letting Satie's melancholy melody wash over her. Eyes closed, she gave herself up to the flow of the music, muscle memory guiding her fingers, the resonant sound keeping the chaos of tonight at bay. While she played, she didn't have to think. She could just be.

A prickling awareness at the back of her neck made her fingers stumble.

Someone was watching.

She opened her eyes to find Zach Falconer in the doorway, half in shadow.

His posture was tense, coiled with an energy she couldn't read. The intensity of his gaze sent an electric tingle down her spine.

She swallowed, waiting for him to speak. But he said nothing.

"I wanted to thank you for—" she began.

"I don't need your thanks."

He stared at her, saying nothing more, the silence stretching until she had to fight the urge to look away.

He stepped in without invitation, and suddenly the room felt too small. The air grew thick with an undefined tension as he approached her, closer than he'd ever been. Now that he wasn't standing twenty feet away or sitting in a mentor's chair, details she'd never noticed assailed her—the breadth of his shoulders, the subtle cologne that lingered around him.

Staring down at her, he crossed his arms. "Sing your audition piece. 'And I'm Telling You.'" His voice was terse, commanding.

"Now?"

"Yes, now. I'm your new mentor, and we're starting work right now. I'll accompany you."

She rose from the piano bench, acutely aware of his physicality as she walked past him. He towered over her, even with her height. He must be, what, six-foot-three?

He settled onto the bench, one leg casually extended, studying her with that same unsettling focus. "Key?"

"E-flat maj—" Her voice trailed off as his fingers were already finding the right chords, his touch carrying a subtle aggression.

She launched into the song, trying to find familiar ground in her professional routine, but the way he watched her made it difficult to settle. Something was brewing beneath his surface that she didn't understand, making her feel exposed despite her years of performance experience.

Still, her voice knew what to do. She was midway through the first verse, hitting a particularly impressive melisma, when Zach stopped playing.

"That's enough."

Kezia faltered. "Is something wrong with the key?"

"No." He turned on the bench to face her fully. "Tell me something, Kezia. Have you ever been in love? Really in love, not just dating someone."

"I'm sorry?" She couldn't be hearing him right.

"It's a simple question," he said. "Have you ever been with someone who made you feel like you couldn't live without him? Someone you'd fight to keep, no matter what?"

Kezia shifted her weight, uncomfortable with the personal turn of the conversation. "I've had relationships."

"That's not what I asked." His gaze remained locked with hers.

"Yes," she finally said. "Once. At Guildhall."

"Are you still with him?"

A beat of silence. "No."

"Did it end badly?"

Her spine stiffened. "He left me for my best friend after three years. Is that relevant to my vocal technique?"

"It's entirely relevant to this song." He turned back to the piano, executing a swift run of arpeggios. "When you were singing just now, and at your audition, every note was perfect. Every run was flawless. The technical execution was..." He gestured vaguely. "...extraordinary."

"Thank you," she said, though she could hear the "but" coming.

"But I didn't believe you meant a word of it."

The criticism stung more than it should have. She shifted her stance. "The song is about desperate love, about refusing to let someone go. I conveyed that."

"No," Zach countered, facing her again. "You performed it. There's a difference." He stood, moving closer. "When your boyfriend left you, how did it feel?"

"This isn't therapy," she said tersely, holding her ground.

"No, it's about connecting you to the material. That song isn't about sounding impressive. It's about the raw desperation of a woman who's about to lose everything that matters to her."

"I understand the emotional context."

"Understanding it isn't enough." He was closer now, his intensity unsettling. "You need to feel it, not analyze it."

He was too close. Kezia took a steadying breath, avoiding the impulse to step back. "I've been doing this professionally for years."

"Yes, you have. And you're extraordinarily good at it." He didn't back down. "You can simulate any emotion a track needs. You can hit every note. You never miss. It's impressive."

"But?"

"But it's empty." The words landed like a punch. "Every time I've watched you perform, it's the same. Beautiful vessel, perfect sound, nothing inside."

Heat rose to her face. "Nothing inside? I've dedicated my life to music. I've trained since I was a child. I've worked when others gave up. I've—"

"Mastered every technical aspect of singing," he finished for her. "What you haven't done is let us see you."

"See me?" She gave a short laugh. "I'm standing right here."

"No, you're not. You're hiding behind perfect pitch and breath control and vocal placement." He stepped even closer, close enough that she caught the warmth of his body and the subtle pull of his cologne.

She had to tilt her chin to hold his gaze, the air between them taut as a wire.

"Tell me how it felt when he left you."

"Terrible," she said flatly.

"That's not good enough. Did you cry? Did you beg? Did you hate him? Did you hate yourself?"

He wasn't going to let up, was he? She crossed her arms. "I was devastated. I thought my life was over. I couldn't eat. Couldn't sleep. Is that what you want to hear?"

"I want to hear that in the song. Channel that into your voice. Don't give me the polite, sanitized version. I want the messy, humiliating truth of it. Even if it sounds raw and unpolished."

"You want me to sacrifice technical precision for emotional display?"

He loomed over her. "I want you to stop seeing emotion as something that compromises technique and start seeing technique as something that serves emotion."

Kezia stood straighter. "I won't deliver a flawed performance just to satisfy some abstract notion of authenticity."

Zach studied her for a long moment. "You know what's interesting? In your audition interview, you were asked about your most emotionally challenging performance. Do you remember what you said?"

She shook her head, but he wasn't waiting for her answer.

He jabbed a finger at her. "You talked about singing with laryngitis. Not a song that moved you, not a connection to an audience. Your biggest emotional challenge was a technical obstacle."

"Because that's what makes a professional. Showing up and delivering a flawless performance, no matter what."

"That's what makes a *session singer*. I'm looking for an artist."

He walked back to the piano. "This is your homework for tomorrow. Think about why perfectly simulated emotion feels safer to you than the real thing."

She bristled. "That's not fair. You don't know anything about how I feel."

"No, I don't," he agreed. "And that's the problem." He played the opening chords of her audition song. "The next time I hear you sing, I want to hear *you*, not just your voice."

Kezia grabbed her tote bag from where she'd left it. She was done with this conversation, and she wasn't going to ask his permission to leave. She walked toward the door, then turned back to face him. "You know, vulnerability can be manufactured, too. Just ask Brianna."

A hint of a smile touched his lips. "I'm not interested in manufactured anything. Not from Brianna, and not from you." His gaze met hers with unsettling directness. "I want to hear what's real. Welcome to Team Zach."

She stepped outside, welcoming the chilling air against her heated face. Was this what working with him would be like? Terrifying, disorienting and...strangely freeing? He might have saved her, but there was nothing safe about being on Team Zach.

Chapter 35

*B*ACK IN HIS OFFICE the next morning, Zach clicked on his Technivorm Moccamaster, loading it with freshly ground Ethiopian Yirgacheffe beans. Only a robust, full-bodied drip coffee would give him the caffeine jolt he needed right now.

He hadn't slept much, his mind cycling through last night's conversations. Lily's grace in accepting his reasons for her elimination. Neil's explosive anger and blustering threats.

But what kept him awake was Kezia. That moment he'd found her playing Satie—the raw honesty in her music before she knew she was being watched, and the confrontation that followed. He'd pushed her hard, deliberately provoking her, trying to crack that perfect façade, jabbing at old wounds in the name of artistic growth. But deep down, he knew it wasn't just about pushing her as a mentor. He wanted to unsettle her the same way she unsettled him.

And she'd pushed back, standing her ground, meeting his challenge even as she retreated behind her professional shield. But now he knew for sure there was something behind that armor.

As soon as he turned his phone on, it lit up with a wave of notifications. He'd kept it off since last night, needing a few hours to decompress after the pressure of the elimination show and everything that followed. Now, watching message after message flood his screen, he wondered if those few hours of peace had been worth it.

Missed calls from Helen in PR, Martha, and Victoria Harlow at Albion. His notifications scrolled like a slot machine spinning out of control.

He thumbed through the entertainment news headlines as the aroma of the coffee filled his office: "DOUBLE ELIMINATION SHOCK." "FALCONER STUNS AUDIENCE." "STARBOUND CONTROVERSY ROCKS LIVE PREMIERE WEEK."

Well. At least no one could say the show was boring.

A text from Martha rose to the top of his screen.

The gamble paid off! Albion execs ecstatic about numbers. Victoria H. wants urgent call.

Zach filled his coffee mug and leaned against his desk, mentally reorganizing his day. The media circus would need managing, but he wasn't going to let it derail what mattered. He'd cracked open a door in Kezia's carefully constructed walls last night. Now he needed to figure out how to keep it from slamming shut again.

A sharp rap on his door was followed immediately by the *Starbound* senior producer Steve bursting in, iPad in hand. "There you are! Have you seen these numbers?" His excitement filled the room as he thrust the tablet at Zach.

"The elimination is trending nationwide. Look at these viewership spikes! And not just last night's live show. Streaming numbers are way up across earlier episodes too. People are playing catchup because they want to see what led to last night's drama."

Zach scanned the overnight metrics, noting the social media engagement graphs climbing sharply upward. The buzz over Kezia's elimination and save had certainly stirred things up.

"We're getting media requests from outlets that weren't even covering us before. Saving her was a stroke of genius." He shot a look at Zach. "Though if someone had told me you were planning to do that, we could have had cameras in position for all the reactions."

"Nice to be called a genius, but I wasn't planning it," Zach said. "I didn't know Ryan intended to eliminate her. This show is unscripted, remember? Simon! Could you come in here, please?"

Zach reached for his desk phone, but his assistant appeared in the doorway before he could dial.

"We need to reschedule today's mentoring sessions. Push Kezia and Jamie to late afternoon. My morning's going to be wall-to-wall media management."

"I was just coming to ask you about that," Simon said, tablet in hand. "Helen from PR is already in the conference room with the team. And Victoria Harlow from Albion has requested a video call at 9:30."

"But we need to film your first session with Kezia while the story is hot," Steve protested. "The audience will be expecting to see that moment."

"That moment already happened. I did some work with her last night."

"What?" Steve slammed a palm to his forehead. "You're killing me, Zach. You cost us golden content, sneaking off to talk to her without cameras."

Zach's mind flashed back to how he'd confronted Kezia about her love life, pushing her to access a genuine connection to her song. "That was a private conversation that needed to happen off-camera."

"Come on, Zach. Give me something to work with here. The ratings prove people want to see the drama of it all. The mentor who saved her from elimination. And the beautiful, talented artist who has to prove herself worthy of that save..." Steve spread his hands. "This is television gold. At least let us recreate the moment and shoot a proper first mentoring session."

"That's exactly what we *won't* do. We can't manufacture that moment." Zach leaned back in his chair, studying Steve. "Look, I understand the business opportunity. I know we need to capitalize on it. But last night's numbers came from something real. The minute we start staging re-actions, we lose that."

Steve narrowed his eyes. "What if we film you explain-ing why you saved her? The audience needs to understand what changed. I mean, you've been her biggest critic from day one. You've ripped into every single performance of hers. They're calling you the 'Maestro of Mean'. Then sud-denly you're throwing out two of your original team to keep her? People want to know why."

"Fine. I'll do an interview about that." Zach took an-other sip of coffee. "And you can film this afternoon's men-toring session. But keep it simple. Two cameras maximum, no boom operators hovering over us. I want her focused on the work, not the production."

"You're going to make this as difficult as possible, aren't you?" Despite his words, Steve was already tapping notes into his iPad. "But keep giving us this kind of gold, and I'll forgive you. Victoria Harlow called me personally this morning. She's talking about potential international format sales if we maintain this momentum. We can't squander that opportunity."

The mention of international sales should have felt like validation of his show concept. Instead, Zach felt that fa-miliar tension between commercial success and artistic in-tegrity. He thought of Kezia at the piano last night, playing Satie with such pure emotion before she noticed him watching. That was what he'd been trying to draw out of her all along.

"We won't squander anything by doing this right," he said firmly. "I'll do that interview with you about the save after I finish up with the network. And I'll see Kezia at half past three. The audience can watch us work together. But remember—minimal crew. This isn't about creating drama. It's about developing an artist."

After Steve left, Zach stared into his coffee, now cooling in the matte black mug. The "Maestro of Mean" saves the technically perfect contestant he's been criticizing. It was the kind of narrative that would drive ratings, and exactly the kind of simplistic story that could derail Kezia's development if he didn't manage it carefully.

He glanced at his schedule, now packed with media and executive obligations. The show needed this success. It was exactly what he'd been hoping and praying for. Albion's excitement was gratifying. This kind of mid-season audience growth was rare and precious, and he understood why they wanted to cash in on it. Wearing his businessman's hat, he wanted that, too.

His family had invested so much in *Starbound's* vision of authentic artist development. *His* vision. But that same vision meant protecting Kezia's emerging artistry from becoming just another reality TV plot point.

Last night, watching her when her guard was down, he'd seen who she was when she stopped hiding behind technical perfection. His job now was to create a space where she could find that authenticity again, media circus or not.

He reached for his phone to call the network executive. Time to start shaping the story so he could get back to what really mattered—Kezia and her music.

Chapter 36

*K*EZIA HEARD MUSIC BEFORE she reached Team Zach's rehearsal space—fragments of melody that started and stopped, like someone thinking through their fingers. She recognized Jamie at the piano before he looked up, his expression shifting from surprise to something more guarded when their gazes met.

"Morning." He lifted his hands from the keys. "If you're here for the team meeting, it's been pushed back. PR crisis management, apparently."

"Oh." Kezia hovered in the doorway, noticing the single mounted camera in the corner. Usually, there were at least three cameras and a boom operator for any scheduled interaction between contestants. "There's a crisis? I hadn't heard."

"Really?" Jamie raised an eyebrow. "Just when I was about to congratulate you. *You're* the *Starbound* story now."

"*I'm* the story?" Kezia moved further into the room. "How?" She'd avoided Brianna—her usual gossip source—by going to bed late and rising extra early this morning.

"Mean judge saves contestant he's been trashing all season? The producers are probably tossing confetti in their offices right now."

"Well, maybe they know more than I do. I'm aware of how much he hates my work." Kezia set her water bottle on a table, memories of last night's confrontation still raw.

"Oh, we've all heard his critiques." Jamie's fingers found a minor chord, held it. "Yeah, he's been pretty brutal. But I'd rather be roasted and then saved by Zach than flattered and dumped by Ryan. At least with Zach, you know where you stand."

Except she still wasn't sure what Zach thought of her. He'd pushed her harder than anyone ever had, demanding honesty about things she'd barely admitted to herself. He'd even got her to talk about getting dumped by Scott. But somehow, his relentless pushing made his save feel more genuine, not less.

Jamie struck another chord, harder this time. "Unlike some people, who smile and nod and tell you that you're improving, right up until they eliminate you."

Jamie had a point.

Despite his abrasive words, intrusive questions, and complete disregard for her personal space, strangely, last night's brief talk with Zach felt much more like real mentoring than all the weeks with Ryan and his smooth talk.

"Zach tells it like it is," Jamie said. "Take Neil, for instance. Be grateful you never had to share a rehearsal space with that ego. You should have heard him last night, going on about betrayal and threatening legal action. But honestly? Good riddance. Zach warned him ages ago about his attitude, so his elimination shouldn't have come as a shock."

He leveled his gaze at her. "What I can't get over is Lily. Why Zach dropped her for you."

Kezia flinched. "I know. I don't get it, either. She's my friend."

"Yes, I thought she was." Jamie crossed his arms. "You used to go to church together and all. So, what does it feel like to take her spot?"

"I didn't take her spot." His accusation cut her to the quick. "Do you think I wanted this? I hate that she's gone. And I resent your implying that I did any of this on purpose. I've spent weeks—no, months, actually—trying to figure out why Zach seems to hate everything I do. He's been on my case right from my audition. I'm just as confused about it as you are. So, for you to sit there and say that I somehow got him to push my friend out—"

She broke off and took a deep breath, pressing her fingers to her temples.

"Look. I'm not here to pick a fight. Since the team meeting's off, I'll get out of your space."

His voice stopped her as she turned to leave. "No, wait. I'm sorry." He stood, pushing a hand through his hair. "I'm just upset about Lily, okay? I was out of order to blame it on you. And Zach's always been a straight shooter. If I have a problem with his decisions, I need to take it up with him."

Kezia's shoulders dropped. "Thanks."

He eyed her. "But of course you realize we're each other's competition for a spot in the semi-finals."

"Yes, we are." Kezia met his gaze directly. "And maybe I'll be sent home first. I already feel as if I'm here on borrowed time. But I want to make the most of however many days I have left. The resources here..." She gestured at the professional setup around them. "After years of self-financing my continual training, it's incredible."

Jamie nodded slowly. "You went to Guildhall, right? And got a master's degree? So what other resources were you paying for? I thought you'd be making decent money from session work."

Kezia leaned against the piano. "I reinvest most of it. Guildhall was just the beginning. Regular vocal coaching doesn't come cheap, and then there's private health insurance because I can't risk NHS waiting times if anything goes wrong. ENT checkups every couple of years, acoustic analysis sessions, remedial work whenever bad habits creep in..." She shrugged. "When your voice is your business, you can't afford to skimp on maintenance."

"Those costs add up fast," Jamie said.

"It does. But it costs even more to lose work because your technique isn't absolutely reliable." Kezia gestured around the studio. "That's what's so incredible about being here. All these resources are just... available. The vocal coaching, the recording facilities, the arrangement support. All of it makes it worth being here."

"Man." Jamie shook his head, a wry smile playing at his lips. "Hearing all that makes me feel like such a slacker. Here's me relying on natural talent and shortcuts since I was ten, and you're doing everything by the book."

Kezia smiled back. "Two platinum albums before you were thirteen? I'd say natural talent got you pretty far."

"Yeah, until it didn't." His fingers picked out a familiar melody, his biggest hit, but with a harder edge than the bubblegum pop version. "Teresa's got me basically rebuilding my technique from the ground up. Says I'm putting strain on my vocal cords." He straightened his spine and adopted Zach's stern expression. "'Raw talent without discipline is just potential going to waste.'" The impression was uncanny.

Kezia chuckled. "That actually sounds exactly like him."

"Right?" Jamie grinned, then grimaced. "But he's not wrong. Some days it feels like I'm learning to sing all over again."

The frustration in his voice was familiar. Kezia had gone through similar retraining at Guildhall.

"What specifically are you working on?" Kezia asked. "With Teresa, I mean."

"This one exercise." Jamie sang a descending phrase that started strong but wavered in the middle register, his voice tightening as he tried to maintain control. "It's about breath support through the phrases, but there's this thing that happens in the middle where—" He broke off, shaking his head. "I'm not explaining it well. Lily used to..." He trailed off, then finished quietly, "She used to help me with it, actually."

"Oh, I know exactly what you mean," Kezia said. "It's that moment where you need to maintain the support while transitioning between registers, right? Without creating tension in your throat?"

Jamie's eyebrows rose. "Yes, that's it exactly."

"I could show you how I approach that, if you'd like."

Jamie studied her for a moment. "Sure," he said finally. "Why not?"

As Kezia moved toward the piano, Jamie added with a half-smile, "Just so we're clear, though, I still plan on beating you even if you help me."

His cheeky candor made her laugh. "I wouldn't expect anything less."

His smile grew, and something shifted between them then. Not friendship exactly, but a kind of professional respect.

The competition was still there, and neither one of them would progress in the show without the other one getting eliminated. Perhaps it ought to bother her, but it didn't. She just saw a fellow singer who needed knowledge that she could share.

She played a few notes on the piano. "So, the trick with this particular run is to think of it like a slide, not stairs. The mistake you're making is you're fighting the natural break points because you're approaching each note separately."

She demonstrated the same phrase Jamie had sung, but her version flowed seamlessly through the middle register. "Try thinking of it as one continuous motion, like you're pouring the sound out."

Jamie gave her a skeptical look. "Pouring the sound?"

"I know it sounds a bit abstract." Kezia smiled. "But sometimes the technical explanations get in our way. When I was retraining at Guildhall, I kept getting stuck because I was thinking too much about the mechanics. My teacher made me visualize it instead." She gestured with her hand, a smooth downward motion. "Like water flowing down steps. It doesn't jump from one level to the next. It follows the contours. Go on, give it another try."

Jamie tried the phrase again, his brow furrowed in concentration. This time, though the transition wasn't perfect, the tension in his throat was noticeably reduced.

"Better," Kezia said. "You're still thinking about it too much, but that's the basic idea."

"Huh." Jamie nodded slowly. "That actually helps. Who knew all those fancy degrees would be good for something?"

"I won't tell Zach you said that."

"And if you did, I'd deny it completely."

Kezia laughed. "Okay, let's try it again."

Chapter 37

*K*EZIA WALKED NEXT TO Jamie as they returned to the rehearsal room in the afternoon. Hanging out with him had been surprisingly fun, despite their rough start this morning.

But now it was time for their delayed session with Zach. Despite Jamie's assurances, Kezia wasn't sure whether she was looking forward to it or dreading it. He hadn't been there last night when Zach was getting in her face, demanding that she dig into the pain of her worst breakup.

Jamie stood aside and let her get into the rehearsal room first.

Her heart thudded. Zach was already there, wearing a fitted gray long-sleeved T-shirt and black jeans. He was deep in conversation with the sound engineer while the camera crew fiddled with their equipment. Were they late? They'd been told the session would start at half-past three, and it was only twenty past. Sheet music and production notes were spread across the piano.

Kezia's stomach tightened when she saw Steve standing at the back of the room. The senior producer and director rarely attended regular mentoring sessions, preferring to focus on the main stage performances and elimination nights. Now he stood, iPad in hand, watching the setup with the kind of focused attention that suggested this wasn't just about capturing a routine coaching session.

Jamie shot her a glance, his eyebrows raised. He'd noticed Steve, too.

Zach looked up, his expression unreadable. "Good, you're here. Right on time, too. Good to see you, Jamie."

A producer signaled that the cameras were rolling, and Steve moved to whisper something to one of the camera operators.

"Kezia." Zach's tone was professionally neutral. "Welcome to Team Zach. Officially this time." He distributed the sheet music. "Today, you'll both work with the same piece. Different focus areas."

She glanced at the music. "Endless Love," made famous by Lionel Richie and Diana Ross, and later covered by Luther Vandross and Mariah Carey.

Jamie kept any comments to himself. The playful mood from their morning session felt very far away.

"Kezia, you'll be there." Zach pointed to a spot about six feet from the piano. "Jamie, just to her right. We'll work without mics for now. I want to hear your natural voices and how they blend."

"Wait." Kezia pulled her portable steam inhaler, a device about the size of a large coffee mug, from her rehearsal bag. "I need to use this first. Two minutes."

Zach frowned. "We're already running behind. We need to make up for lost time this morning."

"Two minutes now could save hours later if I damage my voice." She met his gaze steadily, despite the flutter in her stomach. "I always do this before intensive vocal work. I wasn't aware we'd be singing in this session, or I would have made sure to use it earlier."

Steve shifted by the door, but Kezia kept her focus on Zach. This was about protecting her instrument. Any vocal coach worth their salt would understand that.

Zach's jaw worked for a moment, then he gave a sharp nod. "Fine. Two minutes. Use the dressing room down the hall."

She hurried out, aware of the cameras tracking her exit. In the quiet of the dressing room, she plugged in her My-PurMist steam inhaler and pulled a small towel out of her bag. She draped the towel over her head, creating a tent to trap the warm vapor. Breathing deeply, she could almost feel the tension in her vocal cords easing.

When she returned to the rehearsal room, Zach was discussing arrangement details with Thomas, the session pianist, his drumming fingers betraying his impatience. But she felt centered now, ready to sing.

He shot a glance at her. "Good, you're back. But that was closer to five minutes. Now that your vocal cords have been properly pampered, can we get started?"

Kezia's cheeks warmed, but she kept her expression neutral. She'd learned long ago never to apologize for taking care of her voice. Still, she couldn't help feeling that she'd already started this session on the wrong foot.

Two music stands were already positioned where he'd indicated, angled slightly toward each other. Behind them, one of the camera operators adjusted his position to capture both performers in frame.

"'Endless Love.' Let's take verse one and the first chorus," Zach said. "Thomas?"

Thomas played the opening bars, the familiar melody filling the room. Jamie glanced at Kezia, giving her a slight nod as they began.

Jamie's voice was warm and rich, with a slight gospel inflection. He approached each phrase with an easy, natural style that made technical imperfections feel like artistic choices. But she could hear the tension he'd mentioned this morning as the melody rose.

She joined in with Diana Ross's part, adjusting her usual dynamics for the acoustic space. Where Jamie's style was loose and emotional, hers was precise and controlled, yet somehow they found a complementary balance.

Their voices wove together through the verse and into the chorus. Kezia instinctively compensated when Jamie's pitch wavered slightly, falling back on her years of supporting other vocalists.

Zach's expression remained neutral as they finished the chorus, but his fingers were drumming against his thigh. Never a good sign.

Kezia and Jamie held their final notes, letting the harmony fade naturally in the acoustic space. For a moment, the room was silent except for the soft whir of the cameras.

"Technically, that was fine." Zach straightened from where he'd been leaning against the piano. "But Jamie, you're anticipating those higher notes and tensing up. And Kezia—" He turned to face her. "Where's the vulnerability we talked about last night? You're holding back. You're supposed to be serenading the love of your life, not singing elevator music."

A wave of heat swept Kezia's face, and she forced herself not to clench her fists.

Jamie's gaze flicked to hers, a mix of sympathy and wariness in his expression.

"Let's take it from the top," Zach said.

From his position by the door, Steve leaned forward.

Thomas began the introduction again. Jamie sang his part, but Kezia had barely made it through her first line when Zach held up his hand.

"Stop. Kezia, you're thinking about the notes. I can see it in your face. Start again."

They made it another three bars before Zach called another halt. "Jamie, you're still anticipating that high note. Relax your jaw. Go again."

Halfway through the verse, he lifted a hand. "Kezia, what did I say about vulnerability? I want to hear yearning. Passion. Surely, that steam inhaler should have relaxed your voice, not made it more uptight. Again."

Each interruption was like a paper cut—small but stinging. Kezia could feel Jamie's growing tension beside her, his breathing becoming more labored. Her own throat was starting to feel tight, and not from vocal strain.

"Stop." Zach pushed away from the piano. "This isn't working. You're both getting worse, not better."

They moved to microphones for the next hour, but Zach's critiques were relentless. Every phrase, every note, even every breath, seemed to spark another correction for Kezia, while Jamie's technical struggles earned only gentle suggestions. By the end of the session, she had begun to hate "Endless Love" with a passion she'd never felt for any piece of music before.

"That's enough for today," Zach finally said. He turned to Jamie. "Good work. Don't forget your vocal coaching session. Work on those breathing exercises we discussed."

Jamie nodded, already gathering his things. He shot Kezia a quick look, with a slight shake of his head, then headed out the door.

Zach's attention shifted to Kezia, his expression cooling. "You need to focus on loosening up your delivery. You're still too mechanical."

That did it. The anger that had been simmering finally ticked over. "Why don't I secure world peace and find a cure for cancer while I'm at it? Maybe once I've done that, I'll finally get a good critique from you."

Zach tilted his head, frowning. "Excuse me?"

The camera operators, who had been packing up their gear, suddenly straightened. One nudged the other, and both cameras swung back into position.

Kezia, her face flaming, was beyond caring whether all the cameras on the Starbound Campus were pointed right at her. "You've not had a single positive word to say about what I did today. Nothing has been good enough for you."

Something flickered across his face, but he masked whatever it was. "You're a professional, Kezia," he said after a moment. "You should be able to handle unvarnished critique without taking it personally. If you want someone to coddle you, you picked the wrong mentor."

Kezia crossed her arms. "You told Jamie his pitch issues were 'something we can work on' after he was flat through the entire second verse. Was I the only one who noticed he kept running out of breath at the end of the chorus? Because I don't recall you pointing that out. And I seem to be the only one whose diction bothers you."

Zach opened his mouth to respond, but she continued.

"And just to be clear, I didn't pick you. You picked *me*. You dropped two of your original contestants to bring me onto your team. No one forced you to do that."

Zach's jaw tightened, but he remained silent.

With this outburst, she'd probably earned herself a ticket back home at the next elimination. But she was over this. If he dropped her, at least she could go out with her head held high.

She took a breath, her voice steadying. "Look, I'm a professional. And as a professional, I want honest and fair treatment. I can handle criticism just fine. I don't need my hand held or my ego stroked. But I do need to know I can trust your feedback isn't skewed because I've somehow offended you or you regret your decision. If we're going to work together, I need to know what I'm working with."

Placing his hands on his hips, he dropped his gaze for a moment. "You're right." His tone was more measured than before. "I might have been too soft on people who I think need gentler treatment. But you can trust my feedback."

He paused, meeting her gaze directly. "I don't regret my decision. And you've done nothing to offend me. Your performances come across as stiff and mechanical, and that's my professional opinion."

Kezia nodded once. "Then I'll work on being less stiff and mechanical. Thank you for the clarity."

She gathered her things and left the rehearsal room, leaving Zach standing with Steve and the rolling cameras.

Chapter 38

THE DOOR CLICKED SHUT behind Kezia. Before the sound had even faded, Steve stepped forward, his face lit with the kind of enthusiasm Zach had learned to dread.

"That was absolute gold!" Steve's hands gestured expansively. "The Maestro of Mean strikes again, and Kezia finally claps back. Exactly what we needed. You played her perfectly. Viewers will be glued to their screens."

"This isn't about—"

Steve barreled forward. "The ratings for this will be through the roof! The saved contestant finally standing up to her savior. And you got her to do it on camera. Brilliant timing." He chuckled. "And that whole exchange with her steamer. This girl is the gift that keeps on giving. Did you know she carts that thing around with her?"

Zach's jaw tightened. "This is about artist development, not manufacturing drama." He was ashamed of himself for mocking her steamer. Especially after vocal health was such an issue with Lily.

An uncomfortable thought nagged at him. Was he being unfair with her? Had his critiques crossed a line from development into something else? Steve seemed to think Zach was being tough on her on purpose.

"We can have artist development with drama," Steve said, his grin widening. "That's the beauty of it." He turned toward the door. "Rita, grab Kezia for an OTF about what just happened. I want that interview while her blood is still up. Man, that was a thing of beauty."

As he put his hand on the door handle, he spoke to the camera operators who were disconnecting their equipment. "I need that footage edited by tonight."

Zach stepped forward. "Steve—"

"Don't worry," Steve called over his shoulder. "Conflict makes for better television than harmony."

The door swung shut behind him, leaving Zach alone with his scattered sheet music and growing unease. He gathered his notes mechanically, trying to push aside Kezia's accusations. He'd been maintaining standards, hadn't he? Pushing her because she had the potential to be extraordinary?

But her words kept circling back. She was right about Jamie's pitch issues. And his breathing problems. When had he started going easy on some contestants while being hard on the others?

And Steve's assumption that he'd orchestrated the whole confrontation... That implied that the senior producer had noticed something in his behavior toward Kezia.

His gut twisted. Over an hour going over that song. He stood still, staring at the sheet music in his hands, at the lyrics he'd made her sing over and over.

Something about that woman triggered his critical side. Maybe it was her precision, her technical perfection that made him want to find flaws. And yes, there were flaws—he wasn't imagining them. He could cross-check the footage of their session just to be sure. But if anyone else had made those same mistakes, he'd have let them slide.

He stuffed the music into a folder. No, he wouldn't check the footage. He never wanted to hear "Endless Love" again.

He paused, thinking about the way she'd stood there at the door, her dark eyes flashing, her hand resting on her hip, maintaining her composure even in her anger. Few contestants would dare challenge their mentor, especially after being saved from elimination. And she'd done it with the same measured control she brought to her performances, laying out specific examples to make her case.

That took courage. It wasn't petulance like Neil's. It was the confidence of an intelligent, talented woman who knew her worth.

And it had absolutely no business being as compelling as it was.

He exhaled, rubbing a hand across the back of his neck. If he was starting to notice her for more than her artistry, that was a problem. A serious one.

He gathered his things and headed for the door. Tomorrow, he'd be more balanced. More objective. Make sure she had no cause to question him. He'd be the perfect mentor.

Chapter 39

*K*EZIA STOOD WITH JAMIE in the main hall at the Starbound Campus. They were the final two members of Team Zach. Although she hadn't had a mentoring session since their confrontation over "Endless Love" two days ago, she'd seen Jamie heading to and from his sessions with Zach. Her own schedule showed nothing but vocal coaching, development workshops, and dance training.

Only eight contestants remained of the original sixteen. The production crew bustled around them, positioning lights and checking camera angles. Something was different about the setup today. There were more cameras than usual, and whispered conversations between crew members that suggested this wasn't a typical challenge announcement.

"What do you think they've got planned?" Jamie whispered.

Before Kezia could answer, Olivia Chang strode onto the stage, camera crew tracking her movement. Her silver sequined blazer caught the lights, sending sparkles across the contestants' faces.

"Congratulations on making it to the top eight!" Olivia's voice carried that perfect blend of warmth and authority that had made her such a successful choice as host. "After last week's dramatic eliminations and saves, you've proven yourselves worthy of this next phase of the competition."

Kezia felt eyes and cameras on her and fought the urge to shrink back. Contestants had limited access to social media, but Brianna always found ways to stay informed. She'd backed up Jamie's claim that Kezia's rollercoaster fortunes were making waves.

If Zach hadn't used his save, she'd be back in London right now, probably loading her steamer for another session gig. That, or trying to secure new accommodation so she could get her stuff out of storage.

Wait—Olivia was talking. Kezia really ought to listen to the actual challenge.

"True artists don't just interpret others' work. They create their own," Olivia said. "This week, you'll co-write and perform an original song that reveals something authentic about who you are."

Kezia winced. There was that word again. Authentic. It had become her personal tormentor these past weeks as Zach wielded it like a weapon in critique after critique.

Olivia said, "Your songs must be original compositions created during this challenge period. You can't dig up something you wrote earlier. The lyrics should reveal something personal about your journey or identity. We want to see your artistic vision. You'll have full band and production support for your final performances."

Around her, the other contestants were displaying camera-friendly reactions. Brianna and Dominic exchanged matching grins. Sandra was oohing and aahing and Jamie's eyebrows had shot up to his hairline.

Kezia couldn't muster anything more than a tight-lipped smile. The last time she'd written a song was for a Year One assignment back at Guildhall. Professor Matthews had marked it as "satisfactory, but lacking originality." And now she had to write one to perform on national television. Not just that, but it had to "reveal something personal."

She could already imagine Zach's critique. "Barely adequate, if you were writing elevator music. Where's the emotional connection?"

For the first time since the competition began, she couldn't even count on technical excellence to save her. Because when it came to songwriting, she was average at best.

"To help guide you through this process," Olivia continued, moving toward the wings of the stage, "we've brought in some of the industry's most respected songwriters. Come on out and join us."

Kezia watched as four people walked into the room. Wait, that fourth one was Ezra Falconer, Zach's brother. Her heart rate kicked up.

Olivia introduced them, citing their industry credentials. Mark Hadley's ballads had dominated Radio 1 last year. Sheila Cooper-Marquez, who had her first breakthrough success with Little Mix, and Larry Norton, whose indie sensibilities had earned him critical acclaim.

"Working with Team Ryan, Mark Hadley," Olivia announced. "For Team Diana, Sheila Cooper-Marquez. With Team Tyler, Larry Norton. And with Team Zach, multiple Grammy nominee and chart-topping songwriter, Ezra Falconer."

As Ezra moved to stand next to Zach, Kezia did a quick mental inventory of his credentials. Two Grammy nominations. Multiple number-one hits on the Christian music charts with the Falconers. Songwriting credits for major Christian and mainstream artists, including his wife Morgan. And wasn't he writing the music for some popular TV show?

Plus two solo albums entirely written by him. His reputation was genuine, family connection aside. In fact, he was arguably even more credentialed than Zach.

The cameras swept across their faces, capturing reactions.

Kezia maintained her smile, even as her mind raced through the implications. Would Ezra share his brother's exacting standards? His criticism of her "mechanical" delivery? Or would he perhaps understand what she was trying to achieve with her technical precision?

As Ezra and Zach stood side by side, she noted their similar stance, the easy familiarity between them. Whatever happened this week, it would certainly be interesting.

At Olivia's invitation, each mentor stepped forward, outlining their vision for the challenge. Ryan emphasized commercial appeal, stressing the importance of hooks that would work on radio. That was a shocker. Not.

As he spoke, it struck her how little she'd thought about him since he eliminated her. He'd been her mentor for weeks—but somehow Zach had taken up far more space in her mind in just a few days.

Diana was after authentic storytelling through lyrics, while Tyler focused on melodic originality.

Zach stepped forward last. "Songwriting reveals what makes you unique as an artist." He surveyed the contestants, his gaze sweeping across the stage. "This challenge isn't about writing a hit. It's about writing *your* song."

He faced his team. "I expect both of you to dig deeper than you ever have before."

Then his gaze locked with Kezia's—and she knew exactly what was coming. "No hiding behind clever phrases or technical flourishes."

She kept her face impassive, though her fingers twitched. Always the same critique. Always pushing for vulnerability, never satisfied with what she was willing to give.

"You'll begin working with your songwriters immediately," Olivia announced, her voice cutting through the tension. "You have just over two weeks to write, refine, and prepare your performances. At the end of this challenge, four of you will be eliminated from the competition. The remaining four will go ahead into the semifinals. The stakes are even higher this week. Good luck to you all."

Production assistants began moving forward, clipboards in hand, ready to direct teams to their assigned spaces. The reality of the challenge settled over Kezia like a weight. Two weeks to write something personal, something authentic, something that would satisfy Zach's demand for emotional depth. Or else she'd go home.

As the contestants began to disperse, Zach and Ezra stood conferring quietly. They had the same focused intensity, the same way of gesturing as they spoke, though Ezra's style was more relaxed, his smile easier.

"Ready to write a hit?" Jamie asked, practically bouncing with excitement as they waited for their first meeting with Ezra.

Kezia smoothed her expression into professional calm. "Ready to try," she said, her measured tone smoothing over the churn of anxiety in her gut. How could she write something personal enough to satisfy Zach?

But she'd find a way. She always did.

Chapter 40

*K*EZIA HESITATED AT THE entrance to the Blues Studio, momentarily thrown by how different it looked. The usual rehearsal setup was transformed into something more intimate. Comfortable armchairs formed a circle in the center of the room, with the piano repositioned to one side. Guitars stood ready on stands, and there were whiteboards mounted on two walls.

Only the discreet presence of cameras and production crew reminded her this was still *Starbound*.

She wasn't sure what to expect from Zach today. But then again, when had she ever known? This would be their first session since she'd confronted him. His semi-acknowledgment that he might have been too soft on Jamie hadn't exactly smoothed things over, especially since he'd insisted all his harsh critiques of her were valid.

She could only hope that Ezra's presence would make the group dynamic more positive.

Jamie bounced in behind her. "This is proper songwriter stuff, isn't it? Like those Nashville writing rooms you see on the telly."

Before she could respond, Ezra Falconer walked in with Zach. Where Zach radiated barely leashed energy and laser focus, Ezra's vibe was more relaxed.

"Exactly like Nashville," Ezra said, catching Jamie's comment with a grin. "Though hopefully with better coffee." He gestured to a coffee station. "Help yourselves. Songwriting runs on caffeine."

As Jamie practically sprinted to the coffeemaker, Ezra turned to Kezia with a smile that looked real. "We haven't properly met, although I've been watching you on TV. I'm Ezra, and my wife's a huge fan."

Kezia let out a disbelieving chuckle. "Morgan's a fan? You're having me on."

"Hand on heart. She's always raving about you."

"Wow. I don't even know what to say. She's amazing."

He smiled. "I certainly think so." He faced Jamie, who approached with a cup of coffee. "And you're no slouch, either. Your growth has been a delight to watch."

Jamie beamed. "That's really kind of you, sir."

It appeared that Ezra had inherited all the charm in the family, leaving his brother precious little.

Zach gestured toward the chairs. "Shall we start?" He hadn't even greeted her.

"Absolutely," Ezra said. "But as we begin, Kezia and Jamie, I want you to think of this as a conversation set to music. No pressure, no judgment. We're just exploring ideas together."

No judgment? Someone ought to tell Zach that. But she nodded, keeping a smile on her face. "Thank you. I'm looking forward to learning from your experience."

"Experience is overrated," Ezra said, settling into an armchair. "Fresh perspectives often lead to the most interesting songs. That's why I love co-writing. Everyone brings something unique to the process."

Zach took a seat opposite his brother, his posture more rigid, more focused. He remained silent, clearly intending to let Ezra take the lead today.

"Let's start by exploring potential themes," Ezra said. "What's something you feel strongly about? Something authentic to your experience?"

Jamie didn't hesitate. "Being a child star was pretty intense. The pressure, you know? And then trying to figure out who you are when it all crashes." He settled into his chair. "I had two platinum albums before I was thirteen. Everyone called me the next Bruno Mars. Then puberty hit like a freight train. Voice breaking all over the place, pizza-face acne, grew six inches taller in eight months, all knees, elbows, and misery."

He gave a self-deprecating laugh. "The record label kept pushing back my third album release, waiting for things to 'settle.' By the time I finally put something out, my fan base had moved on to the next cute kid who could actually hit the high notes. You go from selling out arenas to playing shopping centers and being grateful if you can even get those. It's like you become invisible overnight. And that's when you find out who your friends really are."

Ezra nodded. "I'm sure you wish you didn't have to go through it. But you're going to take all of that, use it as creative fuel, and come out of it a much richer artist with depth and resonance that goes far beyond anything you had before. And people will respond to that."

Jamie blinked, his eyes suddenly moist.

Kezia resisted an urge to reach out and squeeze his arm. How was he able to open up so easily?

And now they were all looking at her, waiting for her to say something equally deep.

"What about love?" she said. "You know, lost love, finding love." A safe topic, since her romantic landscape was barren and she wouldn't have to reveal anything too private. Zach had already dragged her breakup with Scott out of her, so this wouldn't be new.

He shifted in his chair, but kept his mouth shut.

"Mm." Ezra stroked his chin. "Love songs are certainly personal, and I've written my share of them. But they're also where most artists go first. For this challenge, let's look for something that reveals you uniquely as an artist."

Blast it. Kezia nodded, mind racing for another safe option. "Perhaps something about perseverance? Working hard despite obstacles." She sat up straighter. "The journey of pursuing music despite setbacks. That's something authentic to my experience."

She caught Zach's slight head shake. He was way too quiet, brooding in his armchair like a storm cloud.

"That's definitely closer to your truth," Ezra said. "But can we dig deeper? What setbacks are we talking about? What makes your journey different from every other musician who's worked hard to get here?"

Now she could see why they were brothers. Ezra had that probing gene, too. It was the same question Zach would have asked, but at least it was gentler, without the edge of frustration she'd grown used to hearing in her mentor's voice.

Still, she hesitated. The cameras were rolling, capturing every word.

Ezra's gaze flicked over to the cameras, then to his brother. "Zach, can we turn those off? It might make it easier for this session."

Zach nodded. Glancing at the camera crew, he made a slicing motion across his throat.

Ezra turned back to Kezia. "You were saying? What challenges and setbacks have you faced?"

"Um...the usual challenges," she said. "Industry pressure, always needing to be better, all that. You know what I mean?"

Zach snorted, speaking for the first time since he'd entered the room. "The usual challenges? You've got perfect pitch, exceptional technical training, and natural abilities most vocalists would kill for. Those aren't real obstacles."

"I've had struggles. It hasn't been easy." She crossed her arms.

His eyes narrowed. "You went to Guildhall. Was that your big struggle? Getting into an elite school with your obvious talent? Then graduating with distinction?"

The challenging edge in his voice made Kezia's spine stiffen. She'd heard that tone too many times before. But how dare he dismiss her experience?

"Paying for it myself because my father wouldn't support a music degree was quite the challenge, actually. Watching him cover every penny of my sisters' tuition and living expenses while I juggled part-time jobs and racked up student debt I'm still paying off."

She pressed her lips together, regretting the admission as soon as it left her mouth.

The studio fell silent.

Only Zach seemed animated, leaning forward, his gaze like a laser on her face. "Your family didn't support your musical ambitions?"

"Zach—" Ezra's voice was soft.

Either Zach didn't hear it, or he pressed on regardless. "Tell me more about that. Your father wanted something different for you?"

"They had different aspirations for me," Kezia said, trying to regain her composure. "Medicine or law. Something respectable."

"And music wasn't respectable enough?" Zach's voice had that edge she recognized. That hunter's instinct. The one that meant he'd sensed something real and wouldn't let it go.

She glanced at the turned-off cameras, then at Jamie, who was watching with his mouth hanging open. This wasn't what she'd planned to reveal today. Or ever.

"I'd rather not put family business on display for entertainment."

"Let's pivot—" Ezra began, but Zach cut him off. He'd grabbed the reins of this session from his brother and he wasn't giving them back.

"It's not about entertainment, Kezia. This—" he gestured at the space between them, "this resistance you're showing right now? That's exactly where your song lives.

In that space between your passion and their expectations."

"I have other experiences I could write about," Kezia said, turning back to Ezra. "My first serious relationship ended badly. That could make a compelling song." She heard the desperate plea in her own voice. She was even willing to offer her sorry history with Scott if Zach would just let this go.

He didn't. "A generic love song won't reveal anything about you that we don't already know about a thousand other artists." Zach pointed to her. "But this thing you're running from? This is real. This is what makes you unique. What do you feel about letting your parents down? Pursuing a career they don't respect?"

She shifted in her seat. "I can't just—you can't expect me to go into that at the drop of a hat in front of—"

"No." Zach's gaze never left Kezia's face. "In the real world, songwriters don't have the luxury of waiting for comfortable inspiration. You're in a room with other writers, on deadline, and you need to deliver something authentic now. That's what separates professionals from hobbyists."

"Zach," Ezra said, louder this time. "This is a good place to pause. Jamie, Kezia, thank you both for being so open with us. Before we break, let me give you some specific directions."

He turned to Jamie. "I want you to write down every detail you can remember about that moment when you realized your childhood success would not carry into adulthood. What did it feel like? What were you thinking?"

Jamie nodded eagerly, already reaching for his notebook.

"Kezia." Ezra's gentle tone made her look up. "Explore those conversations with your family about your music. What did they say? And what did you wish you'd said back?"

She swallowed hard but didn't argue.

"Fifteen minutes," Zach said, "then we get back to work."

"They need more time than that," Ezra cut in. "Take the rest of the morning to get these thoughts on paper. Don't worry about rhymes or structure yet. Just capture the raw experiences. We'll reconvene back here at two to develop lyrics and begin exploring melodies."

Kezia felt a wave of relief at the reprieve. Three hours instead of fifteen minutes. Thank God for Ezra.

"And be specific," Zach said. "Be honest. Generic emotions won't cut it." His gaze fixed on Kezia. "This isn't about crafting the perfect line. It's about finding the truth first."

The implication was clear. He expected more from her next session. That hunter's instinct wasn't satisfied. He was just letting her retreat to regroup.

His gaze tracked her to the door, unreadable as always. Maybe he was planning his next ambush. Or maybe he just liked watching people squirm.

Kezia muttered a quick goodbye and was the first one out the door, Jamie's cheerful "See you later!" following her into the hallway.

Chapter 41

ACH BEGRUDGINGLY ADMITTED TO himself that his brother had been right to give Jamie and Kezia more time to do the deep emotional work they needed. Ezra, with his natural songwriting gift, was more skilled at helping artists open up their creative vulnerability.

And, as he'd told Zach over lunch, "I know you like to push people past their comfort zones, but that's not an end in itself. Sometimes pushing too hard gets in the way of what we're actually trying to do."

Zach settled in his chair. He would do his best to restrain himself and let Ezra take the lead. This session needed to be about the work, not Zach's frustration with Kezia's resistance.

She walked in with the same fluid grace with which she always carried herself. She'd added a jacket against the autumn chill, its light cream contrasting against her dark skin.

He hated that he noticed. Hated more the way something in him responded every time she came into a room.

He swatted the reaction aside before it had a chance to settle. This wasn't about attraction. This was about potential—her untapped, frustrating potential.

She settled into the same armchair she'd occupied that morning, but angled herself away from him, keeping her gaze averted.

He caught himself drumming his fingers on the armrest again and forced them still. He hoped she'd used the time well to come up with useful material for her song. Her stay on this show depended on it.

Jamie walked in soon afterward, and it was time to begin again.

At Ezra's insistence, the camera crew would not film this session, either.

"Welcome back, everyone," Ezra said, his calm presence immediately setting the tone. A calmness Zach couldn't seem to access when dealing with Kezia. "I hope you've had time to process and write. Jamie, would you like to share what you've discovered?"

Jamie pulled out several pages of handwritten notes. "I really got into it," he said, almost apologetically. "Once I started writing, it all just came pouring out."

As Jamie began to read, Zach felt his earlier irritation dissolving into satisfaction. The kid hadn't just described losing his fame. He'd captured raw, specific details that made the experience real. The moment his voice cracked during a Christmas concert and he saw his manager wince. Watching younger artists get the opportunities that used to be his. Industry players who used to court him now no longer taking his calls. His manager dropping him.

"That's powerful stuff, Jamie," Ezra said. "You've given us some really evocative images to work with. Let's start breaking this down into potential verses. Which moments feel most central to the story you want to tell?"

Zach nodded in agreement, content to let Ezra lead the creative direction. But he couldn't help glancing at Kezia, who was listening intently. Was she noting the difference between Jamie's raw honesty and her own careful deflections?

"The emotional specificity is exactly what we need," Zach added when Ezra paused. "Especially that detail about people not taking your calls. That's the kind of image that will resonate with listeners, even if they've never had a hit record."

Jamie beamed at the praise, and Zach caught Kezia shifting in her seat.

Good. Let her see that emotional honesty earned approval, not judgment.

Now it was her turn. And, despite the morning's resistance, he hoped she'd surprise him.

"Kezia?" Ezra's gentle prompt drew everyone's attention to her. "Would you like to share what you've written?"

She straightened in her chair, her notebook barely showing any use compared to Jamie's scattered pages. "Yes, well, I've written about the practical challenges of pursuing music against my parents' wishes. The financial difficulties of self-funding my education, and the strain it put on family relationships."

Her voice was steady, professional—nothing like Jamie's raw honesty.

She might as well have been reading a press release. Even now—talking about something that had clearly wounded her—she was doing it from a safe distance, analyzing instead of feeling. Zach fought the urge to drag the notebook out of her hands and rip it in half. She had a story. Why was she treating it like a case study?

"Can you share a specific moment?" Ezra encouraged. "A conversation that stands out?"

"We had a few discussions about my choice." She glanced down at her sparse notes. "They didn't think music would give me a stable career. We talked about the importance of having a reliable profession."

"Okay," Ezra said. "How did those conversations make you feel?"

"It was... challenging." She shifted in her chair. "Disappointing to not have their support. But at the same time, Mum and Dad were within their rights not to pay for a course they didn't believe in. It's their money and they can choose how to spend it. And lots of my classmates were self-funding their courses, anyway, so that's not really unusual."

Zach frowned. She was backtracking. Making excuses for her parents. Justifying their behavior and talking herself out of feeling the hurt it had caused.

Ezra must have sensed it, too, because he tried another angle. "You were talking earlier about them wanting a different profession for you. You used the word 'respectable'. Don't your parents feel that what you're doing is respectable?"

Kezia's fingers tightened around her notebook. "I...I don't know." Her gaze slid away from Ezra's.

She *did* know. Zach was sure of it. He jumped in before his brother could follow up. "Are your parents ashamed of your choice? Ashamed of you? Of what you're doing with your life?"

She looked up at him for a moment, then back down at her lap, her fingers twisting together. "I wouldn't say that."

Zach couldn't take it anymore. "What would you say, then? What would you say to your father if he were standing right here and there were no consequences?"

His voice was louder than he'd intended, the question landing like a thunderclap in the quiet room.

Kezia clutched her notebook closer to her chest as she stared at him, wide-eyed. She pressed her lips tightly together.

"What would you say?" he pressed.

"I..." She swallowed hard.

The silence stretched out, uncomfortable and electric.

Her gaze darted toward the door, as though looking for an escape.

No. He wasn't letting her off the hook. "Kezia, look at me."

She did, but her body shrank away.

"You got yourself into one of the world's most elite schools of music, and your father is still ashamed of you. What would you tell him?"

"I would tell him..."

Her eyes filled, and Zach's chest tightened as he watched her. But he didn't look away. They were finally getting somewhere.

A knock at the door made everyone jump. A production assistant poked her head in. Really? Interrupting them now?

"I'm sorry to barge in, Mr. Falconer, but Martha is on the phone for both of you." She glanced between Ezra and Zach. "She says it's urgent. It's about Greg."

Zach's irritation at the timing vanished. He exchanged a quick look with Ezra. His brother's face had gone pale.

"We need to take this," Ezra said, already standing. "Let's take a break, everyone. We'll...we'll regroup when we can."

As they hurried out, Zach caught a glimpse of Kezia slumping in her chair, head bowed.

But he couldn't focus on her now. Whatever was happening with Greg, it had to be serious for Martha to pull them both out mid-session.

The production assistant led them to a small office down the hall. "You can take the call in here. She's holding on line two."

Ezra picked up the phone immediately, hitting the speaker button so Zach could hear. "Martha? What's happened?"

"It's Greg." Martha's voice was gentle but direct. "Beth just called. He passed away about an hour ago. She was with him at the prison hospital."

Zach gripped the edge of the desk. Even after everything Greg had done, even when he knew his stepfather was critically ill, the news still landed hard.

"How's Mum?" Ezra asked, his voice rough.

"Holding up. She told me he went peacefully." Martha paused. "She needs someone with her. Do you think one or both of you can head up to Harrowgate? Levi, Adria, and I can handle whatever needs doing on this end."

Ezra looked at Zach, unspoken understanding passing between them. Whatever complicated feelings they had about Greg, Beth needed her sons.

"I'll drive," Zach said, already pulling out his phone. "Give me thirty minutes to sort things here."

Ezra nodded, turning back to the call. "Martha, we'll be there in three and a half to four hours, depending on traffic and how quickly Zach can wrap things up here. Tell Mum we're coming."

Zach stepped out, dialing Hugo as he strode down the hallway. His showrunner picked up immediately.

"Hugo. Greg's died." The words felt unreal. "Ezra and I need to get to Harrowgate. Our mother's alone at the prison hospital."

"I'm sorry, Zach. What do you need?"

"I'll be gone at least two days. Can you step in as my deputy? Jamie and Kezia have barely started their song-writing process. They'll need guidance. Ask one of the other songwriting coaches to step in. Maybe Tyler wouldn't mind sharing hers?"

"Of course. I'll keep everything on track. We've got time before the elimination show."

"Thanks. Meet me in my office in ten? I need to brief you on where we are with the songs. And you'll have to lead tomorrow's production meeting. I think we can postpone everything else until I get back."

He pushed open the studio door. Jamie and Kezia looked up.

He hated the wariness in her eyes. She'd stood toe-to-toe with him, called him out when she thought he'd been unfair to her. And now she looked...scared? No. That couldn't be right. And he didn't have time to think about it.

"Guys, I apologize, but we need to end today's session here." His voice came out steadier than he expected. "A family emergency just came up, and Ezra and I need to leave immediately. We'll be gone at least two days. Hugo will be in touch about your next steps while we're away. In the meantime, Jamie, work with the imagery we discussed. Kezia..."

She swallowed, waiting for him to speak.

He paused. "Keep digging. We'll pick this up when I return."

He turned away, already thinking about the long drive ahead and his mother waiting alone in Harrowgate. The unfinished business with Kezia, the production meeting, the songwriting challenge—all of it would have to wait.

Right now, he needed to be a son, not a mentor or producer.

Chapter 42

IN THE CONTESTANTS' HOUSE, Kezia curled into the corner of the common room sofa, notebook balanced on her knees. The house was quieter than usual. Most of the others had retreated to their rooms after dinner, leaving her what should have been a peaceful spot to work.

"There you are." Brianna's voice shattered that illusion. "I heard about Zach abandoning you guys mid-challenge." She perched on the arm of the sofa. "That must have been so difficult."

Kezia kept the emotion out of her face, though her fingers tightened on her notebook. She knew a fishing expedition when she saw one. "He didn't abandon us. He's left clear instructions and people to help us while he's away."

"But right in the middle of your session? I heard things got pretty intense."

Where did this girl get all her information? If music didn't work out, Brianna could have a promising career in espionage. But today she was way off. She didn't know how relieved Kezia was that Zach was gone.

His absence felt like taking off a too-tight shoe that was pinching on an agonizing blister. She understood what he wanted from her—raw, unfiltered emotion translated into lyrics. But, unlike his brother's gentle probing, Zach's battering-ram tactics only made her walls higher.

And yet...if she didn't produce something that satisfied him, she might as well pack her bags now because she'd be heading home after elimination.

Kezia went for a generic answer. "Songwriting is a vulnerable process. Especially with this challenge. Didn't you find that when you were working with your coach?"

"So what happened, exactly?" Brianna pressed. "Before he left?"

"I should really get back to working on my song." Kezia gathered her materials, tucking her pen into the spiral binding of her notebook. "I'm behind as it is. You know, with my mentor being gone and all."

"Well, let me know if you need any help. I'm pretty near done with mine," Brianna said, her smile bright.

Kezia could imagine what kind of song Brianna was writing. She doubted Ryan was pushing her to reveal her deepest, most festering wounds. The only digging he was doing was probably in the latest market analysis charts.

"Thanks. I'll keep your offer in mind." She needed somewhere private to work, somewhere she could actually process her thoughts without an audience. The rehearsal rooms should be empty this late.

Except they weren't. Jamie was in the first room she tried, hunched over a keyboard, surrounded by crumpled paper. He looked up when she opened the door, offering a weak smile.

"Sorry," she said. "I didn't realize anyone was in here."

"No, it's fine." He ran a hand through his already disheveled hair. "I'm not getting anywhere, anyway."

"Really? You were on fire this afternoon. I thought you'd have your song pretty much finished by now." She was only half-joking.

"I know, right? I had it when Zach and Ezra were here." Jamie gestured at the scattered papers. "But now I can't figure out where to go next. And that songwriter they assigned us...Larry Norton..."

"Did you meet him yet?" Kezia asked.

"Yeah. With his indie background, I thought he'd be helpful, but..." Jamie shrugged. "It wasn't the same. He didn't get what I was trying to say like Ezra did. Not to mention, he was in a rush. He had somewhere else he needed to be. In the end, I just disengaged and nodded along with whatever he suggested."

Kezia hesitated in the doorway. They were competitors, but right now they were also two artists without their mentor, trying to navigate the same challenge. "Maybe I can help," she found herself saying. "What have you been working on since this afternoon?"

Jamie brightened. "Really? I mean, if you don't mind. I know you don't have a bunch of time to spare."

"No, it's fine. I think I'd rather procrastinate, anyway." She crossed the room and pulled a chair close to the keyboard. "What have you got?"

He shuffled through his papers. "Larry tried to help make some lyrics based on my notes. Everything feels flat compared to what I shared with Ezra."

Kezia looked over the pages. While Ezra and Zach had praised the specific moments that crystallized Jamie's painful journey, Larry had reduced it all to abstract ideas. "These lyrics are pretty generic. They feel—I don't know—distant from what you told us earlier."

As the words left her mouth, she realized the irony of her comments. That was exactly what Zach had told her about her own ideas. Too generic. Not deep enough.

"Exactly!" Jamie slumped in his chair. "Larry kept talking about universal themes and broad appeal, but it's lost all the specific moments that made it real."

"Like the moment your voice cracked during that Christmas concert?"

"Yeah. He said that was too particular, that we should focus on more general career setbacks." He frowned, biting the end of his pen. "But that moment—seeing my manager wince—that's when I knew it was all falling apart."

"Then that's your opening." Kezia reached for a fresh sheet of paper. "Start with that specific image. What if we opened with something like…"

She wrote a line, and Jamie leaned in to read it. *Silent night, spotlight fading, I see your smile slip away.*

"Yes," Jamie said. "And then maybe…"

He scribbled quickly. *My strong voice now fragile, failing, will you go or will you stay?*

"That's it," Kezia encouraged. "That's the real story. Not some vague metaphor about closed doors, but the actual moment everything changed. The specific details make it universal, not the other way around. I mean, it's not perfect, but maybe Ezra can help polish it when he gets back. It's better to get something rough, but in the right direction."

They worked through the rest of the verse together, finding words that brought the scene to life. Jamie's earlier raw honesty about his career collapse was now taking shape in concrete images and specific details.

"This feels true," Jamie said, reading over their work. "This is what I was trying to tell Zach and Ezra about. Thanks so much, Kezia. I owe you one." He glanced at her notebook. "How's your song coming along?"

"Still working through some ideas." She shifted in her chair, aware of how empty her pages remained.

A knock at the door saved her from further explanation.

A production assistant poked her head in. "Just to let you know, Zach asked me to send you an update. He and Ezra will definitely be away until the day after tomorrow. He says to just keep working on your songs for now. Try to at least have lyrics in place by tomorrow."

"Okay, thanks," Kezia said.

After the assistant left, Jamie gathered his papers, now filled with honest, hard-hitting lyrics that matched the power of his original story. "Thanks to you, I'm on track for that. I should probably get some sleep. Work on the melody fresh tomorrow. Thanks again, Kezia. Really."

"Any time." She meant it, too. Working with Jamie was really fun.

The door clicked shut behind him, leaving her alone with her blank notebook. The irony of the situation settled over her like a heavy blanket. Here she was, perfectly capable of guiding someone else toward emotional truth, helping him shape his raw honesty into lyrics, while her own pages remained stubbornly empty.

She envied Jamie's natural openness, the way he'd poured out his story to Ezra and Zach without hesitation. Even more, she envied how easily he'd let her help him translate that vulnerability into song. No walls, no deflections. Just truth.

She knew exactly what Zach would say if he were here. That she was hiding behind her professional expertise. That helping Jamie was just another way to avoid dealing with her own story.

And he'd be right.

Because guiding Jamie through his experience was safe. Clinical. Like a vocal coach correcting technique without having to sing the song herself. But facing her own truth? That meant stepping into territory she'd carefully marked off-limits years ago. Places she wished Zach would leave alone.

But he wouldn't. He'd sensed her reluctance to talk about her family. Like a shark who'd tasted blood in the water, it only made him more relentless.

Kezia closed her notebook, pressing it against her chest. Tomorrow. She'd try again tomorrow. Maybe by then she'd understand why Jamie could bare his soul so freely while she built walls with every careful word she chose.

Or maybe she'd just help him polish his lyrics instead.

Chapter 43

*D*USK SETTLED OVER THE M1 motorway, the October evening drawing in early. Zach kept his focus on the road ahead while Ezra checked messages on his phone.

"Levi and Adria are making progress with the funeral arrangements," Ezra said. "And Martha's trying to track down any of Greg's family members who might still be willing to attend the funeral when it eventually happens. Not an easy task, given how many bridges he's burned."

"Good." Zach adjusted his grip on the steering wheel. The situation felt surreal—driving to Harrowgate Prison to collect their mother after their stepfather's death. Not exactly how he'd planned to spend the evening. "How did Mum sound when you spoke to her?"

"Shaken, but holding together."

"Some things never change."

"No," Ezra said. "But I think she'll appreciate our being there with her. There's a lot of red tape when an inmate dies."

They fell into silence. The elephant in the car was Greg's death itself. It was the end of a chapter neither of them quite knew how to feel about.

After several minutes of silence, Zach spoke. "You know, in a twisted way, Greg did me one favor."

Ezra turned from his phone. "Really? How?"

"If he hadn't stolen from us, I might never have seen Verity's true colors."

"Oh."

Zach sensed the question behind Ezra's muted response. He didn't often bring up Verity.

His hands tightened fractionally on the steering wheel. "I was going to propose. Just trying to work out the timing and make it special. But the moment the Greg scandal broke, she was already calculating her exit strategy. So for that clarity, at least, I suppose I should be grateful."

Ezra let out a low whistle. "Man. I never thought about how those two things hit you at the same time." He shook his head slowly. "With everything else going on with Greg—the accident, the missing money, the arrests—I guess Verity breaking up with you just got lost in the chaos."

"Yeah," Zach said. "There was enough going on without adding my relationship problems to the mix."

"We were all so caught up in the larger crisis." Ezra winced. "And Martha and I had our own issues at the time, too. I don't think any of us gave your breakup the attention it deserved."

"It was a long time ago," Zach said, though the words felt hollow even to him. "And, like I said, I dodged a bullet."

"But you can still injure yourself when you're dodging a bullet. And it was a lot to handle all at once." Ezra shifted in his seat to face him better. "The family falling apart, Verity walking out and leaking the whole sordid Greg story to the press. And you had to step up and take charge of everything."

"The timing was...illuminating." Zach checked his mirrors and moved into the outside lane to pass a lorry. "Nothing reveals people's true character like a crisis."

"God works everything together for the good of those who love Him," Ezra said. "Even when we don't see it at the time."

A few moments passed, marked only by the steady thrum of tires on tarmac.

"You know," Ezra said, "you haven't really dated anyone since Verity. Unless I missed it."

"Been busy." Zach kept his eyes fixed on the road. "The Falconers rebuilding, then *Starbound*."

"It's been six years, Zach."

Yes, it had been six years. But whoever said time heals all wounds had lied. Verity blew a crater in his heart, and the fallout was still radioactive.

Which was why he couldn't wrap his head around how Mum still showed so much grace to Greg. What Verity had done to him was nothing compared to Greg's betrayal.

"I don't understand it," Zach said. "How she kept visiting him all these years. Writing to him. After everything he did to us. And I think if he'd lived up to his probation date, she might have even given him a home to return to."

Ezra was silent for a moment. "I never thought about what might happen when Greg got out. But you know Mum. She believes in redemption."

"Redemption requires repentance. Greg never showed any. He was only ever sorry for the fallout of what he did."

"Maybe that's why she kept trying." Ezra's voice was quiet. "She always hoped one day he would."

Zach caught the exit sign for Harrowgate. "Well, now he never will."

"Are you okay with that?"

"I stopped caring about Greg's redemption arc a long time ago." But even as he said it, Zach knew it wasn't entirely true. The anger still burned, which meant some part of him still cared. Levi, his youngest brother, had made peace with Greg a couple of years ago. But Zach hadn't been able to.

Ezra was quiet for a moment. "Sorry we weren't fully present for you when Verity left. We do have your back."

"You've more than proved that with *Starbound*." Zach signaled for the exit. "The way everyone's pitched in."

Ezra looked as if he might say more, but fell quiet as the Harrowgate signs came into view.

Their mother was waiting for them, and whatever complicated feelings they had about Greg would have to wait.

Some wounds never fully healed. Not Greg. Not Verity. But maybe that's what family was for—helping you carry on, anyway.

Chapter 44

HE AMBER GLOW OF the desk lamp cast long shadows across Zach's father's study at Falconhurst, the family's Surrey estate.

This room hadn't changed much since Joshua Falconer used it. Long ago, when Zach and his brothers were little. Greg had preferred to use his own remodeled room in the east wing as his office.

Zach rubbed his eyes, trying to focus on the coroner's paperwork spread before him. Six days. He'd been away from *Starbound* for six days now. Far longer than the overnight trip he'd anticipated when he and Ezra had set off for Harrowgate.

There had been complications. There always were with Greg, even in death. At the prison hospital, they'd found their mother refusing to leave Greg's body, clinging to his hand while the staff stood helplessly by. It had taken them hours to gently convince her to let the medical staff take him away.

They could have brought her home that night, but her emotional state was so fragile they'd worried about the three-hour drive. By morning, it was clear her grief ran deeper than any of them had anticipated. She'd barely spoken, moving only when directed, and even a simple question would trigger overwhelming tears.

With her in that state, they couldn't simply leave. As Greg's next of kin, she was the only one who could sign the necessary paperwork, but she could barely hold a pen without bursting into sobs. Each document became an emotional ordeal—the death certificate, coroner's paperwork, funeral arrangements—requiring them to gently coax her through the bureaucratic requirements while she struggled to process her grief.

Even now, days later, in the safety of the family home, she still had frequent crying spells that surprised and embarrassed her. And she seemed incapable of dealing with the complex logistical challenges of Greg's death in prison custody.

Thank God Zach's brothers and their wives were all here to rally around her and take as much as they could off her shoulders.

Seeing Mum plunged so deep in grief that she could barely function added to the list of Greg's crimes.

The study door opened, and Ezra entered with two steaming mugs, nudging the door closed with his foot.

"Thought you might need this," he said, placing one mug on the desk.

"Thanks." Zach picked it up, letting the warmth seep into his hands. "The coroner's preliminary report confirms what we already knew. The cancer had spread too far. Even if he hadn't been in prison..."

"It would have been the same outcome," Ezra finished, settling into the leather armchair across from the desk.

"Even with the expedited process, they're saying it could be three to five days before they release the body. Why can't we put him into the ground and have done with it?"

Ezra nodded. "Bureaucracy doesn't stop, even for death."

"How's Mum doing?"

"Martha got her to take some tea and toast. She's resting now." Ezra sipped his own tea.

Zach looked up at his brother. "Do you think she'll get through this? I used to hear her crying after Dad died, but I don't think she took it this hard. Maybe I just didn't notice since I was a kid."

Ezra frowned. "It's different, though. Pastor Noah was saying that grief for complicated relationships is often tricky to process. With Dad, she could grieve purely. He was a good man who loved her well. With Greg..." Ezra's voice softened. "There's grief mixed with regret, anger, unresolved questions. She's mourning what was, what could have been, and what never was, all at once."

Zach nodded. That made sense.

"Plus," Ezra added, setting his mug down, "when Dad died, she had three young boys who needed her. That probably gave her focus, kept her moving forward even through the pain."

"And now we're all grown, with our own lives."

"Exactly. She's facing this loss without that same urgent purpose." Ezra leaned back in the chair. "Noah says complicated grief often takes longer to heal. She needs time."

Zach set down the mug and ran a hand through his hair. "I'm really worried about her. And yet there's also my mentees to think of. Jamie and Kezia have been without guidance for days. But at the same time, I feel guilty for even thinking about leaving when Mum's hurting so much."

"You should head back to Glenmere Hall tomorrow. Or even tonight," Ezra said. "We can handle things here. Levi and Adria have insisted Mum stay here in the main house with them, and Martha's not going anywhere. Mum's got plenty of support. There's nothing to be done until the coroner releases the body, anyway."

"It just feels wrong to leave when she needs me."

"Kezia and Jamie need you, too," Ezra said. "Mum has all of us. Go do what you need to do. And you can always come and check on her in the evenings. Between me, Martha, Levi and Adria, we'll handle the funeral arrangements and make sure Mum's not alone."

Zach nodded, grateful for the permission.

They sat in silence for a moment.

"Speaking of Kezia," Ezra said, "I saw the footage of her calling you out for treating her unfairly."

Zach looked up, surprised by the change in topic. "What?"

"She was right, you know," Ezra continued. "Why are you so tough on her? And don't try to spin me that line of not coddling her because she's a pro."

Zach started to defend himself, then closed his mouth when he saw Ezra's look.

"Different contestants need different approaches," he offered finally, the justification sounding weak even to his own ears.

Ezra's raised eyebrow made it clear this explanation would not fly.

"You know," Ezra leaned back, "for someone who literally makes his living developing artists, your approach with Kezia is..." He shook his head with a laugh. "It's like trying to teach someone to swim by throwing them off a cliff and shouting 'Be vulnerable!' on the way down."

Zach's lips twitched reluctantly at the absurd image.

Ezra's face grew more sober. "Even before she was on your team, you were unusually critical of her. That 'dime a dozen session singer' comment at auditions? Brutal. You've ripped into every performance she's done. And then you saved her in the most dramatic way possible."

Zach shifted in his seat, but didn't reply. He wasn't proud of some of the ways he'd expressed his criticism to Kezia.

Ezra tilted his head. "What is it about her specifically, Zach? Because there's something."

Zach dropped his gaze and stared into his tea. What was it? He could deny that there was anything about Kezia, but that would be a complete lie. One that Ezra would see straight through. He tried to work out the truth, feeling it out even as he spoke. "I...I don't know. There's just..."

Ezra continued staring at him as he struggled to wrap his mind around what he was trying to say.

Zach sighed. "I've heard countless technically perfect vocalists. But with her..." He groped for words. "I need to see it," he said finally.

"See what?"

"There's something authentic beneath all that polish," Zach said. "I can hear glimpses of it. But I need her to let it out. I need to know it's there."

"And if you break through and find what you're looking for?" Ezra asked. "She's not a lab rat that you perform a vivisection on so you can observe what's inside her, then go on your merry way. She's a person, and these are deep wounds you're asking her to access. What will you do when she opens up?"

Zach flinched. The image landed hard—because it wasn't far off. Shame curled hot in his stomach. That was exactly what he'd done. Prodded and poked and sliced into her pain. And for what? To prove a point he couldn't even explain to himself?

"When she opens up, I'll do my job as her mentor," he said finally.

Ezra crossed his arms. "That's another thing. You *are* her mentor. And she's strong enough to stand up to you— you saw that on camera. But she shouldn't have to defend herself from you. That power imbalance is real. And it means you have a responsibility to be the safe one in the room. You're using your position against her, whether you mean to or not."

Was Ezra being serious? "I'm not using anything against her. I'm trying to help her reach her potential."

"By demanding she bleed on command? I watched her face during that songwriting session, Zach. That wasn't a breakthrough. That was a breakdown. What does it tell you that she didn't push back this time? You weren't developing her artistry. She was deeply distressed."

Zach shifted uncomfortably. "That's not what I intended."

"Your intentions don't matter if the impact is harm. You can't badger someone into vulnerability. It has to be freely given from a place of safety. And you haven't made it safe for her. Have you thought about the emotional damage you might be doing while trying to break through her defenses?"

Zach felt like someone had kicked the back of his knees. Emotional damage? He'd been so preoccupied with trying to unearth Kezia's buried wound that he hadn't realized he was bulldozing the very person he claimed to be helping.

"It's not just bad mentoring," Ezra added. "It's not even working. In fact, you're getting the opposite of what you're after. She's shutting down. This is the woman who stood up to you in front of the cameras. She's got backbone. But in that songwriting session, she was completely cowed. Couldn't even look you in the eye. If you keep pushing, you won't draw out her artistry—you'll drive it underground. Is that what you want?"

"No. Heaven help me, no." He pushed a hand through his hair. "I've been so focused on what I wanted to hear from her that I didn't consider what it was costing her to try to deliver it." He searched Ezra's face. "You really think I'm hurting her?"

"I don't just think it. I know it."

Zach felt sick.

Ezra continued, "I know she needs to open up. But before she can do that, you need to let her know it's safe. You have to somehow connect with her."

Zach nodded, his mind and heart racing. The last thing he meant to do was hurt Kezia or crush the spark out of her. But that connection—that was exactly what he was afraid of. That pull he felt toward whatever was under Kezia's veneer of technical perfection.

The last time he'd felt that pull to a woman, her name had been Verity. And look where that had led.

"Zach! Ezra!" Martha called from down the hall. "I've made some soup and sandwiches if you're hungry."

"Be right there," Ezra called back. He stood, giving Zach's shoulder a squeeze as he passed. "Think about it, okay?"

Left alone, Zach stared at the coroner's paperwork without seeing it. He didn't need to think about it. Ezra was right. What he'd done to Kezia was foolish at best. Harmful at worst. Was it too late to change?

When he returned to *Starbound*, he would need a different approach. For Kezia's sake.

And maybe for his own.

Chapter 45

THE REHEARSAL ROOM WAS quiet except for Jamie's gentle strumming on his guitar and the soft patter of rain against the windows. Kezia sat at the piano, nodding along as he worked through the chorus of his song for the third time.

"So it goes: 'Every step I take without you, takes me farther from who I was, closer to who I'm meant to be,'" Jamie sang, his voice growing more confident with each run-through.

The melody had come together beautifully over the past few days. What had started as a hesitant idea was now taking shape as something genuine and moving.

As he finished, Kezia smiled. "Wonderful. The only thing I'd suggest is softening that transition into the bridge. Maybe hold that last note a beat longer before you shift keys?"

Jamie tried it, his fingers finding the new pattern easily. "Like that?"

"Perfect." Kezia nodded. "It gives the listener a moment to feel the emotion before you take them somewhere new."

"I couldn't have done this without your help, Kezia." Jamie set his guitar in its case. "Seriously. You've done more for me than that Larry fellow, even though he's the one getting paid to coach us."

"You had all the pieces," she said. "I just helped you arrange them."

Jamie snapped his guitar case closed and turned to her, his expression shifting to concern. "How's your song coming along? Any breakthrough?"

Kezia kept her smile in place, though it felt more like a mask now. "I'm still working through some ideas."

"I could stay and help? Seems only fair after all you've done for me."

"You need rest. That cold sounds worse," she said, noting the raspiness in his voice. "I'll be fine."

Jamie hesitated at the door. "Don't stay too late, okay? I know you've been burning the candle at both ends."

"I won't. Goodnight, Jamie."

As the door closed behind him, Kezia's professional composure crumbled. She turned back to the piano, staring at her own scattered notes and crumpled attempts. Jamie had a completed song ready to go. While she seemed to be paralyzed when she tried to work on hers.

After several discarded drafts and a couple of sessions with their stand-in songwriter, she finally had a song.

But it stank. It was so bland, so derivative, so shallow that she didn't dare share it with Jamie, let alone present it to Zach.

Her notebook lay open to a page where she'd written Zach's instructions in neat block letters, underlined several times, surrounded by doodles of skulls, asterisks, and dark thunderclouds. *Write what you'd say to your father if there were no consequences.*

Simple enough in theory. Impossible in practice.

She placed her fingers on the keys and tried again, playing a few tentative chords. It was no use. The melody was hollow, the lyrics wooden and stiff. Perhaps if she could get the lyrics working, the melody might come easier.

She grabbed a pencil and tried once more to force the words onto the page, rewriting the first verse. Three lines in, she knew it was rubbish. Worse than rubbish. She tore the page from her notebook, crumpled it, and tossed it toward the bin. It bounced off the rim and joined the growing collection of failed attempts on the floor. She couldn't even land it inside the basket.

Turning back to the piano, she pressed random keys with increasing force, the music giving way to noise that matched her inner turmoil.

Finally, she slammed her elbows on the keys and buried her face in her hands.

This challenge would be where her *Starbound* journey ended, after she'd embarrassed herself in front of the whole of Britain with this pile of garbage she was calling a song. Zach's disappointment would confirm what he already believed—that she was just technical skill with nothing authentic beneath. He would eliminate her and there would be no rescue from any of the other mentors.

Worse, her father would be vindicated about her being part of this show at all—a waste of time and money, amounting to nothing. Like her whole career.

The soft sound of the door opening made her look up quickly.

Zach stood in the doorway, silhouetted against the hallway light, raindrops glistening in his dark hair.

A tight fist of dread clenched around her chest. What was he doing here?

She couldn't deal with him tonight. Couldn't face another round of stabbing questions and pressure. Of being pushed into a corner, stripped of composure, forced to expose things to him that she hadn't even faced herself.

"Do you have a minute?" His voice was quiet, almost hesitant.

No, she didn't. Not for him. Not tonight.

But there was no way to say that. Not without consequences.

She nodded, tensing as he stepped into the room.

The scent of him reached her as he came closer—clean rain and a trace of sandalwood that made her stomach tighten. It brought back too much. Their last session. The ache in her throat. The sting behind her eyes. The sickening awareness of how easily he could undo her.

"I met Jamie on the way here," he said. "He told me you've been helping with his song. Thank you for stepping up while I was away." Polite. Measured. Not a hint of the usual edge.

Kezia blinked. Thrown off balance by his approach and desperate to get what was coming over with, she blurted out, "I haven't made any progress on my song. I mean, I have, but it's awful. I might as well have nothing."

The confession felt both terrifying and somehow necessary. She braced herself for the verbal scalpel she'd come to expect.

Zach didn't respond immediately. Instead of speaking, he moved to sit beside her at the piano.

She stiffened. Instinct told her to stand. To not let herself be cornered again.

His nearness prickled across her skin. The warmth of him. His solid weight beside her on the bench. Her heart pounded against her ribs, half-expecting to be dissected.

But he didn't crowd her. Didn't even look at her.

His fingers found the keys, playing soft, flowing chords.

"I know your song is about your family. Family dynamics can be tricky," he said, his voice quiet but clear over the gentle improvisation.

He continued playing, the melody simple but evocative. "I've just come back from planning the funeral of my incarcerated stepfather."

Kezia glanced at him, startled, but his gaze remained on his long, sensitive fingers as they shaped the music.

"He cheated on my mother and nearly bankrupted our family."

The chords darkened, minor keys adding weight to his words. "I've left my mother broken, a shell of herself. His death has devastated her. She can barely speak without crying. I don't know whether she'll ever be the same again."

His fingers never stopped moving as he continued, his voice roughening. "And all that grief, all that pain, is because of a man I despise."

The piano gave emotional texture to his words without drama or self-pity. Kezia sucked in a quick breath. The music was allowing him to access emotions he might not share in silence.

His playing continued, creating space for his words to land. "We all have those painful, dark corners in our lives.

Every one of us. I was asking you to share yours before I'd proven you could trust me with them. That wasn't fair. I realize that now."

She drew in a breath. Was that an apology? It hit her like a hush—unexpected, disarming. Her heart twisted with something tender and raw.

The music flowing from his hands shifted to a more hopeful melody. "Artistry is about accessing our wounds and channeling them into connection." His right hand climbed into a higher register, brushing against her arm. "It's about finding a way to transform our personal pain into something that helps others feel less alone."

She heard him in her soul.

His hands finally stilled on the keys. He stood up, putting distance between them, his gaze searching her face. "Think about it. We'll talk more tomorrow."

He walked out without a backward glance, leaving only the echo of his music and the scent of rain and sandalwood in the air.

Kezia sat motionless on the bench, her pulse still fluttering. He hadn't come to demand. He hadn't dissected. He'd shared something real. Something raw. With his music, he had made his point more powerfully than any words could. He'd shared a deep, living wound, modeling the vulnerability he'd been asking her to show.

She exhaled slowly, her hands moving to the piano al-most without thinking. A single note. Then another. Then a chord that sounded...honest. Not polished. Not perfect. But true. Her song emerged as she began to play, still afraid of what she might find, but determined to do it anyway.

Chapter 46

HE MID-MORNING AUTUMN sunlight cast golden stripes across the polished piano of the rehearsal room. Zach glanced at his watch.

Ezra had come down from Hatbrook, and they'd already spent two productive hours with Jamie, whose song had evolved beautifully. The confidence in the young man's performance was remarkable compared to where he'd started.

"That was excellent work," Ezra said, clapping Jamie on the shoulder as he packed up his guitar. "We'll see you this afternoon with the band."

After Jamie left, Ezra turned to Zach with a raised eyebrow. "So, Kezia's next. Did you think over what I said about your approach?"

Zach nodded. "I know good advice when I hear it. My days of throwing artists off cliffs are over."

"Glad to hear it." Ezra grinned as he arranged his notes. "Think she'll have anything for us?"

"We'll see." Zach kept his tone neutral, not wanting to create expectations. He hadn't told Ezra about his late-night encounter with Kezia, about sitting at the piano beside her and opening up about his stepfather and Mum.

Some moments felt too personal to share, even with his brother. And he wasn't even sure whether any of what he'd said resonated with Kezia.

A soft knock interrupted his thoughts. She walked in, notepad clutched in her hand, the tote bag she carted everywhere slung over her shoulder. She wore a knee-length sweater dress in a dark yellow that made her skin glow, paired with black leggings.

For a moment, Zach forgot what he meant to say. He shuffled his notes to cover it, but the image of her lingered like sunlight behind his eyes.

"Good morning," she said.

Ezra smiled warmly. "Morning, Kezia. Thanks for coming in."

"I wanted to say..." She paused, looking between them. "I'm sorry for your loss."

Zach returned her greetings with a brief nod, noting the genuine sympathy in her voice. Was it because of what he'd told her yesterday?

"Thank you," Ezra said. "I hear you've been helping Jamie with his song. That was good of you."

"He didn't need much help, really. Just someone to listen and bounce ideas around with." The casual conversation seemed to ease some of the tension from her shoulders. She set her notepad on the piano and took a breath.

"I have something," she said hesitantly. "It's rough, but. . ."

"We'd love to hear it," Ezra said.

She sat at the piano, adjusting the bench for her height. Her fingers hovered over the keys for a moment before finding the first chord. She began tentatively, her voice soft as she introduced the opening lines.

"A round peg in a square hole, edges biting, cutting deep. Every corner leaves me bruised, want a place that's mine to keep."

There was no question in Zach's mind. Those lyrics came from a real place inside her.

Ezra settled back in his chair, giving her space, while Zach tilted his head, eyes closed, attentive to every nuance.

As sang, her voice found more confidence, the melody lifting. "I've tried to fit the mold, the one that was designed. But some stories can't be told in straight and perfect lines."

When she reached the chorus, her voice opened up, revealing an emotional authenticity that transcended technique. "Not every shape has four corners. Not every sky is blue. Some truths don't need conformers. More than one dream can come true."

The metaphor of shapes and conformity struck Zach immediately. Of someone being boxed in, constrained, hurt by the limitations placed on her.

He caught Ezra's gaze. A smile played across his brother's face.

The song concluded with a delicate final chord that lingered in the air.

"That's really strong, Kezia," Ezra said.

Though Ezra had spoken first, Kezia turned to Zach, searching his face.

"There's something real there," he said. He didn't press for details about what inspired the lyrics or who they were about. Instead, he focused on the structure. "The lyrics are strong, evocative. And the chorus has a natural flow to it. That moved me. You're definitely on the right track."

As he spoke, her shoulders sank, and she blew out a slow breath. Did his approval matter that much to her?

"Let's work on the arrangement now," he said. "I'd suggest stripping back some of those vocal runs. In fact, don't just strip them back. I'm banning them. Your song lyrics and melody are powerful enough without the technical flourishes."

Ezra nodded in agreement.

Kezia's brow furrowed. "No vocal runs? But that's my thing. It's what I'm known for—what I've trained for."

"It's also what you hide behind," Zach said. "Sometimes a simple, imperfect phrase carries more truth."

He moved to the piano, indicating for her to make space on the bench. "May I?"

Their shoulders brushed as she slid over, a subtle current passing between them—unwelcome, and impossible to ignore.

He forced his focus to the keys, not the woman beside him. "Try it like this," he said, and sang a stripped-back version of her chorus, the melody bare and unadorned.

She repeated the first couple of lines, then stopped, shaking her head. "It sounds...naked."

"That's exactly the point."

Ezra watched the interaction with a half-smile, leaning against the wall with his arms crossed.

"Try it," Zach said, getting off the piano bench and moving back to his seat. "Just the first verse and chorus, without any embellishments."

She played a couple of chords, opened her mouth, then closed it again, face angled down.

Biting her lip, she met his gaze. "Sorry, it's just that...the last time someone asked me to strip back my vocal runs, it was to make me less noticeable so another contestant could shine."

Realization hit Zach. "You mean your duet with Brianna?"

"Yes. Ryan and Mike, the vocal coach, told me to hold back." She hesitated. "They more or less wanted me to be a backup singer again...to disappear. I told myself I'd never do that again."

Zach's stomach dropped as his own words came back to haunt him. *Kezia, you were underwhelming. You disappeared up there. Brianna completely outshone you.* He'd completely ripped into her when she'd been following her mentor's instructions, singing the duet the way Ryan wanted.

And then in her solo performance after that, she'd come out with a vengeance, in a performance of "Vision of Love" so packed with vocal acrobatics that he'd accused her of "out-Mariah-ing Mariah."

I didn't come here to see how many runs you can fit into a three-minute song. I came to discover artists who have something to say. So far, all I'm hearing from you is "look what I can do."

He'd got her so wrong. Totally misread what she was about, what she was doing on that stage.

He ran a hand through his hair. "I...I think I understand where you're coming from, but I want to be sure instead of making assumptions. That day, after your duet, when you sang 'Vision of Love,' I thought you were showing off. That you were just indulging some sort of technical vanity. But it wasn't that, was it? You were reclaiming your voice, asserting your identity and talent after being pushed into the background."

Her gaze locked with his as her eyes widened. "Yes. I guess I overdid it a bit, but I wanted to do something to stand out again."

He leaned forward. "I'm not asking you to hold back to make you disappear. I'm asking you to strip away the technical flourishes so you can be more fully present in the emotion of your song. I don't want to diminish you, but to help you really shine in the way that matters most."

Kezia hesitated, then began again. At first, her delivery was stiff with resistance—but then something shifted. Without the technical flourishes to hide behind, her voice took on a raw quality that brought new meaning to "Every corner leaves me bruised" and the yearning in "Want a place that's mine to keep."

Ezra caught Zach's gaze and gave a small nod. He could hear it, too.

When she reached the last line of the chorus, "More than one dream can be true," the unadorned approach gave it a resonance that hadn't been there before.

"That's it," Zach said quietly. "That's the heart of it."

Her smile warmed him.

"Just so you know," he said, "I'm not banning your vocal tricks permanently. We can bring them back gradually as you learn to rely on them less. Does that make sense?"

She nodded. "Yes. I'm okay with that now that I understand why."

"Good. Now, if Ezra agrees, I want to work a bit more on refining the arrangement. Are you prepared for an extended singing session? Need to use your steamer or something?"

She blinked rapidly. No doubt, she remembered how he'd given her a hard time about it. What a jerk he'd been.

She shook her head. "No, I used it before I came in."

"Good," he said.

They spent the next hour refining the arrangement, discussing instrumentation and emotional pacing.

As Ezra declared the song was developed enough for them to bring in the band tomorrow, Kezia suppressed a yawn.

"You've been up all night working on this, haven't you?" Zach asked.

She yawned again. "Sorry. I was up until dawn. Once the song started coming, I couldn't stop."

Did that mean his talk with her had sparked her creative breakthrough? The thought thrilled him. Maybe a bit more than it should.

As they prepared to leave, Kezia paused at the door, seeking Zach's gaze. "Is this what you were looking for?" she asked hesitantly.

He held her gaze a second too long, struck again by the fire and vulnerability woven through her voice—and the trust she'd placed in him. It stirred something deeper than admiration.

"It's not about what I was looking for," he said. "It's about what you found."

Her face lit up.

"Okay, we're done for today. Make sure you get some rest before our next session."

Glancing at his brother, he caught Ezra's lips twitching in a badly concealed smile.

Ezra checked to ensure Kezia was properly gone and well out of earshot, then turned to face Zach. "She really is extraordinary. There aren't a lot of vocalists who rival Martha, but I have to say, she's right up there."

Zach nodded slowly. Kezia's vocal ability wasn't merely "up there" with Martha's. She was in a class of her own. And she had clawed her way there through sheer grit and relentless training. With natural talent at least equal to

Martha's, Guildhall discipline, and that single-minded hunger to master her craft—she didn't just sing. She earned every note.

Aloud, he said, "Her technical brilliance is a given. But now that we know she also has that kind of potential for emotional depth..."

"It's just the beginning, isn't it?"

"Yes," Zach agreed, gathering his notes. "Just the beginning."

As they left the rehearsal room, he found himself thinking not just about Kezia's song, but about how he understood her so much better now. He'd misjudged her completely, seeing vanity where she'd only wanted her voice to be heard. And the way she'd turned to him first for feedback, seeking his validation—it meant she trusted his judgment. That trust, from an artist of her caliber, especially after he'd judged her so harshly, was a gift he didn't want to lose.

Ezra was right. This was just the beginning, in more ways than one.

Chapter 47

KEZIA PAUSED IN THE doorway of the Broadway Studio, *Starbound*'s showcase recording space, with its gleaming console and perfect acoustics.

The studio buzzed with quiet energy as the drummer adjusted his cymbals, guitarists tuned their strings, and the keyboard player ran scales.

She took in the scene with a mixture of excitement and nerves. She'd been in countless recording sessions before as a session vocalist, and even while recording lead vocals here at *Starbound*, it had always been covers of someone else's song. Today was different. Today she would be recording her own song.

Sam Crawford looked up from the production console and broke into a wide smile. "There she is!" He rose to greet her, headphones dangling around his neck. "How about that, Kezia? I finally get to produce you singing lead."

His enthusiasm was contagious. Sam had given her session work many times over the past few years, and she'd always appreciated his professionalism.

She'd seen him around the Starbound Campus, but since he was assigned to Team Zach, it was the first time she'd be working with him as part of the show.

"And this song is really good, Kezia. Honest." He gestured to the sheet music arranged on stands around the room. "I've been waiting for a chance to work with your voice properly since that session with Verity. By the way, did you hear? That song of hers, 'Higher Ground,' is burning up the charts since it came out last month. Number twelve and climbing."

A thud and a sudden motion made her glance up toward the corner of the room.

Zach sat there, stooping over to pick up a notebook that had fallen to the floor. He straightened and gave her a small nod, but made no move to join them.

Kezia turned back to Sam. "I didn't know how well the song was doing. They keep us pretty sequestered from the outside world."

A small flicker of satisfaction warmed her chest as she set down her bag. "Backing vocals on a top-twenty hit, huh? That'll be a nice addition to my resume if I return to session work."

"Yeah, the label's thrilled with how it turned out." Sam's smile held something Kezia couldn't quite read. "And I have a feeling you won't be returning to session work. Your voice will finally get the credit it deserves."

She returned his smile, but didn't want to get carried away. It was best to keep her expectations realistic.

Now, though, it was time to focus on the present.

As Sam walked her through his arrangement ideas, Kezia glanced toward Zach.

He sat quietly observing, the notebook open on his lap.

"I'm thinking we build this up with backing vocals, maybe some strings," Sam said. He always talked with his hands, and they moved expressively as his enthusiasm grew. "We'll showcase those runs only you can do in the chorus, especially on that final line about dreams being true."

Kezia's gaze sought Zach out as Sam talked about the vocal runs, but he remained silent. Was he letting Sam take the lead in this?

The arrangement Sam outlined was beautiful—professional, radio-ready, exactly what she would have wanted a week ago. It felt familiar, comfortable.

"Let's do a run-through with the full band," Sam suggested, moving back to the console. "Just to get a feel for it."

The band began playing, and Kezia fell into the groove easily. The production was solid, layered with textures that built around her voice. She hit the pre-chorus, adding the vocal embellishments Sam had suggested, everything sounding technically excellent.

But halfway through the chorus, she stopped abruptly, surprising herself as much as everyone else.

The music stumbled to a halt. Sam looked up, frowning. "Something wrong with the arrangement?"

Kezia glanced toward Zach, who sat up straighter, but didn't intervene.

She spoke to Sam. "This song is about the pain of not fitting in. Of learning that the problem isn't you, but the mold you're being squeezed into. It should feel exposed and raw. Like someone finally brave enough to speak an inconvenient truth alone."

She looked toward Zach again. His chin rested on his fist as he gazed at her.

Face warming, she turned back to Sam. "Could we try taking everything away except the piano?"

The band exchanged looks.

Sam considered for a moment, then nodded. "I'm open to testing out new things. Let's try it."

The drummer set down his sticks and the guitarist and bassist stepped back. Only the pianist remained, looking to Kezia for direction.

"From the beginning," she said. "Just follow me."

The pianist began with a simple chord progression. When Kezia started singing, her voice was exposed—no lush production to hide behind, no harmonies to cushion the truth. The vulnerability in the minimal arrangement matched the lyrics in a way the full production hadn't.

As she sang about corners leaving her bruised, about wanting a place that was hers to keep, she connected with the words in a way she never had before.

The room fell completely silent when she finished.

She stole another glance at Zach. A smile played on his lips as he jotted something in his notebook.

Sam broke the silence. "That was...wow. That's a different song entirely." His gaze on her, he tapped thoughtfully on the console. "What if we start with just piano and build slowly throughout the song? Let the production mirror the emotional journey?"

Zach was still silent, and Kezia finally realized what was happening. He was letting her make her own artistic choices. Her stomach fluttered as she answered Sam. "I like that. Begin with vulnerability before adding selective elements."

"Exactly," Sam nodded, already making notes. "We'll keep it stripped back for the verses, then gradually layer in support that enhances rather than masks the emotion."

They ran through the new arrangement from beginning to end. Starting with just voice and piano, exposed and vulnerable, then gradually adding saxophone, guitar, bass. The final chorus incorporated more production while maintaining the emotional core.

As she came to the last repeat of the chorus, Kezia glanced at Zach. His gaze was locked on her—unsettling in its intensity, like he was hearing more than just the notes. The lyrics slipped from her mind like water through her fingers. She blinked, refocused, and found her way back into the song.

What was that about? Why had his look affected her so strongly?

As the final notes faded, Sam's voice came through her headphones. "That's it! That's magic!"

The band members offered genuine compliments as they reviewed the playback.

Kezia accepted their praise, not quite believing what they'd been able to do with her song. But what would Zach think?

As the pianist asked her about a phrase in the second verse, Zach rose from his seat in the corner.

He approached Sam, whispered something to him, and then headed to the door. He offered no words to Kezia, just a brief nod as he slipped out.

She felt deflated as she watched him leave, which made no sense. Shouldn't she be relieved not to have him scrutinizing her every move and making her second-guess her choices?

But she needed to listen to Sam. He was saying something that sounded important.

"Let's record the basic piano track and your guide vocals while it's fresh. Take a couple hours after that to rest your voice, then come back around four for the full vocal session."

He outlined the schedule as he adjusted levels on the console. "Tomorrow we'll have the band lay down any additional elements needed. We'll complete the studio recording well before the live show, but it won't be released until right after your performance on the twentieth."

He tapped something into the computer. "That way, viewers who connect with your song can immediately download or stream it while the emotion is still fresh."

It didn't seem real. People would be able to stream her song. Would they like it?

Sam said, "Here's how I think we should approach both versions. The studio recording can be more polished, but we'll keep the same emotional arc for the live arrangement. I'll let the music director know. The live version will have more room to breathe, of course."

As she prepared to record the guide track, Kezia took a moment to reflect on what had just happened. She'd made a significant artistic choice—stood her ground, shaped the song into something truly hers.

And yet, it wouldn't have become what it was without Zach.

"Ready when you are," Sam called.

"Ready." Adjusting her headphones, Kezia told herself to focus—to stay present, stay grounded in the music.

But as the piano intro began, her thoughts drifted—not to the arrangement or the lyrics or the click of the metronome.

To the look Zach had given her.

To the way it had made her forget the next line.

To the silence he'd left behind.

She started singing right on cue, but part of her followed him out the door, even as an ache lingered. Not for praise, but for something she couldn't quite name.

Chapter 48

ZACH LEANED FORWARD INTO a deep hamstring stretch, one leg extended on the wooden bench that bordered the gravel path. The evening air had a distinct autumn crispness, carrying the scent of fallen leaves and distant woodsmoke.

He'd slipped away from Kezia's recording session to check on Mum, finding her still adrift in grief over Greg's death.

She'd been sitting in the same armchair where he'd left her yesterday, wearing the same cardigan, staring out the window with that vacant, hollow expression that had become so familiar. Martha had whispered that she'd barely eaten or slept.

Although she'd seemed pleased to see him, offering a ghost of a smile, she'd spent most of his visit clutching a photo album, her fingers tracing Greg's face in photos from happier times. She would occasionally start to speak, only to trail off mid-sentence, losing her train of thought as tears silently spilled down her cheeks.

He'd hoped to coax her out into the fresh air. Levi said the doctor suggested gentle activity might help. But she'd turned him down with a barely perceptible shake of her head, clutching the album closer as if it were Greg himself.

Now, back at Glenmere Hall, he carried a heaviness he needed to work through physically as the lengthening shadows stretched across the landscaped gardens. The grounds offered enough secluded paths that he could usually avoid running into *Starbound* contestants or crew.

He shifted to stretch his quadriceps, balancing on one leg, when the rhythmic crunch of footsteps approached on the gravel path.

Kezia jogged toward him, her pace slowing as recognition crossed her face. She wore simple black running leggings and a lightweight blue jacket zipped halfway over a technical shirt.

Zach straightened, weighing whether to acknowledge her or simply nod and continue on his way. Before he could decide, she slowed to a stop several feet away.

"I didn't expect to see anyone out here," she said, slightly breathless, pulling out one earbud. Her face glowed from exercise.

"Me neither."

It was strange seeing her in this context.

She shifted her weight, and he expected her to continue down the path. Instead, she began a stretch of her own, moving through the motions with quiet precision—focused, grounded, like everything else she did. He had the absurd urge to compliment her form, which only made him more determined not to look too long.

"You left before we finished today," she said after a moment of hesitation.

Zach rolled his shoulders, buying himself a moment to consider his response. "I had to leave early. I wanted to spend some time with Mum."

She paused mid-stretch. "Oh. How is she? I've been praying for her."

He glanced down at her face. "Have you? Thanks. She's...struggling. It'll take time."

"I'm sorry. That must be difficult for all of you."

The sincerity in her voice...he couldn't deal with that right now. Not after seeing Mum hurting so deeply while he was powerless to pull her out of it. He shifted his weight to his other leg, stretching his opposite quadriceps.

"How did the session go after I left?" he asked. "Did Sam tell you what the next steps are?"

It took her an extra beat to answer, as though she were thrown by the change of subject. "Yes. We finished the guide vocal and Sam completed the piano arrangement. The rhythm section is coming in tomorrow to build around that foundation."

Kezia began a series of arm stretches. "Was I on the right track? With the arrangement, I mean. You were so quiet today, so I...I wasn't sure what that meant."

The hesitancy in the question surprised him. "I wanted you to learn to trust your own artistic judgment. And you knew what the song needed. You didn't need me there."

"Bit risky, giving all that freedom to a 'dime a dozen session singer.'"

He shot her a look, but her face was angled away. Her tone was light, but the fact that she'd brought it up meant she still thought about it. The things he'd said to this woman... He didn't blame her for calling him out on it. She'd deserved none of his dismissive comments.

He matched her light tone. "I'm getting used to the taste of crow. You just keep serving it up."

She laughed, a sound as musical as her singing. It hit him low in the gut. He wanted to hear it again. Wanted to be the reason for it.

But her face grew sober again as she straightened, releasing her stretch. "In some ways, you were right, though. I'm used to being told exactly what to do, how to sing, what to feel. That's the job—to be technically perfect and completely adaptable."

And now he understood her even more. Session work rewarded technical excellence and conformity to others' visions, not artistic independence.

She met his gaze. "Why did you save me?"

Her question caught him off guard with its directness. He hesitated. There were a dozen answers he could give— and one he couldn't. Should he give her the professional justification he'd used in his interview for the cameras after that infamous double elimination? Talk about her technical skills and her potential? Standing here in the fading light, those explanations felt incomplete.

"For this," he said finally. "For what you did today."

It was both true and yet not the complete truth. Because the fact was, he still didn't fully know why, and he wasn't entirely sure he wanted to.

Something in her shifted at his response. A subtle softening around her eyes, a soft release of breath. Again, he sensed how much his validation mattered to her, and the responsibility that placed on his shoulders.

And yet he'd spent weeks—no, months—heaping unfair and unjustified criticism on her. Not merely unfair. Unkind. Cruel. Shame burned his face like a brand.

"How did you feel during the session with Sam?" he asked. Talking about work was safer, easier than these uncomfortable thoughts.

"Excited. Frustrated at times. Proud, eventually." A slight pause. "Scared."

"Good," he said. "If you're not at least a bit scared, you're not doing it right."

Her eyes widened. "Really?"

"Absolutely. Being an artist means exposing part of your soul for public judgment. You risk being misunderstood. Ridiculed. Dismissed. But you do it anyway because making that connection with the people who get it is worth the risk."

Dusk shrouded her features, but he knew she was watching him intently, processing his words.

"You're a Christian, right?" he added. "It goes even further. Despite the fear, despite the danger, you express that truth in faith that it will touch the people it's supposed to."

Suddenly, standing so close to her in the gathering dark, he realized how long they'd been talking.

"I should let you finish your run," he said, taking a small step back.

"Right." She nodded, straightening her jacket. "I've still got another mile to go."

She gestured down the path, the same direction he'd originally planned to run. The thought of jogging alongside her, continuing this conversation that had already ventured into unexpectedly personal territory... Not a good idea.

"I should actually head back," he said. "Jamie wanted to discuss his arrangement, and I've kept him waiting long enough."

It wasn't entirely untrue. Jamie had mentioned wanting feedback, though they hadn't set a specific time.

"Of course." Her tone was professional, back to contestant-mentor territory. "Thanks for the advice about...everything."

She gave a small smile before replacing her earbud and resuming her pace down the path.

Zach watched her until she was out of sight, the sound of her footfalls lingering longer than they should have.

He hadn't gotten his run. But somehow, his heart was racing all the same.

Chapter 49

SEATED AT THE MENTORS' table, Zach scanned the stage for tonight's third round elimination challenge. The production team had outdone themselves. Gone were the sweeping spotlights and dramatic risers of previous rounds. Instead, the team had created an intimate setting with warm amber lighting, acoustic panels, and a semicircle of stools where the eight remaining contestants now sat, waiting their turn to sing for their place in the semifinal.

Among them, tall and upright, Kezia appeared composed, hands folded on her lap, makeup flawless, her short Afro enhancing her bone structure and the elegant lines of her neck. Was she as calm as she looked? Or was that just the placid veneer that came with years of training and performance experience?

A baby grand piano occupied one side of the stage, with various acoustic instruments arranged nearby.

Zach appreciated the visual statement. Gone was the spectacle. This was about stripping away the production to reveal the artist beneath. Original compositions demanded this kind of setting, where lyrics could be heard and emotional nuances wouldn't be lost.

"First up from Team Zach," Olivia announced, "please welcome Jamie Collins."

Jamie walked to center stage, guitar in hand, looking both nervous and determined. The transformation in him over these past weeks had been remarkable. He'd grown from a former child star, ashamed and defensive about his past, to a young man who now stood with quiet confidence.

As Jamie settled onto the stool and adjusted his microphone, he glanced briefly at Zach, who gave him a nod of encouragement.

"This song is called 'Empty Stages,'" Jamie said, his voice steady and clear. "It's about...well, about what happens when the spotlight moves on and you're left wondering who you are without it."

The opening chords were simple, deliberate, just as they'd practiced.

"Fifteen years old with nowhere to go when the crowds stopped calling my name. Agent's moved on to the next big thing, left me wondering who to blame."

Zach felt a surge of pride. Jamie had come so far from the hesitant young man who'd internalized the sneers and snide comments over his faded fame. Now he was using that very history as the foundation for authentic artistry.

The chorus landed with perfect conviction, Jamie's voice strong and assured on the line about "performing for ghosts on empty stages." He'd embraced every element they'd worked on, owning his story and using his unique background to connect rather than hiding from it.

When Jamie finished, the audience's response was immediate. Not the raucous cheering of previous rounds, but warm, supportive applause from people who understood his journey.

"That was exactly what we've been working toward," Zach told him when it was his turn to speak. "You've taken what once felt like a liability and transformed it into your greatest strength. That's what artists do."

As Jamie returned to his seat, Zach made notes on his tablet. He couldn't have asked for more from his young protégé.

The next hour brought a mix of performances. Brianna delivered a chart-friendly girl power anthem that had Ryan beaming. Young Sandra from Team Diana moved the audience with a tender ballad about her adopted little sister that left Diana dabbing at her eyes.

Zach had to admit that the teen, *Starbound*'s youngest contestant, was a strong contender to go all the way in this show. There was a reason why he'd wanted her on his team early on. Whoever he put through into the semifinal would have to reckon with Sandra's blend of strong vocals and natural charisma.

With each performance, Zach found himself thinking ahead to Kezia's turn. Her journey had been different from the others. She'd already broken through her technical perfectionism in rehearsals, finding the emotional core of her performance. Tonight would be about bringing that vulnerability to the stage in front of an audience.

"And closing tonight's performances," Olivia announced, "from Team Zach, please welcome Kezia Blair."

Zach straightened in his chair as Kezia walked to the piano rather than taking the center mic stand. They'd agreed this setting would best serve her song. Intimate, personal, with nothing to hide behind.

She adjusted the microphone and found the keys with quiet confidence. The opening notes were gentle but assured, matching the honesty of her lyrics.

"A round peg in a square hole, edges biting, cutting deep. Every corner leaves me bruised. Need a place that's mine to keep."

Like they'd agreed, she sang with no vocal embellishments. Her sweet, resonant tone was all she needed, the perfect vehicle to convey the emotion in her lyrics. She was an artist who had learned to trust herself, to believe in the power of her own story.

"I've tried to fit the mold, the one that was designed. But some stories can't be told in straight and perfect lines."

As she moved into the chorus, she let the dynamics build, serving the song rather than showcasing technique.

"Not every shape has four corners. Not every sky is blue. Some truths don't need conformers. More than one dream can come true."

The second verse showed even more confidence, her voice gaining strength as she built toward the bridge. And then it happened. On the line "trying to fold myself smaller," her voice cracked, a tiny imperfection she would never normally have allowed, but which revealed the depth of feeling behind the words.

Zach's chest tightened. He'd heard her rehearse this song a dozen times, but nothing had prepared him for this. That single cracked note was like a hairline fracture in a perfect mask—and it stripped away every defense he thought he had. For a second, he allowed himself to ponder the kind of wound Kezia was singing about, what it might have done to her, choosing a different path despite her parents' pressure and expectations.

She ended the song with none of the vocal pyrotechnics she was fully capable of doing, but with a different kind of power—the power of simple, devastating honesty.

The audience was silent for a beat before erupting in applause.

Diana spoke first. "That moment when your voice broke, that's when I finally met the real Kezia. Everything before was beautiful, but that was the moment I believed you completely."

Tyler nodded agreement. "You've shown us you can do perfect. Today you showed us truthful."

Ryan folded his arms. "It was certainly emotional, but I wonder if that's what the market wants from someone with your technical gifts. For me, that's what made you stand out before. I appreciate vulnerability, but I miss the wow factor you've demonstrated in previous weeks."

When it was Zach's turn, he met Kezia's gaze directly. "Perfection impresses, but vulnerability connects. Today you chose to connect, and you did it beautifully." He kept his feedback brief, knowing she would understand the significance of what she'd accomplished.

As the contestants left the stage and Olivia announced the break before elimination, Zach reviewed his notes.

For the first time in an elimination round, he didn't have complete clarity about what to do. Jamie had delivered what Zach wanted, a confident performance that showed how far he'd come in embracing his unique story.

But Kezia...

Her story, her vulnerability, her performance tonight, moved him on a level so deep that he questioned whether he could be objective about her.

He'd pushed her to dig deep, to break through her technical shell, to make herself vulnerable enough to move her audience.

And now she had—starting with him. How could he make a professional judgment when she'd done exactly what he asked, but done it too well?

The very emotional authenticity he'd demanded from her was clouding his ability to make an impartial decision.

Zach ran a hand through his hair, confronting the irony of his situation. He'd first bullied and then guided Kezia into authenticity. And now he had to deal with his authentic response to her.

His brother Ezra's words came back. *And if you break through and find what you're looking for? What will you do when she opens up?*

He'd created a monster. Not one that lurked in shadows, but one that stood in the spotlight and haunted him with everything he'd ever longed for. Beautiful. Vulnerable. Unstoppable. She stripped him bare, left him breathless, and lingered in the corners of his thoughts like a song he couldn't forget. He should have run. But he wasn't sure he wanted to.

The production assistant signaled five minutes until they'd be back on air for the elimination.

Zach set down his tablet. His notes were useless as the weight of decision settled over him. Only one of his contestants could move forward to the semifinals. And yet both deserved it.

He glanced toward the wings where the contestants waited, catching a glimpse of Kezia's profile as she spoke quietly with Jamie. There was nothing straightforward about this decision.

Chapter 50

KEZIA LEANED AGAINST THE wall of the backstage holding area, trying to control her breathing. The familiar post-performance adrenaline crash was setting in, leaving her hands with a slight tremor.

Something had happened on that stage tonight as she sang from her heart about the deep hurt she'd never articulated before. It wasn't about hitting notes that sounded impressive, but about what Zach had told her. *We all have those painful, dark corners in our lives. Every one of us. Artistry is about accessing that, channeling it into connection.*

His brief critique told her he liked what she'd done. But that didn't mean he would pick her to stay.

Around her, the remaining contestants waited in tense silence for the elimination ceremony to begin.

A production assistant with a clipboard hurried past. "Five minutes, everyone."

Jamie stood a few feet away, catching her glance with a small smile. Only one of them would move on to the semi-final. He moved closer, lowering his voice. "You were amazing out there."

"So were you." She meant it. He might have needed her help early on when writing his song, but its final version was a world away from the rough drafts they'd worked on.

The way he'd embraced his story and transformed it into art...that was exactly what Zach had been looking for, justifying why the young man everyone wrote off as a washed up has been was his first pick for his team. Even from a reality TV perspective, it made a wonderful story. Everyone loved a comeback kid.

Jamie must have read something in her face, because he reached out and squeezed her hand briefly. "Hey, no matter what happens, we both did our best tonight. We made Zach proud."

She nodded, unable to articulate the certainty settling in her stomach like a stone. Jamie would be moving forward. His journey with Zach had been the more dramatic transformation, from shame to acceptance, from hiding to revelation. And she couldn't begrudge him that. He deserved this break.

"Places, please." The stage manager appeared, gesturing them toward the wings.

As they lined up in the darkness beside the stage, Kezia heard Olivia's voice addressing the audience. "After tonight, only four contestants will remain in the competition. Each mentor must make the difficult decision to send one of their remaining team members home."

The stage lights seemed harsher now, designed to capture every flicker of emotion on their faces. Kezia straightened her shoulders, preparing her gracious-elimination-face. The same one she'd worn at the last round. She'd had years of practice maintaining composure through disappointment.

Diana went first, delivering a heartfelt speech before reluctantly eliminating Toby. Tyler followed, choosing to keep Connor over Elliot. Then Ryan, predictably, kept Brianna, whose commercial appeal aligned perfectly with his spreadsheets.

Kezia felt for Dominic as he accepted his elimination.

"And finally," Olivia announced, "Zach must choose between Jamie Collins and Kezia Blair."

Jamie's hand found hers, and their fingers linked as they walked forward together. Despite the odds and under the strangest circumstances, she knew she'd found a friend in him, and she was grateful for that.

Under the intense lights, Zach's expression was unreadable. "Jamie," he began, "when you first auditioned, I saw someone with enormous potential who was hiding from his own story. Your journey has been remarkable. From being defensive about your past to embracing it as the foundation of your artistry. Tonight's performance showed exactly how far you've come."

Jamie nodded, a muscle working in his jaw.

Kezia squeezed his hand.

Zach turned to her. "Kezia, you're perhaps the most skilled vocalist we have in this competition. There's never been any question about your abilities. But what's always been missing for me is that spark, that connection that elevates craft into art. I've been really tough on you because I was so frustrated that you never showed us more than technical precision. Today you finally showed us that you're not a mechanical nightingale. You're the real thing."

Kezia felt the pressure of Jamie's fingers around her own.

The silence stretched as Zach looked between them.

Kezia held her breath.

Zach scrubbed a hand down his face. "This decision has been incredibly difficult. Both of you deserve to continue in this competition. But I can only choose one."

He took a deep breath. "Kezia, you're moving forward to the semifinals."

The words didn't register immediately. She'd been so certain of the opposite outcome that her brain stalled, the audience's applause registering like sound underwater. But Jamie was turning toward her, his arms opening for a hug.

"You deserve it," he whispered as his arms went around her. The genuine warmth in his voice only intensified her confusion.

When she looked past Jamie's shoulder at Zach, his face was averted.

The next few minutes passed in a blur as Jamie said his goodbyes to the other contestants and mentors. She'd been so prepared to be in his position that she felt like an impostor in her own victory.

Again, she searched for Zach's gaze, but he never looked at her.

She looked for Jamie, hoping to say something more meaningful than their stage hug, but he was already being escorted to the exit interviews.

Before she could follow, a production assistant appeared at her elbow. "Kezia, we need you for your semifinalist interview. This way, please."

Semifinalist. She was one of the final four.

As she followed the production assistant toward the interview area, she glanced back at the judges' table. Zach was in conversation with Diana, but for a moment, he looked up and caught her gaze. Then he looked away.

Was he already regretting his choice?

Chapter 51

ACH GLANCED AT HIS watch as he straightened the papers on his desk. Kezia and the other semifinalists would be doing their on-the-fly interviews at the studio for at least another hour, while the eliminated contestants had returned to the Starbound Campus to pack their belongings.

The production schedule was precise. Within a couple of hours, Jamie would be gone, his *Starbound* journey officially over. But Zach wasn't ready to let him go just yet.

"Come in," he said to a knock at the door.

Jamie entered, shoulders tight. He'd changed out of his performance clothes into jeans and a simple t-shirt, looking younger without the stage lighting and makeup.

"You wanted to see me?" Jamie's tone was polite but guarded.

Zach gestured toward a chair. "I wanted to talk before you head out."

Jamie sat, his posture stiff. "About your decision? I get it. Kezia's performance was better."

"This isn't about justifying my decision," Zach said, settling into the chair opposite. "Which wasn't an easy one at all, by the way. You were incredible tonight. This is about what comes next for you."

Jamie's eyes widened. "You think I was incredible? Is there anything I could have done differently to make you put me through to the semifinal?"

Zach considered the question, appreciating Jamie's directness. "Honestly? I don't think so. Not because you weren't good enough. You were the best I've ever seen you."

Jamie frowned. "Then why—"

"Kezia is ready for this right now," Zach said. "She has the technical foundation and has finally broken through emotionally." He gestured with his hands, searching for the words to help Jamie understand. "But for you, I think the spotlight and pressure might actually hinder your development at this stage."

"Okay." Jamie dropped his gaze for a moment, jaw tightening. Then he looked Zach in the eye. "You've always played it straight with me. You think I'm ever going to make it in music again?"

Zach's gut twisted. He hated doing or saying anything that caused this kid to doubt his potential. "I can't predict the future. But I know that your songwriting has a raw authenticity that can't be taught. My brother Ezra agrees with me. That voice, your actual artistic voice, not just your vocals, is rare. And your performance issues were never about talent. They were about discipline and consistency."

Jamie nodded slowly, his shoulders lowering. "I know I messed up a lot. Didn't take it seriously enough at first. Apart from the last couple of weeks."

"I noticed that."

"Believe it or not, Kezia pushed me when you were away," Jamie said.

"Yes, you mentioned she helped with your songwriting."

Jamie nodded. "Not just that. She was on my case about keeping up with my vocal exercises and training sessions. Wouldn't let up. And when I was struggling with the arrangement for my song, she stayed up late helping me work through it."

Another dimension to Kezia that Zach hadn't fully appreciated. As if he needed another reminder that Kezia kept turning out to be more than he'd bargained for. It helped assure him that he'd made the right choice tonight. He thanked God for that confirmation.

He reached behind him to his desk and grabbed a business card, handing it to Jamie. "Sebastian Barry, a good friend of mine. He runs a small label focusing on indie artists."

Jamie took the card, examining it.

"He's looking for singer/songwriters with a unique perspective," Zach said. "I spoke to him about you just before you got here. He was watching the show tonight."

Jamie looked up, genuine surprise in his expression. "You did this for me?"

Zach nodded. "I was torn about letting you go. But I think you need time to develop without the pressure of cameras. Build your song catalog, refine your voice. Prove you can be consistent." He pointed to the card in Jamie's hand. "In six months, call that number. If you've put in the work, Sebastian will listen."

"And there's one more thing," Zach said, reaching for his phone. He pulled up a text message. "I mentioned that Ezra was impressed with your songwriting. He messaged me just after we went off air. He's running a three-day intensive songwriting workshop next month at Hatbrook. Small group, just eight participants working directly with him."

Jamie's eyes widened. "With Ezra Falconer? Those workshops are impossible to get into. I've heard they cost a fortune, too."

"They do," Zach confirmed. "But Ezra wants to offer you a spot. No charge." He turned the phone so Jamie could see the message. "He believes you've got something worth developing."

Jamie stared at the screen, visibly processing this second opportunity. "This is... I don't know what to say."

"Say you'll go," Zach said. "Working with Ezra will help you build that catalog of songs Sebastian will want to hear. My brother's one of the best songwriting mentors in the business."

"Of course I'll go," Jamie said quickly. "That would be amazing. Please thank him for me."

"I'll pass your details to him," Zach said. "He'll contact you directly to sort out the arrangements." He gave a small smile. "Between Ezra's workshop and Sebastian's interest, you'll have the foundation to build something real."

Jamie stared at Sebastian's card for a long moment, then carefully tucked it into his wallet. "Before *Starbound*, I thought I was washed up. Like my chance had passed me by at thirteen." His voice roughened. "Being here, working with you...it made me believe I could still have a career. Thank you for that."

"You've got something real to offer. Now you just need the time and space to build on it."

Jamie nodded, his eyes shining. "I won't waste this opportunity."

"I know you won't." Zach stood, signaling the conversation was nearing its end.

Jamie rose as well, then grinned. "Just make sure Kezia beats Brianna, all right? I'd hate to think I got eliminated so that fake little plastic face could win this thing."

Zach couldn't help smiling at Jamie's jab at Ryan's remaining contestant. He wouldn't be much of a mentor if he couldn't guide Kezia to victory over someone like Brianna, who was all style and no substance, without even Kezia's raw talent to hide behind.

The two women were different in every way that mattered. Where Brianna cos-played authenticity, Kezia fought to reveal her genuine self. Brianna sought the spotlight, but Kezia sought artistic truth, even when it terrified her.

Although Kezia wanted to win *Starbound*, he didn't think she was after fame at all costs. This meant more to her than that. Why else would she help Jamie, a contestant who very well could have beaten her into the semifinal?

He'd taken a beat too long to reply. Jamie was watching him.

Zach blinked and pulled himself back into the moment. "I'll do my best. The rest is up to her."

Jamie offered his hand, but Zach pulled him into a hug instead. "Keep in touch. I mean that. Let me know how it goes with the workshop and with Sebastian."

After Jamie left, Zach remained standing in the middle of his office. He'd made the right decision for Jamie. Of that, he was certain.

But for Kezia?

He could list a dozen reasons why she deserved to move forward—the unflinching vulnerability in her performance tonight. Her impeccable voice. The quiet way she'd carried Jamie behind the scenes, lifting him without expecting credit. All true. All compelling.

But if he was being honest—truly honest—none of those things were the first to surface when she came to mind. Not that she was ever out of his thoughts for long.

It wasn't her voice, or her courage, or her talent.

It was *her*.

And that was the problem.

Chapter 52

*K*EZIA TUCKED HER SHEET music into her folder as she left her new room. With only four contestants left after yesterday's elimination, she and the other semifinalists could now have their own bedrooms, which felt like a luxury after weeks of sharing with Brianna.

The house felt empty compared to the early days, when there were sixteen people living here.

She checked her watch—10:45 AM. Just enough time to get to the rehearsal complex before her scheduled practice session with Sandra at 11:00.

Laura the producer had been clear. Semifinalists were required to have daily "journey content" filmed for next week's episode. Kezia's slot was 11:00 to 12:30, which aligned with her planned vocal technique session with Sandra. The producers were very interested in the cross-team mentoring dynamic that had grown between the oldest and youngest contestants in the show.

Kezia grabbed her dove gray jacket from the hook by the door, shrugging it over her shoulders as she stepped outside. The October morning was chilly, the sky a blanket of gray clouds that threatened rain but hadn't delivered yet.

As expected, a camera operator, sound technician, and producer waited for her at the entrance to the rehearsal complex. The crew members had bundled up against the autumn chill, the sound technician wearing fingerless gloves as he adjusted his equipment.

The producer, Natalie, greeted her with clipboard in hand. "Morning, Kezia. Ready for today's filming?"

"As ready as ever," Kezia replied with a smile, zipping her jacket higher against a gust of cool wind.

Natalie stepped beside the camera. "So what's on the agenda today, Kezia?"

Kezia turned to face the camera. "I'm meeting with Sandra to continue our work on diaphragm control techniques. We've been practicing together regularly since week two."

"Great," Natalie nodded. "Let's find her then."

Kezia checked the first practice room, then the second. No sign of Sandra. Strange. The teenager was usually punctual, especially for their morning sessions.

"She's normally very reliable," Kezia said, checking her watch again. "Let me check the sound booth. Sometimes she likes to warm up in there."

The sound booth was empty, too. When a check of all the practice spaces produced no Sandra, Kezia frowned.

"This is odd. We definitely confirmed for 11:00 yesterday." She glanced at Natalie. "Maybe she's at the outdoor gazebo? Diana sometimes has her practice there for the acoustics."

"Let's check it out," Natalie said. "It'll be good to get some outdoor footage, too. Just walk along the path. Let us know again that you're looking for Sandra, and what you're planning on doing together."

Kezia repeated her spiel of how she and Sandra often did vocal work together, and how she was trying to locate the teen for their 11 o'clock session. As she spoke, walking across the damp grass, her breath formed small clouds in the cool air.

The gazebo sat in the center of the *Starbound* grounds, halfway between the contestants' house and the rehearsal complex. The white wooden structure stood out against the backdrop of autumn trees, their leaves turning amber and gold.

She spotted Sandra sitting alone on the bench inside the gazebo, scribbling in a notebook, her purple jacket zipped up to her chin.

"There she is," Kezia said.

As they drew closer, Kezia noticed another camera crew already positioned near the gazebo, filming Sandra from a distance.

"Looks like we're not the only ones with this location in mind," Natalie murmured, exchanging a glance with her camera operator.

Sandra looked up as they approached, her expression shifting from concentration to something more guarded. She snapped her notebook shut.

"Hey," Kezia said, climbing the two steps into the gazebo as the cameras continued rolling. The wooden structure provided shelter from the breeze, though the air remained crisp. "I was looking for you. Weren't we going to work on diaphragm control at 11?"

Sandra glanced at the camera crews, now positioning themselves to capture both contestants from different angles. Her posture stiffened as her gaze shifted away. "Oh. Sorry, I forgot."

The words hung briefly between them in a puff of white breath before a swirl of wind carried it away.

Kezia stuffed her hands into her pockets. "Um, okay, no problem. We could reschedule for later today if you want?"

Sandra set down her pen, finally meeting Kezia's gaze. "Why are you helping me, Kezia?"

The question caught Kezia off guard. "What do you mean?"

Natalie moved closer, clipboard in hand, waving at the camera operator to move in.

"You know, the breathing exercises, the vocal techniques..." Sandra gestured vaguely. "Why spend time helping someone who could beat you?"

Kezia blinked, glancing at the cameras that moved closer. This wasn't at all the conversation she was expecting. "I enjoy sharing what I know, and you're a wonderful student. And honestly, I learn things when we work together too. You have incredible natural instincts."

Sandra narrowed her eyes. "Brianna said you might have other reasons."

A producer exchanged looks with the camera operator.

Kezia felt her stomach tighten. So that was it. Brianna had been planting ideas in Sandra's head.

Natalie stepped toward Sandra. "What did Brianna say exactly?"

The teen looked embarrassed now, her cheeks flushing pink against the cool air. "She said Kezia might sabotage me with wrong techniques. Or she might be trying to figure out my weaknesses." She looked down at her notebook. "I know it sounds stupid when I say it out loud."

The accusation stung more than Kezia expected. She was acutely aware of the cameras capturing her reaction, the producer nodding supportively at Sandra.

"That's not true," Kezia said carefully, fighting to keep the hurt out of her voice. Sandra was very young, and Brianna knew how to stir the pot. It shouldn't shock her that the teen was questioning Kezia's motives in helping her. "I've been using these vocal techniques for years. I know they work."

Sandra nodded. "I didn't fully believe her, but..." She shrugged, pulling her jacket tighter as a gust of wind whistled through the gazebo. "You know, there are only two spots in the finals. And we all know how good you are. Why would you really be interested in helping your competition?"

Kezia's heart sank. This was the painful risk of forming connections in a zero-sum game. No matter how genuine the relationship, eventually, you became opponents. Two dogs fighting over one bone. She'd hoped they could somehow rise above it. Keep the competition on the performance stage and not behind the scenes.

"I understand why you'd be cautious," Kezia said. "And I guess there's no way to really prove I'm not out to sabotage you. I genuinely enjoy working with you."

Sandra listened, her expression softening slightly, but still conflicted. A fallen leaf skittered across the gazebo floor between them.

After a moment of consideration, the girl shook her head. "I think maybe it's best if we don't work together anymore."

Though Kezia had sensed this was coming, the words still hurt. "I understand."

"It's not that I really think you're actually sabotaging me," Sandra added quickly. "But with the semifinals...everything's just more complicated now." She glanced to where both camera crews captured their conversation. "I really appreciate all your help, but I just think we need to keep the boundaries clear."

Kezia swallowed. Competition had indeed poisoned what was a genuine connection. She'd been naïve to think it could be otherwise. "All right. I...I respect that. Good luck with your preparation."

"Thanks. You too." Sandra gathered her things and left, hurrying down the gazebo steps and along the path back to the house, shoulders hunched against the cold.

As soon as Sandra was gone, Natalie stepped toward Kezia. "Can you give us a quick reaction to what just happened?"

Kezia shook her head, fighting to keep her voice steady. "Not right now. Maybe later."

There was no way she would process what happened while a camera was stuck in her face.

As she walked away, Natalie spoke into her headset. "Get Brianna for an OTF about the Sandra-Kezia situation. We're building this into today's narrative."

Kezia's chest tightened. What had been a private disappointment would now become public entertainment, dissected and dramatized for viewers.

She paused on the path, gazing up at the heavy clouds as the first tiny drops of rain fell.

Lily had been eliminated weeks ago. Jamie was gone. And now Sandra didn't trust her.

She was surrounded by competitors and camera operators. The producers were friendly enough, but every conversation was just them mining for material to weave into her "story."

She really was alone here. No friends. No allies. No buffer. Just the cameras and the cold. And the music. That had always been her refuge. Her sanctuary.

Kezia pulled her collar tighter against the rain and kept walking. Alone or not, she had work to do.

Chapter 53

ACH SHIFTED HIS WEIGHT from one foot to the other as he stood with the other mentors in the main hall of the Starbound Campus.

He'd returned just in time for this morning's semifinal challenge announcement after being away all day yesterday for Greg's funeral. Mum had held up better than expected, a relief to him and his brothers. Perhaps burying Greg would help bring the closure they all needed.

Now it was time to refocus on the competition. And on Kezia. And to figure out how to guide her into the final while ignoring the complex swirl of questions she stirred up inside him.

Things were so much more straightforward when he could just think of her as a singing machine, a voice in human form. But after pushing her to access her emotional core and channel it into artistry, he could no longer unsee the woman behind the technical mechanics.

And yet he had to.

She stood with the three other semifinalists on center stage. But something seemed off. The other contestants chatted to each other as they waited for Steve to call action, but Kezia appeared detached, cut off, staring to the side.

Olivia Chang strode onto the stage with practiced enthusiasm, her silver jumpsuit sparkling in the bright lights.

"Welcome back, everyone!" Her voice carried through the hall. "Today, we're making *Starbound* history as we announce our semifinal challenge."

Steve, directing the shoot, interrupted Olivia. "Great energy, Brianna. Kezia, are you planning on joining us today? We need smiles, please. This is exciting!"

Kezia adjusted her expression enough to please Steve. But Zach didn't buy it.

Olivia continued, "For our semifinal round, each of you will perform two songs that showcase your readiness to be crowned our *Starbound* winner. And, for the first time, it's not up to your mentors to decide who moves forward."

A dramatic pause. "Britain will vote on which two of you will move on to the final. Your future rests in our viewers' hands."

The contestants gave the required over-the-top reactions.

Olivia moved her hands in a dramatic flourish. "This is your chance to prove to the nation that you are complete artists ready for success in today's music industry. Please join your mentors for your first semifinal preparation session."

The contestants broke up their formation, each walking toward their mentor.

"Cut!" Steve called out. "Great work, everyone. Let's move on."

As Kezia approached Zach, a producer intercepted them. "Hey, guys. We need some transition footage of you two. Walk toward the Blues Studio, just chatting naturally about the semifinal."

Kezia glanced at Zach, then fell into step beside him.

A camera operator positioned himself ahead of them, ready to capture walking B-roll without sound recording.

"I never know what to say when they tell us to look natural," Zach said as they moved side by side down the corridor, the awkward "natural walking" that reality TV demanded.

A small smile touched her lips. "Rhubarb, rhubarb, rhubarb?"

Zach chuckled at the old industry joke, what TV and movie extras say to mimic conversation in background scenes. "Rhubarb, rhubarb. Rhubarb," he repeated, laying varied emphasis on the words.

Her smile widened, and she followed his lead. "Rhubarb?" she questioned dramatically, pressing a hand on her heart.

"Rhubarb, rhubarb!" he responded with mock indignation.

She shook her head, pointing a finger as though lecturing him. "Rhubarb. Rhubarb, rhubarb."

They played along, repeating the words with various inflections, just two industry professionals sharing an inside joke.

But when they reached the Blues Studio and the producer and camera crew left, the smile faded from Kezia's face.

Just as well. It was time to focus on work.

He gestured toward the seating area in the corner of the studio. Two comfortable armchairs faced each other across a small coffee table, a more intimate setup than the formal piano arrangement they'd used in earlier sessions.

She took a seat and Zach pulled his notebook from his messenger bag, along with a folder of sheet music.

He sat opposite her and opened his notebook. "Let's start by discussing the strategy behind my song choice."

"Okay."

"I think our best approach will be contrasting pieces that showcase different aspects of your artistry," he began, flipping through his notes. "We want to show you're a complete artist. I'm thinking something like 'All That I

Give' as your first piece. It'll let you unleash your range and vocal firepower while allowing for emotional depth."

The crowd-pleasing power ballad, covered most notably by Whitney Houston, was right in Kezia's comfort zone. The kind of song she could belt out in her sleep.

He pulled out the sheet music and placed it on the table between them. "And for your second piece, I was thinking 'Patterns in Motion.' Neo-soul with a groovy funk-infused pop beat that will show rhythmic finesse and stage presence. I know you haven't done anything like this in the show so far, but that's exactly the point. It's all about proving your versatility, showing you're ready for whatever the industry might demand."

He set another sheet of music beside the first one. "This will be a one-two punch that'll remind viewers of your vocal power and control, but also show them you can do stage presence and personality. 'All That I Give' shouldn't pose any problems, so we can focus our efforts on 'Patterns.' What do you think?"

He glanced up, expecting a response, but she was staring out of the window.

He frowned. "Kezia?"

Startled, her gaze snapped to his face. "Sorry. You think I should sing 'All That I Give'?"

"I said a lot more than that." He folded his arms. "You were distracted earlier as well. Steve had to call you out. Something's clearly bothering you."

She shook her head. "It's nothing. Just some contestant drama. I'm good now. I want to focus on the semifinal."

Zach looked at her for a long moment as she pulled the sheet music toward herself. He could let it go and try to keep on working. Treat her like a singing machine with no inner life, no worries and hurts. That would probably be the safest and smartest thing to do.

But could he really push on, ignoring whatever trouble she was having? He made up his mind.

"If this contestant drama is serious enough to distract you, we need to address it," he said. "I need you at your best for this stage of the competition."

She glanced at his face, then looked away, shaking her head. "I'm sorry I brought it up. Let's get to work. I promise I'll keep my head in the game now."

He knew her well enough now to sniff out deflection. And that told him it definitely wasn't nothing.

"Kezia," he said gently, "if it really is nothing, then it won't matter if you tell me. But if it *is* something, maybe I can help. Either way, I'd like to know."

A moment passed, then she sighed, looking down at her hands. "Okay. It's going to sound really silly. Sandra and I have been working together on vocal exercises and di-aphragm control since week two. We had a practice session scheduled yesterday, but when I went to find her..." She paused. "Apparently Brianna convinced her I might be sab-otaging her with incorrect techniques or trying to discover her weaknesses."

"What?"

"Sandra decided we shouldn't work together anymore. She said with the semifinals, 'we need to be competitors now.' I just didn't expect it to bother me this much." She looked up at him. "See? It's ridiculous."

She tried to keep her tone matter-of-fact, but she couldn't quite hide the hurt behind her words.

He shook his head. "No, it's not ridiculous to be disap-pointed when you're misunderstood, or when someone values winning over genuine connection. This environ-ment isn't designed for sustaining relationships."

And yet, once again, Kezia had been reaching out to help her rivals. The same way she'd helped Jamie. She re-ally was something else. No wonder a person as shallow and calculating as Brianna thought she must have ulterior motives.

"It's not just Sandra," Kezia continued after a moment, her voice softer. "That was just the latest thing. Lily's gone, Jamie's gone... I didn't realize how isolating this would become."

Definitely not ridiculous. Sequestered here over several weeks, she had been watching her small circle of connections shrink further.

With limited phone access and social media restrictions, contestants were largely cut off from their normal support networks. As the eliminations continued, that isolation only intensified. And the competition dynamics threatened whatever friendships she was trying to build. No wonder she was struggling.

He ached for her. But what could he do?

"Hey," he said gently. "We don't have much longer in this weird bubble. Just a few more weeks. Do you think you can hang in there for a while longer?"

She met his gaze, her lips pressed together. "I'll try. Thanks."

Her voice wobbled on the last word. She looked away, drawing a slow breath like she was bracing herself for battle. When she faced him again, her spine had straightened, and her tone was crisp. "Should we get back to work?"

"You sure?"

She nodded. "Yes. Now that I've talked about it and confirmed I'm not being overly sensitive, I think I can focus."

Zach returned to his notes, but something stuck with him. Not just what she'd shared, but the quiet way she'd admitted it. The loneliness. The loss of connection. The effort it took for her to stay soft in a place that rewarded sharp edges. He couldn't stop thinking about how she reached out, how she helped others even when it didn't serve her own interests. That kind of generosity wasn't just rare—it was dangerous. Especially to someone like him, who'd long ago stopped expecting it.

He wanted to do more than just coach her through song selection. He wanted to protect that softness. Be someone she could lean on when the pressure got too much. But he couldn't. Not now. Not while he was her mentor, not while her future in the competition still depended on his judgment. Any personal entanglement would compromise them both.

Keeping it professional was the only thing he could do.

He returned to his notes. "As I was saying, 'All That I Give' would be a good choice for your first performance."

"Isn't that exactly the type of power ballad you were steering me away from?" Kezia asked. "There's no way to do that kind of showcase song without vocal acrobatics. The kind you said I was using as a crutch."

Good. Her focus was returning. "I did say that," he said. "But I think you're ready now to combine both technical elements and emotional depth. 'All That I Give' is the perfect vehicle because it plays to all your strengths. I have no worries about your ability to deliver. What we do need to think about is the second song, 'Patterns in Motion.'"

Her surprise about that title showed him she hadn't been paying attention at all when he'd first brought it up. He went over his reasoning again, noting with satisfaction that Kezia was fully present, offering thoughtful input about performing two such different songs.

But her earlier vulnerability remained in his thoughts. She wasn't just a singing machine to be fine-tuned for competition. He needed to keep her wellbeing in mind as they moved forward. The semifinal would be demanding enough without the added pressure of isolation.

A knock at the door interrupted their discussion.

Maya, the talent producer, poked her head in. "Sorry to interrupt, but Zach, can I speak with you for a moment? It's time sensitive."

"Of course." He turned to Kezia. "Take a few minutes with the sheet music. I'll be right back."

In the hallway, Maya's expression was tense. "There's a problem with Kezia's family," she said quietly.

Zach felt his stomach drop. "What kind of problem?"

Chapter 54

AYA GLANCED PAST ZACH'S shoulder to the studio door behind him.

He stepped closer, keeping his voice low. "Has there been an accident? Are they—"

"It's not that," Maya said. "Can we talk outside? This is somewhat sensitive."

They stepped outside the building, the crisp autumn air chilling Zach's skin.

Maya said, "We're putting the final details in order for the semifinalists' Family Day."

"Yes, I'm aware." It was supposed to be a surprise treat for the four contestants left, having their loved ones come down to hang out with them at the Starbound Campus on Saturday.

Maya said, "Production's been coordinating with their loved ones, arranging travel, making sure everyone arrives at the same time." She sighed. "The Byaruhangas have declined to attend."

"Declined?" Zach frowned. "As in, they can't make it, or they don't want to come?"

"Both, apparently." Maya's expression was grim. "We've made multiple attempts to contact them. First through an assistant producer, then I tried personally. Dr. Byaruhanga gave us a very firm 'no.' Mrs. Byaruhanga was equally clear."

The implications settled over Zach like a heavy cloak. "If they don't come, Kezia will be the only semifinalist without family support."

"Exactly. We're concerned about both her emotional wellbeing and, frankly, how it will look on camera." Maya touched her tablet screen, pulling up notes. "The other contestants will have their moments of joyful reunion while Kezia...what? Stands there alone?"

"Let me see the contact information you've been using."

Maya handed over her tablet, revealing a file with the Byaruhangas' details and carefully documented notes from previous attempts to reach them. The responses were formal, brief, leaving no room for negotiation.

There, in black and white, was Kezia's family's firm refusal to come and spend the day with the daughter they hadn't seen for weeks, who was a semifinalist in a prestigious national music competition.

Maya said, "We've hit a wall with them and I'm not sure what to do next. Maybe we could arrange for Kezia to go to a spa for the day or something? So she doesn't have to be here when the other semifinalists are hanging out with their families. But I'll need you to authorize that."

Zach considered that for a moment, then shook his head. "No, I think it would be better for her if she had her people here, too. I want to try calling them myself."

Maya's eyebrows shot up. "Are you sure?"

"I'm the creator of this show. They might take a call from me more seriously." He started walking toward the main house. "Let's go to my office, and I'll make the call there."

Maya had to trot to keep up with his long strides.

He wasn't entirely sure why he felt so compelled to intervene personally, but he couldn't shake the need to try fixing this. "Who else is on Kezia's approved contacts list?"

Maya checked the file. "Just her former flatmate, Claire Wilson."

A backup plan, just in case.

As they reached his office, he held out his hand for her tablet. "Is that his number? Give me some privacy for this call."

Maya nodded and stepped out.

Alone in his office, Zach stared at Dr. Byaruhanga's number for a long moment before dialing it from his landline. He rehearsed his professional tone as the phone rang.

"Dr. Byaruhanga speaking." The voice was clipped, formal, a hint of a foreign accent.

"Dr. Byaruhanga, this is Zach Falconer, creator and executive producer of *Starbound*."

A slight pause. "Yes, I'm aware of who you are, Mr. Falconer."

A twinge of unease tightened Zach's gut. It didn't sound like Kezia's father was impressed with him. He kept his tone friendly and professional. "Some members of my team have been in touch about an event we're hosting to surprise our semifinal contestants, including your daughter. We have a beautiful venue here on the grounds of a historic house. You'll have the chance to tour Glenmere Hall, spend the day with Kezia, and enjoy a fully catered lunch and high tea. I was hoping you and Mrs. Byaruhanga would be able to join us."

"Mr. Falconer, while your offer sounds...charming, as I already explained to your staff several times, my wife and I have prior commitments that week. As I'm sure you understand, my surgical schedule is arranged months in advance, and my wife has obligations that cannot be altered."

"You carry out surgeries on a Saturday?" As soon as he said the words, Zach wished he could claw them back. Pushing this man into a corner was not the right approach.

Dr. Byaruhanga's tone grew glacial. "I'm best placed to understand the demands on my schedule, Mr. Falconer."

"Yes, of course." Zach hoped his voice sounded apologetic. "I didn't mean to imply otherwise. But this is a significant milestone in Kezia's career. She's one of only four contestants remaining in a national music competition."

"While we're happy to hear that she has progressed so far, this is a career in only the loosest possible terms. As I said, my wife and Kezia's sister have other commitments we can't abandon."

The complete lack of pride or interest in his daughter's achievement made Zach's jaw clench. "Sir, this is more than just a regular visit. The semifinalists' families will be part of a special episode, and it would be a shame if Kezia were the only one whose loved ones aren't present. Your being there would mean a great deal to her."

Dr. Byaruhanga's voice was even more clipped. "Mr. Falconer, I won't be intimidated or emotionally blackmailed into parading my family on a television show. Being part of this spectacle was Kezia's choice. Not ours."

The clear message hung between them—Kezia's professional choices were beneath her family's dignity.

But even if he didn't think much of her career, didn't this man even care about her feelings? Swallowing his anger, Zach tried one final time. "Could you at least record a video message for her? Or allow me to pass along some verbal encouragement?"

"We'll consider it. If that's all, Mr. Falconer, I have other business to attend to. Goodbye."

The line went dead. No greeting for Kezia. No inquiry about how she was doing.

Zach stared at the phone in his hand. Kezia's reluctance to talk about her family in the songwriting challenge now made horrible sense. And if this is how her father spoke to a stranger...

That poor woman.

He saw her face again—tight with distress, jaw clenched, eyes swimming in tears—when he'd pushed her to share about how her family didn't support her music.

A flicker of shame curled low in his gut.

He hadn't just asked her to open a wound. He'd demanded it. And now he'd heard, firsthand, the voice that helped create that wound.

A knock at his door made him look up. Maya stood there, a frown on her face. "Any luck?"

He shook his head. "Nothing. He said he might send a video message for her, but I'm not holding my breath."

"I was afraid of that." She sighed. "So, should I look into the spa day option?"

"Not yet." Zach picked up Maya's tablet. "I want to try one more thing. What about the other person on her approved number list?"

Maya's expression brightened. "Yes! Her former roommate. I'll give you privacy for this call, too."

After she left, Zach stared at Claire's number, rehearsing how to explain the situation without betraying Kezia's dignity.

The dial tone went for a few seconds.

Then, "Hello?" The voice on the other end sounded out of breath.

"Am I speaking to Claire Wilson? This is Zach Falconer."

Claire gasped. "No way! Really? You're not pranking me, are you?" Her voice changed. "Wait, is everything okay with Kezia?"

"I'm not pranking you, and Kezia is fine. I just need to ask you a favor."

Trying his best to blur the details of Dr. Byaruhanga's attitude, Zach explained the Family Day situation, ending with, "I was hoping you might be able to come. Kezia's going to need someone in her corner that day."

Claire was silent for a moment. "They said no, didn't they?"

Zach fumbled for an answer, but Claire continued speaking. "Listen, I've known Kezia for over ten years. I was at UCL while she was at Guildhall. This is nothing new."

Zach's free hand clenched into a fist. "So, it's always been like this?"

"Pretty much," Claire said. "They've never shown up for her performances, even the important ones. Her final recital? Empty chairs where her family should have been. They don't even see how hard she works at this. And the irony is, she's a hundred percent Byaruhanga in her approach to her music. She puts in every single ounce of dedication and her full intellect, same as she would have done if she'd gone into medicine or law. She's so obsessive and anal about it all."

"I've noticed that," Zach said. "I've met her vocal steamer."

Claire laughed. "So you know what I'm talking about, then? She's invested everything into her career and is so crazy talented, and those people couldn't give a flying fig." Her voice hardened. "Of course I'll come for Family Day. What time do you need me?"

The tension in Zach's shoulders eased. "I'll get one of my colleagues to liaise with you about the details. Thanks. I'm sure your being there will mean a lot to her."

"She's been my best friend for years. I wouldn't let her face that alone."

A thought struck Zach. "You wouldn't be the best friend who... I mean, the one she..." His face heated, and he regretted the question before he even got it out.

"Wait, she told you about her best friend running off with Scott? No, that wasn't me."

Scott, huh? Zach filed the name away.

Claire said, "You actually care about her, don't you?"

"I care about all my contestants' wellbeing." His answer was a shade too quick.

"Mm. If you say so. Anyway, just send me the details. I'll be there. Wild horses couldn't keep me away."

Zach sat back in his chair, phone still in hand. Claire's promise echoed in his mind. *I wouldn't let her face that alone.*

Someone had to show up for Kezia. And while he couldn't be that person, at least now she wouldn't be alone in the spotlight, pretending it didn't hurt. Thank God Claire would come.

Chapter 55

KEZIA SAT AT THE piano, waiting for Zach to return from dealing with whatever production issue he was handling.

The sheet music for "All That I Give" lay spread out in front of her. She knew the song inside out, of course. Who didn't? It was a huge Whitney hit, after all. And nailing the big notes and all the vocal runs wasn't an issue, either.

But after weeks of Zach pushing her to connect emotionally with her performances, she was second-guessing whether she could sing it to his exacting standards.

The door opened and Zach strode back in. "Sorry to keep you waiting. That took longer than I expected."

He stared at her for a moment, his hand churning through his hair. Then he looked away. "Where were we?"

She gestured at the music. "I'm struggling with this. I know you think I can give it emotional depth, but I don't know." She broke off with a frustrated sigh. "When I wrote my own song, the emotion flowed naturally. It came from here." She laid a hand on her chest. "I'm just struggling to replicate that with someone else's song. It feels forced."

Zach considered her for a moment, a finger on his chin. "It's natural that it was easier to identify with your own story. You need to identify with the story in this song, even though someone else wrote it. Treat it like it's your own. Think about loving someone deeply. Visualize it, feel it, and let those emotions come through your voice."

She hesitated, then looked up at him. "I'm still not sure. Could you...would you show me what you mean? How you'd interpret it?"

He stared at her, something flickering across his face. He began to shake his head, then said, "Okay. I'll try."

He moved to the piano.

Kezia rose to give him space, walking around so she could watch him.

His fingers hovered above the keys for a moment before beginning the gentle introduction.

"Standing at the edge of everything I know..." His voice caressed each word as his fingers moved across the keys. There was a rawness to his delivery that she hadn't heard from him before.

"Walls around my heart start to crumble so slow..."

Her skin prickled with goosebumps.

His voice. Richer than she remembered from his recordings. More textured. Controlled in the way only a seasoned vocalist could manage—restrained, but laced with unfiltered emotion. His phrasing was masterful, effortless in a way that told her he'd lived through the truth of every line. She caught herself analyzing the placement, the breath control, the husky edge that crept in when he softened a word. But none of it explained the ache blooming in her chest. He wasn't just interpreting the lyrics. He was inhabiting them.

His gaze, initially focused on the keys, gradually lifted until he was looking directly at her.

"I've kept my distance, played it safe for so long. But I'm fighting a losing battle, and the truth is all over my face."

He closed his eyes as he reached the chorus, his voice infused with yearning. "All that I give is all that I am. Nothing held back, nothing left to defend. If loving you means risking everything, then that's the chance I am willing to take."

Kezia couldn't look away. This wasn't the visionary business executive who created *Starbound* or the demanding mentor. He was simply a man, laying his soul bare through the music.

"Because without you, what would remain? Just echoes of a life half-lived in vain." His fingers gentled their touch on the keys as his voice softened. "All that I give is all that I am. Is that enough for you to understand?"

The final notes lingered in the air as Zach opened his eyes again, face flushed, gaze boring into hers. Neither of them moved as the sound faded.

His gaze remained locked with hers. "Haven't you ever loved anyone like this? So much that you'd give everything up? No matter what it cost?"

She swallowed. "Not yet."

"Not even Scott?"

Her heart skidded. How did he know her ex-boyfriend's name?

She shook her head. "No. Not like that."

An unbidden thought formed. What would it be like to be the woman Zach Falconer loved with such intensity?

Kezia's heart hammered against her ribs as she watched emotions flicker across Zach's face. Emotions she couldn't quite name but felt echoing in her own chest.

Then, as if a switch had been flipped, his expression shuttered.

He broke eye contact first, setting her free to breathe again. But the damage was done. Her pulse had quickened, her guard had slipped, and the seal on something private and unspoken had come undone.

"That's the emotional truth I want you to find." His tone had shifted, deliberately professional again. "I'm not saying you should fake it. Try to visualize it. To imagine it. And then draw on that as you sing. I'll accompany you."

As he started to play, Kezia closed her eyes, attempting to visualize the kind of love the song spoke of, and that Zach sang of.

The image that crystallized in her mind, to her surprise, was...him. The way he'd just sung, the raw emotion in his voice, the intensity in his eyes.

She began to sing, and the performance flowed from somewhere genuine.

When she finished, she opened her eyes to find his gaze on her face.

He looked away, fidgeting with the sheet music. "Keep working on it. I think you're well on your way."

"Thanks."

Rising from the piano bench, he threw her a quick glance. "I have another appointment. One of the producers will be in touch about our next session. We need to think about 'Patterns in Motion.' I think that's the song that'll need more work to get performance ready."

She nodded. But after he left, she felt no inclination to go through the groovy neo-soul song he'd chosen to demonstrate her musical versatility.

The resonance of his voice echoed in the back of her mind. The room felt charged, as if something had passed between them.

She wanted to try "All That I Give" again.

She launched into it again, the image of Zach lingering in her mind. Her strong-willed, enigmatic mentor whose passion for music wouldn't let her give anything less than her best. A man who could make a simple song demonstration feel like a declaration of love.

She kept on singing.

Chapter 56

"PLACES, EVERYONE!" STEVE, THE senior producer, herded the four semifinalists toward center stage. "Just stand naturally. Brianna, can you move slightly to your left? Perfect."

Kezia stepped into place between Sandra and Connor, aware of the cameras stationed at calculated angles to catch every flicker of emotion. Another "quick production meeting" that would probably turn into an hour of filming reaction shots.

Olivia Chang strode onto the stage in a striking emerald dress, her smile bright enough to rival the studio lights. "Semifinalists, you've been working incredibly hard. Today, we have a special surprise for you!"

Kezia suppressed a groan. She'd learned to be wary of reality TV surprises.

"Your loved ones are here to spend the day with you!"

As Brianna squealed and Sandra gasped, Kezia could only stare at Olivia, her heart thundering against her ribs as hope flared.

But when it came to her family, hope always heralded pain, like the fraction of a second between when you stubbed your toe and the agony hit.

She crushed the flicker of hope immediately. Of course they weren't here. Her parents had never come to any of her performances, not even her final recital at Guildhall. Their support dried up the moment her music turned into a career. It was one thing to brag to their friends about their high school daughter, a straight-A student who was also a musical prodigy. Quite a different thing when that same daughter wanted to be a professional musician.

The double doors at the back of the stage swung open.

Brianna's squeal of delight pierced the air as her parents rushed forward. "Mummy! Daddy!"

Sandra's mother appeared with Sandra's younger sister, both of them wrapping the teenager in fierce hugs. Connor's wife approached more sedately, their baby son balanced on her hip, but Connor's face transformed at the sight of them.

Kezia kept her smile firmly in place as she scanned the doorway, feeling increasingly exposed. The cameras would be on all of them, capturing every reaction.

Then, through the open doors, Claire appeared—beaming, radiant, like sunlight breaking through storm clouds—as she spotted Kezia.

Her friend's dear face was the most beautiful thing she'd ever seen.

They collided in a tight hug, Claire's familiar perfume washing over her.

"Surprise!" Claire whispered against her ear.

Kezia hugged her friend tighter, joy mixing with the ache of what was missing. But that didn't matter right now. Claire was here.

"What is this? How did you—" Kezia began.

But before Claire could answer, Mark, the spiky-haired producer with horn-rimmed glasses, appeared at their side. "Lovely reunion shots, ladies. Now, if you'll follow me, we've arranged a private space for you to catch up. If you don't mind, please hold off on your conversation until you're settled."

Kezia held back an eye roll. Of course, the cameras wanted to capture all of this.

Mark led them through the main house to the library, its oak-paneled walls lined with leather-bound books. The camera crew was already set up and waiting.

He turned to Kezia and Claire. "You can sit in those armchairs over there and just have a chat. Please act naturally as you catch up, just having a normal conversation. You'll have thirty minutes with cameras, then private time to yourselves for the rest of the day."

As they settled into their chairs, Claire leaned close to whisper, "How exactly does one 'act natural' with three cameras pointed at you?"

Kezia stifled a laugh. "You get used to it. Sort of."

"And...action!" Mark called.

Claire launched into an animated description of her morning, doing a surprisingly good job of being natural. "They sent a car for me and everything. The production team has been so lovely about arranging everything."

"I still can't believe you're actually here," Kezia said.

Mark gestured encouragingly toward Claire. "Talk about watching Kezia on the show. Act as if we're not here and just speak to her."

"She's been absolutely amazing," Claire began, then she caught herself. "Sorry, I mean you've been absolutely amazing, Kezia. That song you wrote? I cried. And things have really changed since those early harsh critiques, haven't they?"

"Thanks," Kezia said. "The mentoring process has helped me grow as an artist."

They continued making small talk with occasional guiding prompts by the producer.

Finally, Mark signaled the crew. "That's great. I think we have enough. We'll leave you two to catch up privately now."

As soon as the door closed behind them, Claire's posture relaxed completely. "How on earth do you live like this? Now that they're gone, I want to know everything they're not showing on TV."

Kezia laughed, feeling the tension release from her own shoulders. At last, she could just be herself. With her best friend and no cameras and no twenty-minute countdown until their conversation had to end.

Claire tucked her feet underneath herself. "But first, tell me if you've sorted out what you're going to do about accommodation when this is over. I know you were worried about that."

Kezia smiled. Trust Claire to cut straight to the practical concerns. "Actually, making it this far into the competition will help a lot. The semifinal bonus is very generous. Even if I don't make it to the finals, it's enough of a cushion to find something. But I might need to crash with someone for a few weeks while I look."

"Our spare room's yours if you need it." Claire's offer was immediate. "Tom's fully on board. Though he might object if you practice your scales at six in the morning like you used to."

"I've reformed. Mostly." Kezia grinned. "How is married life?"

They caught up on mutual friends and news from the outside world, the conversation flowing easily between them. It felt wonderfully normal after weeks in the *Starbound* bubble. Although she noticed Claire didn't ask about her family.

Claire glanced at the door, as though expecting a camera crew to burst through, then turned back to Kezia, her expression shifting to something more playful. "So...what's it really like working with Zach Falconer? I want all the dirty details."

Kezia's face warmed. "There are no dirty details. He's intense. Demanding. But also..." She struggled to find the right words. "There's more to him than what comes across on camera."

A lot more.

Claire's eyes sparkled. "That doesn't sound like the 'insufferable nitpicker' you described after he saved you. But I must say, he seems—dare I say it?—different with you lately."

Kezia tried to keep her tone light. "Maybe he's still insufferable. Just...in a more nuanced way."

Claire tilted her head, clearly unconvinced. "Hmm. Because from where I'm sitting, it looks an awful lot like he's rooting for you. Like he sees you."

The words hit a little too close. Kezia looked away, pretending to straighten the napkin on her lap. "He's my mentor. That's his job."

"Right," Claire said, drawing the word out just long enough to make her skepticism obvious. "Mentor. Got it."

"We've reached a professional understanding."

"If you say so." Claire watched her face carefully. "Well, he sounded nice enough on the phone when—" She snapped her mouth shut.

Kezia's head jerked up. "You talked to him? When?"

"Oh, you know, when the production team called to arrange everything." Claire waved a hand dismissively. "He just happened to be there. Anyway, tell me more about this song you're working on for the semifinal."

Kezia let her friend change the subject, but Claire's slip nagged at her. Zach was involved in arranging Claire's visit? She would have thought he was too senior an executive to handle things like that.

The afternoon passed too quickly, lunch and then high tea going by in a blur of delicious food and the healing laughter and comfort that only a long chat with a dear friend could bring.

But all too soon, a production assistant appeared to remind them that Claire needed to leave.

"Already?" Kezia glanced at her watch. Where had the time gone?

Claire stood, gathering her handbag. "If it's anything like how I came, they're sending me back to London in one of their fancy cars. Very posh." She wrapped Kezia in another tight hug. "I'm praying for you. And rooting for you, too. I'm so proud of what you're doing here."

"Having you here today means more than you know," Kezia whispered back.

Claire pulled away, holding Kezia at arm's length. "Show them all what you can do. You've got this."

Kezia watched her friend walk away, feeling both refreshed and oddly unsettled. The production team had asked Claire to come. But she couldn't have been the first person they called. Not when the other contestants' family members were here.

They must have called her parents first. And, when they couldn't—or wouldn't—come, they'd asked Claire.

The ache was a physical thing clawing into her heart. She shouldn't be surprised, though. Even if by some miracle they wanted to be part of anything music-related she was doing, her parents would recoil at being filmed on a reality show.

And they might have just been busy. They had packed schedules, after all, especially with Salome's engagement.

Claire's visit had been exactly what she needed—a reminder of who she was beyond the competition, beyond her family's disapproval. For that, she could be very grateful. With how alone she'd felt lately, it meant the world to have this warming slice of friendship to hang onto throughout whatever time she had left on this show.

But as she headed to the contestant quarters in the growing dusk, Claire's interest in Zach kept replaying in her mind. Considering how eager her friend had been in digging for details about him, it was odd that she couldn't change the subject fast enough after mentioning she'd actually spoken with him. What was that about?

She walked in silence, hugging her arms around herself against the growing chill. Claire's visit had filled her with light, but it had also cracked open a door she wasn't sure she was ready to walk through.

Behind that door was Zach Falconer. Brilliant. Demanding. Unreadable. One moment a fortress of control, the next...singing a love song like the lyrics were carved into his soul. The soulful intensity. The contradictions. The maddening, whiplash-inducing complexity of it all.

His complete and utter...Zachness.

How was she supposed to make sense of a man like that?

Chapter 57

ZACH SLIPPED INTO THE production monitoring area, nodding to the crew members who glanced his way. Banks of monitors filled the space, each screen showing a different angle of Family Day unfolding across the Starbound Campus.

Dr. Elise Wilson, the Contestant Welfare Coordinator, sat at one of the monitoring stations, making notes as she reviewed the footage of semifinalists spending time with their loved ones.

Zach settled into the chair beside her. "Just following up on our conversation about contestant mental health," he said. "I know the isolation is intensifying as we get closer to the finale. I want to make sure we're on top of it."

"Family Day was well timed," she said, settling her tortoiseshell spectacles more firmly on her nose. "And we're implementing increased phone contact starting next week."

Zach made himself scan each monitor methodically, resisting the pull toward one in particular. There was Sandra with her mother and sister in the conservatory, the teenager looking animated. Brianna and her parents occupied one of the smaller reception rooms. Connor sat with his baby son on his lap in a cozy alcove, looking more re-laxed than Zach had seen him in weeks.

Only after this careful review did Zach allow himself to look at the screen showing Kezia and Claire in the library. His gaze settled on Kezia's face as she listened to what Claire was saying. She needed this, being able to spend time with someone who knew her and cared for her, with-out having to worry about being judged, criticized, or misunderstood.

All things *he'd* done to her, too. He winced at the thought.

He prayed this visit with Claire would ease the feelings of isolation Kezia had told him about.

Dr. Wilson's clinical tone broke into his thoughts. "We've briefed the families on sending care packages, though internet access will remain restricted, of course."

Zach nodded his approval. Would Claire be sending care packages, too? That was a lot more than she'd signed on for when he'd called her to step in and visit Kezia today.

He could follow up, make sure Claire understood how much her support meant to Kezia...

No. He caught himself, tightening his grip on the arm of his chair. He shouldn't pester Claire. Whatever Dr. Wilson said would have to be enough. And, as Kezia's best friend, Claire would understand.

"The child psychologist reports Sandra is adjusting well," Dr. Wilson continued, drawing his attention back to the monitors. "She's actually showing better resilience than some of our older contestants."

Right. There were other contestants who needed his concern, too. Zach tore his gaze away from the Kezia monitor. "How's Brianna handling the pressure?"

Dr. Wilson consulted her notes. "Some anxiety about the semifinals, but her support system is solid." She added, "Contestants often experience an emotional dip after these visits. We'll be monitoring everyone closely."

Maya appeared beside them, tablet in hand. "All the family visits are running smoothly. We've arranged lunch in different locations to give everyone privacy."

"Good." Zach forced himself to focus on the logistics. "Any issues getting everyone here? Accommodations working out?"

"Everything's going according to plan." Maya glanced at her tablet. "Only Connor and Sandra's families need overnight accommodation, which we've booked at Fodder-wick Lodge down the road. The other guests will be driven home."

Finally, Zach allowed himself to ask what he really wanted to know. "And Kezia? Her situation was a bit different."

"It looks like Claire's providing excellent support," Maya said. "They're not miked up, of course, but they've been talking non-stop for hours."

He hesitated, then made himself ask. "Any last-minute word from the Byaruhangas? Will they be sending that video message?"

Maya shook her head. "Nothing. I followed up yesterday, but they declined."

Zach nodded, maintaining his professional demeanor despite his disappointment. What kind of people were these? They couldn't even spare five minutes to record a simple video message to let Kezia know they cared?

His gaze drifted back to Kezia and Claire, still deep in conversation. At least he'd been able to provide this connection for her. He prayed it would be some consolation.

He forced his attention to the other monitors. "Make sure we document any signs of stress in all contestants over the next few days," he told Dr. Wilson. "If you need me to authorize extra counseling support or anything like that, just let me know." They'd make room in the budget somehow.

"Of course." Dr. Wilson made another note. "We've scheduled extra check-ins with everyone after their families leave."

Zach stood, gathering the papers he hadn't actually looked at. "Good. Keep me updated."

His gaze was drawn one more time to Kezia's monitor. She laughed at something Claire had said, her face transformed by genuine joy.

The memory of yesterday's rehearsal flashed through his mind, the way she'd looked at him as he performed "All That I Give," the charged silence after he'd finished.

He'd let himself get carried away, the lyrics striking too close to home, the song's emotion sweeping him into dangerous territory. What had he been thinking agreeing to sing that song, with *those* words, to *her*? That couldn't happen again.

"Zach?" Maya held out a scheduling update that needed his signature.

"Right." He took the paper, grateful for the distraction. There were dozens of production details requiring his attention.

The semifinals were less than two weeks away. He had no business dwelling on one contestant's smile.

Chapter 58

ZACH GATHERED HIS COAT and the stack of sponsorship proposals he needed to review. He'd look them over at the cottage tonight. He'd been staring at contract negotiations about international franchising all afternoon and couldn't face another hour in his office.

The day had been a marathon, Family Day's emotional weight followed by hours of calls with a major American network interested in franchising the show. They were being squirrely about the commitment to artist development that made the *Starbound* format unique. He wasn't ready to sign over the franchise unless they agreed to include vocal health experts and training programs. At least the deals with Denmark and Australia were almost ready to sign.

As he crossed the grounds toward his cottage, a sound caught his attention. Singing coming from the rehearsal complex—Kezia's voice, singing "All That I Give." Or, rather, repeating the same line over and over.

He should keep walking. But instead, his feet carried him up the steps and into the building. She worked through the same phrase again and again, making minute adjustments each time.

He stood in the doorway, watching her at the piano. Her focus was absolute, as though her whole world hinged on that single sequence of notes.

When she finally stopped to grab a sip of water, he spoke. "You've sung that same line seventeen times. I counted."

She startled slightly, her gaze flying to his face, then straightened her posture. "I just want to get it right."

"It was right the first time. Technically, anyway." He entered the room fully, closing the door behind him.

She shifted her weight on the piano bench. "I need to be better than technically right."

Zach stepped closer. There were a thousand reasons to turn back. None outweighed his need to know she was okay.

"How was Family Day?" he asked, shifting his stack of folders to his other hand.

"It was fine. Although my best friend came instead of my family." Her voice took on a carefully measured tone. "I know it looks unusual, but they're busy people. My father's a surgeon, my mother has her charity work. My sister's working hundred-hour weeks as a surgical resident and they've also got a family wedding to plan."

"Kezia." Each word of her rationalizing their absence made his heart ache. "You don't have to explain why they didn't come."

She looked downward. "I've always had to explain."

"Not to me."

"You... You knew they weren't coming, didn't you?" She lifted her gaze to his face. "Claire mentioned you called her. It was because you knew my family wouldn't be here."

Zach hesitated, then simply said, "Yes." No need to tell her about his conversation with her father, to add that wound to the others.

"You know, the real surprise would have been if they did come." Her eyes glistened even as she attempted a chuckle. "I've been doing this on my own since I went to Guildhall. My father would have agreed with your assessment of me, you know. He thinks session singers are a dime a dozen, too."

The words knifed Zach's conscience. His own dismissive critique echoed her father's judgment, reinforcing the very wounds he was now desperate to heal. How many times had she heard that message? That her extraordinary gift wasn't enough? That she had to prove herself worthy of approval?

"You know what the worst part is?" Her hand went up, rubbing the back of her neck. "I still think if I win this thing, if I get that contract, if I show up on the charts...then they'll finally see I made the right choice."

Zach spoke gently. "And if they don't?"

She frowned. "What do you mean?"

"What if you win *Starbound*, get the contract, top the charts, and they still think you made the wrong choice?"

"I..." she began, then stopped, blinking quickly, her lips pressed tightly together.

"Kezia, I've worked with artists who've won Grammys and still couldn't please their families." He held her gaze, looking straight into her beautiful, pain-filled eyes. "Some people, even the ones who should love us most, will never give us what we're looking for from them."

"So, what am I doing all this for?" Her voice cracked.

"That's what you need to figure out." Zach moved closer. "Because if you're performing to earn your father's approval, I guarantee you'll never feel like you've succeeded. No matter how perfect your technique is or how many awards you win."

Tears welled in her eyes, but she blinked them back. "What if I don't know how to do it for any other reason?" she whispered.

He fought the urge to reach for her, to stroke her cheek. "Then that's what we need to work on. Not your voice. We both know that's extraordinary. But finding your reason. Your authentic *why*."

He'd already spoken enough, but with all the harsh, unthinking things he'd said to her over the past weeks, he had to do something to mend the wound his words had caused. "Your father and I were both wrong. You're not a dime-a-dozen. You're one in a million."

"Wow." A tear escaped despite her efforts to hold it back. "You're making me cry."

Good. It was reckless and completely unwise, but he wanted to make her feel something.

"Don't ever question how outstanding you are," he said. "The whole of Britain has seen what you can do now."

Another tear followed that first one, and his fingers itched to wipe it away.

Instead, he tried to do it with his words. "Your gift wasn't given to you so you could prove something to people who might never see its value. It was given to you to connect—with yourself, with your audience, with the music. That's the part no one can take away from you."

She met his gaze, tears still shining in her eyes. "Do you really believe that?"

He did. Too much, probably. He wanted to reach for her—just a brush of his knuckles against her cheek. But kept his hands at his sides.

"I believe in *you*," he said simply.

She smiled then, tears making her eyes luminous, a real smile that transformed her whole face.

His heart sang.

He'd crossed a line with those words. With this entire conversation. This wasn't mentor-to-mentee guidance. That was many freeway exits ago. He'd blown past the last off-ramp, tossed his GPS out the window, and was careening straight ahead with no plan.

There was no question anymore. He had fallen for this woman. Face-planted hard. And he had no idea how to protect her from what that meant.

Chapter 59

THE MORNING AFTER FAMILY Day, Kezia sat in her usual back-row seat at Grace Community Church, her Bible open in her lap, though her thoughts were a million miles from the weekly announcements.

Last night's conversation with Zach kept replaying in her mind. The way he'd found her in the rehearsal room. How he'd known about her family not coming and done something about it. His words still echoed in her thoughts in the gentle tone he'd used.

Some people, even the ones who should love us most, will never give us what we're looking for from them.

Kezia scanned the congregation, unable to stop herself from searching him out. She'd spotted Ezra and his wife sitting near the front when she'd arrived, but there was still no sign of Zach. Part of her had expected—maybe even hoped—to see him here today. Another part was relieved he wasn't.

Critical, demanding, suffer-no-fools Zach, she could handle. She'd dealt with exacting musical directors her entire career. But tender, supportive Zach who saw into her core and knew exactly what to say to soothe her heart and brush away her shame? That Zach terrified her.

Your gift wasn't given to you so you could prove something to people who might never see its value.

It was as if he'd reached inside her and put gentle fingers directly on the bruise she'd been carrying for years. The bruise she pretended didn't hurt anymore.

What would it mean to stop striving for her parents' validation, for approval that might never come? To accept that she didn't need to prove her choices to them? The very idea felt foreign, almost rebellious.

The congregation rose for the final hymn, startling Kezia from her thoughts.

As the benediction ended, she gathered her things quickly. Her Sunday routine since joining *Starbound* never varied. Arrive just as the service began, sit in the back, and slip out before anyone could engage her in conversation. It kept church as a sanctuary, free from the pressures of the show.

She was nearly at the door when a voice called out, "Kezia? Kezia! Wait a moment, please."

Turning, she found herself face to face with a petite, slender woman with dark hair and warm eyes, her flawless skin a shade darker than Kezia's.

No way. It was Morgan—the chart-topping artist married to Ezra Falconer.

"I'm Martha, Zach's sister-in-law," she said, extending her hand as she introduced herself by her real name.

As if Kezia didn't know exactly who she was.

"You worked with my husband when you wrote your song."

"Hi! It's lovely to meet you." She fought to keep the fan-girl grin from escaping. Because if it did, so would the squeal.

Martha's smile was genuine. "I've been watching the show since the first episode. Your performances have been stunning. That song you wrote moved me to tears."

"Wow, you have no idea what that means." Kezia pressed a hand to her heart. "Ezra was incredibly helpful during the songwriting process."

"He mentioned how impressive your work ethic is," Martha said. "I'm rooting for you, and not just because you're Zach's mentee."

The warmth in Martha's voice was so real, so different from the disinterest her family showed. Here was a bona fide chart-topping star complimenting her performances. It filled a space inside her she usually tried to ignore.

"Thank you so much."

Ezra approached, slipping an arm around his wife's shoulders. "I see you've met our *Starbound* favorite and arrested her before she could sneak out the door," he said with an easy smile. "Hello again, Kezia."

"Hello." Our favorite. The casual inclusion in their world sent a strange flutter through Kezia's chest.

"We were just saying how much we enjoyed Kezia's songwriting performance," Martha said.

"It was extraordinary," Ezra agreed. "Looking forward to seeing what you do in the semifinals."

"Will we see you in church next Sunday?" Martha asked.

"I expect so, all being well," she said. "I feel so refreshed and blessed when I come here."

"Wonderful," Martha said. "I know you're stuck on the campus during the show's run, or else I'd have totally asked you to grab a coffee afterward."

Kezia managed another smile and a polite goodbye before heading out to where the car waited to take her back to Glenmere Hall.

Her heart felt full and achy at the same time. The Falconers' warmth was intoxicating, along with their genuine interest in her music, and their lavish praise of her talent.

But she couldn't allow herself to get caught up in how good it felt. These weren't just any friendly church people. This was Zach's family.

And he wasn't just any guy. He was her mentor, the show's creator.

No matter how her heart leaned into their warmth, or melted under the tenderness Zach had shown, she had to remember who she was and what this was—a contestant on his show. Nothing more.

Even if the way he'd looked at her last night made her wish things could be different.

Chapter 60

HE LATE AFTERNOON SUN shone through the windows of Glenmere Hall's library, casting warm rectangles across the polished oak table where Kezia sat. This room, with its leather-bound books lining the walls and cozy reading alcove, had become one of her favorite spaces at the Starbound Campus. Ever since she'd spent Saturday here visiting with Claire.

And now she was going to have a meeting with Zach. Which should have started three minutes ago. Not that she'd been counting down the hours since last night. The man was taking up so much head space, it wasn't even funny. Every thought was Zach-flavored or Zach-related. His gentle words to her the evening after Family Day, his voice in her mind whenever she rehearsed "All That I Give," the memory of his gaze on her face... Good thing the cameras couldn't film inside her mind, or she'd be sunk.

But she needed to force her mind to focus on business, on the purpose of today's meeting. She flipped through the binder embossed with the *Starbound* logo that all semifinalists had received that morning: *Post-Competition Career Planning*. They certainly took all this stuff seriously, going far above and beyond any reality music show she'd heard of.

The door opened and Zach entered, a tablet under his arm, a camera operator and producer following.

Kezia sat up straighter, smoothing out her blouse.

"Sorry to keep you waiting," he said, settling into the chair across from her, a wave of his tangy fresh cologne teasing her senses. "My production meeting ran long, but I wanted to clear the decks so we can get through today's agenda uninterrupted."

"No problem." Kezia glanced at the camera, now positioned to capture their meeting.

Laura, the producer, moved to the side of the table. "We're just after about fifteen minutes of you two discussing the career planning materials, then we'll get out of your hair. As always, keep it natural, and don't worry about the camera."

Zach placed his tablet on the table between himself and Kezia. "Shall we get started? I know we've not even reached the semifinals, but it's not too early to think about what happens when the competition is over."

"That makes sense," Kezia said, opening the binder to the list of agents. She would not let herself be distracted by those blue eyes. But had his eyelashes always been that long?

"Our hope with *Starbound* is that everyone who participates can have a chance at a career in music, whether or not they win the show," Zach said.

Kezia believed that. And she was certain he was the driving force behind that focus. Unlike too many in this industry who would squeeze what they could out of artists, then drop them and move on to the next promising prospect. *Starbound* would look very different if someone like Ryan Sterling were calling all the shots.

"Have you had an agent before?" Zach asked.

"Yes." Kezia hesitated. How much should she say? Best to keep it positive. "He's the reason I built up a stable income with my session work. He was excellent at booking those jobs, and I'm grateful because I've been able to earn a living doing something I love. But we had different visions for my career. We recorded a demo EP three years ago that didn't go anywhere and decided it was best to part ways because I really wanted to break through as a solo artist."

Zach nodded. "That happens a lot. Some agents prefer keeping talented vocalists in the session world because it's steady income for everyone involved. Less risk than developing a solo artist."

"I can understand that. I mean, why throw away a steady gig for a pipe dream?"

"This time will be different," Zach said. "For your next agent, you want someone who sees your full potential and will invest in building your career for the long term. Which is why we're having this meeting."

He pointed at her binder. "We've compiled a list of pre-vetted agents whom we recommend for all our semifinal-ists. Our goal is to connect you with someone who will help you build on what you've accomplished here and carve out a sustainable career for yourself."

Kezia looked at the list of names and agencies while Zach continued speaking.

"There are other practical things to think about once the show's run is over."

For the next fifteen minutes, the conversation flowed naturally as Zach advised her on what she should look for in an agent. As the cameras rolled, they talked about post-show planning and building a career beyond session work.

He met her gaze with a smile. "Of course, I hope you'll win and all of this will be moot, but it's smart to at least think about it."

Laura spoke up. "I think we've got what we need. Thanks, you two. Carry on as you need to, but we're off to film Sandra's session now."

"Of course. See you soon," Zach said.

The camera operator packed up efficiently, and within moments, Kezia and Zach were alone in the library, the heavy door closing behind the production team with a soft click.

Her shoulders relaxed as he set down his tablet.

"Tea?" he asked, moving to the window where a service had been set up on a side table. "The cameras are gone now, so we can be more comfortable."

"Yes, please." She watched as he prepared two cups. "Milk, no sugar."

No cameras. Just the two of them, a wood fire, and a cozy library. It felt...suspiciously like a date.

Her cheeks warmed as he handed her the cup of tea and collected his tablet. She needed to get a grip and not be silly. This was still a mentoring session, cameras or not.

"Let's move to that alcove," he said, gesturing toward the cozy reading nook by the bay window. "It's more comfortable for a proper conversation."

With suggestions like that, he wasn't helping her quest to keep her mind on mentoring. "Okay," she said, heading toward the pair of wingback chairs bathed in the warm glow of late afternoon sunlight.

Zach settled into his chair and tapped his tablet screen. "Your resume is quite eclectic. I'm curious to know how you've pieced together your career so far. I know it's been session work primarily, but I see a lot more."

"It's a patchwork," Kezia said, gripping the warm cup to still the tingling in her fingers. "Session work is my bread and butter, but I also do regular zero-hours contract work for a production music company."

"Production music?"

"Yes. Library music, advertising jingles, corporate videos. And hold music."

"Hold music?" His eyebrows rose.

"My voice is what a lot of people hear during that forty-five-minute wait to make a claim with their insurance company." She laughed. "I've probably been heard by more people than many chart-toppers, between assurances of how their call is important and how they're number fifty-three in the queue."

Zach chuckled. "That's quite a thought. Your voice as the soundtrack to customer service frustration across Britain."

"It pays the bills, so I can't grumble too much." She sipped her tea. It was perfect. "I also pick up wedding and corporate gigs when they come along. Good money, but unpredictable."

"And before that? Your file mentioned something about Disneyland Paris?"

She groaned. "You've seen that? Yes, I did a six-month stint there after university. Then a cruise ship, then a summer at Butlins." She shook her head. "I've paid my dues."

"We all start somewhere."

"Where did you start?"

His eyes widened, as though he hadn't expected her to ask about him. "Making music with my brothers. We were blessed to build a fan base very early on. The longer I've been in the industry, the more I realize what unicorns we were." He set his cup on the wide windowsill. "But that came with its own challenges."

She tucked her feet under her. "Like what?"

"Remaining grounded in our church community when success came. Having the spotlight on us while trying to live out our faith authentically." He hesitated. "And having some of our worst tragedies play out in the media."

"I've read some things."

His younger brother Levi's scandal about fathering a child out of wedlock sent shockwaves across the Christian community. And, more recently, Ezra had been involved in another controversy, thankfully cleared up.

Zach made a face. "I won't ask what you've read. But you know what I mean. My family and church support were everything to me growing up and still are. That's why I'm extra impressed with what you've accomplished without that kind of foundation."

He held her gaze for a moment, his smile making her insides flutter.

"Do you ever wonder," she asked after a moment, "if you would have chosen music if you hadn't grown up in that environment? If it hadn't been, well, the family business?"

"No one's ever asked me that, so I have to think for a minute." He stared up in the air, a finger on his chin.

"I'd like to say yes," he said finally. "Music has always been essential to me—an outlet, something that comes as easily as breathing. But would I have had the courage to pursue it as a career without that safety net? That built-in support system? That early success? Could I have pushed on despite the kind of opposition and discouragement you've faced?" He shook his head slightly. "I honestly don't know."

His words threw her. "That's not the answer I was expecting."

"Does it...make you think any less of me?" His face was suddenly serious.

The vulnerability of his question, the almost hesitant way he asked it, hit her square in the chest. The man who'd built an empire was asking if she respected him?

She answered from her heart. "You may have been blessed with early success and a somewhat easier road. But look at what you're doing with it." She gestured around her. "You've built all this. You're paving the way for other artists to have a shot they might never have had. No, I don't think less of you because you haven't had to claw your way from paycheck to paycheck and lend your voice to hold music and sing at weddings where you're only background noise."

"That means a lot. Thank you." That smile again, making her tummy flutter like a swarm of butterflies.

"What about you?" he asked. "What gave you the grit to choose and stay on this path, especially without family support?"

"I couldn't imagine doing anything else." It was that simple. "There was never a Plan B. Even when it would have been easier to give in and follow my father's plans for me."

He studied her for a moment. "That takes remarkable courage."

"Or remarkable stubbornness," she said with a laugh. "Sometimes I can't tell which is which."

His smile warmed her, made her bold enough to say, "Can I ask you something I've been wondering about?"

"Of course."

"Why didn't you ever record a solo album? Both of your brothers have. And your voice is...well, it's extraordinary. I know you sing most of the Falconer Brothers' lead vocals."

"Thank you. I started one, actually. About six years ago."

"What happened?"

A shadow crossed his face, and she wondered whether she'd made a mistake in asking.

"A woman happened. I was twenty-five and dumb. Mistook charisma for character." He attempted a lighthearted tone that didn't quite land. "Let's just say when things ended with Verity, so did my enthusiasm for baring my soul through music."

"Wait—no way." She was too stunned to be diplomatic. "Verity? You dated Verity James?"

His mouth twisted. "One and the same. You didn't know about us? It was all over the tabloids. Just how she liked it."

"I honestly didn't realize that. You just seem so...so different." She would never have thought Zach would have anything in common with the entitled, lazy, unprofessional woman she'd met at the studio. And then she remembered who she was talking to, and how she might be overstepping.

She waved her hands. "I'm sorry. I didn't mean to pry."

"It's ancient history now." He stood, taking their cups back to the tea table. But the flush in his cheeks told her it wasn't. "In any case, perhaps I was better suited to the production side of things anyway. I'm not interested in being a recording artist anymore, unless it's with my brothers."

That surprised her. Not interested? After the way he'd sung "All That I Give" and the way it had made her feel?

Either he was lying to himself, or he'd buried that part of him so deeply he'd forgotten it was still there.

He passed her a second cup of tea and settled back into his chair.

"Careful," she said, accepting it with a smile. "If you keep bringing me perfect tea in cozy libraries, I might start thinking this is your standard mentoring package."

"Only for contestants who ask questions that make me rethink my entire life path," he said with a chuckle. "And I thought I was supposed to be the mentor here."

"Maybe we're mentoring each other." Her own words, blurted out before she had a chance to think, shocked her. But not as much as the way his expression changed, something unguarded flickering in his eyes before he looked away.

Again, she worried she'd crossed a line. Said too much.

Then he chuckled. "Well, I could probably use some mentoring. Though I'm not used to it. Firstborn guinea pig and family trailblazer, that's me."

She tilted her head, smiling. "I'm a firstborn too. Of three girls. But less guinea pig, more cautionary tale."

His smile faded into something gentler. "You're the one who kept going anyway. That's a different kind of legacy."

The warmth of his words settled around her like a blanket. She hadn't expected understanding, affirmation, encouragement. Not like that. And certainly not from him.

They talked about his experience as the nominal head of an old English family that could trace its roots back to the Tudor Era and the English Reformation, while she was a second-generation African immigrant.

Their conversation flowed into the faith that shaped them. His, always vibrant and deeply personal, nurtured by his family and lived out through community, scripture, and quiet conviction. Hers forged in a stricter church, where starched collars and polished shoes seemed to matter more than authenticity, until she learned—slowly, painfully— that God cared more about the state of her heart than the crease in her Sunday dress. Their journeys looked nothing alike, yet they met on the same foundation of grace.

And then back to music, as the shadows lengthened across the library floor and the embers of the fire glowed. She told him about the Ugandan folk music that her grandmother had once sung to her and the classical training that was her technical foundation, and they discussed the contemporary artists who inspired them both.

They discovered a shared appreciation for Nina Simone's raw authenticity and Stevie Wonder's technical brilliance.

Kezia would never have imagined how easy he was to talk to, how much they had in common despite coming from different worlds. Beneath the authority, the name, the clout of an industry powerhouse, Zach was far more thoughtful and layered than she'd expected. More humble. And even...vulnerable? A man used to control, command, and scrutiny...yet here he was, offering her glimpses of something unguarded.

The library door swung open abruptly, and Ryan Sterling appeared.

A smile spread across his face, but something about it set her on edge.

"Oh, my, I didn't expect to find anyone here," Ryan said, his gaze moving between them. "Look at you still having a *tête-à-tête* in the dusk. The other mentor sessions ended hours ago."

"We were just wrapping up," Zach said.

Ryan's gaze lingered a moment too long on their tea cups. "Don't let me interrupt. No doubt you had quite a lot to say about agent representation. There was certainly a lot of ground to cover with Brianna on that score."

Kezia stood, gathering her binder. "I should get going." She nodded to Ryan before turning back to Zach. "I've been working on a new song and I'd love to hear your feedback on it sometime."

"Sure. Let's run through it at tomorrow's rehearsal." He stood as well. "Anything I can do for you, Ryan? Did you need to use the library?"

She didn't catch Ryan's answer as she left. Despite that awkward interruption, she found herself smiling once she was in the corridor.

Talking with Zach had been wonderful. Inspiring. Just like talking to a friend. Who'd have thought spending time with him could feel like that?

For the first time since Lily had left, she didn't feel so alone here.

Chapter 61

ACH SAT AT HIS desk, spreadsheets in front of his eyes, but his mind on this morning's meeting with Kezia. What was supposed to be a half-hour career mentoring session had turned into something far more personal. He'd meant to talk shop. Instead, he'd spent hours in conversation that left him warmed, disarmed, and...more than a little undone.

Now, alone at his desk, trying to focus on the numbers from Sunday's Family Day episode, he could still picture the curve of her smile, the way sunlight had spilled across her face, the softness in her voice when she told him there had never been a Plan B.

He shook his head. He'd let things drift too far. He needed to put her out of his thoughts. Compartmentalize. Focus on work.

Like these ratings.

As the numbers came into focus, he couldn't hold back a smile and a quiet air punch. Viewership had spiked after the Family Day show, with especially strong engagement in key demographics. It had been a hit—not just for the semi-finalists' wellbeing, but with the audience, too. And streaming numbers were growing.

A knock at his door made him look up. Ryan Sterling stood in the doorway, casual stance belying a narrowing of his eyes. "Got a minute? Just saw the ratings. Impressive numbers."

Something in Ryan's tone set off warning bells. Or perhaps it was just the man himself. Ryan seeking him out was never good news.

"Come in," Zach said.

Ryan closed the door behind him, confirming Zach's suspicion that this wasn't just a friendly chat about viewing figures. Ryan didn't want to be overheard.

They discussed the statistics for a few moments before Ryan's real purpose emerged.

Sitting back and steepling his fingers, he said too casually, "Your girl Kezia is becoming quite popular. Her segments are getting the most social media engagement, even more than Sandra with her three million followers."

"She's not 'my girl,'" Zach said automatically, then silently kicked himself for falling into Ryan's trap.

Ryan's teeth flashed. "Interesting mentoring technique you've developed with her. Very...how shall I put it? Hands-on."

Zach's muscles tensed. He knew exactly what Ryan was implying. "Excuse me?"

"Come on, Zach. I've been in this industry long enough to recognize when there's something brewing between a mentor and contestant." Ryan's smile was all predator now. "It's quite entertaining, actually. Mr. Family Values himself breaking the most basic rule in the *Starbound* handbook."

"My relationship with Kezia is completely professional."

"For now, maybe." Ryan was not even bothering to hide how much he was enjoying Zach's discomfort. "But we both know where it's heading. Just interesting to see how your Christian principles seem to...flex...when it's your own interests at stake. Scandalous outfits for my contestants? Tsk, tsk. Absolutely not. Developing feelings for one of yours? Apparently that's different."

He leaned forward in his chair.

"Personal calls to her family, late night *tête-à-tête* chats...oops, pardon me. 'Career advice.'" He made air quotes with his fingers. "And I hear she's been attending your church every Sunday. How...wholesome."

Zach's jaw clenched. Everything Ryan mentioned had an innocent explanation, but together, they formed an incriminating pattern.

"I'm just looking out for the show, Zach." Ryan's concern was as phony as his smile. "Making sure your intentions aren't misunderstood."

The implicit threat hung in the air between them. Ryan tapped the ratings report on Zach's desk. "These numbers are too good to risk with a scandal. The viewers are loving the show."

"I appreciate your concern, but it's misplaced." Zach kept his voice carefully steady. "My focus is on developing her as an artist."

"Of course." Ryan's smirk widened. "That's exactly what everyone is saying...for now."

The casual reference to staff gossip cut Zach's knees out from under him. As Ryan no doubt knew it would.

"Just be careful," Ryan said, rising from his chair. "*Starbound* is still establishing its reputation. It would be a shame if its creator became known for...questionable ethics. Especially when his reputation depends on being squeaky clean. Not that I'm saying that, of course. I just want to put you on your guard."

He paused at the door. "I'm sure the Albion executives wouldn't want that kind of attention for their flagship show."

Ryan left, and Zach allowed his shoulders to slump. Every missile of Ryan's precision attack had landed.

Slimy as he was, he wasn't wrong. Zach's feelings for Kezia had crossed professional boundaries. If even Ryan could see through him, how transparent was he being?

What had he been thinking, letting himself get so close to Kezia? That late-night conversation in the rehearsal room, letting his emotions run wild while singing "All That I Give" to her, arranging Claire's visit, lingering for hours in the library...that created an opportunity for Ryan to walk in on them. He'd been indulging his growing feelings while telling himself he was just being a good mentor.

And now his self-indulgence could derail her career before it even began. He was the one who'd crossed boundaries, not her. She shouldn't suffer because he couldn't control his feelings.

This could reflect badly on *Starbound* too. Everything he'd built, the artist development focus he'd fought so hard to maintain, the high ethical standards—all of it could be undermined by whispers of scandal.

The bitter irony of it. Just when Kezia was beginning to trust him, when she'd finally opened up about her family's rejection, he would have to retreat behind professional formality. But there was no other ethical choice. He had to protect her career from any hint of impropriety, no matter how difficult or painful it might be for both of them.

Here he'd been worrying about her isolation, her family's rejection, arranging for Claire to visit, all while his own behavior was becoming the biggest threat to her wellbeing. One hint of scandal, one whisper of impropriety, and her extraordinary talent would be overshadowed by gossip about her relationship with her mentor.

He'd told her she didn't need to prove anything to people who might never value her gift. Yet his inability to maintain professional boundaries could force her to prove herself all over again, to defend her achievements against accusations of favoritism.

Or worse, have people suggesting she'd advanced in the competition for reasons other than her talent.

Zach's hand clenched into a fist. He would not have her integrity questioned. She deserved so much better than that.

He needed to squash any hint of his attraction to her, deny Ryan any further ammo, and do all he could to help her succeed.

He reached for the stack of papers Maya had left earlier. He would do his job and review the semifinal arrangements, coordinate with the performance coaches, and ensure every technical aspect of her semifinal showing was perfect.

Kezia would make it to the finals. And he would maintain enough distance to ensure no one would ever question how she got there.

She didn't need a man who loved her recklessly. She needed a mentor who would guard her future. Even if that meant killing the part of himself that wanted more.

Chapter 62

*K*EZIA HURRIED INTO THE Broadway Studio on Tuesday afternoon, her arrangement notes clutched to her chest. She couldn't wait to show Zach and Sam her idea for the key change in "All That I Give." The modulation would create exactly the kind of dramatic climax the song needed, something that would let her connect with the emotion they'd discussed.

Zach was already there, standing at the console with Sam. He glanced at her, then looked down at his phone.

"Perfect timing," Sam said. "We were just going over the semifinal arrangements. I've got a few ideas, but I'm more than happy to hear what you've got in mind. You're going to do some incredible things with this song."

Kezia smiled. "I hope so. Zach, I've been thinking about what we talked about," she said, moving toward him. "About balancing the emotional core of the song with all the vocal power. What if we modulated up for that final chorus?"

He crossed his arms, his gaze moving to a point over her left shoulder. "Mm hm."

Her hands sketched the musical pattern in the air. "I thought it would give us that lift we've been looking for, really emphasize the emotional progression of the song."

"The technical execution would be challenging," Zach said, speaking to Sam rather than looking at her. "Miss Blair will need to ensure her upper register doesn't become shrill in the new key."

Miss Blair? Since when did he call her that? And speak past her as though she wasn't in the room?

"I've rehearsed it on my own. I can keep it clean. Let me show you what I mean," she said, trying and failing to catch his gaze. "Sam, could we run through that section?"

"Of course." Sam motioned to the session pianist. "From the bridge? From F minor to A minor?"

Kezia sang the passage, demonstrating how the key change would lift the emotion of the final chorus. Even to her own ears, her voice soared perfectly into the modulation, her tone still resonant and perfectly controlled.

"Nice!" Sam's enthusiasm filled the room. "That works even better than I imagined. Zach?"

Zach didn't look up from his phone. "The transition needs work. Otherwise, it's adequate."

Adequate? After he'd called her one in a million just two nights ago?

"Is something wrong?" The words escaped before she could stop them.

"We're on a tight schedule." His gaze swept the area around her head, darting past her face. "Let's focus on the arrangement. Time is limited."

She sang the phrase again, almost defiantly perfect this time, not a single note out of place in the transition.

"Okay, the key change works," he said, checking his watch. "Let's go with it. Sam, I think it'll be straightforward from here."

As Zach gathered his papers, Kezia took a step toward him. "Before you go, I wanted to ask about our session this afternoon. You said I could show you the new song I've been working on."

Something flickered in his eyes before his expression went blank. "That session is canceled. You need to focus entirely on your semifinal preparation. You have a lot of work to do on choreography and stage blocking. For 'Patterns in Motion' especially, but this song could also use some more rehearsal. I expect you to spend most of today and tomorrow working on that."

"But I thought—"

"You can't afford to get distracted by side projects," he said, cutting her off, as he headed toward the door. "The competition is very tight, and don't forget, it's up to an audience vote now. Your progress isn't guaranteed." He paused at the door. "We'll reassess any other projects after the semifinal. Assuming you're not eliminated."

His words struck her silent. Was this really the same man who'd gazed into her eyes two nights ago and told her she was extraordinary? He'd barely even looked at her today. What happened to the man who'd spent hours yesterday asking about her journey and sharing his, confessing his own uncertainty about whether he would have chosen music without his family's support? The man who'd made her feel truly seen in a way no one ever had?

Sam cleared his throat after Zach closed the door behind him. "Hey, don't take it personally. The semifinals make everyone tense. Should we finish working on that arrangement?"

Sam's kindness only made it worse. He'd noticed Zach's coldness, which meant it wasn't all in her head. She wasn't just imagining the return of the Maestro of Mean.

"Of course." Years of practice meant her voice came out steady, professional. Just another client, just another session. "Let's nail down those transitions, shall we?"

But as Sam worked through the technical details, she couldn't stop hearing Zach's words. *Your progress isn't guaranteed.* Of course she knew it wasn't, especially with the wildcard element of an audience vote. But she'd expected encouragement from him, especially after this weekend and how kind and nurturing he'd been.

She focused mechanically on the arrangement, her professional training taking over while her mind spun. What had changed? Saturday night he'd seen straight into her soul, understood exactly what she needed to hear about her family's rejection. He'd been gentle, supportive, telling her she didn't need to prove herself to anyone.

And just yesterday afternoon in the library, they'd talked for hours—about their journeys, their faith, the music that shaped them. He'd made her tea. And smiled like she mattered. Told her she had courage. Made her feel like she wasn't alone.

Now he treated her like she was just another name on a schedule. Worse—like she was a particularly tiresome mentee who might not even make it through the semifinals.

Had she imagined the warmth in his eyes when he told her she was one in a million? Had she read too much into his arranging for Claire to visit?

"Kezia?" Sam's voice broke through her thoughts. "Want to try that modulation one more time?"

She nodded, grateful that years of session work had taught her to perform even when her heart was aching. At least she could still do that much right.

Zach had warned her not to depend on anyone for approval. She just hadn't realized he was warning her about himself.

Chapter 63

"*O*KAY, KEZIA." LAURA, THE producer, ushered her into the mirrored rehearsal room the day after Zach's latest weirdness.

"We've arranged a special coach to help with your choreography and stage presence for the semifinals. They're on their way over with your mentor. When they arrive, we need a great reaction from you. You know the drill by now—excitement, enthusiasm, gratitude for this amazing opportunity. Big energy."

Kezia suppressed a sigh as she took in the cameras already set up to document her "spontaneous" response. After yesterday's cold studio session with Zach, she wasn't sure she had another performance in her.

"Viewers love seeing the preparation process and the cameras are already set up for the whole session. We want to document this coaching segment for next week's episode. Just stand here." Laura positioned her near the ballet barre. "And remember, big reaction."

Footsteps approached in the hallway. Kezia plastered on her camera-ready smile as Laura signaled "action."

Zach entered first, his posture and face stiff and formal in his dark jeans and blue button-down. Why didn't Laura instruct *him* to fake excitement and enthusiasm?

But her plastic smile softened into something real as Martha Falconer appeared in the doorway just behind Zach. The petite woman, looking impossibly cute in a loose denim shirt dress over black leggings, wore her dark hair pulled back in a simple ponytail. The size difference between her and her brother-in-law was striking. Martha didn't even reach Zach's shoulder.

"Miss Blair," Zach said, his voice formal, gaze fixed somewhere above her head. "This is Morgan, who'll be working with you on stage presence today."

Kezia fought to keep her Brianna-grade grin straight. Miss Blair again? And should she act as though she were meeting Martha for the first time? She glanced at Martha, who offered a warm smile in return.

Kezia summoned her most enthusiastic expression. "It's such an honor to work with you, Mar—sorry, Morgan." She hoped Laura wouldn't make her repeat the greeting because of her verbal stumble. It was awkward enough as it was.

Martha stepped forward, extending her hand. As the cameras zoomed in to capture their interaction, she said, "Martha's fine." Leaning in closer, she whispered, "And we don't need to pretend we haven't met."

Kezia's smile once again relaxed into its genuine form at Martha's straightforward approach. Unlike Zach, whose every movement screamed discomfort, Martha seemed completely at ease.

"I have meetings to attend," Zach said, backing toward the door. "I'll check in later to see how things are progressing."

As he left, he took the tension in the room with him, and Kezia released a slow breath. Martha noticed the energy shift, too, judging by the slight raise of her eyebrow as her gaze tracked him and flew back to Kezia.

"Well," Martha said, setting her notebook on the piano, "we've got a lot to cover today. We'll be working on both your semifinal songs—'All That I Give' and 'Patterns in Motion.' Each requires very different physical expression, but Zach tells me he's most concerned about 'Patterns,' because you've not yet performed something quite as uptempo on the show."

Kezia nodded. "Yeah, I'm a bit worried about that, too. Both of them, to be honest." Not as much as she was worried about what was going on with Zach, though.

"Well, we're more than halfway ready for the semifinals. Your vocal technique is flawless. You could teach me a thing or two there." Martha's eyes sparkled with amusement. "Do you really bring a steamer everywhere with you?"

Kezia laughed. "I don't think I'll ever live that down, will I? But, yes, I never leave home without it."

"Well, today we're going to work on everything except vocal technique." Martha settled into a casual stance, her energy inviting conversation rather than formal instruction. "I know you've got extensive studio experience, but how much stage work have you done?"

"Well..." Kezia felt her face warm. "I did a six-month contract on a cruise ship. Played the Fairy Godmother in their pantomime."

"Really? Please tell me there were wings involved."

"And a light-up wand." Kezia chuckled. "The costume department went all out."

"Can't skimp on a good wand. You know, I've always wanted to do pantomime? Maybe one day. From Fairy Godmother to semifinalist." Martha's smile warmed Kezia from the inside. "Unfortunately, I don't think we'll be busting any Cinderella moves today, but at least you know what it means to have your movements tell a story. Let's start with 'Patterns in Motion' since it needs more choreography. The upbeat rhythm will help you loosen up before we tackle the emotional ballad."

Martha moved to the center of the cleared floor space. "The key with this song is finding a groove that feels natural. I've been watching your performances since day one of *Starbound*. You tend to stay very still when you sing."

"Force of habit from session work," Kezia admitted. "In the booth, any movement can affect the sound."

It still felt unreal—getting one-on-one coaching from Martha Falconer, whose voice had ruled the radio for the past three years. Yet here was this incredible artist, teaching her as naturally as if they were friends practicing together.

"Well, today we're breaking those habits." Martha demonstrated a simple step sequence. "Try this. Let the rhythm move through your whole body. Don't worry about looking perfect."

Kezia attempted to copy Martha's fluid movements, feeling stiff and awkward.

"Relax your shoulders," Martha said, moving forward and gently adjusting Kezia's posture. "You're still thinking like you're in a recording booth. Think about how you'd dance if no one was watching."

Kezia winced. "I'm not much of a dancer."

"Neither was I when I started. My label made me take months of dance training. Ask Ezra about my early performances." Martha's self-deprecating humor made Kezia smile. "The secret is to stop worrying about looking silly and just feel the music."

Two hours slipped by in intensive work. Under Martha's encouraging guidance, Kezia gradually released the self-consciousness that usually kept her movements contained and mannequin-like.

Kezia's studio recording of "Patterns in Motion" played through the speakers as they worked on the last particularly challenging sequence, where Kezia still kept freezing during the bridge transition, her body stiffening as she concentrated on the vocal runs.

"That's it," Martha said as Kezia managed a tricky transition. "You're connecting the movement to the emotion rather than just executing steps. So, let's just try to—"

Martha broke off, pressing the back of her hand to her forehead.

"Sorry, I'm feeling a bit... I just need a moment..."

Her voice trailed off as beads of sweat appeared at her hairline. Tottering backward, she reached for the ballet barre but missed, and her knees began to buckle.

Kezia sprang forward, grabbing Martha's arm before she could fall. "Whoa, I've got you."

Swaying on her feet, the smaller woman clung to Kezia's sleeve.

Kezia wrapped her other arm firmly around Martha's shoulders, supporting her weight. "It's okay, I've got you. Here, let's sit down."

Thanking God for that cruise ship emergency response training, Kezia eased Martha to the floor. "Pull your legs up and put your head between your knees. That's it. Just sit like that for a moment. Deep breaths."

She rubbed Martha's back.

The door opened and Zach entered, a folder of papers in his hand. He stopped in his tracks, his face tight.

Setting his papers on the piano, he bounded across the room. "What happened?"

"I just got lightheaded," Martha said, her head still lowered between her knees. "I'm fine. Kezia caught me and knew what to do."

Kezia glanced up at him. "She nearly fainted."

"Stop recording," Zach snapped at the camera operators. He crouched down next to Martha, one hand on her shoulder. "Have you eaten today?"

Kezia rose and grabbed Martha's water bottle from her bag by the piano.

Martha lifted her head enough to glare at her brother-in-law. "Yes, Zach, I've eaten. Breakfast and lunch."

She looked between Zach and Kezia as she accepted the water bottle, then glanced at the camera operators who were powering down their equipment. "I suppose now's as good a time as any to tell you, because it'll come out soon. I'm pregnant."

The transformation in Zach's expression was instant, concern melting into pure joy. "Martha! That's incredible! Ezra's going to be a dad? But let's get you off the floor."

He turned to Kezia. "There's a bench against the wall. Would it be safe to move her?"

"Yes, but she should lie down with her feet elevated," Kezia said. "Martha, has the dizziness passed?"

"Mostly." Martha attempted a smile. "Really, I'm fine."

"Let's get you up," Zach said. "Kezia, help me?"

As she reached for Martha's arm, her hand brushed Zach's. The touch was brief and accidental, but a jolt of awareness shot through Kezia.

He didn't react. Neither did she. But the contact lingered in the air between them as tangibly as the sandalwood-tinged scent of his cologne.

Together, they helped Martha to her feet and guided her to the bench.

Kezia quickly arranged her cardigan over her tote bag to create a makeshift cushion to elevate Martha's feet.

"You're all being ridiculous," Martha said, but her smile was warm as she allowed them to help her lie down. "I'm pregnant, not ill."

Zach glanced toward the camera crew, his tone urgent but composed. "Can one of you go find the on-site medic?"

The camera operator nodded and quickly exited the room, his movements swift and professional.

"Does Ezra know?" Zach asked, still hovering.

"Of course Ezra knows." Martha adjusted the cardigan under her feet. "We found out about a month ago, but kept it quiet because of everything with Greg's death and Beth taking it so hard. We were waiting for the right time to tell everyone."

"You shouldn't be pushing yourself like this," Zach said, already pulling out his phone. "I'd never have asked you to coach if I'd known this could happen. I'm calling Ezra."

"You'll only worry him," Martha protested. "I just got a bit light-headed. Thank God Kezia was here to help me."

"He'd kill me if he found out I didn't tell him immediately." Zach was already dialing. "Ezra? Good, you're already on the grounds. You need to come to the rehearsal complex. Martha nearly fainted during a coaching session."

Martha took the phone from his hand. "Sweetheart, I'm fine. Don't panic." She listened for a moment, a smile tugging at her lips. "Hand on heart, I'm okay." Another pause. "You Falconer men. Always so dramatic."

Kezia lingered at the edge of the room, feeling like an intruder on a family moment in which she had no rightful place. She began gathering her sheet music from the piano.

"We're done for today," Zach said, his tone shifting as he glanced at her. The warmth from their shared concern for Martha vanished, replaced by cold professionalism. "Thank you for helping her."

"Of course," Kezia said quietly.

"Let's talk about tomorrow," Martha said, looking at Kezia. "We still have work to do on the staging."

"Absolutely not, Martha," Zach interrupted firmly. "Not until you've checked with your doctor. I'm not having you push yourself and risk something happening to you or the baby. And I'm certainly not going to be the one explaining to Ezra why I let you right back to work after this. If I know anything about him, he'll agree with me that you won't be doing any more coaching."

The silence that followed was thick with tension. Kezia wasn't sure what would be less awkward—staying, or sneaking away.

"Fine," Martha said, finally. "Kezia, would you mind grabbing my notebook from the piano? I jotted down some notes I wanted to talk through with you."

As Kezia moved across the room, she overheard Martha's quiet words to Zach. "What's going on with you two? The temperature dropped about twenty degrees when you remembered she was in the room."

"Nothing," Zach replied. "Just maintaining professional boundaries."

"Mmm-hmm."

Kezia returned with the notebook, pretending she hadn't heard.

The door burst open, and Ezra rushed in, his gaze instantly fixed on his wife. The medic, a silver-haired woman in scrubs, followed on his heels.

"I should go," Kezia said softly as Ezra pulled Martha close.

As the medic told Martha to get into a sitting position, Kezia retrieved her bag and cardigan from the bench.

She was almost at the door when Martha called out. "I'll get those notes to you somehow, okay?"

Bless her. Having nearly fainted, surrounded by worried family and the attentions of the medic, Martha was still thinking about Kezia's performance notes.

Kezia nodded and slipped out of the room.

In the hallway, she paused, her mind spinning from the jarring contrast between Zach's joy at Martha's news and his coldness toward her. For those few moments when they'd worked together to help Martha, everything had felt natural...and right. Then the walls had slammed back into place. What did it all mean? Maintaining professional boundaries? She didn't buy it one bit.

She sighed. She had semifinals to prepare for. Brianna, Connor, and Sandra were probably hard at work on their songs, free of distractions and stupid heart entanglements. And yet here she was, still thinking about the brush of her mentor's hand.

He'd hit peak *Zachness* again—that maddening bundle of mixed signals that left her reeling from the whiplash between warmth and frost.

She squared her shoulders. If she was going to make it into the finals, she couldn't afford to waste energy trying to decode Zach Falconer's mood swings.

Chapter 64

ZACH WALKED BESIDE MARTHA and Ezra toward the parking area, late afternoon sun stretching long shadows across the gravel. Despite her protests that she could walk perfectly well on her own, Ezra kept a protective arm around her shoulders.

"I meant what I said about the coaching," Ezra said. "It's too much risk."

Martha looked at her husband for a long moment. "Okay, I'll stop. I think I would have been fine, but I don't want you worrying."

"Good," Zach said. "I'll reassign one of the other movement coaches to Kezia."

He felt a surge of relief that they'd managed to get the cameras turned off before Martha's pregnancy announcement. And all the *Starbound* staff members present were bound by a strict NDA. The last thing she and Ezra needed was that news breaking before they were ready to share it.

As they reached Ezra's car, Martha turned to face Zach. "Now, are you going to tell us what that was about with Kezia?"

"What do you mean?" Zach kept his tone deliberately casual.

"You know exactly what I mean. The North Pole act whenever she's in the room."

"Oh, are we back to that?" Ezra raised an eyebrow. "I thought you'd moved beyond your issues with her."

Zach shifted uncomfortably. "I'm just maintaining appropriate professional boundaries."

Martha shook her head. "That's not going to fly with me. This isn't about professionalism. This is about you retreating from something that scares you." She studied his face for a moment. "You like her, don't you?"

The question hung in the air between them. Zach couldn't find the words to deny it.

His mind flashed to Kezia at the piano that night, her vulnerability as she'd talked about her family's rejection. His overwhelming urge to comfort her, to make her see she didn't have to be defined by her family's standards. The way they'd connected that afternoon at the library.

"Oh, boy." Ezra blew out a low whistle. "I'll be praying for you, brother."

The understanding in his eyes both comforted and embarrassed Zach. They'd always been able to read each other.

"We're here if you need to talk," Ezra added simply.

Martha squeezed Zach's arm. "I know the timing's tricky, but it's not the end of the world to fall for someone, you know. You're only human, Zach. And she's incredible."

"It's not that simple." Zach ran a hand through his hair. "There's the show, her career, the non-fraternization clause... I've made a total hash of things."

"Having feelings for her isn't a breach of contract," Ezra pointed out. "The clause is about actions, not emotions. So, as long as you're not acting on your feelings, you're good. The competition ends in a few weeks and then the non-fraternization clause won't be an issue, anyway. There is life after *Starbound*."

"You don't understand." Zach's voice was tight. "This goes beyond that. Ryan Sterling's already making insinuations...about favoritism, about my intentions. If there's even a hint of impropriety, it could destroy her career before it begins. Everything she's worked for, her reputation, her credibility...it would all be overshadowed by gossip about how she moved forward in the competition."

"Ryan Sterling's a snake," Martha said.

"But he's a snake with influence." Zach leaned against Ezra's car. "And he's not wrong about the optics. I'm the show's creator, her mentor. If anyone even suspects there's something between us..."

"So you're protecting her by treating her like she has the plague? That's your master plan?" Martha put her hands on her hips, stretching herself to her full five-foot one inch height. "I have to tell you, Zach, if you keep up this repellent cold shoulder act, you won't have to worry about what happens after the show. She'll want nothing to do with you."

Zach winced. "I know I'm handling it badly."

"There's a middle ground between inappropriate involvement and Arctic frost," Martha said. "You can maintain professional boundaries without making her feel like she's done something wrong. Right now, you're hurting her, and you're not exactly being subtle about your feelings, anyway."

"She's right," Ezra said. "You're many things, brother, but a good actor isn't one of them."

Martha added to the pile-on. "Anyone watching you two today could see the connection and the way you're fighting it."

Zach pushed away from the car, frustration tightening his shoulders. "I don't know how to do this. How to be around her without..." He trailed off.

"Without falling harder?" Martha's voice was gentle. "Maybe you can't. But you can at least treat her with basic human warmth. Otherwise, even if everything works out perfectly after the show ends, you might have already destroyed any chance with her. And you'd better not, because I like her."

"I like her too," Ezra said. "She's got substance and grit."

Zach closed his eyes briefly. Every word they said just confirmed what he already knew. Kezia was extraordinary in ways that went far beyond her voice.

"I'll work on the Arctic frost," he said finally. "But I must maintain some distance. There's too much at stake."

Martha squeezed his hand. "Just remember, there's a difference between keeping appropriate boundaries and emotional cruelty. You're better than that, Zach."

After they drove off, Zach remained in the parking area, the setting sun streaking the sky in amber and rose. The weight of the situation settled over him anew. His family's support helped, but they couldn't fully understand the tightrope he walked.

Emotional cruelty. The words hung over him like a shroud of dread. He was hurting Kezia, but he didn't know how to avoid causing her pain. He offered up a brief prayer for wisdom and for strength to find that middle ground Martha talked about. To protect Kezia and her career without crushing her spirit in the process.

He straightened, resolve settling over him like a weight he had to carry. And he would carry it. Not just for his sake, but hers.

He had a production meeting in ten minutes. Time to focus on what he could control. Such as running this show and giving every contestant, including Kezia, their best chance at success.

Even if that meant keeping his heart firmly in check.

Chapter 65

WO DAYS HAD PASSED since Kezia had last seen Zach, and now here she was, sitting in the makeup chair while Lisa, one of *Starbound's* beauty team, made final adjustments to her eye shadow.

Getting glammed up like this was one of the fun parts of the show—but not when her stomach was tied in knots.

The bright lights around the mirror highlighted every detail of her carefully crafted appearance. Subtle contouring to emphasize her bone structure, false lashes to make her eyes camera-ready, lips glossed to perfection. For once, she actually looked like she belonged in a photo shoot.

Through the mirror's reflection, she could see the photography setup behind her. The main stage area of Glenmere Hall had been transformed for this publicity shoot, with multiple shooting stations arranged around vintage musical instruments. An exquisite grand piano occupied one corner, while other areas featured artfully arranged guitars, microphones on classic chrome stands, and a Hammond organ that looked like it had stories to tell. Light stands and reflectors created pools of perfect illumination throughout the space.

"The semifinals promotional shoot is pretty intense," Lisa said, blending another layer of shimmer across Kezia's cheekbones. "Individual portraits first, then shots with your mentor, followed by the group shots. They're going all out with the artistic vision."

Shots with her mentor? Kezia's stomach tightened. After days of Zach's avoidance, they'd be forced into close proximity, pretending connection where there was only confusion and coldness. How would he square that with his famous quest for authenticity?

"You need to look relaxed," Lisa said, frowning at the tension in Kezia's face. "Can you manage that?"

Relaxed was the last thing she felt. But if she'd learned anything in her weeks on this show, it was how to bring it in front of a camera.

Across the room, Brianna posed with Ryan by the grand piano, their easy rapport on display as she laughed at something he'd said. The photographer captured their interaction, calling out encouragement. "That's it! Beautiful energy between you two!"

Lisa brushed a final dusting of powder across Kezia's face. "All done. And just in time, because I think you're up next."

Kezia rose from the chair, smoothing her cream-colored blouse. Naomi, the wardrobe stylist, had paired it with tailored black trousers and classic heels, going for what she called "timeless sophistication."

The photographer, Antoine, waved her over to an area where vintage microphones created a backdrop of chrome and shadow. "Let's get your individual shots first, then we'll bring Zach in for the mentor poses."

Her heart kicked up at the mention of his name. Through the studio's open doors, she saw him in the hall-way, speaking with Hugo, the showrunner, looking like the hair and wardrobe team had finished their magic on him. He looked incredible.

"Beautiful, darling!" Antoine called as Kezia moved through a series of poses. "Now pull that mic stand toward you as though you're crooning a love song. Tilt your chin up and turn your head to the left. Just look at me with your head still turned. Give me some gorgeous side-eye. Perfect. Give me sophisticated. Give me artistry."

She followed his directions automatically, her mind more focused on the fact that Zach had entered the room. He stood talking with Ryan near the entrance.

"Excellent!" Antoine lowered his camera. "Now, let's get you with your mentor. Zach?"

Zach approached, moving with the grace of a panther, his gaze avoiding Kezia. "Antoine. How are we doing this?"

"Let's start by the piano. I'm thinking a mentoring moment with you guiding her through something musical."

Antoine gestured them into position. "Kezia, you sit at the stool while Zach looks on, standing just behind you. We want to capture that special connection between mentor and artist."

Kezia fought back a laugh. Connection? When Zach had spent the past week rebuilding the Berlin Wall between them?

"Excellent," Antoine said as they arranged themselves at the piano. "Now, Zach, maybe guide her hand like you're showing her something on the keys."

Zach's fingers were warm as they settled over hers, his touch sending a jolt up her arm. She kept her smile in place as Antoine's camera clicked, but her heart thundered against her ribs.

"Natural conversation," Antoine encouraged. "Kezia, turn toward him. Pretend you're discussing strategy."

The perfect opening. "How's Martha?" Kezia asked quietly, turning slightly toward Zach as the camera clicked again. "She and the baby all right?"

"They're both fine." Zach matched her quiet tone while maintaining his photo-ready smile. "The doctor cleared her, but she's taking it easy."

"Great chemistry!" Antoine called. "Now, angle toward each other a bit more."

As they shifted closer, Kezia seized her chance while he was here, trapped. "What's going on, Zach?" she whispered, her lips hardly moving. "Did I do something wrong?"

His fingers tensed over hers, but his expression remained perfect for the cameras as he pitched his voice for her ears only. "We need to focus on the competition."

"Lovely!" Antoine circled them, camera clicking. "Now, Zach, lean in, and Kezia, move closer to his ear, like you're sharing a secret."

Kezia took full advantage of the pose, still holding her smile steady. "This isn't about the competition," she breathed. "Something changed. It's as if... As if I've made you angry. As if you hate me."

"Perfect! Hold that connection!" Antoine beamed. "This is the money shot."

"Hang on a minute," Lisa called, hurrying over with her makeup brush. "Sorry, but Mr. Falconer's starting to shine under these lights."

They waited in charged silence as Lisa powdered Zach's forehead, still positioned intimately close, his hand still covering hers on the keys.

"Right, let's try something different," Antoine said after Lisa stepped away. "Kezia, stand up and move away from the piano. Over here. I want you to face each other, like you're having a chat about musical secrets."

The new position brought them even closer, and face to face. The intimacy of the pose felt like both torture and revelation.

"I don't hate you," Zach said, his voice so quiet she barely caught it.

"Give me more," Antoine commanded. "Look at each other. Lock eyes."

"Then what is it?" she whispered as she held his gaze. "You've spent weeks telling me to be real. To be open. And now you've shut down completely. Why?"

"Gorgeous intensity!" Antoine called. "Whatever you're doing, keep going!"

A muscle twitched in Zach's jaw. He murmured around his photogenic grin, "Because what I feel isn't just professional anymore."

The words hung between them as Antoine captured the moment. Kezia's heart seemed to stop, then restart with a thundering rush.

"You know it, don't you?" His voice was barely audible, his blue eyes intense.

Drowning in his gaze, she swallowed, her answer as quiet as a breath. "Yes."

Antoine directed them to move to a new setup near the vintage microphones. Away from Zach's immediate presence and his intoxicating gaze, Kezia took a moment to catch her breath, to process what had just passed between them.

When they came back together, the intensity in Zach's eyes nearly undid her carefully maintained composure.

"Stand close together," Antoine instructed. "Like you're reviewing performance notes."

Zach held a piece of sheet music between them. "There are other people who've noticed," he said quietly. "People who could use it against you."

He angled the sheet music toward Ryan, who stood on the sidelines, acting as though he were scrolling his phone, but clearly watching them.

Kezia drew a sharp breath as the pieces clicked into place. She and Zach getting closer, then his abrupt change back to icy professionalism.

"Everything you've worked for is at risk," he said, smoldering for the cameras as he pointed at a spot on the sheet music. "And so is everything I've built."

"That's a wrap," Antoine called. "Great chemistry, you two. Totally nailed the mentor-mentee dynamic."

Kezia almost laughed. If only he knew.

As Ryan approached Zach, her heart hammered.

Was his timing just coincidental? He couldn't have heard what they'd said. Antoine, who was right here, hadn't.

"Zach," Ryan said, "I need to speak with you about the semifinal set design for Brianna's performance. I'm told you need to sign off on my request for pyrotechnics."

"Of course." Zach's professional mask slid instantly back into place, and he walked away from her without a backward glance.

She watched him go, unable to tear her gaze away from him, their unfinished conversation hanging between them.

Lisa clapped her hands. "Semifinalists, group shot! Over there by the guitars."

Kezia's mind spun as she walked to where Lisa pointed. Brianna, Sandra, and Connor already stood there.

Every interaction of the past week shifted in her memory, recalibrating with this new understanding. Zach's distance hadn't been rejection—it had been protection. Not just of the show or his reputation, but of her career.

Her heart soared even as reality pressed in. They'd barely scratched the surface of this complicated situation. Any future conversation would have to navigate the dangers Zach had hinted at, the watchful eyes of people like Ryan who could twist their connection into something tawdry and damaging.

But none of that changed the fundamental truth that had been exposed today. The memory of his hand over hers at the piano tingled across her skin.

This thing between them was real. She wasn't alone in feeling it. And now that the truth had surfaced—barely whispered but blazing between them—there was no going back. Not to denial. Not to distance. Because everything had changed.

Chapter 66

THE DAY AFTER THE photo shoot, Zach stood at the back of the stage area as Kezia's semifinal rehearsal wrapped up. Combining the choreography and stagecraft from Martha's coaching with the full band and live vocals, she was incredible. There was no doubt in his mind that she would be one of the final two in the show.

But all he could think about was the warmth of her hand beneath his at the photo shoot yesterday and her widening eyes as he'd told her, "Because what I feel isn't just professional anymore."

She'd said she knew. But how much did she really understand? Could she discern that he had feelings for her? And did she grasp that he was maintaining his distance to protect them both? That he didn't mean to hurt her?

He should have been focused on the network's latest demands about the live finale format, which was now to be held at a different, bigger venue. On the international licensing negotiations that were heating up. On anything except the look on her face at his confession. And torturing himself with wondering how she felt about him.

The musicians began packing their instruments while the sound crew secured their gear.

Kezia lingered at the piano, shuffling through some sheet music, apparently in no hurry to leave.

Zach collected his notes, nodding a professional good-night in her direction as he prepared to escape to his office and the stack of production meetings that would keep his thoughts buried—and too busy to brood over her.

"Zach?"

His name on her lips stopped him mid-step.

Her voice wasn't loud. But it wrapped around him with a gentle gravity that bent his will without asking, drawing him back toward her.

He turned, schooling his features into neutrality even as something in his chest pulled taut. "Yes?"

"Before you go, I have a song I've been working on."

She glanced at the crew members still working around them. Her tone remained calm, loud enough to be overheard, but carefully professional. "I told you about it a few days ago, and it's almost done. Would you mind taking a look?"

He shouldn't. But her calling him back like that—saying his name like it meant something—left him too exposed to walk away.

"Yes, I remember you mentioning it. I said you didn't have time for side projects."

She held his gaze. "Yes, but since I felt like we were on top of things for the live show, I did a bit more work on it. It's mostly done, but I'm a bit stuck with the second verse."

He walked up to her and leaned on the piano, nodding a goodbye to a couple of guitarists as they left the stage. "I can spare a couple of minutes. What's the song called?"

"'Old Town Symphony.'" She smoothed the handwritten sheet music on the piano's music stand. "Would you like to hear what I have so far? Or look at the lyrics first?"

"I'll listen first."

Her fingers moved across the keys, playing a short jazz-influenced intro. Then her voice came in.

Old Town Symphony

A melody in a minor key

Notes from our past, songs that shaped who we are

A reason for every crack, a purpose in every scar.

She glanced up at him as she sang the chorus.

It doesn't have to be perfect, it just has to be real

The brokenness will be worth it, if we have the courage to heal.

From a bittersweet yesterday, our tomorrow will start

Singing solo, till you joined in, playing straight to my heart.

His heartbeat thundered in his ears as she let the final notes fade.

"What's the song about?" he asked, though his heart already knew.

"About what you've been teaching me all along." She met his gaze steadily. "Telling the truth. Being authentic. That's what I've got so far. I need help with the second verse."

She pushed the lyric sheet toward him, a pencil sitting on top of it. "I thought maybe you could help find the right words."

He moved closer. For one reckless moment, he almost reached for her hand instead of the pencil—just to feel the connection again, to let her know what he couldn't say aloud. But instead, he took the pencil, careful to keep the contact purely professional.

"Play the accompaniment for me while I think."

The music washed over him again, quiet and full of longing, as he studied the page.

He could barely breathe around the emotion swelling in his chest. He wanted to tell her everything: how much he admired her courage, how deeply he felt this impossible thing between them. But he couldn't. Not here. Not yet. This was the one place he could speak freely—and only if he did so in lyrics.

Taking a steadying breath, he wrote:

Faded harmonies

Echoes linger in empty streets

We've sung alone, now we're stronger as two

Every broken chord brought me closer to you.

He handed the sheet back to her.

Face angled downward, she bit her lip as she read what he'd written. Then she began to play again, singing the lines he'd added. The way her voice invested his words with such meaning while maintaining perfect professional composure for anyone watching... It nearly undid him.

He fought to keep his expression neutral as a crew member passed nearby, but joy surged through him. She hadn't just understood his confession from the photo shoot.

She felt the same way.

She looked up at him after she finished singing his verse. "It's perfect. Says exactly what I hoped it would. Thank you."

"Thank you for letting me hear that. It's a beautiful song." As he busied himself gathering up his papers, he spoke quietly. "Let's work hard and get through this competition. Do it right."

He met her gaze, letting the moment stretch longer than it should have. "You're under enough pressure. We shouldn't add to it." He tapped the sheet music gently, the gesture loaded with meaning. "Let's put this aside for now and focus on the show."

Please understand.

His voice dropped just enough to keep their conversation private. "The show will end in just a few weeks."

He couldn't say more with crew still nearby. Couldn't say "I think about you constantly" or "I'm trying not to fall harder every time you sing". Couldn't tell her how fiercely he wanted a future beyond cameras and contracts. But maybe she'd hear it anyway—in the quiet spaces between his words.

She held his gaze, the corner of her mouth lifting just slightly.

"I understand," she said, and something in her voice told him she'd heard all of it.

"Goodbye, Miss Blair," he said, the formality a thin veil over everything unspoken.

As he turned to leave, she returned to the piano and began playing the song again. The melody rose behind him. Gentle and unfinished, like a promise.

His steps slowed for just a moment.

She hadn't just understood.

She'd answered—with music, with grace, with something like faith.

And that hope—unspoken, mutual, and fiercely protected—would be enough to carry him through the weeks ahead.

Chapter 67

*T*HE STUDIO AUDIENCE CRACKLED with nervous energy as Zach sat at the judges' panel, Martha beside him as his guest for tonight's semifinal performances.

He barely registered the cameras anymore, but knew they would track every reaction, every nuance of this live broadcast.

During the break, Hugo had updated him on early viewing figures, the highest ever this season. Millions of viewers had tuned in to watch the four semifinalists. But Zach had eyes for only one performer.

Kezia had already dazzled everyone with "Patterns in Motion," showing a command of rhythm and stage presence that had the audience on their feet. Now came the real test. Not just of her vocal ability, but whether he could keep his feelings for her off his face while she sang a song that hit so close to home.

He needed to hold it together because Ryan, two seats away, seemed more interested in watching Zach than the stage.

Olivia took position, speaking directly into the camera. "For those just joining us, welcome to the *Starbound* semifinal. Tonight, for the first time, our mentors have no say in who moves forward to the final. That decision is entirely in your hands. Your votes will determine which two artists continue their *Starbound* journey. Remember you can vote by text to the number at the bottom of your screen, online at starbound.tv, or through the official *Starbound* app. Lines close in one hour!"

She turned back to the studio audience. "And now, for her second song of the evening, performing 'All That I Give,' please welcome back to the stage... Kezia Blair!"

The studio went dark. Zach's heart pounded as the spotlight found her at center stage. She stood perfectly still, the simplicity of her sheath dress emphasizing her statuesque grace. But it was her face that pulled him in. For the briefest instant, their gazes connected and his breath caught.

The first notes from the orchestra began.

"Standing at the edge of everything I know. Walls around my heart start to crumble so slow."

He'd heard her rehearse this song countless times, but the lyrics landed differently after the past few days, since their whispered exchange at the photo shoot and their coded messages that confirmed that she felt something for him, too.

"I've kept my distance, played it safe for so long. This feeling inside is too mighty, too strong."

His mind registered the resonance of her tone, the masterful way she built the dynamics, but his heart heard only the meaning behind the lyrics.

"I've never surrendered. Held back just in case. But with you, I'm fighting a losing battle and the truth is written all over my face."

He schooled his own features to remain impassive, even as he gripped the arm of his chair.

"All that I give is all that I am, nothing held back, nothing left to defend. If loving you means risking everything, then that's the chance that I'm willing to take."

The force of emotion in her voice cracked something open in his chest, making his heart race as she continued through the chorus.

"Because without you, what would remain? Just echoes of a life half-lived in vain. All that I give is all that I am. Is it enough for you to understand?"

Those words... Would she one day feel that way for him? After the spotlights dimmed and the cameras were gone, when the *Starbound* season wrapped up, could they explore this connection between them and see where it led?

"My heart is in free-fall, there's no safety net. It was a lost cause since the day that we met."

He knew what that felt like all too well. But he couldn't let his heart run away with him, much as it wanted to charge ahead. Slow, measured, applying wisdom at every step. That was the only way to navigate this treacherous sea without getting shipwrecked.

As the final notes faded, her gaze found his across the distance, the briefest connection before she turned to acknowledge the thunderous applause. The audience rose to their feet, and Zach stood with them, grateful for the chance to hide his emotional reaction behind the standing ovation.

Burning eyes, heated face, face-splitting grin? Everyone around him looked like that, so he fit right in. Thankfully, his thundering heart wasn't visible, and nobody could hear the blood rushing in his ears.

Draping an arm around Kezia's shoulders, Olivia invited the mentors to share their thoughts.

"Diana, let's start with you."

"What we just witnessed was extraordinary." Diana pressed a hand to her heart. "The control, the emotion, the artistry, all of it coming together in perfect harmony. That's what happens when technical excellence serves the heart of a song."

Kezia bowed her head, her face radiant.

"Tyler?" Olivia said.

"I have to agree with Diana." The mentor spread out her hands. "Honestly, tonight you seem unstoppable. Bravo, Kezia."

"Ryan?"

"This is exactly what I saw in you from that first audition." Ryan's smile was camera-perfect. "The potential to deliver performances like this. I'm not ashamed to admit I have big regrets."

The audience chuckled along with him, and Kezia's lips curved in a gracious smile.

"And finally, Zach?"

He gathered his professional composure like a cloak, measuring each word. "What we've just witnessed is the emergence of a complete artist. That performance showed the whole reason *Starbound* exists. To discover not just talent, but authentic artistic voice. Like Ryan, I have regrets, too. My regret is not making you one of my first picks."

Kezia's smile warmed him, even as laughter spread across the audience.

"But I'm honored to be part of your journey now," he concluded. "You were fantastic tonight, Kezia."

Oh, dear. The way her face glowed as she beamed at him, as though she were lit up from inside.

He forced himself to look away before his own face did something reckless. His gaze landed on Diana, catching her watching him, a finger on her cheek.

"Thank you, mentors," Olivia said, moving to center stage as Kezia glided off into the wings. "And remember, viewers at home—your votes tonight will shape the final. Two artists move forward. The lines are open now!"

Chapter 68

THE BACKSTAGE SPEAKERS PIPED in the guest artist's performance as Kezia slipped down the corridor toward the ladies' room. The crowd roared as Damian "King Flow" Reynolds, the chart-topping rapper, launched into his latest hit "Strong Medicine." Its signature pounding bass line shook the walls like a heartbeat.

After pouring her heart out through "All That I Give," Kezia needed a moment alone, just a brief respite from the cameras that had documented her every breath for weeks.

The semifinal performances had left her emotionally drained. First "Patterns in Motion," where she'd pushed her body and stage presence beyond her comfort zone, then the raw vulnerability of singing a love song while fighting not to look directly at Zach. She had left everything out there on that stage. All while knowing millions of viewers were deciding her fate with their votes.

The bathroom door closed behind her with a soft click, and Kezia released a long breath, grateful to find the space empty.

She approached the sink, staring at her reflection in the harsh fluorescent light. The makeup team's work remained flawless despite her performance, her stage makeup emphasizing her eyes and giving her skin a camera-ready glow. She looked like a different person, one who was polished, confident, poised for success.

But she knew the truth behind that mask. It was in the tremble in her hands as she turned on the tap.

What had she done tonight? Standing on that stage, baring her heart in a love song whose authenticity was only possible because she sang it while thinking of Zach. As he watched from the judges' panel, it felt like confessing in code, hidden in plain sight. Every word about risk and surrender had been meant for him, and from the intensity in his eyes, he'd understood.

Kezia splashed cool water on her wrists, a technique she'd learned years ago to calm her racing pulse before performances. She needed to center herself before returning for the results announcement. Two contestants would advance to the finals. Two would go home. After everything she'd poured into tonight's performances, she desperately wanted to be one of those moving forward.

Or did she?

Perhaps it wouldn't be such a bad thing to be cut now. If she were gone from *Starbound*, Zach would no longer be her mentor. Her face warmed. And maybe, if he meant what he said, they could...

The bathroom door swung open. Kezia glanced up to see Diana Morris entering, elegant in her designer pantsuit, statement earrings glittering as she approached.

With her gray hair piled on top of her head in a chignon and her flawless mahogany skin, the veteran recording artist defied time itself.

"There you are," Diana said, her warm voice filling the quiet space. "That was quite a performance."

"Thank you," Kezia said. She'd always admired Diana. The woman had maintained a forty-year career in an industry that typically discarded female artists after their first hints of aging.

Diana moved to the sink beside Kezia, checking her reflection as she pulled out a powder compact. "You've come so far since your audition. The vulnerability in that second piece was remarkable."

"Coming from you, that means a lot."

Diana's gaze met hers in the mirror, her expression shifting subtly as she pressed a powder puff to her nose. "I hope you don't mind my saying this, but I've been noticing something that concerns me."

Something in Diana's tone made Kezia's stomach tighten. "What do you mean?"

Diana turned, facing her directly. "I'll be blunt. The way you and Zach look at each other. There's more than mentorship there."

The question struck Kezia like a two-by-four to the head. She opened her mouth to deny it, panic flaring in her chest. "I don't—"

Diana raised a hand gently. "I'm not judging you, Kezia. Forty years ago, I *was* you."

"What?" Kezia's heartbeat thundered in her ears. Had she heard Diana right?

"Different setting, same story." Diana leaned against the counter, her voice softening. "He was a powerful producer, I was the promising new talent. We thought we were being so careful, so discreet." She gave a small, bitter laugh. "We weren't."

Kezia stood frozen, unable to form a response.

Diana's eyes misted. "It ended, of course. And when it did, his career continued uninterrupted. While I spent years rebuilding mine, fighting rumors about how I'd got my first record deal. It took five years to get my second."

She slid her compact back into her clutch. When she looked up again at Kezia, her eyes were hard. "The industry has a very specific narrative for women who become involved with men in positions of power. And it can be very hard to shake that off once it sticks to you, no matter how talented you are."

The fluorescent lights hummed overhead as Kezia absorbed Diana's words, her mouth dry.

This wasn't idle gossip or a mentor flexing her authority. And Diana didn't seem to be threatening her. This was a woman sharing a hard-won warning.

Kezia's hand went up to her throat. "I don't know what to say."

"Ryan has been watching you both," Diana said. "Asking discreet questions. I recognized the look—he's gathering ammunition. He's not subtle when he thinks he has leverage."

A wave of cold washed over Kezia. That's exactly what Zach had told her, that Ryan had noticed something between them. Zach had tried to protect them both by acting cold and distant again. But she'd pushed him, hinting at her feelings in such a reckless way. She'd been so stupid. Of course watchful eyes couldn't fail to pick something up. And Zach had seen it coming. All of it.

"This show represents everything Zach has worked for," Diana said quietly, her gaze intense. "His reputation, his investment, his family's support. His future. One hint of scandal could undermine it all."

She dropped her voice even further, her gaze locked with Kezia's. "Whatever happens tonight, remember that sometimes protecting someone means making tough choices."

The bathroom door swung open before Kezia could respond, and a production assistant poked her head in.

"There you are, Kezia! Results in five minutes. We need you backstage now. Ms. Morris, you too, please."

Diana gave her one last meaningful look before she straightened her jacket and moved toward the door, leaving Kezia to follow.

Stepping back into the corridor felt like emerging from an underwater cave. The bright lights, the hurried production crew, the pounding music, it all drilled into Kezia's skull after the quiet intimacy of Diana's revelation.

Kezia hurried toward the stage, the weight of Diana's words pressing down on her. Zach had talked about the danger to her emerging career. But he had so much more to lose. He had *everything* to lose.

She joined the other semifinalists, their nervous energy crackling between them. Brianna bounced on her toes, while Sandra stood perfectly still, eyes closed. Connor paced in a tight circle, mouthing what looked like a prayer.

Scanning the crowded backstage area, Kezia spotted Zach deep in conversation with Hugo and Steve, his focus completely on whatever production issue required his attention. Not just a mentor. The creator of this whole show. Professional. Dedicated. Everything he'd built could be jeopardized by whispers about them.

Then she caught Ryan watching her from across the room. A chill ran down her spine as she recognized exactly what Diana had described. The look of someone who thought he had leverage.

The potential fallout suddenly crystallized in her mind. Not just gossip about how she'd advanced in the competition, but damage to Zach's reputation, questions about his integrity and his judgment, accusations that would undermine everything he stood for.

She startled as Laura touched her arm. "We're back from commercial in thirty seconds," the producer said, ushering the mentors out. "Places, everyone."

Kezia allowed herself to be guided into position, standing between Sandra and Brianna.

Diana was right. She needed to be careful. Not just for her sake, but for Zach's.

The stage manager signaled five seconds with his fingers. The spotlights blazed. Olivia took her mark.

"Welcome back to the *Starbound* semifinal results!" Olivia's voice rang out. "Your votes are in, and we're about to reveal which two artists will compete in next week's grand finale!"

Kezia stood tall, her professional mask firmly in place as the camera panned across the four semifinalists.

Whatever happened next, Diana's warning had changed everything. Behind her camera-ready smile, Kezia sent up a desperate prayer for wisdom.

Chapter 69

BACK IN HIS MENTOR'S seat, Zach gripped the arm of the chair as the commercial break ended. Across the stage, Kezia stood in line with the other semifinalists, her perfect posture belying the electric tension filling the studio. The bright lights highlighted her dark skin's radiance, giving her the appearance of someone already crowned with success.

She should be. Her performances tonight had been nothing short of spectacular.

Beside him, Martha leaned over. "She was incredible," she whispered. "You've done amazing work with her."

He nodded, careful to keep his expression neutral as cameras swept across the judges' panel. Something about Diana caught his eye. She seemed unusually attentive to him rather than the contestants. Ryan stared at him, too.

He shrugged it off as Olivia took center stage, envelope clutched dramatically in her manicured fingers.

"Welcome back to the *Starbound* semifinal results!" She held up the envelope. "Britain, your votes are in, and we're about to reveal which two artists will compete head-to-head in next week's grand finale!"

The audience fell silent. Even the camera operators seemed to hold their breath.

"With the largest share of audience votes, the first finalist is..." Olivia paused, the practiced dramatic timing perfect as she opened the envelope. "Kezia Blair!"

Martha squeezed his arm in excitement. "I knew it!"

The audience erupted. Zach allowed himself a small smile as Kezia stepped forward, eyes wide, her hands covering her mouth. She wasn't expecting this. The most votes, huh? Relief and pride surged through him. Her talent deserved this recognition.

Their gazes met briefly across the distance, and he caught the sheen of tears in her eyes.

"And joining Kezia in the finale is..." Another dramatic pause. "Sandra Cassidy!"

Diana let out a whoop beside him, her professional composure momentarily forgotten as her young mentee stepped forward. Sixteen-year-old Sandra's face transformed with shock and joy as she moved to stand beside Kezia.

"Congratulations," Zach said to Diana while applauding.

Olivia's expression transformed to professional sympathy. "Which means, Connor and Brianna, that your *Starbound* journey ends here. But I'm sure this won't be the last we hear of you. Any final words for us? Brianna?"

Zach tuned out Brianna's farewell speech as his thoughts clustered around Kezia. They could win this. Tonight's performance had proven what she was capable of when she let her technical precision serve her emotional truth. Not to mention her movement during "Patterns of Motion." With just a few hours of Martha's coaching, she could do up-tempo songs, too. There seemed to be no limit to her versatility.

His mind went back to the stage as Olivia waved Brianna and Connor away.

"Congratulations to our finalists," the host said. "But your journey isn't quite finished yet. We have one surprise in store for you."

Zach straightened in his chair. This wasn't in the format they'd discussed in production meetings.

Martha glanced at him questioningly.

He gave a barely perceptible shrug in response. Whatever it was, Albion had kept this well under wraps.

"Kezia, Sandra, as you go into the *Starbound* finale, you now have a choice to make. And you must make it right now," Olivia said.

The studio lighting changed to a dramatic red hue.

Olivia paused for effect as all eyes focused on her. "Ladies, you can continue your *Starbound* journey with your current mentor. Or you can choose another to guide you through the finale. Ryan, Tyler, since your mentees are out, you can make your case to steal Kezia or Sandra onto your team."

An icy finger of alarm traced down Zach's spine as the audience murmured. This must be one of the format twists Albion Broadcasting Network had reserved the right to implement. A twist that was kept secret even from him. He glanced toward the wings where Hugo stood, receiving only an apologetic shrug in return.

Martha leaned closer. "This is new," she whispered.

He took a deep breath, forcing his shoulders to relax. This was just the network adding drama for ratings. There was no actual concern here. After the breakthrough Kezia had made under his guidance, after their shared song, there was no question about her continuing with him.

"As the contestant with the second-highest scores, Sandra, you're up first," Olivia announced. "Tyler, Ryan, would either of you like to make a pitch for Sandra to join your team for the finale?"

Tyler leaned forward. "Sandra, I've admired your natural talent from day one. I know you've had a good thing going with Diana. But if you want to add some edge to your finale performances, I'm your mentor. I'd love to have you on my team."

Ryan spoke next. "You've got the raw material to be extraordinary, Sandra. You're already extraordinary. I can make sure the industry sees that."

"I'm really flattered, but I'll stay with Diana," Sandra announced without hesitation. "She's believed in me from the beginning."

Zach nodded with professional satisfaction as the audience applauded. He had nothing against Tyler, but Sandra was better off with Diana's sure hand. And as for Ryan... No. Just no.

"Now, Kezia, it's your turn," Olivia said. "Ryan, Tyler, would either of you like to try to convince Kezia to join your team?"

Tyler shook her head with a laugh. "I know how to pick my battles. I'll sit this one out."

Ryan, however, straightened in his chair. "I don't know how to pick battles. I fight them all."

The audience chuckled as he flashed a grin.

"I've always lived by the principle, 'If you don't ask, you don't get.' Maybe it's a longshot, but why not ask? Kezia, I'd love to work with you in the finale. I believe I have what it takes to get you over the finish line and win this thing."

Zach couldn't hold back a smirk. You could never accuse Ryan of lacking guts. The man's brass neck was legendary. He was just playing to the cameras, making a show of ambition that would look good in the edit. There was no chance Kezia would go back to him after what he'd done.

"Kezia," Olivia asked, "you have a choice to make. It's a unique one, because you've worked with both these mentors. Who will guide you through the final stage of your *Starbound* journey? Ryan, or Zach?"

The camera swung toward him, and Zach maintained his composed expression.

Kezia looked directly at him, something unreadable in her eyes.

He gave her a small nod of encouragement.

She took a deep breath. "I choose to work with Ryan for the finale."

The words didn't make sense at first. They echoed in the air, incomprehensible, like they were spoken in a language he didn't understand. Ryan?

The studio erupted in shocked gasps. Camera operators swung wildly to capture reactions. Even Olivia, consummate professional that she was, blinked rapidly, mouth hanging open, before recovering.

Martha gripped his arm, her small gasp barely audible beneath the audience's reaction.

A hollow sensation expanded in Zach's chest, as if someone had punched a hole straight through him. Someone had. Kezia had.

This couldn't be happening. The cameras were on his face. Britain was watching him live and in ultra-HD. They wouldn't see him crumble.

Every fiber of his performing experience activated at once, forcing his features to settle into something resembling composure. He nodded, his smile tight but intact.

He searched her face for explanation, for the smallest hint that would make sense of this public rejection. But Kezia was already looking away, her gaze fixed on some middle distance as Ryan rose from his chair.

The audience's continued reaction—murmurs, gasps, scattered applause—confirmed this wasn't a nightmare. It was real.

"A surprising turn as we head to our finale!" Olivia said. "Ryan, you threw your hat in the ring, but I think you're probably as shocked as any of us. Your thoughts on working with Kezia for the finale?"

Breaking protocol, Ryan strutted like a peacock to join Kezia on stage. "I've believed in Kezia's commercial potential from day one. And I'm honored that she believes in me, too. I'm thrilled she's chosen to return to my guidance for the final push."

His hand settled on Kezia's shoulder, a physical claim that was salt in Zach's open wound.

Zach couldn't make sense of any of it. Had he completely misinterpreted everything? The song they'd worked on together, the whispered confessions during the photo shoot, her performance of "All That I Give" just hours ago. Had it all meant nothing?

Then, like a poisoned dart, one word pierced through the fog of shock: Verity. Of course. It was happening again. Like her, Kezia was thinking about advancing her career. Ryan had a lot more industry pull than he did. He knew how to make chart topping artists.

"Zach..." Olivia turned to him. "Your reaction to this surprising development?"

For one splintering moment, he couldn't speak. Then the mask slid into place.

"I respect Kezia's choice." He was shocked at how steady his voice was. "This is all about her journey, what will serve her career ambitions best. That's what *Starbound* is about. Artists making their own decisions and taking charge of their own destiny. I wish her all the best."

Martha's hand stayed on his arm, and he was grateful for her support. She knew what this was doing to him.

"What a shocking evening. Am I right?" Olivia beamed at the cameras, already moving to the closing segment. "The drama never stops on *Starbound*. Join us next week for our live finale! Two extraordinary artists, one life-changing prize. Who will be crowned our first *Starbound* winner? The decision is in your hands, Britain!"

The closing music swelled. Zach remained seated as the cameras captured final reaction shots, the excruciating eternity of remaining on camera while processing betrayal stretching each second into hours.

When the floor director finally signaled they were clear, Zach stood smoothly, Martha rising beside him with concern written across her face.

"Are you okay?" she whispered.

He gave a nearly imperceptible nod as they moved to congratulate Sandra and Diana. He kept his path carefully plotted to avoid Ryan and Kezia, who were now surrounded by production staff.

As he shook Sandra's hand, offering genuine congratulations, he caught sight of Kezia across the stage. For a brief moment, their gazes met, her dark eyes wide.

Then she turned away—just like Verity had all those years ago—and let Ryan steer her toward the spotlight.

"Zach," Martha said softly beside him.

The hollow feeling in Zach's chest expanded. Had everything between them been fiction? A professional actress playing a part? Or had something changed to make her reject him so publicly, so completely?

He didn't know which answer would hurt less.

Chapter 70

"TEN SECONDS, EVERYONE." THE floor director signaled as Kezia was ushered to the interview area, a plush sofa with the *Starbound* logo behind it.

A makeup artist darted in, dabbing powder across her forehead and nose as she fell to pieces inside.

The look on Zach's face as she'd chosen Ryan...

"Congratulations, Kezia!" Laura gushed, clipping a microphone to the front of her dress. "We just need the standard reaction to advancing to the finale. Isn't this so exciting?"

Kezia's hands were ice cold as she clasped them together to stop the trembling. Around her, the studio had transformed from performance space to a maze of post-show interviews.

Ryan appeared at her side, taking up way too much room on the sofa. His satisfaction radiated from every pore. It was in his posture, his smile, the proprietary way he patted her knee. He'd won, and he wanted everyone to know it.

She angled her body away, edging farther from him.

Across the studio, Sandra sat with Diana for her own interview, looking stunned but happy. No complications clouding her joy at making the finale.

"We're live in three, two…"

The interviewer of the post-show companion program, a woman whose name tag read "Melanie," beamed at them as the red light blinked on. "I'm here live with finalist Kezia Blair and her mentor. Or should I say, her newly chosen mentor, Ryan Sterling! Kezia, congratulations on making it to the finale! How are you feeling right now?"

She had to sell this and sell it well, or there was no point in what she'd done. She forced her wooden lips to smile. "Thank you. It's absolutely surreal. I can't believe I made it this far."

"She's being modest," Ryan interjected, leaning forward. "I always knew she had this potential from the moment I first selected her. That's why I was so determined to get her back on my team."

His revisionist history made her stomach twist, but her smile remained fixed in place.

"You must have felt you would make it into the final after your performances tonight. They were absolutely spectacular," Melanie said. "'All That I Give' brought the audience to their feet, including your former mentor, Zach. If I'm not mistaken, I think that's your first standing ovation from him."

The question was a knife-twist in Kezia's gut. Her fingers tightened into a fist, but she kept her voice steady. "Thank you. It was a really special song for me."

"I knew she would be among the last two," Ryan said. "We're going to focus on making sure she connects with the audience on an even deeper level."

As Ryan continued blathering on, Kezia's gaze drifted past Melanie, scanning the bustling studio. Somewhere among the crowd of producers, crew members, and contestants, Zach was handling his post-show responsibilities.

What did he think of her after what she'd done? Would she get a chance to tell him this wasn't what it seemed?

Her attention whipped back to Melanie as the interviewer said her name.

"Kezia, let's get to the question I'm sure everyone's asking." Melanie leaned forward, her expression turning serious. "Why did you decide to work with Ryan again even though he dropped you after Round Two?"

Ice flooded her veins. She should have known this was coming. Why hadn't she prepared an answer? The cameras would catch every hesitation, every flicker of doubt.

"I, um..." She faltered, then drew a deep breath. "When I came to *Starbound*, Ryan was the first one who believed in me and took a chance on me. I was his number one pick. So it's full circle, in a sense."

The words made her want to gag. Instead, she smiled. She had to make sure Ryan believed her, even if nobody else did.

He nodded, grinning widely. "Exactly. I've always believed that with her talent and my knowledge of the market, the sky's the limit for Kezia. We make a great team."

His hand settled on her shoulder, heavy and possessive. It took everything in her not to shrug it off.

"Ryan," Melanie said, "It's true Kezia's always been a frontrunner, but she's kept getting better and better every week. And, arguably, working with Zach Falconer has elevated her so much further. Do you feel you're benefiting from his hard work?"

If the question offended Ryan, he didn't show it. His laugh was practiced and smooth. "I planted the seeds of Kezia's success from day one. Zach simply watered what I had already cultivated. Now I'm back to harvest the fruits of my initial vision."

Kezia's nails dug into her palms. The audacity of his claim almost made her drop the charade. She'd grown almost as much under Zach's guidance in a few weeks than in all her years of formal training.

There—near the exit. She finally saw him.

Zach stood with Martha, deep in conversation. Was she imagining the tension in his shoulders, the rigid line of his spine as he nodded at something his sister-in-law was saying?

"Kezia?" Melanie's voice pulled her back. "I asked about your strategy for the finale?"

"I'm sorry." She refocused with effort. *Fix your posture, find your light, fake the joy.* "I think consistency will be key. Continuing to challenge myself while staying true to who I am as an artist."

As Ryan launched into his own finale strategy, Kezia's gaze drifted back to where Zach stood.

Martha laid a hand briefly on his back in a gesture of comfort. The simple action confirmed what Kezia already knew. She'd hurt him deeply.

And now he was leaving without even a glance in her direction. She'd probably lost Martha's friendship, too.

"Kezia and I have a special musical connection that's going to bring out something extraordinary in the finale," Ryan said, squeezing her shoulder. "Just wait and see."

There was no musical connection between them. None. Just the threat he posed to Zach, and her desperate ploy to protect the man she considered her real mentor. Would Zach ever understand why she'd done this?

"Well, I think all of Britain agrees when I say I can't wait to see what you bring to the finale," Melanie said. "Best of luck to both of you."

"And we're clear," called the floor director.

The relief of being off camera lasted only seconds.

Ryan turned to her with an oily smile that made her feel dirty. "Well, Kezia, for a while there I questioned your judgment. Now I can see you're a smart girl." His voice dropped to a level only meant for her ears. "A very smart girl. Play your cards right, and the sky really is the limit for you."

It was almost funny how little he understood her. He thought she'd chosen him for career advancement, completely unaware she'd made this choice to protect Zach and everything he'd worked so hard to build.

Ryan stood. "Let's meet bright and early tomorrow and discuss our strategy for winning this thing. My office, nine AM."

She nodded, managing another smile. She was becoming a pro at being phony.

Ryan strode away to speak with a group of producers, leaving her alone in the glare of the studio lights.

She stared at the exit where Zach had stood moments before. He was gone now.

And maybe that was for the best. Because if he stayed close, she wasn't sure she could keep pretending she didn't care. But she did. So much. Enough to let him think the worst of her, if that's what it took to shield him from the fallout.

The full weight of what she'd done settled on her shoulders, weighing her down like a physical burden.

But beneath the ache, determination began to form. She'd made this choice to protect Zach, and now she would see it through to the end.

The most important thing was to get through this competition with Zach's reputation intact. With her on his team, Ryan had no reason, no leverage to accuse Zach of inappropriate behavior. Somehow, someday, she'd have the chance to explain to Zach.

She had to believe that.

Chapter 71

ACH GUIDED MARTHA THROUGH the backstage labyrinth of the Albion Broadcasting Network studio complex, home of the *Starbound* live shows.

The chaos of post-show activity swirled around them, but it didn't come close to the turmoil raging within him. Crew members rushed past, buzzing about the night's dramatic conclusion.

Zach kept his neutral mask on, nodding at those who caught his eye. He was still the show's creator and executive producer. He couldn't let them see how deeply the knife had twisted.

Each step away from the stage, away from Kezia and Ryan, felt like escape and exile simultaneously.

But his first priority now was getting his sister-in-law to Ezra, who waited in the parking lot to take her home.

"Are you sure you're feeling all right?" he asked, studying Martha's face for signs of fatigue or dizziness. "We can stop if you need to rest."

The memory of her fainting spell during Kezia's coaching session remained vivid. He still wasn't sure whether she should be here tonight, but she'd wanted to watch Kezia's performance.

A performance which had led to...no. He would not think about that. Not yet.

"I'm fine, Zach. Don't fuss." Martha patted the hand which rested on her elbow.

They finally reached the exit doors, the chilly November air striking his face as they stepped outside.

As they walked slowly toward the parking area, Martha looked up at him. "Zach, I'm sure there's a reason why she—"

"Don't say anything." His voice came out raw, far harsher than he'd intended.

He immediately regretted his tone. Martha didn't need him barking at her. Especially when her presence was the only thing keeping him anchored. "I'm sorry. That was uncalled for. What were you going to say?"

She squeezed his arm. "I just wanted to say that I'm sure she had a reason for going back to Ryan."

A bitter laugh escaped him. "Of course she has a reason. She wants to win." They walked around a puddle, the reflection of studio lights shimmering in the dark water. "It's all about the public vote from here on out, and Ryan knows exactly how to play that game."

Martha glanced up at him, her eyes big and dark in the dim security lighting. "Does she know how you feel about her?"

The blade-sharp accuracy of her question cut through his defenses, leaving him momentarily speechless. Trust Martha to see straight to the heart of it.

"Oh, she knows. She knows very well." The words almost choked him. "Just like Verity."

Martha shivered in the frosty night air, and Zach was instantly alert. She had only a shawl over her evening gown.

Removing his jacket, he placed it around her shoulders.

"Zach, I'm fine. We're almost to the car, aren't we?"

"I'm not delivering you to Ezra freezing and shivering. Do you have any idea the tongue-lashing I'd get? Do it for me, if not for yourself." He adjusted the jacket to cover her properly.

"Thanks." She accepted the jacket, studying his face as she pulled it around herself. "I didn't know Verity that well, but I don't think Kezia is anything like her."

"How well do you know Kezia?" His words were as bitter as the cold wind that sliced into them as they reached Ezra's car.

His brother stepped out from the driver's side. "There you are. How'd it go?" His gaze settled on Zach's face. "That bad? Oh, no. Did Kezia get voted out?"

Martha slipped Zach's jacket off her shoulders and handed it back to him as she spoke to her husband. "Kezia made it through to the final. But she's switched back to Ryan to mentor her."

"What?" Ezra's eyebrows shot up. "Why?"

Martha touched his arm. "We're trying not to jump to conclusions." She faced Zach again. "We'll be praying for you."

As she slid into the passenger seat, Ezra placed a hand on Zach's shoulder. "Hang in there. We're here if you need to talk."

"Thanks."

But he didn't plan on doing any more talking about Kezia Blair. He'd thought she was different, that she understood what he was trying to do for her. He'd thought they had a connection. Had it all been one-sided? Or worse, merely strategic on her part?

Because at the first opportunity, she'd chosen to work with Ryan and his surface-level approach to artistry.

"I'm fine," Zach said, his words automatic even though he knew the lie was as flimsy a covering as Martha's shawl. Ezra could see right through it.

But his brother didn't challenge him. Ezra just squeezed his shoulder and got into his car without another word.

As Ezra's car pulled away, Zach headed toward his own vehicle, his shoulders finally slumping now that he no longer needed to put up a front. All he wanted was to slink away home and lick his wounds where nobody could see him.

But before he could reach his car, Steve Wilson, the senior producer, appeared from between two parked vehicles.

"There you are, Zach! I missed a chance to catch up with you after the show." Steve was nearly hugging himself with delight. "That Kezia really is the gift that keeps on giving. All that drama! She's the *Starbound* MVP."

The clash between Steve's excitement and Zach's devastation was almost surreal. For a moment, Zach couldn't even form a response. And yet he had to, even though the different worlds he inhabited—show creator and wounded man—collided with the violence of a thundercloud.

As executive producer, he had to celebrate that tonight would be a ratings bonanza. He forced a smile. "It certainly adds another layer to the finale narrative."

"The social media team is already reporting record engagement," Steve said, scrolling through his phone. "Everyone's talking about the shocking twist. We couldn't have scripted it better."

"No, none of us could have made that up."

Steve clapped Zach's shoulder. "This is exactly what we need heading into the finale. See you in tomorrow's meeting."

As Steve finally walked away, Zach stood alone in the darkened parking lot. He couldn't get the image out of his mind of Ryan's hand settled possessively on Kezia's shoulder, claiming his prize. Tomorrow, in his role as a savvy businessman, he'd need to figure out how to capitalize on that to promote his show. His investment.

As he unlocked his car, his gaze slid back to the brightly lit studio building where Kezia remained with Ryan.

His plans had crumbled into ash. And not just his plans for guiding Kezia through to a potential victory. His hopes to explore their connection when the show was over were dead, too. The song she'd shown him, lyrics revealing what he thought was her understanding of what was growing between them. Was all that a lie?

And yet...did he really have a right to be upset with her?

There wasn't even supposed to be anything between them. For all he knew, Kezia might have felt trapped with him after he, her mentor and the show's creator, told her he had more than a professional interest in her. Maybe she'd switched to Ryan so she could get away from him.

The idea burned like acid in his brain, and, feeling suddenly dizzy, he braced himself against the cold metal of his car.

The only thing he had left was the show. But, ironically, *Starbound* was now all about Kezia and the man she'd chosen.

But maybe it hadn't been a choice. Maybe she hadn't been reaching for something better...but pulling away from Zach. From the power imbalance. From pressure she never asked for. From the feelings he never should have confessed.

Because he'd looked at her with eyes that said "I want" when she was depending on him to say "you're safe."

And she wasn't. Not really. Not if the person meant to protect her was tangled up in his own hopes and feelings.

Zach climbed into his car, gripping the wheel like it might hold him together. Tomorrow, he'd do his job. He'd make the finale shine.

But tonight, all he could feel was the shame of having crossed a line he never meant to cross...and the quiet, devastating possibility that in her mind, what he'd offered her hadn't been love at all.

It had been pressure she needed to escape.

Chapter 72

KEZIA ARRIVED AT RYAN'S office precisely on time, on an overcast Monday morning.

It was telling that he wanted their finale strategy session to be here rather than in a rehearsal room or even in a relaxing space like the library.

This was unmistakably Ryan's domain—meticulously ordered, dominated by presentation boards and market data pinned to a sleek bulletin board.

"There she is! The future *Starbound* winner." He gestured for her to sit. "Congratulations once again. I've been looking over those semifinal performance statistics. You outscored Sandra by a significant margin. The voting audience loves you."

"Thank you," Kezia said. If they loved her, it was because of all the work she had done with Zach. The way he'd encouraged her to dig deep inside herself to connect with the audience. And because the only way she could infuse such emotion into that power ballad was by thinking of him as she sang it. And yet here was Ryan, acting as though all the credit was his.

He tapped his tablet with a manicured finger. "But you can't rest on your laurels. Word on the street is Sandra's social media army is mobilizing to flood the voting lines for the finale. We need to strategize on how to make sure we convince even more people to vote for you."

Typical Ryan. Instead of working on artistic authenticity and emotional connection, he wanted to focus on audience metrics and market positioning.

He moved to a large board covered with magazine cutouts, charts, and photographs. "Off the record, because we're not really supposed to be having this conversation unless you win, but I was in touch with Harmony Records this morning. They're extremely interested in your commercial potential."

He spread several market analysis reports across the desk between them. "The diva vocalist market has a significant gap right now. That's where we're positioning you."

Kezia nodded, trying to appear engaged as Ryan outlined his vision.

"For the finale, after a lot of thought, I recommend one power ballad to showcase your range, and one upbeat Beyoncé-style track to show your versatility," he said, making notes on his tablet.

She bit back the observation that this followed exactly what Zach had planned for her semifinals strategy. Ryan was presenting it as though he'd thought it all up himself.

"This combination will show your marketability across multiple formats," he continued. "The record label executives are looking for someone who can sell both albums and streaming singles. That versatility will hook a wider voting base. Your vocal skills are a product we need to package correctly for maximum commercial appeal. And because you can sing literally anything, we have a lot of scope to play with."

Ryan flashed a condescending smile. "I'm not too proud to admit I was wrong about your look, by the way. The natural Afro hair and neo-soul styling was a genius move. Fans are responding extremely well, according to our social media metrics. Even the younger voters who we might have otherwise lost to Sandra think you look cool."

Kezia's jaw tightened. She'd fought so hard for that authentic styling when she was Ryan's mentee the first time around, and now he was acting as though he was being generous in "allowing" her to keep it when it served his purposes.

"We'll maintain that aesthetic while elevating it to a more commercial level," he said, his patronizing tone making her skin crawl. "Just because we're selling to the masses doesn't mean we can't look distinctive."

He pulled out his phone to show her voting and engagement statistics. "The audience responds to packaging as much as performance. That's just business reality."

The hollow feeling in her chest grew as Ryan continued outlining his marketing approach. Her professional mask remained in place, hiding the struggle beneath. Was Diana's warning enough to justify this painful choice? Did she even want to win anymore if it meant being tied to Ryan and his vision of music?

The weight of her decision felt heavier with each of Ryan's suggestions. She'd made this sacrifice to protect Zach and everything he'd built, but sitting here listening to Ryan reduce her artistry to sales figures and streaming numbers made her question whether she could endure the finale.

Ryan checked his watch. "We need to get to the main hall. They need to do a new photo shoot for promo images since I'm your mentor now."

A new photo shoot. The memory of her last photo shoot with Zach threatened to unravel Kezia's tightly wound control. What did he think of her? How was he feeling about what she'd done?

Ryan gathered his materials, still outlining marketing strategies as they walked through the office wing of Glenmere Hall.

Kezia half-listened, part of her still aching over the look on Zach's face when she'd announced her choice. The place was busier than usual with finale preparations underway; production staff hurried past with equipment and overflowing binders.

As they rounded a corner, Ryan was mid-sentence about album release timing when they nearly collided with someone coming from the opposite direction.

Kezia's heart lurched as she found herself face to face with Zach. She wasn't prepared for this moment, and her professional mask slipped briefly before she forced it back in place.

A spasm flashed across his face as his gaze met hers, then slid away, his expression shifting to careful neutrality. They stood suspended in time, neither of them speaking.

Ryan's trademark smirk emerged. "Zach! Perfect timing. I was just telling Kezia how the Harmony Records execs are thrilled with her commercial potential." His gloating was barely disguised as professional courtesy.

"Ryan. Miss Blair." His voice was as bland as a robocall. "I know you must be very busy. Excuse me, I have a meeting to attend."

He stepped aside to let them pass, his gaze focused slightly past her shoulder.

"We were just discussing Kezia's market positioning," Ryan said, motioning for Kezia to move ahead of him. "The label is very excited."

Zach glanced at him. "Oh, I'm sure you'll package her perfectly for the commercial market."

Kezia's throat tightened at the coldness in his words.

As they continued down the hallway, Ryan chuckled, not bothering to lower his volume. "Looks like someone's still smarting from being dumped on national television."

He leaned toward her ear. "Don't worry, the viewers loved the drama. Great for ratings."

Kezia's face burned. Had Zach heard that? She didn't dare turn around to check. He must think she was choosing Ryan and everything he stood for. Everything that now felt fake and shallow.

Just days ago, Zach had acted as though he didn't like her. She was the one doing the acting now, pretending she didn't care, pretending she'd chosen Ryan.

For a moment, she let herself hope he might understand. That maybe this distance between them was just another performance, two actors playing roles to protect something fragile and unspoken.

But no. He was being real. The fakeness was all hers. He'd been the one to teach her how liberating authenticity could be. How truth in art and in life was what made everything matter.

And now, in front of the one person she most longed to be real with, she was wearing her heaviest mask yet. Losing Zach's friendship, his good regard, cut deeper than she had imagined it would.

Yet beneath the pain, a renewed determination took hold. His coldness and Ryan's smugness meant that her sacrifice had worked. She was protecting Zach by removing herself from his orbit. And she would see this through.

No matter how much it hurt her.

Chapter 73

*K*EZIA SAT AT THE piano in the empty rehearsal room. The solitude was a life-giving oasis after days of Ryan in full-blown commercial strategizing mode.

Of course, she couldn't escape him completely. Sheet music lay scattered across the piano—Ryan's market-calibrated song selection for the finale—but she wasn't playing any of them.

Instead, her fingers moved over the keys, picking out the melody of "Old Town Symphony," the song she'd written with Zach. *For* Zach. The one she'd played for him when they'd silently acknowledged what was growing between them.

Singing solo till you joined in, playing straight to my heart. ..

Playing it was torture, but she couldn't help tracing that last meaningful connection they'd shared. Better to remember it and sit with the pain than to bury herself in the meaningless, soul-numbing vision Ryan had for her finale performance. And not just her next performance, but her career afterward.

He'd made it clear that he wanted to be her manager if she won the show, which he was sure she would.

She hadn't heard from Zach since that painful hallway encounter. Why would she? There was no reason for him to reach out. And if she tried to contact him, it would only arouse the very suspicions she was trying to avoid. It was better this way. Cleaner. Like an amputation with clinical precision.

One small blessing was how much easier it was to find pockets of alone time, even during this week of intensive rehearsals. Since the next episode would be the live finale, the *Starbound* crew was no longer as interested in recording "behind the scenes" footage to edit and put on air. The constant presence of cameras documenting every interaction had diminished significantly.

Kezia jumped as the door swung open.

Sandra, eyes wide, hovered in the doorway, sheet music clutched in her hands. "Sorry, I didn't know anyone was in here." The teenager turned to retreat.

"It's fine," Kezia called after her. "I was just taking a break. In fact, I'm done if you want to use this place."

Sandra paused, then entered hesitantly. "Are you sure? I can go somewhere else. There are loads of other rooms."

"Really, it's okay." Kezia stood, gathering up her music.

Although the other rehearsal rooms at the Starbound Campus were more than adequate, Kezia had always thought this one had the best acoustic setup, with its high ceilings. Not to mention the Steinway grand piano. No wonder Sandra had sought it out.

The younger girl moved closer, watching Kezia put her things together.

A charged silence stretched between them, heavy with awkward feelings.

As Kezia slid her music into her tote bag, Sandra said, "There's no way anyone could pull off an act for this long."

Kezia froze. "Excuse me?"

"That 'nice girl' act. Being so helpful and generous and selfless." Sandra busied herself with her papers, not looking up. "Letting the competition use the best rehearsal space in finals week. I didn't think anyone could really be that kind. I thought you were just playing 4D chess at the reality show game."

Kezia *was* playing 4D reality TV chess...just not the kind Sandra imagined.

"Seriously," Kezia said, "the room's all yours." She couldn't handle any more drama.

She headed toward the door, but Sandra spoke again.

"I wanted to apologize, actually."

Okay, this conversation was officially weird. Kezia faced her. "Apologize? For what?"

"For believing what Brianna said about you." Sandra finally met her gaze. "That you were just pretending to help me with vocal technique so you could figure out my weaknesses."

"Oh." Kezia was floored by the teen's words. "You don't need to apologize for that."

"I do, though." Sandra tucked a strand of hair behind her ear. "I asked Diana about those exercises you showed me. She said they were not just legit, but were making a big difference. Said I should carry on with them. I should have trusted my gut instincts about you."

"It's a competition," Kezia said. "Makes everyone a bit suspicious. And I wasn't just a stranger, but a competitor. Why wouldn't you wonder about my intentions?"

Sandra's posture grew more relaxed. "Brianna had everyone believing the worst about each other." She shook her head. "Ryan and Brianna, they just fit together, you know? But you're not like that."

"I try my best not to be."

"Diana says Zach was bringing out something really special in you." Sandra scanned her face. "So, why'd you leave him?"

Kezia's stomach dropped. Of all the awkward questions to ask, Kezia had no idea how to handle this one. Especially with the teen's gaze exposing her like a two-thousand-watt spotlight.

Kezia groped for words that wouldn't reveal too much, that wouldn't hint at the real reason behind her choice. But she came up with nothing. "It's...hard to explain."

Sandra sighed. "You mean because I'm just sixteen? I get that a lot." She rolled her eyes. "I can't wait to get older."

The comment offered an unexpected escape route from dangerous territory, and Kezia seized it like a lifeline. "Being sixteen is a gift I didn't appreciate while I had it," she said. "Don't be in too much of a hurry to grow up."

Sandra's lips curved into a smirk. "Because things get complicated?"

Kezia laughed. "Yes, because things get complicated. Like trigonometry and calculus complicated. Stick with music. It's much more fun."

Sandra's laughter joined hers, the sound bright in the quiet room.

"No one ever talks to me like this," Sandra said. "Everyone either treats me like I'm five or expects me to act forty. I mean, Diana is wonderful and all, but she's more like a mum."

"Sixteen is sixteen," Kezia said. "Not a child, not quite an adult. It's its own thing."

"There you are!" A production assistant appeared at the door. "Ryan's looking everywhere for you, Kezia. Something about some market analysis he wants to discuss."

The brief respite ended as quickly as it had begun. Now she had to listen to more of Ryan's bloviating over commercial strategies and calculated image crafting.

Kezia gave Sandra a shrug. "See? I really was done here. I wasn't just being nice. I'd better go."

"Hey, do you want to do some more work together sometime?" Sandra asked. "I really miss doing that."

This girl was full of surprises today. Kezia smiled. "I'd love that. Let's set up a time later."

As Kezia followed the production assistant out, she felt lighter than she had for the first time in days. The finale was approaching fast. And Ryan's shadow loomed over not just that, but her future career as well. But there were still ways she could find meaning and joy in her time here. She still had some agency.

Maybe she hadn't lost everything after all.

Chapter 74

CAMERA FLASHES EXPLODED LIKE strobe lights, blurring Kezia's vision as she stepped out of the sleek black production car and onto the red carpet outside London's Royal Victoria Theater.

The noise assaulted her—reporters shouting questions from behind safety barriers and fans screaming her name from the designated viewing areas.

The grand Victorian-era playhouse, with its imposing stone columns and ornate facade, had hosted Britain's greatest musical legends since 1889, from opera divas to The Beatles to Adele. Tonight, the first *Starbound* champion would be crowned on its storied stage.

She knew she looked her best, dressed in a floor-length Duro Olowu evening gown, with the designer's distinctive bold African patterns and long voluminous sleeves. Thousands of music fans knew her by name, by sight, by her sound. It should have been exciting. This was the pinnacle of her career so far.

Instead, she felt hunted. Exposed. Trapped.

Ryan exited the car behind her, immediately placing his hand on the small of her back. "Big smile," he murmured, breath warm against her ear. "This is your moment. Follow my lead."

Every nerve screamed to escape from the presumptuous ownership of his touch, but the cameras were everywhere, documenting every movement, every expression. Instead, she fixed her camera-ready smile in place as Ryan expertly navigated the carpet, steering her toward strategic photo opportunities.

"Over here, Kezia!"

"Ryan, this way!"

"Give us a smile together!"

The photographers' directions blurred into shrill, meaningless chatter as Ryan maneuvered them into position after position. His hand never left her back, a physical reminder of his claim on her.

Another car pulled up, and Sandra emerged, looking both excited and overwhelmed in her elegant blue gown. Diana followed, immediately providing protective guidance through the media gauntlet. The veteran singer moved with practiced ease, shielding her young mentee from the pushiest photographers while still ensuring Sandra got plenty of coverage.

Production assistants appeared, guiding Kezia and Ryan further along the carpet's path. Ryan's charm switched on like a spotlight as they approached the waiting reporters.

"Ryan! How confident are you feeling about tonight's finale?"

His smile widened. "Extremely confident. Kezia and I have been working tirelessly on finale performances that will showcase her extraordinary commercial potential."

He could speak for himself about the work being "tireless". She was exhausted. Mentally and physically drained. Mostly mentally.

Kezia played her part while counting the minutes until she could step away from him and seek solace in the routine of performance.

His hand remained firmly on her back as they fielded questions about outfit choices and excitement levels.

"What's it like to be back with your original mentor, Kezia?"

Before she could answer, Ryan jumped in. "It's been a seamless transition. We've always had an exceptional creative rapport."

She nodded along, letting him dominate the responses. Every answer emphasized his role in her journey as he claimed credit for her growth and success, as though her life-changing weeks with Zach had never happened.

"Ryan! Kezia! Over here!"

The voice cut through the chaos, commanding attention. They turned to see Imogen Hunter, the incisive entertainment host from Albion Network, sleek and polished with microphone in hand. The network's logo gleamed on the microphone.

This interview mattered. It would likely be broadcast during the pre-show coverage and would probably influence voters.

Kezia caught herself. She was starting to think like Ryan. She died a little inside.

Ryan immediately pivoted toward the reporter. "Imogen! Always a pleasure." His hand pressed Kezia forward as if presenting a prized possession.

Imogen's professional smile was dazzling. "*Starbound*'s breakout finalist and her mentor! The story everyone's talking about."

She began with seemingly innocuous questions about finale preparation, and Ryan delivered polished responses about their "natural alignment" and "shared vision."

Then came the subtle shift as Imogen turned directly to Kezia. "Britain was stunned when you chose Ryan over Zach Falconer to guide you into the finale. Some say you successfully turned the tables on 'The Maestro of Mean,' the mentor who always gave you a hard time. But now, after proving you can win the public vote, you're returning to the market-savvy mentor who dropped you after round two."

Kezia's smile didn't waver, though the question made her feel sick.

"Many are calling it the most strategic move in reality TV history," Imogen said. "Was it always your plan to use Zach to elevate your profile before returning to Ryan?"

Panic flashed through Kezia, even as the insinuations hurt like a knife to the gut. Any response to this loaded question could be twisted to sound calculating. There *was* no plan to use Zach.

Thankfully, Ryan was eager to answer, jumping in immediately. "Kezia recognized who could best position her for commercial success."

But Imogen wasn't so easily put off. "I'd love to hear from Kezia herself."

Kezia took a steadying breath. "The decision was difficult and personal. Both Zach and Ryan have contributed enormously to my journey on *Starbound*."

"But now, at the end of that journey, you think Ryan will advance your post-show career?" Imogen pressed.

Kezia chose her words with extreme care, knowing Zach and his family might hear this. "I made the choice I believed was necessary at the time."

"And have you had any contact with Zach since making your choice?"

The personal interest was barely disguised as professional inquiry. Kezia answered honestly, "No, I haven't had that opportunity."

A production assistant signaled it was time to move on.

Ryan smoothly stepped in. "Always a pleasure, Imogen. We should catch up after the show."

As they moved away, he squeezed Kezia's waist and whispered, "Perfect. You handled that beautifully."

They proceeded toward the theater entrance, Ryan still maintaining physical contact.

Across the carpet, time slowed as Kezia spotted Zach. His gaze connected with hers for a fleeting second before he deliberately turned away, speaking to the woman next to him. The physical ache of that deliberate dismissal was worse than Kezia ever imagined.

That woman...she was older, maybe in her late fifties, with beautifully styled graying hair and a black evening gown. Her jawline, the shape of her eyes, were so much like Zach's. Was that his mother? She was well enough to be here tonight? He had been so worried about her.

Ryan pressed her waist. "Focus, Kezia. Tonight is about your future, not the past."

As though the future were something to look forward to. She edged away from him as they entered the theater, the doors closing behind them like a final decision. Would she ever have the chance to explain herself to Zach? To tell him she'd made her choice to protect him, not to advance her career?

As they moved into the bustling backstage area, that possibility seemed to shrink with every step. Tonight she would either win *Starbound* and be locked into Ryan's vision for her career, or lose and face an uncertain future without the connection that had come to mean so much to her.

She had only just begun paying the cost of her choice.

Chapter 75

ACH STOOD NEXT TO Mum near the Royal Victoria Theater entrance, her hand looped through the crook of his elbow. Her presence here tonight was both comfort and concern. This was her first public event since Greg's death, and she'd chosen a huge night on which to come out.

Grief had hollowed her cheeks and sharpened the lines of her figure, but tonight there was a warmth in her complexion he hadn't seen in weeks. He was grateful she was taking an interest in things again.

"I've had this date in my diary for months, Zach," she'd said when he'd suggested she might find it too taxing not just to attend the finale, but to appear on the red carpet with him. "I'm not missing my son's big night."

Now, as she asked him who was who and listened as he identified all the VIPs as they arrived, he was grateful she was here. She reminded him of what mattered most in his life: faith and family.

A cluster of network executives approached, animated with pre-show excitement. Victoria Harlow, Head of Albion Entertainment Programming, glowed with delight. This was her triumph, too. She had championed *Starbound* before the network, convincing her bosses to take a chance on Zach's concept. Its success reflected very well on her instincts.

She leaned toward Zach, including him in the conversation. "The finale projections are through the roof. You've exceeded every expectation, Zach."

He nodded, offering the appropriate smile. "The contestants have given us exceptional performances to work with."

"Your mother must be very proud," Victoria said, extending her hand to Mum. "Mrs. Falconer, it's a pleasure to finally meet you."

"Please, call me Beth," Mum said with the gentle smile that reassured him she was really back. "And yes, I'm very proud of Zach. Although, I have to say, I'm not at all surprised."

As Victoria and Mum exchanged pleasantries, Zach's gaze drifted to the red carpet arrivals.

The crowds surged as another car pulled up, cameras flashing in anticipation.

And there she was.

His heart bounded as Kezia stepped onto the red carpet, so beautiful that watching her was exquisite torture. Regal in a floor-length gown with bold patterns, she stood elegant and poised as cameras clicked and fans called her name. A star was being born in front of his eyes.

Then Ryan emerged behind her, placing his hand on her back like a man claiming what he owned.

A flicker of fury flared in Zach's gut until shame crept in behind it. Had he been any better, imposing his feelings on her? Had he mistaken guidance for ownership, protection with possession?

"Is that the girl everyone's been talking about?" Mum asked, following his gaze.

Zach clenched his fist. "Yes." He didn't trust himself to say more.

"She's lovely," Mum said.

Zach watched Ryan working the media line like a pro, keeping Kezia close as they posed for photographers. Ryan was steering her through the media like a PR puppet-master. And Zach could only wonder—had she turned to him to escape Zach's own strings?

"Zach, I was so excited about everything that I can't believe I didn't tell you about this," Victoria said, drawing Zach's attention back. "We've had to call in a lot of favors, but it's confirmed that Verity James will be our special guest performer tonight. She'll perform her new top ten single during the intermission."

The hits just kept on coming tonight. Verity. Of course. The woman who had duped him into trusting her before she broke his heart six years ago would be performing at the *Starbound* finale. On the same night he was watching history repeat itself with Kezia. If God was trying to teach him a lesson, Zach was currently flunking out.

Mum squeezed his arm. Bless her...she understood.

"I'm sure she'll be a crowd-pleaser," he managed. "What's the song, again?"

"'Higher Ground,'" Victoria said. "Have you heard it? Critics are saying it's her best yet."

As though he wanted the self-flagellation, his gaze turned to the other side of the carpet, where Imogen Hunter was interviewing Ryan and Kezia. No doubt, Imogen's provocative questions would be crafting the narrative of Kezia's strategic mentor switch for the viewers at home.

For a fleeting moment, Zach considered escaping inside the theater, away from the spectacle. But the creator of *Starbound* couldn't be seen avoiding his own red carpet.

He breathed a prayer of thanks that Mum was here. Focusing on her gave him something beyond his own turmoil to think about.

"How are you holding up, Mum? Are you tired?" he asked, noticing the slight tremor in her fingers as she brushed back a strand of hair.

"Not yet." She patted his hand. "There'll be lots of time to sit when we're inside. And I'm enjoying watching you in your element."

Yet again, Zach couldn't keep from glancing at Ryan and Kezia as they moved toward the theater entrance.

Suddenly, she looked in Zach's direction. Their gazes tangled across the distance, and his heart flinched.

He looked away, not out of anger, but out of shame. Shame that he wasn't the mentor she could trust, but the man she'd needed to get away from.

When she'd sung "Old Town Symphony" to him and asked him to help shape it, he'd taken it as a sign. That she felt what he felt. That she was choosing him, quietly but clearly.

But maybe she'd come to realize just how tangled things had become. How unbalanced things were, how exposed she was, depending on him for her future, while he stood above her with all the power. Maybe she'd panicked and hadn't known how to pull back until the mentor switch gave her an out.

And maybe, worst of all, he hadn't seen it because he hadn't wanted to.

He turned to Mum, grasping for words to still the noise in his head. "You know, we owe a lot to the production team. They're the unsung heroes of this show."

"Zach!" Sir Giles Wentworth, the network president, approached, hand extended.

Zach had been so preoccupied with Kezia that he hadn't even seen the tall, gray-haired man appear on the red carpet.

"There's our golden boy." Sir Giles' grip was firm. "*Starbound* is the breakout hit of the season. You've created something extraordinary."

The praise should have felt triumphant. Instead, it rang hollow. Still, he smiled and shook hands, accepting congratulations for the show's success while the woman who had inspired some of its best moments moved past him, led by the man who had threatened to destroy her career and this show just to get some leverage over Zach.

"Mum, let's get you seated," Zach said, spotting the slight sag in his mother's shoulders. All the VIP guests had arrived, and it was finally acceptable to escape the red carpet circus.

They moved toward the entrance, Mum squeezing his arm as though she sensed more than she was saying.

He might be a total loser at love, but at least *Starbound* was the runaway success he'd hoped for. He hadn't let down any of the people who staked their money and their reputations on his show.

And if his heart ached over Kezia, he had only himself to blame for opening up to the possibility of something more. He should have remembered the lessons learned from Verity—how easily artistic connection could be mistaken for something deeper, how quickly that connection could be discarded if it no longer served.

At least his public dignity remained intact. Nobody but his family knew Kezia had meant more to him than just a mentee. From now on, *Starbound* would be his only heartbeat. He would reclaim his professional detachment and never make the same mistake again.

They entered the theater's grand foyer, the *Starbound* logo prominently displayed on banners hanging from the ornate ceiling. This—the show, the format, the business success—was always the real goal. Everything else was just a temporary distraction, a detour to a dead end.

As they made their way into the packed auditorium, the excited buzz of the audience washed over them. The historic venue hummed with anticipation. This was a big night, and if the bookies were to be believed, it was a toss-up who would win, although they gave Kezia the edge.

Audience members pointed and whispered as they recognized him, the creator of the show they'd been following for months. Camera crews positioned throughout captured the pre-show atmosphere, the energy building toward the broadcast that would begin in less than thirty minutes.

Backstage, Kezia would be getting ready for her performance. Probably working that vocal steamer for all it was worth.

Martha and Ezra were already seated in the front row when he and Mum got to their reserved seats.

"Quite the spectacle out there," Ezra murmured.

"Just part of the job," Zach replied, settling Mum between him and his brother.

He fixed his gaze straight ahead, toward the stage where tonight's finale would unfold. He would focus only on what truly mattered—his faith, his family, and his work. Those were the only things he could count on.

Chapter 76

THUNDEROUS APPLAUSE RANG IN her ears as Kezia rushed offstage after opening the *Starbound* finale. The audience had gone wild over her performance of Destiny's Child's "Survivor," but her heart pounded from the exertion of the song's demanding choreography and vocals. She was just grateful that she'd remembered all the steps and not tripped over one of the backing dancers.

Especially after seeing her parents in the audience, seated in the VIP area. Apparently, Maya had pulled off the impossible, getting Dr. and Mrs. Byaruhanga to attend a performance by their daughter for the first time in years.

"Brilliant job!" Chelsea, a wardrobe assistant, intercepted her, guiding her toward the dressing room. "We need to hustle through your wardrobe change. Sandra's up next, then a commercial break, then the special guest performer. You're on after that."

Two makeup artists and another costume assistant were already waiting, hands reaching to help Kezia out of the sparkly gold outfit she'd worn for the high-energy opener.

"That was electric!" One of the makeup artists dabbed at the perspiration on her forehead. "The way you moved across that stage, I got chills."

Kezia nodded, still catching her breath as they helped her into the elegant midnight-blue gown chosen for her power ballad. The structured bodice gave her the support she'd need for the demanding vocal performance of "I Will Always Love You," while the flowing skirt would create the dramatic silhouette Ryan had insisted upon.

"Hair touch-up," someone called, and Kezia tilted her head obediently as they refreshed her carefully styled Afro curls.

Sandra's first performance filtered through the dressing room speakers. She sang a soulful rendition of Tevin Campbell's "Tomorrow" that gave Kezia goosebumps. The teenager's remarkable vocal control and tone were breathtaking, and the children's choir was an inspired touch for backing vocals. Bravo, Diana.

Ryan was confident that this competition was in the bag, but with Sandra performing like this, Kezia wasn't so sure.

As the makeup team finished their work, Kezia's mind shifted to the technical challenges ahead. The a cappella opening of "I Will Always Love You" would put her immediately in the spotlight. Just her voice, alone and exposed, before the instruments joined. Then the famous key change and the sustained high notes that would demonstrate her range.

Ryan had chosen it specifically as her technical showcase, and he wanted her to unleash her full vocal arsenal.

"Drop it like a nuclear bomb," he'd said. "Make sure that little Sandra sounds like she brought a plastic knife to a gunfight."

The green room television displayed the live broadcast feed as Sandra concluded her performance to enthusiastic applause.

Kezia clapped along with them, adding her private tribute to the teen's artistry.

That was a shot across the bow. Sandra was bringing it tonight, and if Kezia wanted to win, she needed to step it up.

Olivia Chang returned to center stage, her sequined gown throwing a constellation of sparkles around her. "What an incredible start to our finale," Olivia exclaimed. "I don't know about you, but after both performances we've seen, I am totally blown away. What a high bar they've set tonight. We'll be right back after this short break, and then we have a special treat. Chart-topping artist Verity James will perform while our finalists catch their breath!"

Verity James? Kezia stared at the screen. Hopefully she was better prepared than when she showed up hung over for that studio session months ago. Wait—that was the day when Simon invited Kezia to audition for *Starbound*. So weird that things had come full circle.

The feed switched to commercials and Kezia made her way to the side stage area, her mind already rehearsing that crucial opening note of "I Will Always Love You," visualizing how she would sing it.

"Perfect timing." Ryan appeared beside her in the corridor. "Well done with that first number. You did exactly what we discussed. The energy and the attitude were absolutely spot on. You owned that stage."

His smile was triumphant, eyes gleaming with satisfaction. "The technical showcase will seal the win. You gave them entertainment with 'Survivor,' now you'll give them artistry with Whitney."

Kezia accepted a flask of throat coat tea from a production assistant. "Thanks. I don't know, Ryan. Sandra is on fire tonight."

"The label executives are ecstatic about you." Ryan continued as though he hadn't heard her, checking something on his phone. "They're already discussing album concepts. Your performance metrics are off the charts, and you're dominating the hashtag engagement, too. Sandra was okay, but the only way she'll take this is if those three million social media followers of hers pull off that mobilization campaign they've been talking about. But if you bring the house down the way I know you can, we have nothing to worry about."

Ryan continued rattling off statistics and market positioning and Kezia eventually tuned him out. She needed to quiet her mind and her heart in order to perform, and Ryan's pep talk was as welcome and useful as a fly buzzing in her ear.

The television monitors flickered back to the live broadcast. Olivia stood center stage once more. "And now, please welcome chart-topping sensation Verity James, performing her number one hit 'Higher Ground'!"

Kezia nearly choked on her throat coat tea. "Higher Ground"? And the song had reached number one?

"Perfect," Ryan said, gesturing toward the wings. "Let's watch from there. This is the level of production value you'll be getting soon."

In a daze, Kezia followed him to the side stage area, where they could watch Verity's performance directly. The pop star emerged from a cloud of stage fog to deafening applause, her entrance accompanied by elaborate lighting effects and a troupe of dancers.

But wait. Was she hearing right?

Although a pianist sat at the grand piano on stage right, Kezia could tell they were using a backing track. Then her breath caught—those harmonies were hers. The guide vocals she'd recorded months ago weren't just on the track; they *were* the track. And now they were coming out of Verity's mouth.

Kezia walked forward, stunned. She'd known when she signed the release form that this kind of thing might happen in the studio release of "Higher Ground." But for Verity, a chart-topping artist, to go ahead and lip-sync to another singer's voice in a live performance?

The production was impressive, full of pyrotechnics, choreographed dancers, and costume reveals. Verity moved confidently across the stage, striking poses and working the audience, who were lapping it all up, unaware they were hearing someone else's voice, not hers. But given Verity's level of showmanship, would they even care?

"That could be you topping the charts in six months," Ryan said beside her. "Same level of production, same market positioning. We'll build on your technical abilities while surrounding you with this kind of spectacle."

Horror washed over her as the future Ryan envisioned suddenly crystallized before her eyes. This was his plan for her—to become another manufactured pop product, technically perfect but fundamentally empty. A "vocalist" who was just a shell, whose actual singing didn't matter at all as long as she could be a vehicle for whatever was trending most on the market.

Zach's words echoed in her mind. *Artistry is about accessing your pain and channeling it into connection. It's about finding a way to transform that personal pain into something that helps others feel less alone.*

No. She couldn't—wouldn't—proceed with Ryan's plan. Not after everything she'd learned about herself, about what truly mattered in music.

Not after what Zach had taught her.

Verity's performance concluded to an enthusiastic audience response. As she took her bows, stagehands were already preparing for Kezia's second performance, adjusting the microphone stand at center stage.

An assistant adjusted the train of Kezia's gown while another checked her in-ear monitor.

Ryan approached with last-minute instructions. "Remember, this is your Whitney Houston moment. Pull out all the stops. That a cappella opening will capture everyone's attention, and the key change is your money note. That's where you'll lock in the votes."

"Ready, Kezia? You're on in five seconds." The floor director's voice came through her in-ear monitor.

Kezia glanced at the piano sitting at the side of the stage, a sudden clarity washing over her. She knew exactly what to do.

Ryan squeezed her arm. "You've got this. Show them what a real vocalist can do."

Before she could respond, Olivia's voice rang out. "And now, for her final performance, singing the Whitney Houston classic 'I Will Always Love You,' please welcome back Kezia Blair!"

Kezia walked onto the stage, the applause washing over her as the lights found her. The orchestra was poised to begin the iconic ballad, only waiting for her to deliver that famous a cappella opening line.

She approached the microphone, heart pounding but mind surprisingly clear. Gazing out over the audience, her gaze landed on Zach. She hadn't allowed herself to look at him earlier. His face was a professional mask. Not angry, not hurt, just...blank.

Her parents sat in the row behind him. Mum with a polite smile. Dad's face was as expressionless as Zach's. She'd auditioned for *Starbound,* hoping that winning this show and earning a record contract would finally get her parents to accept her choices, to acknowledge that she wasn't "less than" just because she'd forged her own path.

A quiet piano note played in her in-ear monitor—her starting pitch for "I Will Always Love You." It hung in her mind, waiting for her.

She could sing that technical showcase just how Ryan wanted. It would impress her parents. It might even win her the competition. But it would be a hollow victory, even if it earned her the validation that she'd always craved. It wouldn't be true to who she'd become, or the voice she was meant to share.

What had Zach told her? *I don't want to diminish you, but to help you really shine in the way that matters most.* And what mattered most was authenticity. Vulnerability. Telling the truth.

She took a deep breath.

"Thank you." Her voice was steady despite the magnitude of what she was about to do. "Before I begin, could someone from the production team please make sure the piano microphone is active? I'd like to make a change."

A murmur rippled through the audience. In the wings, she caught a jerky movement from Ryan. A stagehand rushed to adjust the piano microphone, giving her a thumbs up when it was ready.

Kezia continued speaking. "Like Olivia said, I had prepared to sing 'I Will Always Love You' tonight. But instead, I'd like to share something more personal with you."

She turned and moved toward the grand piano. Through the monitor cameras, she glimpsed Ryan's face in the wings, a mixture of shock and fury as he realized what was happening. She was going off script. Way off script.

The audience knew it, too. The entire theater held its breath.

Chapter 77

*K*EZIA SETTLED ONTO THE piano bench, adjusting the microphone to the right height. Her heart thundered in her chest, but her hands were surprisingly steady as they played a gentle jazz-influenced introduction.

When she began to sing, her voice was softer than the power vocals she'd delivered in her first performance, but it carried a depth of emotion that immediately commanded attention.

"Old Town Symphony, a melody in a minor key. Notes from our past, songs that shaped who we are. A reason for every crack, a purpose in every scar."

Her voice gained strength as she sang, the words carrying a double meaning. For the audience who heard a song about resilience and authenticity, and for Zach, wherever he was sitting, who she prayed would recognize the truth behind every line.

"It doesn't have to be perfect, it just has to be real," she sang, her voice clear and unwavering. "The brokenness will be worth it if we have the courage to heal. From a bittersweet yesterday, our tomorrow will start. Singing solo till you joined in, playing straight to my heart."

Through the stage lights, she could make out faces in the audience. Somewhere among them sat Zach, who had written part of this song with her. Who had understood her when no one else did.

As she approached the second verse, the lines Zach had written for her that day in the rehearsal room, her heart swelled, the emotion spilling into her voice. This was the verse that had sealed their unspoken understanding, where they had communicated through music what they couldn't say directly.

"Faded harmonies, echoes linger in empty streets."

She glanced toward the section where she knew Zach was sitting, but she couldn't make out his face through the lights. "We've sung alone, now we're stronger as two. Every broken chord brought me closer to you."

The words drifted across the hushed theater, stripping away every pretense. No pyrotechnics, no glitter, no clever tricks—just raw, trembling honesty laid bare.

The final choruses built naturally, her voice finding new depths of feeling she hadn't known she possessed. She wasn't trying to impress anyone—not the judges, not the audience, not the millions watching on TV, not even her parents or Zach. She was simply telling the truth through music, the way Zach had taught her to.

As the final notes faded from the piano, a breathless silence hung in the air. For one terrifying moment, Kezia wondered if she'd made a terrible mistake.

Then the theater erupted.

The applause began in one section and spread like wildfire until the entire audience was on their feet.

Kezia stood from the piano bench, overwhelmed by the response. Through a sheen of her own tears, she could see people wiping their eyes in the front rows.

Diana was on her feet, clapping hard. Tyler, too.

She didn't dare search for Zach's face. She couldn't bear to see if he'd remained expressionless, if her second musical confession had meant nothing to him.

Ryan stood in the wings, his face red, but his eyes narrowing as he watched the audience's reaction.

A few feet behind him, Sandra beamed, clapping hard.

Olivia Chang returned to the stage, visibly moved as she approached Kezia. "That was...extraordinary," she said. "Completely unexpected and absolutely beautiful. Am I right, everyone?"

A fresh wave of applause filled the hall, warming Kezia's heart.

"Thank you," Kezia said quietly into the microphone.

As she walked off stage, a profound sense of peace settled over her. For the first time since joining *Starbound*, she felt complete alignment between her exterior performance and her inner truth. Whatever happened next, whether she won or lost, whether Ryan abandoned her career or not, whether Zach had understood her message, she had finally performed with complete authenticity.

Backstage, Ryan stepped into her path, his expression tightly controlled but eyes blazing.

"What was that lunacy?" he hissed. "We had a plan. We rehearsed the Whitney number for days. You yourself talked about how Sandra was stepping things up and you go and pull a stunt like that? What even *was* that?"

Kezia met his gaze, her voice calm but firm, despite her racing heart. "I needed to perform something authentic tonight. All this—the music, the performance—it's all pointless if I can't perform songs that mean something. What you...what we originally planned just wasn't real. I might as well go back to being a session singer and record hold music if I'm going to sing to order."

His face turned an ugly shade of purple as he started to speak again, but she held up a hand. "I know we need to discuss this, but let's do it later. Right now, I need a moment."

She stepped around him and continued toward the dressing room, her head held high.

Chapter 78

POLISHED. PERFECT. AND ABOUT as authentic as a £3 note. While the audience roared around him, Zach went through the motions of applauding as Verity James took her final bow. With this chart-topping single, his ex-girlfriend had truly arrived.

This was the commercial success she had dumped him for, ditching him when their relationship was hindering rather than serving her ambitions. When she'd discovered that the Falconer name wasn't a ticket to instant fame, she'd dropped him like last season's Jimmy Choos.

How blind was he not to see what she really was?

"She certainly knows how to work a crowd," Ezra murmured beside him.

Zach nodded. "She always has."

Mum remained in her seat, stony-faced. She had no interest in cheering Verity on; not even her innate politeness could make her pretend to clap.

It stung that his business agreement gave Albion the right to decide which guest performers would appear on his show. But their inviting Verity made sense. Her latest single was topping the charts, and her presence added star power to the finale. And the crowd loved her.

As Verity exited to enthusiastic applause, Zach exhaled slowly. He was making it through this evening, clawing up the cliff handgrip by painful handgrip.

He'd maintained his composure during Kezia's power-house performance of "Survivor," even as Martha had leaned over to comment, "She can do anything she wants, can't she?"

He'd even kept his professional mask in place while watching Verity perform. The only hurdle left was Kezia's second song.

Olivia returned to center stage. "Wasn't that incredible? Thank you, Verity. And now, for her final performance, singing the Whitney Houston classic 'I Will Always Love You,' please welcome back Kezia Blair!"

The audience applauded and whistled as Kezia appeared in an elegant midnight-blue gown. Ryan's influence was evident in every detail of her presentation tonight—the song choice, the styling, the emphasis on commercial appeal. So far, she'd followed her mentor's playbook perfectly.

Zach took another deep breath. He could do this.

Then Kezia spoke words that weren't in the script.

"Thank you," she said. She looked over her shoulder, toward the wings. "Before I begin, could someone please make sure the piano microphone is active? I'd like to make a change."

Zach caught the ripple of confusion that passed through the production team near the stage.

"What's she doing?" Martha whispered beside him, echoing the question suddenly buzzing through the audience.

Kezia spoke again, commanding silence. "I had prepared to sing 'I Will Always Love You' tonight. But instead, I'd like to share something more personal with you."

Zach's entire body tensed as she moved toward the piano. This wasn't planned—she was clearly winging it. He could only imagine the chaos unfolding in the production booth, the director frantically adjusting camera cues, the stage manager scrambling to communicate with the lighting team.

And Ryan? He was probably having a fit right now.

She settled onto the piano bench, arranging the long skirt of her gown while a production assistant adjusted the microphone.

Her fingers touched the keys, a gentle introduction weaving over the auditorium.

As she began to sing, the entire theater fell silent. No one whispered, no one moved. The audience collectively held their breath as this unexpected, intimate performance unfolded.

"Old Town Symphony, a melody in a minor key."

What? Zach sat motionless. That song? On national television, in the finale of the whole competition?

"Notes from our past, songs that shaped who we are. A reason for every crack, a purpose in every scar."

He couldn't take his eyes off her. Emotional truth reverberated in every note, every chord. But what did it mean?

"It doesn't have to be perfect, it just has to be real. The brokenness will be worth it if we have the courage to heal. From a bittersweet yesterday our tomorrow will start. Singing solo till you joined in, playing straight to my heart."

The audience was transfixed, even as Zach's heartbeat thundered in his ears.

As she approached the second verse, the verse he had written, Zach's hands throttled the armrests of his seat.

"Faded harmonies, echoes linger in empty streets..."

Could this be a message to him? Like the first time she'd sung it? Or was it just a performance choice that would showcase her skill and showmanship to the viewers? He didn't dare allow himself to hope, not after her public rejection at the semifinals, not after watching Verity perform just minutes ago, another painful reminder of how badly he could misread people. When it came to women, his radar was way off.

"We've sung alone, now we're stronger as two. Every broken chord brought me closer to you."

The lyrics he'd written hit him with unexpected force.

She looked toward this section of the audience now, though the stage lights would make it impossible for her to see him clearly.

His throat tightened. What did she mean by this?

As the final notes faded into silence, Zach sat reeling.

The theater ignited in thunderous applause, the audience rising to their feet around him.

He stood, too, though he barely felt his legs beneath him.

"That was extraordinary," Ezra murmured beside him as they applauded. "Where did that song come from?"

Zach fought to keep his voice steady. "She wrote it." He didn't add that some of those lyrics were his own. Or that the song had been a private conversation between him and Kezia, now broadcast for the world to witness.

On stage, Olivia approached Kezia, hand pressed to her heart. "Wow. That was...extraordinary. Completely unexpected and absolutely beautiful. Am I right, everyone?"

The audience roared their agreement.

Whatever had just happened, Zach knew it had been Kezia's choice alone. Ryan would never have approved such a deviation from his plan, a complete abandonment of the commercial strategy he'd mapped out for Kezia since choosing her for his team.

Kezia had done the musical equivalent of spitting in her mentor's eye. But why? Why risk everything at this crucial moment? Why share something so personal, so raw, so.. .theirs?

As Kezia left the stage, Zach remained standing, applauding mechanically while his mind raced. He shouldn't read anything into this. But how could he *not*?

But then perhaps this was just a strategic choice to differentiate herself from an evening of over-produced performances. She was such a skilled musician that she would have had the confidence to pull off a power move like this, performing with nothing but piano, accompanying herself, layering on the drama to reel in the votes.

Yet even as he tried to rationalize her actions—telling himself this was a clever gambit by a savvy, ambitious artist—a dangerous spark of hope flickered to life. Whatever her reasons, she had chosen their song, their shared creation, as her statement to the world.

He just wished he knew what that meant.

Chapter 79

ADRENALINE COURSED THROUGH KEZIA'S veins as she sat in the green room, waiting for the rest of tonight to play out.

It was all out of her hands now. Millions might have been listening, but she'd sung "Old Town Symphony" to just one man. But had he understood? The answer to that question mattered more to her than whether or not she'd win the competition.

With a final venomous glare in her direction, Ryan stalked off to take his seat among the other mentors. He'd barely spoken to her since their brief confrontation backstage, but his expression made his feelings unmistakable. Her deviation from his carefully choreographed plan had burned whatever professional bridge might have remained between them. Good.

Production assistants buzzed around, making final preparations for the results announcement. The television screens in the green room showed Sandra performing an outstanding rendition of Andra Day's "Rise Up," showcasing her incredible range and vocal control with that beautiful anthem to perseverance. The teenager had absolutely delivered tonight.

As Sandra came into the green room after her performance, flushed with excitement, Kezia greeted her with a spontaneous hug.

"That was incredible," Kezia said. "You really brought the house down."

Sandra beamed. "So did you. I've never heard anything like that song you performed."

Makeup artists descended on them both, making final touch-ups for the results announcement. As the brush swept across her cheeks, Kezia's mind drifted back to Zach. Had he recognized the message in her performance?

Whatever happened next was up to him. She'd said what she needed to say, in the only way she knew how— through music. She had no regrets about her choice, no matter what the fallout. Ryan might drop her, the label might lose interest, but for the first time since joining *Starbound*, she felt an unexpected peace beneath her nervousness, even if it meant going back to being a session singer. She'd finally found her voice.

"Two minutes until results. Places, please," the stage manager announced, appearing in the doorway.

Sandra reached for Kezia's hand, her confident stage persona momentarily giving way to the sixteen-year-old beneath. "Whatever happens, I'm glad we got to know each other."

Kezia squeezed back. "Me too."

They walked toward the stage together, hearing the audience's excited murmurs, standing in the wings as Olivia built up the audience anticipation with practiced skill.

"I'm terrified," Sandra whispered, her voice barely audible over the audience's applause.

Kezia turned to her with a genuine smile. "You're going to be fine, no matter what happens."

The certainty in her own words surprised her. Somehow, in the midst of everything, the competition itself now mattered less than the journey.

"And...go," the stage manager directed.

They stepped onto the stage together, momentarily blinded by the bright lights. The audience erupted into applause as Olivia's arms spread wide in welcome.

"Our two extraordinary finalists, after an incredible journey," Olivia proclaimed, her enthusiasm infectious. The energy in the theater was electric, the culmination of months of competition distilled into this single moment.

They took their positions center stage, instinctively joining hands. Kezia's gaze found Zach. His face was angled downward as he sat next to his mother. Just behind them, her parents watched her with polite expressions, the epitome of polite British restraint.

"Before I announce who has won tonight, I need to explain that the result combines votes from our studio audience here at the Royal Victoria Theater, and viewers at home." Olivia held up two sealed envelopes. "First, the studio audience vote..."

She opened the first envelope with dramatic flair.

"Our studio audience here in the Royal Victoria Theater has chosen...Kezia Blair!"

A wave of applause washed over Kezia. She had won the studio audience vote? The one that was all about the live performance and audience connection?

Sandra squeezed her hand, her smile unwavering.

Olivia waited for the applause to subside before continuing. "And now, the viewers' vote from home..."

Kezia felt a strange detachment. She knew Sandra's massive online following could change everything, given how hard they'd been mobilizing, if Ryan was to be believed. But somehow she cared about the outcome less than she would have imagined just days ago.

"The viewers at home have chosen...Sandra Cassidy!"

The audience's reaction shifted to uncertainty, then renewed applause as they understood the significance. The competition had split between the live audience and home viewers. What did that mean?

Olivia's dramatic pause stretched the moment. "Which means that, based on an aggregation of the votes, the winner of *Starbound* is..."

Every heartbeat stretched into eternity.

"Sandra Cassidy!"

The theater exploded in cheers as confetti cannons fired and golden streamers rained onto the stage. Sandra's expression froze in disbelief, her hands flying over her mouth.

Kezia felt an immediate, instinctive joy for the younger girl as she pulled Sandra into a heartfelt hug.

"You deserve this," she whispered fiercely. "I'm so proud of you!"

There was no disappointment, no regret, only celebration for Sandra's achievement. As they separated, Sandra looked almost dazed by the moment, tears glistening in her eyes.

Kezia's heart froze as she caught Zach watching her rather than Sandra. Something in his expression had shifted, though she couldn't define exactly what had changed.

"Kezia," Olivia said, turning to her with a warm smile. "Although you're our runner-up tonight, I can tell you that this went right down to the wire. Would you like to say a few words while Sandra composes herself?"

Kezia stepped forward, the microphone feeling lighter in her hand than it had all season.

"I couldn't be happier for Sandra tonight. She fully deserves this win. From the first time I heard her sing, I knew she had something special. Not just an incredible voice, but a pure, genuine connection to music and a hunger to excel." She turned toward Sandra. "You've grown so much during this competition, and Britain has fallen in love with you for all the right reasons. This is just the beginning of an amazing journey."

The audience applauded, and Kezia could see Diana beaming from the judges' panel. Ryan wore a grin that was probably as fake as it was wide.

Her parents clapped politely, their faces blank and unreadable. She knew she'd let them down yet again, but in this moment, she couldn't bring herself to care.

"Thank you for those very gracious words, Kezia," Olivia said, then turned to the winner. "And now, Sandra, would you like to perform 'Rise Up' one more time as our first *Starbound* champion?"

Sandra nodded, dabbing at her eyes as the opening notes began to play.

Kezia stepped back, allowing the spotlight to focus entirely on Sandra where it belonged.

As Kezia moved to the side of the stage, she cast one last look toward the judges' panel. Zach was no longer in his seat.

Chapter 80

HE *STARBOUND* FINALE AFTER-party glowed with champagne and crystal light as Kezia stood beside her parents in the Royal Victoria Theater's grand foyer, her polite smile a shield against the growing ache in her chest.

She'd been aware of Zach the entire time as he worked the room, speaking to network executives and music reps with practiced ease—never once looking her way. She couldn't tell if he'd understood the message in her song, or if he was choosing to ignore it, and the uncertainty gnawed at the fragile hope she'd carried offstage, eroding it into quiet despair.

Chandeliers sparkled overhead, illuminating the crowd of industry executives, contestants, and *Starbound* staff celebrating the end of a triumphant season. After months of restricted internet access, Kezia was only beginning to realize just what a big hit the show was.

Maybe that's why Mum and Dad had decided to attend the finale, the first time they'd shown up at any of her musical performances since her piano recitals at school. And it couldn't have hurt that the event was being held in such a prestigious venue.

"You did well to reach far," Mum said, adjusting her designer handbag. "And you sang very well. Though I wonder if this is a young person's game. That Sandra girl is only sixteen, after all."

Dad nodded. "This was probably the biggest chance you can expect to come your way. Perhaps it's time to put this to rest and do something more substantial."

A month ago, no, even a week ago, their words would have crushed her. She'd spent years chasing their approval, hoping her success would finally make them see the value in her chosen path. Now, their disapproval no longer held the power it once did.

"Thank you for coming tonight," she said. "And for your advice. But I've actually got some promising options, even though I didn't win." She tapped her clutch, where several business cards from agents and indie labels rested. "A lot of people seem interested in what I have to offer."

The cards were tangible proof that her authentic voice had value in the industry. Each one represented someone who wanted to work with her after seeing what she did tonight. And that meant something huge.

Her father glanced at his watch, as though the conversation bored him. "We should be going. Your mother has that charity breakfast tomorrow."

"Of course." She accepted their perfunctory embraces, watching as they made their way toward the exit with the same efficient purpose that characterized everything they did.

Across the room, Ryan stood with a group of industry executives, his anger visible only in his eyes while his smile remained fixed in place. She knew he was already working to salvage his reputation after her impromptu performance had upended his carefully orchestrated plan.

She felt a strange lightness, a newfound freedom in no longer seeking approval from Ryan or her parents.

For a moment, she stood alone, scanning the crowded room. Where was Zach?

"Kezia!"

She turned to see two executives approaching—Lena Morales, A&R director for Solstice Records, and Doug Chin, VP of Artist Development at Harmonix. Both had introduced themselves earlier in the evening.

"Didn't want to leave without saying goodbye," Lena said, smiling. "We're leaving now to catch a flight to New York, but your performance? Absolutely stunning."

"Agreed," Doug said. "Though I still say we were the first ones to spot her potential."

"Please." Lena rolled her eyes. "You only approached her after she detonated a finale set list on live television. I've had my eye on her since episode six."

"Only because you hoard the indie circuit like it's your personal vineyard." Doug turned to Kezia. "Ignore us. Just remember you've got options, and we're serious about wanting to work with you."

"Both of us are," Lena said, her expression warm. "And for what it's worth, that song tonight? That's the kind of thing that builds a legacy."

Gratitude bloomed in Kezia's chest, tempered by a quiet steadiness. "Thank you," she said. "I'm still catching my breath from all of it. I think I need to take some time to just center myself, pray, and figure out what's next."

"Smart girl," Doug said with a grin.

"We'll be in touch," Lena added, already moving toward the doors. "Don't sign with anyone else while we're in the air."

Kezia laughed as they disappeared into the crowd. Her heart lifted, not just because they'd said all the right things, but because for once, she believed she had the freedom to choose what came next.

As Kezia turned away from the executives, Martha Falconer stepped quietly into her path, her smile warm.

"I'm so glad to see you, Martha. Are you feeling okay after the other day?"

Martha waved a hand. "Oh, I'm fine. Ezra's after me to go home, but I wanted to congratulate you on your performance tonight. You have a truly beautiful voice. But more importantly, you have something to say with it."

The unexpected validation from someone she admired caught Kezia off guard. "That means a lot, especially coming from you."

"It's the truth." Her gaze sharpened. "That second song you sang seemed very personal."

Kezia hesitated. The temptation to explain the song to Martha, knowing she would tell Zach, was almost too much to resist. She searched for the right words, a way to send him a message through his sister-in-law, but stopped herself. Some conversations needed to happen directly, not through intermediaries. It wouldn't be appropriate to put Martha in that position.

"It was," she said simply.

Ezra appeared beside them, resting his hands on Martha's shoulders. "Sorry to interrupt you, Kezia, but I'm here to enforce a curfew on this beautiful wife of mine. Congratulations, by the way. Martha, we really should get you home to rest."

Martha sighed but nodded at her husband's gentle reminder of her condition. "You're right. I'm pretty shattered." She turned back to Kezia. "I'll be watching for whatever you do next, Kezia."

"Thank you for everything," Kezia said.

She watched them walk away. That was the end of yet another connection, cut short before it could deepen. If only she could have known the Falconers better, under different circumstances.

"Kezia." Maya approached, tablet in hand. "I know it's been a really long day for you, so I wanted to let you know I've arranged transport back to the Starbound Campus whenever you're ready. No need to wait for Sandra. The driver will take you alone."

"Thank you."

"There'll be no early wake-up call tomorrow. You can have a good long lie in, and then you'll have all day to pack your things properly," Maya said. "Oh, and Claire called. She says her spare room is ready whenever you need it." Maya smiled. "Don't worry, you'll get your phone and any other devices back when we sign you out."

The mention of Claire provided a welcome touchstone amid the uncertainty of what came next. At least she had somewhere to go while she sorted through the business cards and possibilities before her.

Maya's professional demeanor softened. "You've been extraordinary to work with. Whatever comes next, I'd love to stay in touch."

Maya's friendly words touched Kezia deeply. "I'd like that."

She glanced around, the fatigue suddenly hitting now that she had the option to leave. "You're right. It has been a long day. I think I'd like to go now."

"Of course. Follow me. I'll get Robert to escort you to the parking garage."

Kezia took one last scan of the room as she prepared to leave. She finally saw Zach. He stood with his mother near the main entrance, deep in conversation. Her chest tightened with hope, foolish and fragile.

But he never looked up.

She didn't dare intrude on him. His careful avoidance of looking in her direction was obvious even at this distance, the clear message in his body language unmistakable. Whatever connection they had was broken.

The realization brought a bittersweet acceptance of what her choice had cost. Yet she had no regrets despite the pain. She had protected him when it mattered most, standing between him and Ryan's threats, just as Diana had advised.

The semifinal and final bonuses would provide security while she figured out her next steps. A future opened before her, unburdened by Ryan's slick machinations or Zach's creative expectations. It was a future entirely her own.

As she moved toward the exit, the sadness was tempered by a profound peace.

She was used to this feeling. All her life, choosing what felt right had come at a cost—of approval, connection, even belonging. From the day she turned down a medical degree and chose Guildhall to the moment she'd gone off-script tonight, her choices had always led to disapproval and isolation. But she regretted nothing.

She allowed herself one final glance at Zach before turning away.

Chapter 81

THE AFTER-PARTY BUZZED around Zach as he worked the room, his professional smile locked firmly in place while the sparkling grape juice in his hand remained untouched.

Small talk with industry players, light banter with network reps—he could run that script on autopilot. It was the only way to keep his mind from replaying Kezia's song, her voice threading through every beat of his heart. If he thought too hard about her, he'd fall apart.

He hadn't stayed to listen to Sandra's victory encore. He'd needed a moment to collect himself. Now he was back in executive mode, performing his duties as *Starbound's* creator and his mother's escort. He'd left Mum chatting with Tyler while he circulated among the VIPs.

Sir Giles Wentworth, the network president, clapped him on the shoulder. "Such a brilliant finale. I was on the edge of my seat the whole time. The ratings are through the roof!"

"Thank you." Zach offered a practiced smile. "Sandra will make an excellent first champion."

"Absolutely," Victoria Harlow chimed in. "Though I must say, both finalists were exceptional. Kezia's unexpected piano performance was pure television gold! Ryan claims that the song switch was planned all along, but I'm not convinced."

Zach nodded, his gaze drifting across the room to where Kezia stood with her parents. Although it was wonderful that they had come, the stiff formality in their posture, the polite distance despite the crowded room, told its own story.

Her father repeatedly checked his watch. Apparently, even his daughter's runner-up status at a nationally televised competition wasn't worth disrupting his schedule for long.

As Victoria continued talking about streaming numbers and social media engagement, Zach excused himself to congratulate Sandra and her family. The teenager beamed as photographers captured the moment, her mother dabbing away proud tears beside her.

"Diana has been incredible," Sandra said, "but I learned so much from watching everyone, especially Kezia."

"You deserved the win," Zach said sincerely. "Your journey on this show has been remarkable."

Even as he made small talk, Zach tracked Kezia's movements around the room. She now stood talking with representatives from two record labels. Runner-up status still attracted industry attention. Her smile was gracious, her posture confident despite everything. The same quiet dignity she'd shown on stage.

Across the foyer, Verity held court among a circle of admirers, her laughter carrying over the ambient noise. The sound grated on his nerves almost as much as Ryan's barely contained fury as he spoke with Albion executives. The mentor's rigid posture and tight smile confirmed what Zach had already guessed—Kezia's song choice hadn't been part of Ryan's carefully orchestrated plan.

The melody of "Old Town Symphony" still echoed in Zach's mind, the lyrics playing on repeat. Had she been singing to him? The hope that kindled in his chest warred with the memory of her public rejection at the semifinals. If only he could have a moment to ask her.

Wait, the label executives were gone, and Martha was with Kezia now. This might be his chance to speak with her, even if it was just one word.

He stepped in her direction, only to have his path intercepted by an all-too-familiar figure.

"Quite the dramatic finale, Zach." Verity's perfectly made-up face tilted up toward his. "You always had a flair for the unexpected."

Zach's jaw tightened. "Thank you for performing tonight. The audience clearly enjoyed it."

"I have to hand it to you. When I turned down your offer to be a mentor, I had no idea it would get this exciting." She sipped her drink, watching him over the rim of her glass.

"The offer came from Albion, not me," Zach corrected her, taking small satisfaction in her momentary surprise. "I didn't request you as a show mentor."

Blinking at him for a moment, she quickly recovered. "Well, that explains it. But now that I've seen what a success *Starbound* has become, I might reconsider for next season."

"We're not looking for anyone else. The mentor slots are all filled."

Verity smirked. "Are they? Because Ryan doesn't look particularly secure after tonight's little incident. Are you sure he'll stay on? And I might have more influence with Albion than you think." She leaned closer. "Gone are the days when Zach Falconer held all the power. Your finalist seemed to sense it too, hence her joining with Ryan. Although she seems to be a bit of a wildcard."

Zach deliberately kept his expression neutral. "Kezia makes her own choices."

"Oh, I'll say. Ryan looked ready to combust." Verity's laugh was practiced, designed to carry just far enough. "Though I suppose she needed some kind of dramatic moment after that mess with her vocals."

"What are you talking about?" Zach asked.

"Well, let's just say her technical execution wasn't quite up to par on those high notes. Too much emotion, not enough control." Verity's dismissive wave was infuriating. "But that's to be expected from an amateur, I suppose."

"Amateur? I guess that's what they're now calling five years at Guildhall and six years of wall-to-wall professional session work," Zach said, his voice low but intense. "And even without any of that, Kezia has more raw talent and artistic integrity than you could ever dream of."

Verity's eyes flashed. "Is that why I have the UK's number one hit, and she's just a runner-up of some knock-off, low-rent reality show?"

"Strange." Zach crossed his arms. "You seemed pretty keen to be a mentor on my knock-off, low-rent reality show."

Verity's face turned red. "You know what? Maybe it's a good thing she lost. You seem to prefer women you can control, Zach. Face it—you can't handle an ambitious, successful woman."

She spun on her heel and walked away before he could respond.

Zach watched her retreating figure, the bitter reminder of how she'd used their relationship to advance her career settling like acid in his stomach. The possibility that she might actually have the industry pull to muscle her way onto his show next season added insult to injury.

"What did that woman want?"

His mother stood beside him, staring after Verity.

"Just to remind me that some things never change," he replied flatly.

She touched his arm. "You know something, Zach? In all your life, she was the only bad choice you've made." She looked up into his face, her eyes glistening. "And I thank God every day you found that out before it went too far."

His mind flew to her heartbreaking marriage to Greg and all the pain it had caused her. Was still causing her. Pulling her into a hug, he kissed the top of her head. "Thanks for the reminder, Mum."

She stepped back, studying his face, then glanced around the room. "I'm feeling rather tired. Would you mind terribly if I headed home soon?"

He noticed the fatigue in her eyes, the slight droop to her shoulders. "Of course not. Let me get your coat."

"No, no." She held up a hand. "I don't want to pull you away from your big night. You've earned this. You should stay and enjoy yourself."

"Mum—"

"She's right," Ezra's voice came from behind them. "I'll take Mum home. Martha's ready to go, too. Pregnancy fatigue is hitting her hard tonight."

After a brief discussion, Zach agreed, kissing his mother's cheek goodbye and watching as Ezra escorted her toward the exit.

He turned back to scan the room. Kezia was gone. She must have left while Verity was wasting his time.

Lord, what am I supposed to do now? The desperate prayer rose unbidden as he stood alone amid the celebrating crowd.

"Quite the finale, wasn't it?" Diana Morris walked toward him, elegant in her designer pantsuit. "Congratulations on a successful first season."

"And congratulations to you on Sandra's win," Zach said. "You should be very proud of her development."

"I am," Diana smiled. "Though I genuinely expected Kezia to win tonight. She's full of surprises, that one. First choosing Ryan over you, then that remarkable finale performance." Diana swirled her glass thoughtfully. "When I talked to her before the semifinal results, I had no idea she'd solve your little problem the way she did."

She had Zach's full attention. "What little problem?"

Diana stared at him, her head tilted. "The Ryan situation, of course."

Zach frowned. It felt like he was trying to put together a puzzle with half the pieces missing and the other half upside down. "What do you mean? What exactly did you say to her that night?"

But before Diana could speak, an executive from Harmony Records approached.

"There you are, Diana. We're trying to arrange a lunch meeting with Sandra next week, but we need to find out when you're free."

Diana turned to Zach with an apologetic smile. "We'll have to continue this conversation another time." She touched his arm. "Or better yet, if you really want to understand what she did for you...talk to Kezia yourself."

As Diana was led away, Zach stood motionless, his mind racing to piece together the fragments of information. What had Diana meant about Kezia solving "the Ryan situation"? What had Kezia done for him? Did all this have something to do with her actions at the semifinals?

Most importantly, where was she now?

Chapter 82

ZACH RAN UP THE steps to the Starbound offices at Glenmere Hall early the morning after the finale. His first, reckless idea had been to come and find Kezia last night. But reflection had brought sanity; going to the contestant house at that time of night and demanding to speak with her would have been completely inappropriate.

As he walked down the hall, his eyes were gritty from a sleepless night spent replaying Diana's cryptic words. *When I talked to her before the semifinal results, I had no idea she'd solve your little problem the way she did... The Ryan situation, of course.*

What exactly had Diana said to Kezia that night? And what did it have to do with Kezia's sudden switch to Ryan's team?

He rubbed his temples, desperate for answers. The need to speak with Kezia had grown from a whisper to a shout that drowned out all other thoughts. He needed to catch her before she left.

As he approached his office, he spotted Maya walking down the corridor, tablet in hand.

"Maya," he called, keeping his tone casual. "Good morning."

She looked up, eyes widening. "Morning. You're in early. I didn't expect you in until the production debrief meeting."

"Just catching up on a few things." He paused, weighing his words carefully. "The contestants—I imagine they're both preparing to return home?"

She nodded. "Sandra's in the process of packing up. She'll leave after breakfast. But Kezia decided to check out last night straight after the after-party. One of the production assistants signed her out."

The news slammed into Zach's gut like a fist. "I see. Wasn't it rather late to be making a journey?"

"Well, she mentioned staying with her friend Claire, since it's not too far from here. I guess she decided she wanted to get back to the real world among real people." Maya's lips twisted. "I can't say I blame her. The contestant house was getting pretty empty."

"I think we'll all be glad to get back home," Zach said. "Speak to you later, Maya."

In his office, he sat at his desk, staring at his phone. Kezia was staying with Claire. He still had Claire's number from when he'd arranged for her to visit during Family Day. He could reach out to Claire, ask her to connect him with Kezia.

But would she want to talk to him?

His finger hovered over the screen for a long moment before he pressed call.

The phone rang three times before Claire answered.

"Hello?"

"Claire, this is Zach Falconer from *Starbound*."

"Zach!" Her voice brightened with recognition. "I didn't think I'd hear from you again. That was quite a finale last night."

He moved the phone to his other ear. "Yes, it was. All of us are still unpacking all that happened. Look, I'm calling because I need to speak with Kezia. My talent producer mentioned she's staying with you."

"She is," Claire said. "She got in really late last night. I watched the whole finale—her song was incredible, the one she sang instead of 'I Will Always Love You'. When she arrived, I tried to ask her about it, but she was completely exhausted. Just needed to sleep. We haven't even had a chance to talk about any of it yet."

Zach's pulse jumped. "That song...there's so much more behind it than what the audience saw. That's part of why I need to see her."

"I see," Claire said slowly. A pause stretched between them.

"Like I said, she's still sleeping," Claire said finally. "She's normally up at the crack of dawn, but I haven't heard a peep from her."

Zach took a deep breath. "Claire, it's really important that I speak with her. There are things I need to understand, things I think only Kezia can explain."

"About why she switched mentors?" Claire asked.

This woman was way too perceptive. "Among other things."

Another pause. "Sounds like this is about more than business."

Busted. He took a deep breath. "It is."

"Okay." Claire dragged out the word as though she were thinking. "I'll tell her you called, and if she wants to speak with you, I'll let you know."

"Of course," he agreed immediately. "I completely understand."

"Can I call you back after she wakes up?"

"Actually..." Zach hesitated, then decided to take the chance. "I'd rather speak to her in person. But only if she's completely okay with it. If she doesn't mind, would it be okay with you if I came by your place later today?"

"Oh." Claire's surprise came clearly across the line. "I see. I'll ask her and let you know what she says."

"Thank you. And, Claire, I can't emphasize this enough...I don't want to put any pressure on her. I won't come unless she's completely fine with it. Please make it clear to her that she doesn't have to see me."

"I will." Claire's voice softened. "For what it's worth, I think she *will* want to talk. But I'll check with her."

"Thank you, Claire. I'll wait for your call."

After hanging up, Zach leaned back in his chair, both relieved and anxious. The ball was in Kezia's court now, as it should be. He'd respect her boundaries and give her the choice about whether to speak with him.

Now all he could do was wait. And pray that she would give him the chance to understand what had really happened.

Chapter 83

*K*EZIA BLINKED AWAKE IN Claire's spare bedroom, momentarily confused by the unfamiliar surroundings. Pale yellow walls, a framed botanical print, and Claire's exercise bike crammed in the corner—not the pristine contestant quarters at Starbound. Reality came flooding back. The finale. Sandra's win. Her performance of "Old Town Symphony." Zach's indifference.

The ache was just as sharp as when she'd left Glenmere Hall.

She glanced at her phone—10:37 AM. She couldn't remember the last time she'd slept this late. Then again, after months of *Starbound*'s strict schedules and last night's emotional marathon, her body had apparently decided it needed recovery time.

Sitting up, she passed a hand over her tangled hair. The first day of the rest of her life. She had so much to figure out—finding a place to live, following up with those agents and label executives who'd given her their cards, deciding what kind of music she wanted to pursue now that she was free of Ryan's commercial vision.

And how to move on after laying her heart bare before millions, only to have her offering go unanswered.

A gentle knock interrupted her thoughts.

"Come in," she called, pulling the duvet up slightly.

Claire appeared in the doorway, balancing a steaming cup of tea on a saucer. "Morning, superstar. You told me to wake you if you weren't up by 10:30, so technically, I'm late. Fortunately, I brought a peace offering."

Smiling, Kezia accepted the delicate cup and saucer. "Thanks for this, but I'm not sure about the 'superstar' bit."

"Runner-up in a national television competition qualifies you for breakfast in bed privileges," Claire said, perching on the edge of the bed. "You're getting the royal treatment today with my special wedding tea set—Wedgwood china, no less. "

Kezia smiled, sniffing the fragrant Earl Gray. "I could get used to this."

"Hey, don't." Claire nudged her foot through the covers. "This is strictly a twenty-four-hour service."

The familiar banter felt wonderfully normal after weeks in the *Starbound* bubble. Claire was the one constant in her life, the friend who'd stood by her through every career disappointment and small victory. Every heartbreak.

Claire's expression shifted slightly. "So, I got an interesting call a couple of hours ago. From Zach Falconer."

Kezia sloshed her tea into the saucer. She set the cup on the bedside table, her hands suddenly unsteady.

"That bad, huh?" Claire raised an eyebrow, studying Kezia's reaction.

"Did he..." Kezia swallowed, trying to collect herself. "Did he say why he called?"

"He mentioned something about that song you performed last night. Said there was more to it than what people saw on TV." Claire tilted her head. "He seemed pretty intent on talking to you in person. I told him I'd check if you were okay with that."

Her heart pounded so hard she felt it in her fingertips. Zach wanted to talk about the song? *Their* song? So, he wasn't indifferent, after all.

"What exactly did he say?" she asked, trying to keep her voice even.

"Not much, to be honest. Just that he needed to understand some things that only you could explain." Claire watched her closely. "He also mentioned something about why you switched mentors. And when I asked if this was about more than business, he admitted it was."

Kezia's breath got stuck somewhere between her chest and her throat. Zach had acknowledged to Claire that this wasn't just professional?

"But he gave me the strictest instructions to tell you that he'll only come over if you're a thousand percent okay with it. His exact words, were, and I quote, 'I don't want to put any pressure on her.' And from the way he said it, I don't think he'll set foot near you unless you really mean yes."

Claire examined Kezia's burning face. "So, sweetheart. Should I tell him it's okay to come by? He sounded like he wanted to come as soon as possible."

Kezia's mind raced, only outpaced by her thundering heart. Did she dare hope what this might mean?

"Okay," she said finally. "I just need to hop in the shower first."

"I'll call him back," Claire said, squeezing Kezia's hand. "Whatever this is about, I'm here for you."

Twenty minutes later, freshly showered and dressed in jeans and a simple sweater, Kezia emerged from the bathroom to find Claire waiting in the hallway.

"He's on his way," Claire said. "Should be here in about half an hour."

Thirty minutes. Thirty minutes until she would face Zach for the first time since the finale. Whatever happened next would be entirely outside the structure of *Starbound*. Just two people without cameras, contracts, or a competition between them.

Kezia took a deep breath. She'd been brave last night. She could be brave now.

Chapter 84

ZACH STOOD ON CLAIRE'S doorstep, the bite in the December air bracing him for the conversation ahead. The modest terraced house in Worcester Park was a far cry from Glenmere Hall's grandeur or the Royal Victoria Theater's opulence—a reminder that they were now firmly outside the Starbound bubble.

He rang the bell, heart pounding as he waited. When the door swung open Claire, a pretty, open-faced brunette, greeted him with a cautious smile. "Lovely to finally meet you, Zach. I'm Claire."

It was odd seeing her in person rather than through the production monitors that had filmed the Family Day visit.

He took the hand she offered. "Hi. Thanks for having me."

"She's in the living room," Claire said, stepping aside to let him enter. She grabbed an orange leash from a hook by the door. "Just go straight through. I need to take Otis for his walk. I'll be back in about forty-five minutes."

A small black terrier appeared at her feet, looking expectantly up at its owner.

"Thank you," Zach said, understanding Claire's tactful exit was giving them privacy.

As Claire and Otis slipped out, Zach moved down the hallway, pausing at the living room door. He took a steadying breath, praying for the wisdom and clarity he so desperately needed.

Kezia stood by the window, her silhouette etched in mid-morning light. No stage makeup. No cameras. No styling team. Just Kezia—in jeans and a soft navy sweater, her natural curls tousled, looking up at him with those deep, soulful eyes.

"Hi," she said, tugging at the hem of her sweater.

"Hi." He moved further into the room but maintained his distance, suddenly unsure how to begin despite rehearsing this conversation all night. "Are... Are you okay?"

She nodded, gesturing toward a beige sofa with plaid throw pillows. "You?"

"I'm good." He sat on the edge of the sofa while she lowered herself onto an armchair, hugging a cushion to her chest.

The silence stretched, both of them suspended in it, until Zach found the courage to speak the question that had haunted him since Diana's cryptic words. "Why did you do it?"

"I've done a lot of things lately," she said. "Which one do you mean?"

Her words threw him for a second, until he noticed her small, rueful smile. "I want to hear about all of them," he said. "But how about starting with the things involving Ryan?"

"I've been working out how to explain everything. But now that you're here..." Her arms tightened around the cushion. "It's hard to know where to start without a camera in my face. I may have gotten too used to the confessional interviews at *Starbound*."

He appreciated her attempt at humor, understood her hesitation. The weight of everything was hard to endure.

"I'm not as good as Laura or Mark, but maybe I can help throw out some interview questions," he said, relieved at the smile that drew from her. "Diana said something last night at the reception. She mentioned talking to you before the semifinal results. She said something about you solving 'the Ryan situation.'"

Kezia's eyes widened. "She told you about that?"

"Not much. She just hinted and said I ought to ask you to explain."

Something shifted in Kezia's expression. Relief, perhaps, at having somewhere to start. "She warned me that Ryan had been watching us and talking to people. That he was gathering ammunition to use as leverage. She said *Starbound* represents everything you've worked for. I remembered what you said, about how Ryan could use our..."

She gestured with her hand. "Our connection against us. I thought if I removed myself from your team, removed the appearance of anything between us, he couldn't use it against you." She hesitated. "It seemed like the only option at the time."

Each word hit Zach with the force of revelation. All these weeks he'd assumed the worst.

"At first I thought you joined his team because he would give your career more of a commercial edge," he said. He struggled to voice his more painful thoughts. "And then I thought maybe you were creating space between us be-cause I...because I put too much pressure on you by telling you how I felt about you."

"What?" Shock was written on her face. "No, that wasn't it at all. What you told me, what we said with that song..." She grew flustered, breaking eye contact. "I meant all that."

Relief flooded him. "That's what I was most afraid of. That I took advantage of you. Made you say things you came to regret."

"No." She raised her gaze to meet his. "No, you didn't. And I don't regret anything I said to you. It was all about Ryan. I didn't care about any sort of commercial edge. I didn't even care about the competition anymore, whether or not I won. I was just trying to...trying to make sure he had no reason to threaten what you'd built."

Zach couldn't find words to respond. Her integrity, her concern for him, blew him away.

"When I joined his team, I tried to toe the line," Kezia continued into Zach's silence. "I worked on the songs he wanted. I was all prepared to do the Whitney song. To do what he said and 'drop it like a nuclear bomb.'" A wry smile crossed her face. "And then Verity performed."

"Verity?" Zach asked. "What did she have to do with anything?"

"I did the backing vocals on 'Higher Ground,'" Kezia said. "I recorded them months ago, before *Starbound*. Watching her perform at the finale, I realized she was lip-syncing to the track I did with Sam."

"I overheard you and Sam talking about you singing backing vocals on that song." The song for which Verity was getting unprecedented praise, her best chart success ever...with a voice that wasn't hers. A voice whose cadence and tone Zach knew intimately.

A flash of understanding hit him. "They used your voice for more than just backing vocals, didn't they?"

Kezia bit her lip, her gaze flickering away.

"I know you don't want to violate any NDAs," Zach said quietly. The implications were clear. "You don't need to say anything else about that. Tell me the rest of it."

Her shoulders relaxed. "Watching her on that stage, lip-syncing, I saw a manufactured performance being cele-brated as authentic. It horrified me, the complete discon-nect between what the audience was seeing and what was actually real."

Her fingers twisted together. "I saw my future laid out in front of me with Ryan as my manager. All the careful packaging, the focus on image over substance. That's when I knew I couldn't go through with the Whitney song just to show off. I had to sing something real, a song that actually held meaning for me." Her voice softened. "And that's why I sang our song. I couldn't think of anything more real. I was hoping you would remember the first time I sang it and understand."

The ground shifted beneath him as the pieces finally slotted into place. "I remembered. But I didn't understand what you meant. I thought I did, but I was afraid to hope."

Her expression softened with a smile. "That's the prob-lem with singing in code. The message doesn't always land the way you want it to."

"That's true. But I'm not speaking in code now." He leaned forward. "I want to be crystal clear. Ryan was right about one thing—the way I feel about you hasn't been pro-fessional for a long time. In fact, if I'm completely honest with myself, maybe it never was."

Kezia's eyes widened as she held his gaze.

"You got under my skin the moment I first heard you sing," he said, a tentative smile flickering. "So, naturally, I acted like a nine-year-old and picked on the girl I liked."

A startled laugh slipped from her lips.

"But seriously..." He couldn't joke about it anymore, as the truth lit up all the corners of his heart, including the shameful parts he'd rather were kept hidden. "I judged you so harshly in those first weeks. I told myself I was just pushing you to be real, to drop the polish. But the truth is, I was punishing you. For being everything I didn't expect. For making me feel what I knew I shouldn't."

His voice roughened. "I'm ashamed of the way I treated you. The cruel critiques. The way I picked apart everything you did, called your work shallow when it wasn't. I undermined your confidence under the guise of artistic purity. I tried to bulldoze you into sharing things I had no right to know. And I made you prove yourself over and over when you shouldn't have had to."

Kezia opened her mouth to respond, but he raised a hand gently.

"And then I tried to tell myself I was demanding because you had so much potential. But if I'm honest—really honest—it was because I didn't know how to handle the fact that I was attracted to you from day one. You were always the real deal. And I was the one lying to myself. Can you forgive me for that?"

Her eyes glistened. "I forgave you long ago. Back on that night when you came back, after your stepfather died. When you talked to me about how artistry is about channeling our pain into connection."

He winced. "Yeah, that was just after Ezra called me out. Made me see what I was doing and how I was bullying you. I really am sorry."

"Thank you."

Her smile dissolved the last of his restraint, and he spoke from his heart. "I've never met anyone like you, Kezia. I already thought you were amazing. Your courage, your grit, your generosity. And now when you tell me what you did for me, what you gave up to protect my show, my work—"

He paused, his voice catching. "I'm in pretty deep. I want you in my life. But we both know how pushy I can get. The last thing I want to do is pressure you into something you don't want."

"You're not pressuring me into anything," Kezia said. "If I wasn't interested, I wouldn't have sung that song. And I wouldn't be talking to you now."

Zach exhaled slowly, her words ringing in his ears like sweet music from heaven. For the first time in days, the knot in his chest began to ease.

"I don't want to assume anything," he said, his voice low. "So let me ask—what do you want, Kezia? After everything that's happened between us."

"What do I want?" she repeated softly, her eyes glistening. "Can I have a moment?"

"Of course."

She stood and crossed to the window, wrapping her arms tightly around herself as she stared out at Claire's narrow garden. The bare branches of an oak tree trembled in the breeze.

Seconds stretched. He didn't move. Just waited. And prayed.

Finally, she turned to face him. "This... this thing we have, I want it to breathe. To grow. I want you in my life."

A slow warmth uncurled in his chest, quiet and sure.

"But I don't date casually, Zach. I never have. Not because I'm old-fashioned or trying to be intense. Just...the stakes are too high. For me. For where I've come from." Her voice trembled. "For the kind of heart I have."

He started to speak, but she lifted a hand.

"I'm not giving you an ultimatum. I'm not asking for promises you're not ready to make. I just need you to know how I'm built. When I date, it's intentional. It's about heading toward marriage. About building a future, a family. I don't do placeholders or distractions. If I let someone in, it's because I've thought and prayed seriously about where it could lead."

She paused, searching his face. "But then *you* happened. We started in this weird, high-pressure, completely artificial environment. I let you in without meaning to. And now here we are. None of this has been normal for me."

He understood her. She wasn't giving him some sort of twisted loyalty test, the kind Verity loved to pull. She wasn't speaking out of fear. It was clarity. And it was the most beautiful thing he'd ever heard.

Something fierce and steady rose in his chest. This—*this*—was what he'd been afraid to hope for. And now she was offering it freely.

He stood slowly, as if rising to meet the truth of her.

"I don't do placeholders either," he said. "And I don't play games. I'm here because I mean it, too." He held her gaze, voice low and certain. "Make no mistake. I have very clear intentions for you, Miss Blair."

She stepped toward him, eyes shining, and slipped her hands into his. "Then I want to start again. Properly this time. Not with cameras and mentors and producers circling like sharks. Just us."

"I want that. With all my heart." He squeezed her hands, searching her face. "But it may not be that simple. There's something you should know."

Her brow furrowed slightly. "Go on."

"You're not anonymous anymore, Kezia. Not just a background voice or a name in the credits. The show changed that. People know your face now. They're paying attention." He drew in a breath. "And if we're together...they'll pay attention to that, too."

She didn't speak, but he saw her shoulders lift with a quiet inhale.

"There's a tour coming," he said. "Albion greenlit it last night. We're doing twelve cities over six weeks. You'll be called back to Glenmere Hall just after New Year's to start rehearsals. I'll be on the tour team." He held her gaze. "So if we do this, we won't be starting in private. Not really."

She nodded slowly, her expression sobering.

He cupped her hands against his chest. "I want you to know what you're signing up for if we do this." He paused. "And you need to be sure you're okay with that. Because once we step into the spotlight together, we don't get to step out again."

She closed her eyes for a moment.

He resisted the urge to speak, giving her time to process his words.

"Diana warned me," she said at last. "She said that dating a powerful man in this industry can brand a woman for life. That no matter what she achieves, people will say she didn't earn it. That he made her."

Zach's heart clenched. "She's right," he said quietly. "People will say a lot of things. It's completely unfair, but that's just the nature of it. So if that sounds like too much, I'll understand. I won't pressure you. You don't owe me anything."

Her eyes filled. "That's exactly why I feel safe enough to try," she whispered. "Because you understand, and you'd give me that choice. Because we can talk about it and be real. Maybe 'normal' doesn't exist for us anymore. But I think we can make something better—a new kind of normal. One we choose...together."

He scoured her face for any hint of uncertainty, his voice low but firm. "Are you sure?"

"Yes. I'm sure."

Relief surged through him, fierce and overwhelming. She'd chosen him—really chosen him—with her eyes wide open.

His hands moved to cradle her face, slowly and reverently, like she was something sacred he didn't quite dare to touch.

But then she leaned into him.

And that was all it took. As their lips met, the emotion behind it nearly brought him to his knees.

He kissed her deeply, urgently, like a drowning man who'd just been thrown a lifeline. An eternity of restraint, of fighting what he felt, of learning she wanted him, too, of despairing that he'd lost her—it all poured out in that desperate connection.

For a heartbeat, Zach couldn't believe it was real—after all the walls, all the misunderstandings, all the aching distance. But then she was kissing him back with a fierce intensity that matched his own, hands sliding up his chest, fingers curling into his shirt, and he knew this wasn't a dream.

This was nothing like the careful control he'd built his life around. This was surrender—complete and terrifying and more right than anything he'd ever known. Every careful barrier he'd constructed crumbled as she pressed closer, angling her neck, inviting him to deepen the kiss as her fingertips rested against his racing pulse.

His heart swelled, overflowing with everything they'd carried in silence. Every unspoken feeling. Every sacrifice. Every impossibly brave choice she'd made to protect him. The taste of her, the exquisite wonder of her in his arms—it was like coming home to a place he'd never dared imagine existed.

He pressed a kiss to her temple. "You have no idea what you mean to me."

"I think I do," she whispered as she brushed her fingers along his jaw.

Her lips found his again, tender and achingly sweet. Her breath caught against his, and he felt it—the same burning hope he hadn't dared allow to take root in his heart. They took their time, the world expanding into this one luminous moment—each brush of their lips a promise, each breath a quiet vow. No rush. No performance. Just the slow, sacred wonder of being fully seen and still chosen.

When they finally parted, he rested his forehead against hers, stunned, shaken, exhilarated.

"Worth every second of the wait," he whispered.

Chapter 85

Two Months Later

S NOW DUSTED THE LAWNS of Glenmere Hall like icing sugar, softening the estate's sharp edges and lending it the hush of a fairytale. It was eight weeks since the Starbound finale, and the top eight contestants had returned to rehearse for the tour, bringing laughter and music to its once-silent halls.

Zach's phone buzzed with another venue confirmation. Eighteen cities now—up from twelve—thanks to overwhelming ticket demand. His desk was a battlefield of production spreadsheets and travel schedules, but the chaos was a kind he welcomed. This time, he wasn't chasing a vision alone.

Success still mattered. But these days, it wasn't the only thing that did.

He glanced out the frosted window, watching his breath fog the glass, and smiled at the sound drifting from the rehearsal wing—a blend of laughter and imperfect harmonies. The cast was bonding. The energy was hopeful. And somehow, amid the madness of tour prep, everything felt grounded.

Maybe because, for the first time in years, he did too.

Kezia had brought him back to himself. For the past two months, they'd been dating quietly—long walks through Wimbledon Common and Cannizaro Park when he came into town, late dinners in her rented studio flat above a florist's shop in the Village. No drama. No press. Just space to know each other outside of cameras and contracts.

She'd spent Christmas at Falconhurst with his family, slipping effortlessly into the rhythms of their joyful chaos. His mum had taken to her instantly, and Levi had pulled him aside after dinner to say, "She's exactly the kind of woman who makes a man braver."

Zach hadn't disagreed.

They were still learning each other, still navigating what it meant to build something lasting in a world that rarely slowed down. But it was real. Steady. Sacred, even.

There'd been no press announcements, no red carpet debuts. Just texts that made him smile mid-meeting and a playlist they'd started building together, adding songs that reminded them of stolen glances and quiet rehearsals. She'd even teased him last week about adding her finale performance of "Old Town Symphony" to it, half-joking, "Only if you leave the rough edges in. That's where the truth is."

He hadn't promised. And he hadn't needed to.

Because every note between them, whether spoken or sung, was already pitch perfect.

He'd made dinner reservations for tonight at a small Italian restaurant in Guildford that Ezra had recommended. Something casual but intimate, where they could continue building this relationship that had started under such unusual circumstances.

But before he could get to that, there was a lot of work to do. He was settling back at his desk when a knock sounded at his door, a perfunctory gesture as the door was already swinging open.

Ryan Sterling stepped inside, shutting the door behind him with just a bit too much confidence.

"Didn't mean to interrupt," he said, tone breezy. "Thought we should catch up."

Zach gestured toward the chair across from his desk. "What's on your mind?"

But Ryan didn't sit. He wandered toward the bookshelves, his gaze drifting across framed tour posters and mentor plaques like a man browsing a résumé. "The tour's looking good. Strong lineup. Kezia's pulling the crowds."

"She's earned them," Zach said evenly.

"Oh, I know," Ryan replied. "The numbers don't lie. Sandra may have won, but Kezia's got the buzz. More streams, more press, more heat. Not bad for a runner-up."

Zach said nothing, letting him spool it out.

Ryan turned back, hands in his pockets. "Anyway, I hear things. Albion's close to finalizing the US franchise deal. Big network, big rollout. They'll want someone who knows how to scale this thing—someone with experience on both sides of the Atlantic."

Zach waited.

"I'm not after a spotlight," Ryan continued. "Just a seat at the table. Something advisory, maybe. Quiet influence. You've got Albion's ear. A good word from you, and I'm in the room."

Zach leaned back slightly. "And if I don't give it?"

Ryan smiled. "Then the rollout might get...complicated."

"Complicated in what way?"

Ryan stepped forward. "You and Kezia. There's chemistry there. Everyone saw it. The mentorship shift, the finale performance, the way she looked at you on stage. If someone were inclined to frame that poorly, well...it might raise questions. About fairness. About the brand."

Zach didn't flinch. "Yes, we're together. That's no secret."

Ryan blinked. This was clearly not the answer he was expecting.

Zach continued, voice calm. "Our relationship didn't start until after the finale. She never crossed a line. Nothing happened during the show. Diana Morris will back me up. The timeline is clean. If you're looking for leverage, leave her out of it. You want something from me? Come at me. Directly."

Ryan's smile faded. "Kezia still threw the finale. We spent ages rehearsing a showstopper, which she swapped for that impromptu and overwrought ballad. A song about *you*. Don't pretend it's not and don't pretend it didn't work. You think that performance didn't sway the vote?"

"She sang a song she wrote," Zach said, tone even. "And it resonated with people more than anything else that night. It's the most streamed performance of the *Starbound* season. The most downloaded track on StreamTune. That hardly looks like an act of self-sabotage or throwing the finale. And, don't forget, she won the studio audience vote. She was a finalist because of her voice, her choices, her work."

Ryan crossed his arms. "And now you're managing her career. Her face is everywhere, and somehow yours keeps showing up next to it. You really think that looks clean?"

"I'm not managing her," Zach said. "She makes her own decisions. Just like she did when she walked away from my mentorship and chose you for the finale."

The words weren't loud, but they landed.

Ryan's jaw clenched. "Sponsors don't like mess. Neither do networks. You're trying to tell me there's no conflict of interest here? A little doubt, a little drama—that's all it takes to rattle a deal."

"Then, rattle it." Zach stood, not to threaten, just to finish. "There's no scandal. The press might speculate, but Albion has the timeline and Diana has the receipts. And the truth is simple: Kezia earned every step forward. On her own."

He held Ryan's gaze. "If you think you belong in the US launch, pitch your value. If you have concerns about optics, bring them to Albion. But you won't use Kezia or me to muscle your way in."

Ryan studied him for a long moment, then adjusted his cuffs with exaggerated ease. "You always did enjoy the high road," he said, his lip curling.

Zach didn't blink. "It's the only way I can look a woman like Kezia in the eye."

Ryan gave a thin smile and yanked the door open.

Kezia stood just outside, hand raised to knock. She froze for a beat, eyes flicking from Ryan to Zach. "Oh," she said. "Sorry, I didn't realize you were in a meeting."

Ryan recovered quickly, flashing her that press-ready smile. "Not at all. We were just wrapping up." His gaze lingered a little too long, but he didn't say more. He slipped past her and disappeared down the corridor.

Kezia stepped inside and closed the door behind herself.

Zach remained where he was, jaw tight, the heat of Ryan's insinuations still pulsing beneath his collar.

He hadn't raised his voice. Hadn't let Ryan provoke him. But watching that man try to weaponize Kezia's reputation, try to reduce her to a bargaining chip, had ignited a fury he was still fighting to hold back.

Kezia approached slowly. "Do I want to know what that was about?"

He exhaled through his nose, tension still simmering beneath the surface. "It's dealt with. I'll fill you in, but just not right this second."

He should tell her. And he would—soon. But not when his blood was still running hot and the words would come out as fire instead of truth. She deserved better than secondhand rage. When he told her, it would be clear. Calm. About respect, not reaction.

Her brow arched. "So...the usual?"

That tugged a smile from him, but it didn't hold.

"Hey." She stepped closer, studying his face, a hand reaching toward him. "You okay?"

Zach didn't answer with words. He simply pulled her close and wrapped his arms around her.

She melted into him, her head resting on his shoulder.

This was what centered him. Not the charts or the contracts or the press cycles. Just *her*. Kezia. Steady, real, and his.

He let out a slow breath against her hair, the last of his anger easing into something deeper. Protective. Certain.

"I've got you," he murmured.

"Mm." Her arms tightened around him. "And I'm not going anywhere."

They stood there for a moment, the world outside the office forgotten.

Then she leaned back slightly, looking up at him. "This is really nice," she said, lips curving. "But I actually came in here to tell you something."

He didn't let go. "You want to tell me now, or after I'm done using you as a human reset button?"

She laughed softly. "Now, before I forget."

He raised an eyebrow.

"Claire just called. She and Tom are inviting us to dinner this weekend. Nothing fancy—just takeaway and board games. Otis will be there to supervise."

Zach smiled. "Wasn't he the one who tried to eat my shoelaces last time?"

"He has a complicated relationship with footwear," she said solemnly. "And a vendetta against anything resembling authority."

Zach let out a quiet breath. "Dinner with Tom and Claire sounds perfect."

"I thought it might." She slipped her arms back around him, nestling against his chest. "Carry on with your reset."

Smiling, he closed his eyes and let the simplicity of the moment settle around him as he held her. God was so good to him. After all the noise, all the maneuvering, this was what mattered. Not the spotlight. Not the power plays. Just the woman he loved.

Dinner with friends. A mischievous terrier. A life unscripted, unpolished, and real.

And finally, fully, his.

Epilogue

11 Months Later

*K*EZIA CAREFULLY LIFTED THE roasting pan to baste the turkey, the savory aroma filling the Falconhurst kitchen. Around her, the cheerful chaos of Christmas Day preparations buzzed with activity.

"Is this too much thyme, do you think?" Martha asked from the island counter, sniffing at a bowl of stuffing.

"Never too much thyme for Christmas," Kezia replied with a smile, returning the turkey to the oven.

Eight-month-old David sat happily in his highchair, banging a wooden spoon against the tray with impressive rhythm for someone who couldn't yet walk.

"He's going to be a drummer, not a singer," Martha laughed, ruffling her son's dark curls.

In the adjacent room, Ezra was arranging presents under the magnificent Christmas tree. Through the doorway, Kezia could hear Levi and Adria debating—again—about the proper timing for Yorkshire puddings.

Beth's voice called from the living room, "Kezia, dear, could you stir the cranberry sauce? I don't want it to stick."

"On it."

Kezia moved toward the stove, marveling at how naturally she navigated this space now. The formal Christmases of her childhood couldn't have been more different from the warm, noisy generosity of the Falconer family.

"Remember last Christmas when you were still so nervous around everyone?" Martha asked, bumping her hip playfully against Kezia's. "Now you're Zach's secret weapon in the family gingerbread house competition."

"Speaking of which," Kezia said with a conspiratorial smile, "I've been practicing some structural reinforcement techniques since last year. The flying buttresses on our cathedral are going to blow Ezra and Levi's minds."

Martha laughed. "They're still bitter about losing their two-year winning streak when you joined the family."

Joined the family. Her throat grew too tight to speak. Blinking quickly, she turned her attention to the cranberry sauce.

Martha, who never missed anything, squeezed Kezia's shoulder before she changed the subject. "Hey, you didn't tell me—how are the Royal Albert Hall rehearsals going?"

Kezia cleared her throat. "Almost done finalizing the setlist, but I wouldn't mind your eyes on it before we lock in the song order. I still can't believe I'm headlining six sold-out shows."

"Not bad for your first major performance series. Though after your featured vocals on my album, I'm not surprised."

That collaboration had changed everything. Their natural musical chemistry had led to Kezia performing on three tracks of Martha's latest album, creating buzz far beyond the *Starbound* fanbase.

"How's your own album coming?" Martha asked, wiping her hands on a tea towel.

"Slowly but surely. I want to take my time and get it right."

Martha gave her a knowing smile. "The royalties from 'Old Town Symphony' make that easier, I'm guessing."

The song's success still left Kezia a little breathless. More than a year on, it remained the most-streamed performance from *Starbound's* history and had become something of an underground anthem for honesty and healing.

"Zach still insists I take full credit," Kezia said, shaking her head. "Even though half those lyrics are his."

"Those moments on tour when you performed it together were absolute magic." Martha's eyes softened. "The audiences went absolutely wild."

"When the tabloids finally caught on about us, I was terrified," Kezia admitted. "I mean, I know there could still be a backlash, but thank God that hasn't happened yet."

"Now, that was a real answer to prayer," Martha said. "What did the *Sun* say? 'TV's Most Authentic Love Story?' Thank God the news broke when everyone was in the mood for a feel-good story and all the media decided to run with that angle."

The irony wasn't lost on Kezia that the most authentic moment of the competition had become the foundation of her career. Meanwhile, Zach's vision for *Starbound* had been validated with a successful second season just concluded and a third in pre-production. The format had been sold internationally, exactly as he'd hoped.

David started to fuss, dropping his wooden spoon.

"He's going to need a feed soon," Martha said. "I wanted to finish the stuffing first."

"I can take him," Kezia offered, lifting him out of his high chair as Martha smiled gratefully.

David settled against Kezia's chest with a happy sigh, grabbing at the silver tinsel on her jumper.

"I'll show him the Christmas tree," Kezia said, heading toward the living room.

Her own parents hadn't come this year, though she'd invited them. They'd opted to spend the holidays with Salome in Geneva. She no longer waited for Mum and Dad to become people they weren't, or to show her love in ways they never would. Instead, she'd learned to receive what they were willing to give, and to stop grieving the rest.

It was so much easier now that she was surrounded by Zach's family—the kind that didn't measure worth in trophies or titles. The kind that welcomed her, flaws and all.

She found Zach in the living room, adding a fresh log onto the fire. His eyes lit up when he saw her.

Even after over a year together, the warmth of his gaze could make her pulse stumble. He rose, taking the baby from her arms with practiced ease.

"Hello, little man," he murmured, lifting David high, earning delighted squeals.

Kezia's heart melted all over again as she watched him.

They'd been deliberate about building their relationship, taking time to do it right. When the *Starbound* national tour wrapped up, she'd found an apartment in Hatbrook, just fifteen minutes from Falconhurst. She'd joined Grace Community Church and their lives continued to weave together. Beyond a shadow of a doubt, she knew Zach Falconer was her person.

Kezia adjusted an ornament on the tree—a miniature piano Zach had given her last Christmas.

"A nod to the song that started it all," she said, running a finger over the polished surface.

He smiled. "Still think you could've won if you'd stuck with the Whitney ballad?"

"Maybe. But I wouldn't change a thing," she said softly.

Because everything that mattered had begun the moment she chose to be real.

Dinner had been perfect.

Full plates, full laughter, full hearts. Kezia couldn't remember the last time she'd felt quite so...held. Not managed, not tolerated, not even celebrated, but known, in the way that only came with time and tenderness.

As the sky faded to indigo outside the tall windows of Falconhurst, the household gradually settled into its evening rhythm. Beth sat in front of the fire putting together a Lego set with Owen, Levi's little boy. Adria sat curled up on the sofa with a book while Levi and Ezra debated some obscure football statistic over mince pies. Martha had vanished upstairs to put David down for a nap.

Kezia and Zach sat together at the cleared dining table, hunting down the edge pieces of a one-thousand-piece jigsaw puzzle.

She caught Zach's gaze lingering on his mother. "She looks happy."

He smiled. "I really believe she is. There was a time I never thought she could be again. I spent years angry on her behalf, holding the line when our family nearly broke apart. I used to think I had to make up for what Greg destroyed. That if I built something strong enough, successful enough, it would undo the damage. But she didn't need me to fix it. She just needed time. And the people who never walked away."

Kezia leaned her head against his shoulder. "You gave her that. You gave her space to heal."

He exhaled. "And somewhere along the way, I think I did, too."

They sat quietly for a moment, until he said, "Come for a walk with me?"

She sat up. "Now?"

"Now." He held out a hand. "Ten minutes. Just us. Let's go get some fresh air."

Outside, she slid her hand into his, letting him guide her into the cold night.

The Falconhurst grounds stretched quiet and serene beneath a star-washed sky, the air biting but dry. They walked in silence at first, their boots crunching lightly over frosted gravel.

Zach led her toward the back of the property, along the familiar stone path past the garden hedge and down toward the gazebo at the edge of the orchard.

Tonight, it glowed with fairy lights strung through the rafters, their soft golden warmth casting a circle of quiet magic.

"Pretty," Kezia murmured as they stepped beneath the arched roof.

Zach turned to her, taking both her hands. "It's where Ezra and Martha got married. And a few years ago, Levi and Adria."

"I can imagine why. It's stunning here."

"You know, a couple of years ago, Mum asked if I could picture myself standing here with my forever girl. Back then, the answer was no." His voice softened. "But now...I dream about it every day."

Her throat tightened as she stared at his face.

He pressed her hands to his lips. "I've loved you quietly, and then all at once. I love your voice, your courage, your faith, your ridiculous overuse of vocal steamers." He chuckled. "I love that you sang our song to the world. And I want to spend my life writing every next verse with you."

Zach reached into his coat pocket and pulled out a small box. She could hardly see it through her tears. He held it between them, cupped in his hands like something fragile and sacred.

"I've been carrying this around for weeks," he said quietly. "Waiting for the right time."

He opened the box, revealing a vintage-cut diamond set in warm gold. Then he got down on one knee.

"I can't imagine life without you by my side. Kezia Blair Byaruhanga, will you marry me?"

She dropped to her knees in front of him before she even realized she was moving, throwing her arms around him, laughter and tears catching in the same breath.

"Yes," she whispered against his shoulder. "Yes. A thousand times, yes."

He kissed her there on the gazebo floor, soft and sure and smiling against her lips.

When they finally stood, he slid the ring onto her finger. It was a perfect fit.

He drew her close, and they stood holding each other as the first snowflakes began to fall.

"I thought about waiting until New Year's," he murmured against her hair. "But then I saw you in the kitchen, holding David and blending so beautifully in our family, I thought, 'What on earth am I waiting for?'"

She chuckled. "I'm glad you didn't wait."

They stood there for a long time, wrapped in each other and the hush of the winter night. Not rushed, not scripted. Just real.

Just them. Just right.

The End

Encore!

Thanks for being part of Kezia and Zach's story in *Old Town Symphony*. If you'd like to linger a little longer in their world, I've put together something you won't find anywhere else.

The songs that shaped their journey—including "Old Town Symphony" and "All That I Give"—are more than just words on a page. You can actually hear them performed, just as I imagined them while writing.

And because I couldn't resist fast-forwarding to see where life and love take them, I've written a special bonus epilogue that offers a glimpse into their future together.

In your private bonus collection, you'll be able to:

- Hear "Old Town Symphony" performed by Kezia and covered by Zach
- Listen to "All That I Give" in Kezia's voice
- Download the bonus epilogue set after the events of the book

Claim your exclusive access here:

https://millaholt.com/oldtownsymphonybonus

Note: When I first imagined Kezia's semifinals performance, I pictured her singing Whitney Houston's powerhouse ballad "I Have Nothing." Unfortunately, quoting the lyrics would have required permissions that aren't easy to come by, so I created an original song instead: "All That I Give." It's fictional in our world, but in Kezia's, it's a Whitney classic with the same heart and sentiment.

More in the Rhapsody of Grace Series

Three brothers. Three love stories. One faith that holds them together when everything else falls apart.

From the spotlight's glare to the quiet ache behind closed doors, the Falconer brothers' lives are bound by music, family, and a God who can redeem even the most broken chords.

In *Home Town Melody*, a chance reunion forces Levi to face the child he never knew and the woman who's never stopped guarding her heart.

In *Small Town Harmony*, Ezra and Martha must rediscover their marriage in the middle of music careers pulling them in opposite directions.

And in *Old Town Symphony*, Zach must decide if love is worth the risk when the woman who captivates him could also cost him everything he's built.

Tender, deeply emotional, and brimming with heartfelt romance, these faith-filled stories celebrate grace, second chances, and the music that plays when love finds its way home.

Find out more on:

https://millaholt.com/book-series/rhapsody-of-grace/

About the Author

Milla Holt writes heartfelt Christian fiction that blends faith, hope, and romance. She loves crafting stories where heroes and heroines face sometimes hard—but always life-changing—truths, and where happy endings feel both hard-won and deeply satisfying. Her aim is to uplift and encourage readers while taking them on an emotional journey they won't forget.

Milla lives in the east of England with her husband and their four children. When she's not writing, you'll find her rambling through the countryside, reading good books, or making up ridiculous lyrics to favourite songs with her family. She is also a self-confessed lover of strong cups of milky tea, long outlines, and the occasional binge of true crime podcasts.

Discover more of Milla's books at https://shop.millaholt.com.